THE TASTE *of* ASHES

Caitlin Press Inc.
8100 Alderwood Road,
Halfmoon Bay, BC V0N 1Y1
www.caitlin-press.com

Text design by Vici Johnstone.
Cover design by Vici Johnstone.
Cover photograph by Alicia Fox.
Printed in Canada

Caitlin Press Inc. acknowledges financial support from the Government of Canada
through the Canada Book Fund and the Canada Council for the Arts, and from the
Province of British Columbia through the British Columbia Arts Council and the
Book Publisher's Tax Credit.

Library and Archives Canada Cataloguing in Publication

Peters, Sheila, 1953-
    The taste of ashes / Sheila Peters.

ISBN 978-1-894759-77-9

    I. Title.

PS8581.E84113T34 2012   C813'.6   C2012-900634-3

THE TASTE *of* ASHES

a novel by
SHEILA PETERS

CAITLIN PRESS

for Marie Manrique

Part I

1

When the radio clicked on at 6:15, Isabel Lee was still half-asleep. Clear skies. Temperatures rising to the mid-twenties. Current temperature, one degree. A danger of frost in low-lying areas. She jolted awake. Throwing off the covers, she pulled a sweater over her nightie, stuck her bare feet into her clogs, and rushed outside to rescue her flowers.

Sunlight touched the peak of the mountain across Railway Avenue, but her house was in shadow. The heavy dew soaking the grass froze her feet and cold air coiled around her legs snaking right up under her nightie as she turned on the tap and unwound the hose. Determined to trick the cold into leaving another few days of life to the frost-tender lobelia, the tubs full of nasturtiums, and the dahlias that would look glorious if they were given a couple more weeks, she sprayed them all. The summer in this small town tucked between three mountain ranges five hundred miles north of Vancouver had held so little heat this year, everything had come so slowly, that each flower was worth fighting for in spite of the chill that had tunnelled its way deep into her bones by the time she went back inside.

She turned up the heat and waited, standing over the hot air vent as the furnace rattled and coughed, forcing warm air up between her feet. They were still lovely feet, she thought, with long toes and perfectly polished red toenails. Her ankles and calves were slender, and the shape revealed as the blue-flowered nightie billowed and subsided showed a flat stomach and breasts still holding their own against gravity. She grimaced as her feet prickled into warmth and scrubbed her fingers through the dark blonde hair that sleep had spiked into a frazzle.

The radio blared upstairs, the only other presence in her small house. The announcer reminded drivers to slow down for the children returning to school and she groaned to think of the store swarming with list-packing mothers and kids already wired from a couple of hours in a classroom. Instead of a day ringing up sales, she longed for a cigarette, a drink, and a man's warm body. It had been almost three years since she'd given them all up. Three years since she had tried, unsuccessfully, to stop her daughter from packing up and driving away. She was moving, Janna had screamed, to a town where no one knew her. Or, more specifically, where no one knew her mother.

Trudging back up the stairs for a shower, Isabel felt the same helpless anger she always felt when she thought about that day. Every one of her forty-eight years made itself felt in the way her hips ached after spending hours just the day before hunkered down weeding the same flowers she was trying so hard to save. She wondered if she'd ever limber up again.

†

By the time the early afternoon lull hit the store, Isabel was wishing the morning frost hadn't tricked her into putting on a long-sleeved cotton sweater and heavy denim skirt. Sun slanted across the checkout counter where she leaned to take the weight off her feet. She sorted through the jumble of security tags, sale price stickers, and the stack of bulletins sent out from head office over the long weekend. The store sweltered under racks of dark fall fashions — burgundy and green velour everywhere. The only summer clothes left were mustard yellow shorts sets in the discount bin, outfits so ugly they'd been marked down to $1.99 and still weren't moving.

She was thinking of ducking into the washroom to peel off her pantyhose when Lily Thomas, bent almost double by a disintegrating spine, wandered in. Thin grey hair curled out from under a black felt cap, and a once-fine pink wool coat, belted at the waist, drooped below her knees. White ankle socks and black high-top runners completed the ensemble. Squashing an old beaded purse under one arm, she sifted through the shorts sets, held one pair up to the light, shook them out, fingered the tags, and dropped them back into the pile. She drifted toward another sales rack, then doubled back. Rooting around underneath, she pulled out the eyelet lace tank top Isabel had tucked in the bin as treasure for the sharp sighted. Mrs. Thomas had scored, though God only knew who would wear it.

Isabel was on her way over to ask her how best to protect her dahlias from the frost when a bright flock of girls twittered in and scattered among the fake leather tops and tiny skirts. Grade eights, probably, fresh from their first day at the high school, and somebody had a clothing allowance. Before the door had even closed behind the girls, three young men tumbled into the store, laughing at the tag line of a joke. Friends of her boys, they'd filled the house with their unfinished voices as they played hours of video games and munched through a thousand plates of nachos. Whenever they needed wool socks or long underwear and were strapped for the kind of cash the higher-end stores charged, they'd come to see Isabel.

"Hey, Mrs. Lee. Heard from Trevor?"

"He's drilling in Mexico, raking in the dough. You boys got yourselves some work?"

"Going into the bush for Ajax. Need some new woollies is all."

She sent them over to one of the younger clerks. Isabel often forgot she wasn't nineteen and had to hold back from flirting, from making God knows what kind of fool of herself. She remembered her confusion when her younger son, Trevor, away for months on his first job diamond drilling for a mining company up north, came home and picked her up with his new muscles. She could barely think who or where she was as he swung her around. His big dream since he was a kid, he'd said, was to pay off the house. Slapped down six thousand dollars to put against the mortgage. No more turning out pockets for cash on the first of the month. No more begging the bank for a few more days.

Isabel struggled against sudden tears. Here she was, forty-eight, six years the assistant manager of the store, making $12.50 an hour. The chemical smell of new running shoes made her sneeze. Her back ached from lugging box after box, year after year, of limp clothes, of pillowcases and duvet covers, of fuzzy slippers and rubber boots, moving a mound surely as high as the mountain across the railway tracks from her house. Her dreams she had to keep small. That her oldest child, Jason, would leave his idiot wife. That her second, Trevor, wouldn't be killed on the drill rigs. That her baby daughter, Janna, would one day screw up her perfect life plan and need her mother's help. That when she did, Isabel would still be clean and sober and ready.

A young couple dropped a pile of towels, sheets, and dishcloths on the counter. Isabel was ringing up the sale when the man grinned and pulled a black satin nightie from under his jean jacket. The girl shrieked and held it up to her cheek while one of his hands crept around to do a little dance on the side of her breast.

Isabel looked away. She ordered her own nipples to lie down as she bagged their purchases and tried not to look at the man's hand sliding across the girl's butt on their way out the door. While she rang in three pairs of yellow rubber boots for the little blond kids lined up like Russian dolls behind their mother, her thoughts wandered to the new shipment waiting in the back. She'd heard there were some slinky skirts coming in, long with a slit up the side. And those shiny sweaters that sit low on the shoulders. She ran a hand up and down her neck. With a nice chain to sit here — she rubbed a spot just above her breasts — she could put together a pretty outfit. Pretty enough to imagine herself as young and hopeful as the schoolgirls who, in little groups, began to appear at the counter wearing their new clothes. One girl's black lace T-shirt flashed peeks at a red bra and enough cleavage to make a swimsuit edition.

"No returns if you wear them out of here," Isabel warned. "Your folks might not like everything you've picked."

They frowned and insisted, twisting and turning as Isabel cut off their tags and rang them in. She gave them bags for the clothes they'd worn into the store and watched them convulse into giggles as they brushed by the boys picking socks out of a bin by the door.

A clerk whispered in her ear, "Radousky's snuck in."

Isabel sighed. Once they'd found Richard Radousky stretched out drunk under one of the racks in the teen section looking up the empty dresses, no doubt imagining them full of warm and moving flesh. Isabel hadn't been surprised. She remembered sitting on his lap in her father's office at the back of the house, liking the tobacco smell of him. Later, her mother at her elbow, fingers a circle of pain pressing her bones, saying, "He is not your friend, Isabel. Remember that. Never is he your friend."

"He's watching the girls." The clerk nodded toward the change rooms.

Isabel inhaled her anger. When her mother went into the hospital, her father's friends had spilled out of his office and filled the house with beer and smoke. She was sixteen then. Her boyfriend, Jason's soon-to-be father, swaggered in there with them. Her elbow hard in Radousky's face as he wrestled with her in the hall. She looked across the store. From a distance he looked younger than he was, and with the sports jacket over the black T-shirt and the grey hair swept back, he looked like somebody famous. He was about the same age her dad would have been if the booze hadn't finally killed him. Her dad who was as indiscriminate in his choice of friends as he had been brilliant in his choice of a wife.

She planted herself to block Radousky's view of a girl pirouetting in front of her friends, her little body flashing in and out of the mirrors on the pillars. A flounced velour skirt with a v-neck top, all dark green.

"Very nice, honey, but the shoes aren't quite right," Isabel said.

The girls and Richard Radousky looked down at the new Nikes, bright against the ratty brown carpet.

"Go pick yourself a nice pair to match. We can lay away whatever you don't have the money for. Give you a couple of days to work on your mom. Now who's next?"

Another girl danced out of the change room in a fake leather violet mini and matching jacket over a slinky silver shirt tight across her tiny breasts. Isabel backed up, sending Radousky scuttling into the oversize lingerie. She took his elbow and steered him toward the door.

"The Legion'll be open by now, Richard. You must be feeling thirsty after watching that little show." She squeezed hard, her gardener's hand a vise.

He wrenched his arm away. "There's things I could say, Isabel."

"No doubt," she spat. "But you're not going to because both you and I know the fathers of those lovely little girls and, what's more, they know you."

His old eyes drifted over her body as he backed out the door, a cigarette in his hand. "Couple of them probably know you, too." He flicked his lighter and blew smoke through the closing door.

She felt the same helpless anger she'd felt that morning. Anger, too, at the longing for the bar that Radousky's smoke blew through her. For the feeling she got halfway through the first glass of draft, the sliding into a long amber silkiness. A muscled arm reaching out to keep her steady.

†

As the day dragged to a close and the last girl flounced out the door with her bag of dreams, the clerk came up from the back with her jacket on. "Mrs. Thomas is asleep in that chair in the linen section. She's got piles of stuff in her lap. Should I wake her up before you cash out?"

Isabel had forgotten her. "You go on home. I'll take care of her."

As the door snicked shut behind the clerk, sweet children's faces smiled down on Isabel from the walls above the Girls and Boys department. She moved between the crowded racks, running her hands across the neat stacks of towels, pillows, and duvets. Sometimes she wished for an earthquake or a storm to trap her in the store with the other clerks. They'd build a camp with all the bedding, wrap themselves in flannel nightgowns and fleecy jackets, laugh and tell stories.

She drifted from rack to rack, held up a dress shot with silver thread, and draped a glittering scarf around her neck. She wondered what outfit she would buy if she could afford anything in the world. Some little Yves Saint Laurent shift for a few thousand dollars? Italian leather pumps, dark red, maybe. Or a pale yellow dress and tan leather sandals. As if there'd ever been much call in her social circles for Armani frocks.

She fluffed up a pink housecoat. Maybe she and Mrs. Thomas could have a pajama party, leaf through *Vogue* or *Cosmo* and talk about the days when Mrs. Thomas was the mystery woman from the New York fashion house who presided over the Fifth Avenue Salon. Isabel had been afraid of her severe black dresses and harsh voice. She hated the stiff clothes — quality, her mother insisted — that felt wrong on her little girl's body. She longed to try on something soft and swirly from the rack of party dresses: shimmering silk or glittering chiffon. Sweetheart necklines. One of them the perfect dress that would finally reveal her in all her beauty. When she was old enough, her mother promised.

By the time she was old enough, her mother was dying and their beautiful lakeside home was a ratty lounge where all the drinks were free. The Fifth Avenue Salon had become a video store, and Mrs. Thomas had given up on the town's women and retired to her little house beside St. Mary's Church to create a tangled garden stuffed full of anything and everything that could bloom before it froze.

When had she become this soft crumpled creature snoring in a chair at the back of a third-rate chain store? Someone who never seemed to know exactly who Isabel was. The floor around her was strewn with dresses, nightgowns, sweat pants, and two winter jackets. Her own coat, as worn and dingy as Janna's abandoned plush pig, fell open to reveal a food-stained white blouse and black skirt. Her scalp showed pink beneath the thin frizz of hair.

"Mrs. Thomas," Isabel whispered, and the grey eyes fluttered open, blurry behind the glasses. One hand clutched the purse. The other opened, dropping a crumpled tissue.

"I need a tent," she said. "Do you have any bargains on tents?"

"Most folks are thinking about putting away their camping gear, Mrs. Thomas. The nights are getting cold."

The old lady started upright. "Is it going to freeze tonight, Isabel?"

She did know her name, Isabel thought. Did she remember seeing her that night so long ago now? Standing in her dahlias, semen running down her leg onto her feet, bare in the warm black dirt.

"The radio gave out a frost warning. We should get ourselves home and start covering things up. After this terrible summer, it would be a shame to lose everything so early."

The old woman's eyes slid over Isabel's face. "I don't remember a worse."

"How are your dahlias? Mine still need a couple of good warm weeks to be at their best."

"My dahlias." The old woman's face froze in distrust.

Isabel struggled on. "Those old varieties are the best. That one with the bronze leaves, what's it called? Bishop something?"

"I have a dress, a nice red and white cotton print, it would look lovely on your mother."

"I've managed to get hold of some of those apricot Masquerades. Maybe we could do a swap." Isabel tried to keep the longing out of her voice. "I could give you a hand lifting all the tubers, once the frost does come."

Mrs. Thomas's fingers brushed Isabel's sweater. "You don't have the same eye for style your mother has."

All the tiredness of the long day gathered in Isabel's legs; she slid down to sit at Mrs. Thomas's feet. Sometime she'd ask her about her mother. About the beautiful dresses still hanging in the closet after her father died. They were probably worth good money now, the ones she hadn't worn out. After she'd made the down payment on her house with what little was left of her father's estate, she'd sat Jason and Trevor down on the couch in their new living room. She'd modelled dress after dress and told them where their grandmother had worn each one. Her picture on the mantel. The eight-year-old Jason kicked his skinny legs at the coffee table. Little Trevor, solid and serious, watched her every move. When she came through the door in the white cotton print, his dimples appeared. White cotton strewn with tiny blue and black flowers, a blue belt. A square neckline, and sleeves that were hardly there.

The new me, Isabel had thought, stretching to fasten the buttons at the back the next day. My chance to start again.

She'd worn it to her first confession since her mother's funeral, felt its pressure across her shoulder blades as she knelt and bent her head to tell the stranger behind the screen of her plans to get her Grade 12 now that both boys were in school. She was going to get off welfare and become a teacher. She spilled out all the ways she'd failed her mother's memory. Her too-young marriage to Jason's father. Her hopeless fling with Trevor's father. Her fights with her own dad. She'd had to lean close to catch the conditions of her forgiveness, the English awkward in the priest's mouth. Purified, she'd worn the dress the next morning to take communion. Her mouth open to the long fingers of the young priest visiting, they said, from Central America. The wafer dissolving on her tongue.

"You haven't put your mother in a home, have you?" Mrs. Thomas was angry.

She'd worn it a few weeks later, that night in the parking lot behind St. Mary's. She'd watched that same hand move across the space between them, wondering, as it trembled in the dark like some moth, where it was going to land. Finally, two fingers on her lips. Her mouth had opened, tasting soap and the smell of a steering wheel. She'd taken the fingers inside and run her tongue around them, over the nails, the ridges of the knuckles, and he was helpless. It was all up to her — his fear, intoxicating.

"No, Mrs. Thomas, I haven't put my mother in a home. I would never do that."

From a blanket under the willows down by the river, they'd moved into the bedroom he shared with the other priest. How crazy they'd been. Parishioners knocking, frantic with loss. She, curled up deep in the bed, listening to them on the other side of the bedroom door. He coming in all dark with Spanish anguish, looking for his shoes, the secrets of the parish lodged in his throat. And that last time, the other priest back early from his road trip, the key in the door. She'd tumbled out the window and scurried across the wet grass to pull on her clothes in the shadow of Mrs. Thomas's house. Her shoes forgotten in the hurry and his sperm inside her because the sound of the key startled him, his fear exploding. Nothing as exciting as that fear. She'd been vibrating as she stood there, her bare feet in the dark soil, careful of the plants. Waiting for him to call her back in. Certain that nothing could keep them apart. Janna, taking root inside her.

Mrs. Thomas had come to her mother's funeral and stood at the back in a black dress and jacket, a white lace handkerchief tucked in her sleeve. The shine of ironing on the stiff skirt even then marked the beginning of her long slide. Why, Isabel had raged as the handkerchief came out to dab at the reddened eyes, did that old lady still live when Isabel's own mother was gone? Why was her father, the rotten orange smell of Scotch on his breath as he clutched her and sobbed, why was he still alive? The old priest, the one who had baptized her, why was he doddering over to give her another blessing when her mother was already decomposing in the huge gilt coffin sliding into the back of the hearse?

Isabel pushed herself up from the floor, blew her nose and wiped her eyes. The first day of school was over. She called Mrs. Thomas a taxi.

†

Isabel walked home in the deepening dusk. People were moving through their houses, some heads bent over dinner, others watching television. The early darkness caught them unaware. They weren't yet in the wintertime habit of closing the drapes. A door opened somewhere and a man whistled for a dog. Behind him, music floated into the street, a woman singing some high sad song. She stopped to listen, her heart opening to the music's sorrow, thinking she should check in on Mrs. Thomas and make sure she'd got home okay. Her garden was beautiful, but the house was a death trap.

That night, twenty years ago, she'd looked in through the window and seen the old woman looking right back at her from between tilting piles of junk: papers, magazines, dolls, racks of clothes, jars of home preserves, and dusty plants climbing everywhere. A path just wide enough for her hips, the window almost blocked. She'd shaken her head in what looked like disapproval.

Isabel went the long way around, avoiding the inevitable invitations from the smokers sitting at the tables on the sidewalk outside the Imperial Hotel. She crossed through the playground of the elementary school where she and later all three of her kids had gone. She'd dreamed once of being a teacher and decorating a classroom with bright construction paper cut-outs and dangling mobiles. Of wearing pretty dresses and bright jewellery to welcome the little ones back to school each year.

She kept going past the liquor store, the grocery story and across Main Street until the cross on St. Mary's appeared. It had been years since she'd walked here, years since she'd pushed Janna in her stroller at least once a week, the boys trailing behind, down the street in front of the church, the school, and the rectory. Dawdling until the old priest came out and climbed into the same car she'd ridden in a dozen times, to a dozen secret places. Forcing the old bastard to stop as she walked across his path and looked him in the eye. She hated him, but it wasn't until he left that she realized how much it meant to her that at least one other person in this town knew where Janna came from.

She turned and forced herself to pass the school, bright with "welcome back" posters and balloons. She cut across the parking lot, walked around the corner of the rectory, and stopped. For a moment she didn't know where she was. She turned, scanning the nearby houses, wondering at the small square of tilled soil littered with bright tatters of flower petals and ragged stems. Shards of glass glinted in the last rays of light. Then she realized she was looking at all that was left of Lily Thomas's place. The house was gone but for a few splinters of wood and shattered Mason jars. The garden, obliterated. She cried out and knelt there, her fingers deep in the dirt that was still warm from the heat of the day.

Where had they moved her? Her mind drifted around the vague mental map she had of the town. Pleasant Haven. Those small rooms and the halls smelling of urine. No wonder she'd fallen asleep in the store. After all those years in her own place, safe behind a wall of things, safe in the jungle of her garden. Things that would breathe in the night around her.

Isabel worked her fingers through the soil, careful of the glass, until she found what she was looking for. A brown fragment — a dahlia tuber. She kept looking until she had a dozen in her pocket. She couldn't seem to stop. She gathered seeds, roots, anything that looked like it might harbour life, stuffed her pockets, filled her purse with dirt. She was furious at the waste. Lily Thomas's plants held so much knowledge about what it took to survive through the long winters and the treacherous summers, knowledge that shouldn't be lost.

It was dark when she stumbled to her feet. A light clicked on in the priest's bedroom. A man moved across the room, opened the closet door, and picked out a shirt. He threw it on the bed and turned toward her, unbuttoning the one he was wearing. All those years, all those priests, staring out the window, unseeing. Those beautiful dahlias, wasted. Such rage jolted through Isabel that one hand closed around a stone the bulldozer had turned up. It was cold and heavy, rough with dirt. Her arm drew back as if some powerful force had formed its own intent, and flung the rock toward the light shining on the man's face. She was already running when the glass shattered behind her.

2

Wasps, he thought, curled tight into greyness. Wasps, stinging him. He was bound and blind in a paper nest, and they were stinging him. As he tried to cry out, the paper squeezed tighter and filled his open mouth. He struggled, but his arms were bound to his sides, his legs tight against each other. The pain grew stronger. He choked and flailed, his fist suddenly breaking through. A hand on his shoulder, holding him. He froze.

"Hey, buddy."

English. Álvaro sputtered and gulped great breaths of air. Diesel and the man's tired crumpled shirt smell.

"Wake up. You're here."

Álvaro cowered, eyes down. The man's pants were the grey of a wasp's nest.

"Come on." The hand slipped under his arm, tugging. Álvaro hunched down further, covering the back of his head with his hands. The man's black shoes glinted in the darkness below. He pulled his feet up out of their reach, the pain like knives in his knees, and waited for a blow.

The man turned at the sound of a voice, released his arm, and walked away down a long tunnel toward a distant light.

Slowly unclenching his body, Álvaro set his feet back on the floor and let his head fall back against the dark softness. A big chair, the upholstery swirling in blue and grey lines just visible in the dimness. A bus. A bus at night. He looked around. Behind him, the shadows of empty seats. Across the aisle, a crumpled paper bag and cup. Outside his own window, orange light illuminated a deserted parking lot. In small red letters on the windowsill, instructions on how to open the emergency exit. The man had disappeared, but he would be back and Álvaro did not want to be trapped. He was fumbling with the window latch when the lights flickered on. A man called out. A different man. He called Álvaro's name.

Huddling now against the half-open window, Álvaro prepared to fling himself out. He could not let them catch him again.

"Welcome," the man sang in clumsy Spanish. Tall and ungainly in flapping tan pants and a red windbreaker, he walked toward Álvaro, arms outstretched. Light hair and eyes. "Welcome to Vancouver."

Álvaro let the window fall shut and slumped against it. His hand felt for the rosary in his pocket. He remembered now. He had, himself, called from the Seattle bus depot and told the priests what bus he'd be on. It felt like a hundred thousand years ago, but the Oblate community of St. Paul's Province here in British Columbia had been his first home as a priest and it was to its refuge he had been invited. He was, for the moment, safe.

He reached out to the hand coming to take his, the hand that pulled him into an embrace he could hardly bear, the grey paper suffocating him again. He began to list the names as he had been doing for months now, and he started as he always did with Ana Elisabeth. Ana Elisabeth Yax, Moises Osorio, Juan Tzul, Armand Guzman, Emilia Estuardo, Marta Barillas, and Lucía Madriela — the quiet music of their names drew all his concentration. But even as he muttered the soft cadences he was unsure. He was always unsure as he came to the end — had he missed anyone? He looked up to the pale blue eyes.

"What a time you've had of it, Al."

He couldn't control his wince at the hand clapping his back.

"Thank the Lord you're here in one piece. Now come on. It's late and you must be wanting to stretch your legs."

Álvaro followed the man to the front of the bus. He nodded to the driver and apologized.

"No trouble at all, Father, no trouble at all."

He helped him down the stairs and Álvaro hurried after the red windbreaker. He struggled to remember the man's name as they collected his small bag inside the bus station.

"Shall we walk?" the man asked in Spanish. "It's not far and I thought you'd need a stretch."

The words echoed in his head like pain. "No Spanish." He tried to make it sound like a joke. "I need to get my English back." And because the other man so obviously preferred it, he agreed to walk even though his knees were swollen and his feet burning. It had been over twenty years since he'd been in Vancouver and the walk would give him time to reclaim some memory of this place. Of this man.

In the darkness under the trees across from the station, the sweet smell of rain cut him adrift; he paused and closed his eyes trying to identify one familiar scent stirring in hidden flowers, in the water on the pavement, in the exhaust of the cars passing under the streetlights.

"Over this way." The hand on him again, directing him to a path through a circle of rain-soaked benches; the water shimmered and fractured in the passing headlights.

"Friend," he said, "you need to tell me your name." The man's eyes surprised, hurt. His other hand on the man's wrist. "Please forgive me. I have been gone a long time."

His suitcase bumping between them, Álvaro listened as they walked under overpasses of streaming cars, past chain-link fences and people ducked into doorways. George told him about the novitiate year he'd spent in Winnipeg, working with Álvaro. He told him about the parish in the centre of the city, the kids they'd rescued, the ones they'd lost. The Ukrainian feasts. The Indian funerals. And then the waves of Central American refugees and the Spanish lessons.

"Winnipeg's where they were going to send you," he said, "but we thought we could do a better job with you. There are some good programs here."

A fat woman, lips swollen and bruised, sucked on a cigarette outside a doorway. George greeted her and moved on.

"Where you going in such a hurry, honey?" she asked Álvaro.

The way the flesh sagged under her pitted skin distressed him. The cut on her mouth.

"I'm with him," he said.

The woman laughed, derisive, and called out to a car slowing beside the curb.

Álvaro's distress for the woman propelled his exhausted body around a corner onto a street of red banners and gold letters. Strange vegetables shimmered behind the bars covering the shop windows. It carried him past the stores and into the dimness of side streets. It carried him until, just ahead, he saw a large brick building illuminated in the bright beam of a spotlight behind a chain-link fence. Acid flooded his mouth with saliva. He tried to swallow it. He tried to keep walking. But he could not follow George through the gate in the fence, and he could not call out as George walked on, chattering into the quiet night. He stepped into the shadow of a tree and retched. The vomit from his empty stomach came up thin and sour and splattered on an exposed root.

He was a boy back in his village in Guatemala, hiding with Vinicio, surrounded by the night sounds of the mountains, the wind in the leaves, the bright moon, and watching the men gathered to prepare the corn for planting. Wanting to be in the house with them for the corn seed vigil, afraid to be out in the night with Vinicio, who didn't know how to behave properly. Who laughed at the rituals. Laughed at the men when they stepped out to piss into the darkness beyond the light filtering from the open door. The old one looking right in their direction and calling the mountain god by his saint's name. The owl hooting from the tree above their heads sent the boys crashing away through the thick brush, Vinicio never more angry than when he was afraid.

The fat brown root glittering from his vomit uncoiled itself into a snake, the mountain's anger unleashed, uncoiling higher and higher until the whole tree became the body of the snake, hissing. He backed away, terrified, and ran toward the lights of Chinatown, toward what little traffic there was. He heard George yelling after him but didn't stop until his way was blocked by a Chinese family arguing outside a restaurant. He hovered nearby, hoping for some safety in their presence. They shifted away from him, still yelling at each other. A child looked up at him, eyes huge. He cried out. Her eyes slanted like the one they'd named Emilia, her dying body wrapped in blue plastic and tipped into a ravine. Her eyes, scrubbed clean of makeup, opened only long enough to look at him with this same fear as he blessed her passing. The old prayers still rising like comforting breath even when he raged against them. His stomach lurched again and he turned away, not wanting to scare the little girl.

"Al, what happened?" George's pale face blotched in red streaks. He reached out to take his shoulder. Álvaro twisted away.

"Don't touch me!" His breath was ragged, his mouth full of paper. The family hurried away.

"What's happening?" George's hair was wet, his jacket streaked with what was now a proper rain.

Álvaro explained as if to a child that he must not be touched suddenly. That certain buildings frightened him. Brick. Fences. As he spoke, Álvaro's panic leaked away. George led him into the bright red and golden restaurant, ordered tea and went to phone. Álvaro hunched over the white pot, his hands wrapped around it for warmth. It wasn't until George returned that he realized he'd burnt his fingers. They were red and sore as he struggled to lift the small cup to his lips. The surface of the green liquid cracked and shivered with his trembling. Like water during an earthquake. The cup of water on the table in his mother's house, its surface fractured, a mirror to the plaster cracking in the ceiling.

Álvaro tried to talk himself into calmness. He was safe here. There was a house prepared to take him in where he could live quietly and help some of the older priests with their chores. There would be no reminders, fewer triggers to his relapses. He just needed to give himself time. He was tired and the bus trip had been difficult. He thought he'd left fear behind when he crossed the Guatemalan border into Mexico. But at the American border, the man driving him had been turned back, forcing Álvaro to take the bus across alone. By the time immigration was through with his Canadian passport, the stiff new pages were bent and dog-eared and so were his defences. The remainder of his journey turned into a long hungry hallucination north. He dozed sitting up, in and out of nightmare. It was worse when he slept. Coming awake into normal sleepy confusion, the holiday feeling of a bus trip made him smile and then the memories slipped through. The razor and Ana Elisabeth. The electric current opening incandescent lines of pain. The smell of the morgue. One kind woman had given him something for the nausea but it had dropped him into a terrifying sleep of remembering. He'd woken screaming. The bus driver had been ready to throw him off, but the small Indian woman sitting beside him had slipped him a pamphlet. *El Corazón de Jesús. Llamada de Emergencia. Oración para una grave necesidad.* He stared at the picture of the heart, a bright light under Jesus's parted robe, thinking a prayer to St. Jude might be better. Cases despaired of.

She'd stayed beside him until she got off in Los Angeles. An accompaniment, he realized as she showed him where the bus north waited. He whispered his thanks, and she'd hoisted her packages to her head to trudge out into the city, unmet, alone, the flimsy papers that gave her passage tucked inside her *huipil*. It had only been a few years since he had accompanied busloads of *campesinos* going in the other direction, returning to homes they'd fled in terror. Hundreds came out to slap the bus's hot metal, to shake the hands extended through the open windows. He'd given what comfort he could to women returning to reclaim the hillsides where their men had been shot. The villages where their children had been hacked to death with machetes. Their sisters and mothers and daughters raped. Burned alive. He should, he told himself, be able to sit quietly on a bus taking him away from those hillsides. Away from those windowless rooms and rain-soaked courtyards.

And he did. Somehow he had lived through the next thirty-six hours, through the progressive cleanliness of the washrooms and the sparkling fast food places where he had looked hopelessly at the menus and walked out again. He had managed to change buses in Seattle and phone the number where the woman who answered seemed to know him. He kept his eyes shut and his fingers on the rosary in his pocket as they crossed the border into Canada. Safe at last, he'd thought, and let down his guard to fall asleep for the ride into Vancouver. To be met by this fool who dragged him through the rain, chattering like a tour guide. As if he were on some nostalgic journey into his past. He slurped the tea until the taxi came.

It dropped them five minutes later at the bottom of steps hedged by dark shrubs.

"Just start walking," George said, "and a light will come on." His eyes bright with the pleasure of a surprise. "Walter Prytuluk's in there."

If the taxi hadn't already driven off, Álvaro would have jumped back inside to escape. It was as if tonight he was doomed to relive every mistake he'd ever made. Every humiliation. Every failure. Father Walter Prytuluk.

After his ordination, Álvaro assumed he'd be sent to work somewhere in Latin America. But a request had come from Canada, a diocese in northern British Columbia where the Oblate priests had been baptising, confirming, marrying, and burying the Indians for over a hundred years. They'd been looking a role model for the local tribes. Álvaro had some of his mother's Mayan features and the English he'd learned at the plantation she'd worked for. *La finca.*

Walter Prytuluk had been his mentor. All had gone well for the first months and the initial welcome grew into trust and mutual respect. But Álvaro had destroyed that within a few short weeks. Walter's tolerance and derision had been worse than anger. You stick your little candlestick where it doesn't belong and all of a sudden you're ready to throw it all away, he'd said. On a woman who's already got two babies by two different men. How are you going to support them and any more she might pop out? Give Spanish lessons to men who want to ride motorbikes on Mexican beaches and screw little Mexican girls?

All this time Walter had been holding Isabel's shoes. Dangling them from his thumb. Red leather sandals with high cork platforms. The insoles imprinted with the mark of each toe. The indentation of her heels. Isabel, who had taught Álvaro what a priest's vows really meant. Because when a priest makes love, he breaks them all. Celibacy. Obedience. And the vow of poverty. He didn't truly understand the concept of poverty until he lost Isabel. With her, all the knees and elbows and forehead of prayer were clothed in the radiance of flesh. With her, there was not a single patch of skin that didn't have nerve endings. You were inside your own body and inside hers at the same time, you became the tongue in her mouth and the mouth drinking her tongue. It was only when you were without her, back inside your bones, your skin a nerveless paper envelope, that you understood poverty, a fasting penance your belly could never teach you. And began to truly understand the Oblates' fourth vow. Persistence.

Which Walter embodied. Here again to witness his failure. Álvaro stood in the dark, all the shreds of his life fluttering around him. The Guatemalan boy hiding in the bush and the seasoned voice of God on Winnipeg's coldest streets. A scoured hull, smoldering in the fires of the city dump, beyond the reach of Guatemala City's most resourceful scavengers. And still the young priest, sticky from his lover.

How wise Walter had seemed that summer. How tough. When Álvaro had tried to go out the door after Isabel, stricken by the thought of her walking across town at night on her tender feet, Walter wrestled him up against the wall, his breath in his face, his eyes fierce. Oh, no you don't, boy, he'd said. There's always some who like the priests and if you're not a priest they don't want you anymore. So, what'll you do then? Come back into the fold, dip your pecker in the holy water and begin again? You're worth a thousand Isabels and don't you forget it.

How flattered he'd felt in the midst of his longing. How full of love.

He moved forward and a light came on, illuminating the narrow path and the stairs up to the tall narrow house. How noble he'd felt to walk away from her without a whimper.

Walter would have been in his fifties then, about the same age Álvaro was now. Over twenty years ago.

"Alvie, old buddy! What are you waiting for?"

The voice, the nasal garrulous pleasure, rolled over him like water.

"Haul your ass up here and give an old man a hug." Glasses winked as the man pushed his walker to the edge of the stairs. "I'm warning you. If I have to come any further, I'll be right in your lap."

It was the surprise of joy that sent Álvaro up the stairs. The old man cackled, gleeful, put one hand out, warm and strong, and grabbed Álvaro's.

"Help me get this turned around and come inside out of this rain. You look like crap."

Álvaro knew what he looked like. The bathrooms in American bus stations were wallpapered with mirrors. Over the sinks and beside the doors. He was surprised each time by the stranger who turned out to be him. The hair, shot with grey now and longer than it had ever been, curling down onto his neck — he could feel it there, startling him, as if someone was brushing against him. The pouches of skin that pushed up under his eyes. One scar sending an eyebrow awry, the other one drawing a question mark along his chin and down his throat.

Inside the small house, the smell of fresh bread drove everything out of his head but his sudden, sickening hunger. He staggered.

"Hang on there," Walter said. "Let's get you into the kitchen. I don't know what's with George, making you walk. There's a perfectly good car around here somewhere. He thinks a walk will cure everything. A walk or a swim. Just be glad you didn't have to cross False Creek."

A loaf of bread stood on a wooden board, a knife ready. A big chipped teapot and thick mugs were set out on a turquoise Formica table. The plastic mat under the salt, pepper, sugar, chrome napkin dispenser, and toothpicks in the centre of the table released Álvaro. This was his past come back, the years vanished. He was in trouble, but for that moment it seemed like nothing the kindly bulldozer of Walter's talk couldn't set straight.

The tea was spiked with whiskey, the bread slathered in butter and honey, and within half an hour Álvaro was feeling the warmth of food and liquor right to his fingertips. His eyes drooped. George and the others had come, eaten, and gone, not saying much, attentive, uncertain. Walter pulled himself upright into his walker, and Álvaro followed him into a small bedroom off the kitchen. The covers were pulled back, the sheets white, the quilt's squares framing little stars, flowers, moons, and crosses. Curtains drawn and a small lamp on a bedside table. A big easy chair at the foot of the bed. His bag waited on the low dresser.

After he had washed, he pulled on the pajamas George had given him and stood beside the bed. It was always a toss-up between the pain and the dreams — he'd flip from one to the other. What he really wanted was oblivion. He put the vial of morphine tablets on the table; a glass of water was already there. He stretched out beneath the covers and waited, afraid as always of what would come. The sudden starts. The lurching awake. The small birds pecking his head.

Walter knocked and came in wearing pajamas and a shabby cardigan. He settled himself in the chair.

"I'll be here," he said, pulling a blanket over his legs. He brushed aside Álvaro's protests, saying if he lay down he coughed — he often dozed in the chair all night. "Is there a place I can touch you?" he asked. "If you need waking?"

There was no safe place on Álvaro's body, no place that did not remember. When they'd shoved him out onto the road, he could not stand on his shredded feet. His broken ribs made every breath agony. To be alive had come to mean the same thing as to be in pain. He'd made a cave of his body and balanced on the edges of his limbs in a whimpering mound until someone whispered, "Come!" The arms trying to lift him. "Hurry!" In the hospital, they'd said he'd been in a car accident.

He slid one foot out from under the quilt. In the dim light Walter's old eyes would not see the scars. Walter put out his hand and rested it on Álvaro's heel, his rough thumb on the anklebone. The calluses were a comfort. Gardening, Álvaro remembered. Walter always liked to put his hands in the earth. And for a few miraculous hours, his body still weaving in the currents of travel, hope fluttering against the jagged lines of his ribs, Álvaro escaped.

3

The sun was already warm when Janna Catherine Lee joined the stream of students leaving residence for morning classes. Boys in hoodies and low-slung jeans. Girls in capri pants, sleeveless shirts, and flip-flops. Her tan bell-bottoms, black blouse, and fleece vest felt out of place, but she was glad for them when the cool ocean air filtered between the thick shrubs that seemed to cluster around every building and line every path. Huge trees, their leaves still glossy and green, shaded much of the grass. Chestnuts split open on the path.

Up north, the grass would be slick with frost this early in the morning, the leaves yellow in the ditches. In Smithers, the smell of fresh-cut logs from the sawmill down the tracks would ride the thermals past Janna's mother's house right into town. Two hundred and fifty miles east in Prince George, just where the highway turned south toward Vancouver, the high-pressure sunshine would trap the stink of the pulp mills and squeeze it into every corner of the community college where she'd done her business diploma, where she'd topped her class and won the scholarship that brought her to the University of British Columbia to finish her degree and the chance for jobs with some of the city's biggest financial firms. Janna Lee, chartered accountant.

She turned into the lane leading to the back entrance of the commerce building. Today began with a statistics lecture, then a workout at the gym, an entrepreneurship seminar, a statistics tutorial, the grocery store, dinner, and the orientation to the accounting recruitment program. Only two classes tomorrow; she could fit in laundry and, if the weather stayed good, a jog on the forest trails.

She dodged a delivery truck backing up to a service door and walked into the dim hallway still holding yesterday's stale heat. Halfway up three flights of stairs, she decided to forget the platform shoes for daytime wear. She was more of a track and field girl, really, and this UBC Asian look with the stretch bell-bottoms flapping over three-inch heels didn't feel right. Though for all she knew, Asian was exactly what she was. Her mother had steadfastly refused to inform her about the source of the colour in her skin, the slant in her brown eyes, the little dab of white in her straight black hair, and her insistence that everything be kept in its proper place. Her brothers swore they knew nothing. After all, Isabel had had quite a few boyfriends over the years. The less said, they insisted, the better.

She stared at the handwritten note taped to the door. Class cancelled. Other students were already walking away, calling stragglers to come for coffee, isn't it sweet, let's go downtown, I don't have another class until tomorrow, oh no, I already missed one, will there be a makeup, and it would have been nice if someone had phoned and saved me two fucking hours on the bus. The chatter pinged around her, bouncing off what felt like an invisible force shield from a bad space movie. A barrier she could see through, breathe through, hear through, one she'd felt from her first day on campus.

Small town nerves, she told herself. Just give it a bit more time. She had worked methodically to make herself fit in. The campus alone was almost as big as the city of Prince George, so she'd spent the first couple of days walking with the university orientation guide in her hand, making a mental map of her residence, her classrooms, the faculty offices, the gym, the grocery story, and the bank. She'd listened to the conversations as students waited for lectures to start and used the information to pinpoint a few classmates she thought would be good study partners. But it had been three weeks now and she hadn't connected with anyone.

She ducked into the washroom to find three of her classmates clustered in front of the mirror, one talking on a cellphone in a language she didn't understand. Their eyes slid over her as if she were a poster advertising a product they didn't want. As if the pulp mill stink still clung to her hair. She went into one of the stalls to hide until they left and sat on the toilet staring at a picture of a blonde woman wearing a sun visor, the caption encouraging female business students to learn to play golf.

Outside, she wandered toward the Student Union Building's club day displays with a half-formed idea of going to find the golf club's table. She stopped to stare at a bulletin board in the bus shelter. Desolation washed over her with the exhaust from buses idling at the loop. A cancelled class gave her two free hours and she was thinking of tacking on another self-improvement project. How pathetic. One poster advertised an introduction to rowing. She'd seen the boats sculling across the inlet down at Granville Island. Maybe she'd just go sit on the docks and listen to the seagulls. A misshapen pumpkin invited students to a Halloween pub crawl. Nuns were being tortured in Tibet. A fist called for the end of oppression of gays, lesbians, transvestites, the transgendered, and transsexuals. First-year psychology had covered those terms but she couldn't keep the last three straight. She laughed out loud at her own pun. A girl trying to find a place to put up another poster turned to look at her.

Janna looked back. The girl had short streaked blond hair, a pudgy face with bright blue eyes, and a pouty little mouth. She wore layers of T-shirts and a pair of plaid harem pants that sagged to reveal a little roll of fat and a belly button ring. Janna shifted her pack.

"You got a problem?" the girl said. Janna read the girl's poster. Overlaying the photo of a bedraggled little boy, text in a barbed wire font invited people to crash a guest lecture on international business — one she laughed to see was part of her international studies course.

"Can I have one of those?" she asked. She could bring it to class.

"Janna?" the girl asked.

Hot blood rose to her face as if the girl had read her mind. Janna struggled to place her.

"It's Janna Lee, isn't it?" The girl smiled. "I'm Amy Myerson. From Smithers. What's it been? Two, three years?"

Janna remembered. Amy's mother was an accountant who always spoke at careers day — an elegant woman with this daughter who wore clothes with rivets and chains. Heavy boots. Amy been a couple of years ahead of Janna in high school.

"I roomed with your mom this summer. She told me you'd be down here, or I don't think I'd have recognized you."

She startled Janna by pulling her into a jangling hug. She smelled like sweat, vitamin B, and some kind of lemon shampoo. Janna's trapped knuckles dug into Amy's breasts. She pushed herself away, crumpled and sweaty. "Weren't you going to South America or somewhere?"

"*Si m'ija.* Somewhere *Latino.*" Her hips wiggled. "That's where I went." She tucked the posters under her arm. "Now I'm back and I've got to put some of these up in the SUB — how about a cup of tea?"

Diesel fumes fluttered through the bus loop as the accordion-pleated B-line pulled away.

"I've got a seminar in half an hour," Janna lied. Amy's familiarity confused her. She hadn't been hugged by another human being since she'd hugged her older brother goodbye in Prince George in August. Hugs he always received reluctantly.

"That gives us about twenty-five minutes. Come on. I'm thinking of taking in that Halloween pub crawl. What do you think? I have to keep this journal for my twenty-first century culture seminar and it would be a perfect experience. I'd probably have to borrow some clothes to fit in because most of the kids will be jocks or business types, I figure." She prattled on, one hot hand on Janna's arm.

"I could probably lend you some — I have just the type you mean." Janna didn't try to keep the irritation out of her voice.

"Like they'd fit me." Amy reached to pinch Janna's waist and her fingers slid across the tight shirt under the fleece. She dropped her hand. "God, sorry. You're here on some business scholarship, aren't you? Me and my mouth."

She grabbed her hand. "Come on. I'm going to have to buy you that tea. And maybe a brownie to go with it."

Janna didn't pull away. Something about Amy's unflappable chattiness worked its way under her defences. That and the fact that Amy knew her mom, undoubtedly knew they rarely communicated, and apparently didn't seem to think it was a big deal.

They never got any tea. Amy elbowed their way through all the tables and displays to find the food booths plugged with line-ups. They ducked out of the crush into a consignment clothing store tucked into a corner. The clothes were no Value Village cast-offs. Faculty and rich students unloaded here. Lots of wool blazers and flowing rayon skirts and tops. Satchels. Very nice cotton sweaters and shirts. Solid-colour T-shirts with small brands embroidered on the sleeves. One mannequin in a black cocktail dress. Another in designer jeans and a leather jacket Janna immediately wanted.

"I had no idea this place was so upmarket," Amy said, scanning the racks. "It might be perfect. Maybe you can give me a hand, pick out something that isn't too kooky for a commerce department type like yourself."

Janna stroked the leather jacket and a clerk appeared.

"Isn't leather great?" she said, pulling it off the mannequin. "Try it on."

"What do you think?" Janna asked. "What club would take me if I wore this outfit?"

"The faculty club," Amy said. "Or the golf and country club. It's pretty swish."

Janna slipped off the jacket. $150. No way could she spring for that. At least not now. She pulled some clothes off the racks for Amy. She'd be about a twelve. Stretch black bell-bottoms. A white translucent shirt and one in a blue check, a couple of fleece vests. "Try these on," she ordered.

Amy looked at them dubiously, but ducked behind the curtain.

"What look is she going for?" the clerk asked.

Janna picked out a pair of running shoes and some black platforms and tossed them in.

"Me. She wants to look like me."

The clerk shook her head.

Janna rummaged through the bags dangling from one wall. She found a pack like hers, this one baby blue with a clear plastic cellphone slot. Amy stepped out into the middle of the store, giggling. The pants stretched over her butt and accentuated the heavy thighs her skirt had hidden.

"Give me your comb," Janna ordered. She zigged and zagged the straight part and messed it up a little at the back. Pulling two bobby pins out of her pocket, she pinned Amy's short bangs back. "Now take these out." She pointed to the nose ring, two eyebrow rings, and five studs up one ear. "Leave in these," — the two high on her ear and a little one down on the lobe — "and have a look."

Amy was delighted. "You are so like Isabel," she laughed, undoing the bottom button of the little shirt so her belly showed.

"It's about the only thing we have in common, my mom and me. Stuff that really matters. Clothes."

Amy ignored Janna's sarcasm. She put one foot forward and turned her hip out. "Who am I?"

Janna handed her the pack. "Put this on and you'll be perfect."

The clerk applauded as Amy completed the transformation into a slightly overweight and sexually eager business student.

"But it will be useless for Halloween. No one'll know you're in costume."

Amy staggered on the platform heels, laughing. "You're right. This is a disguise."

"A costume?" the clerk said. She dragged them over to a rack of sequins, glitter, and red velvet. A plush leopard skin coat. "Get a blond Marilyn wig, this coat, and butterfly glasses with little diamonds in the tips."

"And I'll bet you carry butterfly glasses," Janna said.

The clerk pointed.

"I can never think of leopard skin as sexy," Amy said. "Not after that year I worked at your mom's store."

That was when she first heard Amy's name. Through those last weeks at home, Janna's mom had kept talking about this crazy kid, about how much she liked her. The night Janna walked out, she'd said Amy could have her room. Screamed it.

"We carried extra size leopard skin nighties. Mrs. Dankley came in looking for something sexy to wear for her second honeymoon."

Mrs. Dankley, a very large woman, had been a janitor at the high school.

"We found her stretched out on the floor of the change room. She couldn't get up without our help because she was afraid she'd rip the nightgown. We asked her what she was doing down there and she said she needed to try it lying down. We should provide couches, she said. How could you tell how a nightie would feel unless you lay down?"

Amy threaded her rings back into their various holes as the clerk and Janna tried to stop laughing. "Even the living felines themselves have never looked the same since that day."

Maybe it was the release of laughter that made Janna speak. Or the sudden longing for the familiarity of home. A place where she wasn't invisible.

"Forget Halloween," she said. "You can put your little water pistol in there," she pointed to the pack, "and you'll be all ready to crash the globalization seminar. Just do me a favour and don't sit beside me."

Amy stared at her. "Is that one of your classes?" She clapped her hands like a child. "Too cool." Without bothering to close the curtain on the change room, she peeled off the clothes and tossed them to the clerk. "Ring those up for me, will you? A business expense, I think."

As Janna watched her pull on her skirt, layer the shirts and vests, take the bobby pins out of her hair and twist it up into a couple of pig tails, she envied Amy even as she disdained the roll of fat at her waist, the thickness of her thighs, and the loose elastic in her panties. Imagine not caring.

†

Janna walked back to residence through the grounds of the First Nations House of Learning. She liked the way they'd tried to reconstruct the bush: river stones piled in a little wild and weedy area beside a manufactured waterfall. If she closed her eyes, she could imagine playing tag in among the totem poles in Kispiox, down by the river, the sound of water always in the background. She used to go there with her brother, Trevor, whose father was Gitxsan. Maybe she was too, she'd say. She tried to understand the language the older women spoke and loved the orderliness of the smokehouse, red filaments of salmon hanging in neat rows, all facing upstream so their spirits could continue where their bodies could no longer go. No, the women had said. They'd know if one of their boys had any hand in her making and there'd be half a dozen aunties on Isabel's doorstep claiming ownership and jurisdiction.

No one had ever come, she reminded herself as she walked through the trees to her residence. A counsellor once had offered to approach her mother about what she called her identity issues. Janna didn't realize she'd snorted right out loud at the memory until one of the smokers sitting outside the residence door on a disintegrating lawn chair said, What? She waved him off, laughing. She already had one parent she wished she didn't; what if her father was a dud too? What if she got all her DNA from losers?

It didn't have to mean she'd be one too, she told herself. Look at Amy — she wasn't anything like her mom. And they probably didn't get along either — after all, she'd stayed with Isabel last summer, not with her own mom. Maybe they could trade mothers, she thought, staring at the smoker bending to butt out his cigarette in the metal bucket under his chair. She held the door open as he came in behind her. His name was Benny, he said. What was hers?

4

When Isabel was a girl, her family connections meant something. Her grand-father was a Bulkley Valley hotel owner who had started business back in 1912 running a roadhouse and pack train operation on the old telegraph trail through northwestern BC. He'd expanded by opening small hotels and liquor establishments in the new towns that grew along the railway between Prince George and Prince Rupert. He'd helped out many settlers by giving them a few dollars for their farms so they could get the hell out of the north and then rented the farms out until land prices went up to make a sale worth his while. He grubstaked prospectors and gyppo sawmill operators, a sideline that made good use of his only son's enormous physical energy. At the logger sports, David Lee would compete for the Bull of the Woods prize with the same men who cut the timber for his mills and then use his winnings to buy them all drinks at the family hotels his sisters ran.

He was skating across Lake Kathlyn to a Christmas party in 1951 when he spotted Catherine Black lacing on her skates at the edge of the lake. She came from a Prince Rupert family that had financed the railway that underpinned the Lee family money. Her grandfather had built himself a log house on the small lake near Smithers where prosperous Prince Rupert families escaped the coastal fogs to get a little heat in the summer and snow in the winter. Dave insisted he accompany Catherine around the lake to her home because he'd just missed stumbling into a newly opened crack out in the middle. Whether or not the crack truly existed depended upon who told the story, but his strat-egy worked because they were married within a year and Isabel came along the next.

Until her mother was hospitalized the first time, Isabel grew up in the midst of a welcoming network of aunts, uncles, and cousins who gathered in large lakeside houses, ski hill cabins, Babine Lake fishing lodges, and the big Lee family home up on the hill above town or the Black summer lakeside home that had been given to her parents when she was born. It wasn't

Vancouver posh by any means, but there were always cars and boats and ski passes and lots of food and liquor. Favours given and favours returned, children moving in packs from place to place. But during the two years her mother struggled to stay alive, Isabel separated herself from them all; she couldn't stand their pity. She hated the way the men insinuated themselves into a house that had a man in need of consolation and no wife to keep them in line. By the time Catherine Black Lee died on New Year's Day in 1969, Dave Lee had sold the family sawmill to the big industrial mills and Isabel was looking for her own consolation in all the wrong places. At the funeral, she stood her ground, silent and raging in her stiff black dress, her hair twisted back so tightly the tears couldn't leak out, as the priest droned on about God's will, patting her shoulder until she screamed at him not to touch her and slapped his hand so hard it flapped back into his own face. The beginning of her long withdrawal from the family.

A couple of decades later, none of that history mattered except to the old families themselves. And hardly even to them. So it amused Isabel to find her local knowledge in demand. Instead of gathering for Thanksgiving at the family cabins out at Babine Lake, here she was hefting bales of straw up to a young woman, Jasmine, standing in the back of a pickup pulled up beside an old barn. She was explaining that the straw stacked behind two antique trucks and dusty stage sets abandoned by a defunct amateur theatre group had likely been baled by one of Isabel's uncles twenty or thirty years ago.

"It was a family legend how my grandfather, old man Lee, conned the Indians out of about three quarter-sections up this way," she said. "That tack shed down by the creek used to be theirs, and they'd come out every fall to take a few trout. My aunt, when she brought her new husband out here to live, put an end to that. The Indians acted like they owned the place, she used to say."

After her aunt and uncle sold out to a German professor, the place moved through the hands of a series of ever more grandiose and doomed dreamers who built experimental living quarters that included a geodesic dome and a tree house, as well as a more useful group of log cabins. Jasmine and her brother, Frank, bought the place during a real estate slump a couple of years ago that coincided with a boom in the silviculture business their little company was perfectly situated to cash in on. They shared it with an eclectic mix of even more recent arrivals: a social worker, two teachers, and a biologist. They all loved Isabel's stories about riding with her mother to check on the big herd of cattle that grazed right up into the mountains. How in the winter, they'd drive out once a week to pick up a few bales of hay for the horses they stabled

in town. Her mother about Jasmine's age. The car's leather seats coated in
dust that made them sneeze big whooping joyous explosions. She wasn't sure
if it was a memory of that joy or its loss that sent the next bale barrelling right
into Jasmine.

A hand landed hot on her shoulder, a rumble in her ear. "Don't overdo it,
Isabel, my love. We've got more than enough manpower here."

She sneezed and stepped out of reach. It was only lately that she'd figured
out how to work hard physically. How the discomfort eased if you kept going,
slowly, through it. But Frank, Jasmine's brother, would like nothing better than
for her to ask for help. He was older than the others, late thirties, with at least
one wife in his past. While the others treated her as a surrogate mother, Frank
courted her. The last thing she needed. She always figured it wasn't the booze,
really, that caused her grief; it was drinking in the company of well-built men.

She walked beside the truck as Jasmine drove down the rutted track toward a small, cultivated field. In the remnant afternoon heat, a rare heat
for the second Monday in October, she could smell the girl's sweat. Light
caught the copper hair on her thin muscular arm where it bent at the open
window, and her beautiful young breasts bounced under the tie-dyed shirt
as she backed to the edge of the dirt. Three men bent over curved plots that
radiated out in dark spokes from a centre circle. They were planting garlic,
hundreds of cloves of garlic. Three bare backs bent to the work. Isabel swallowed. There was something beautiful about their shoulder blades, the way
the shadowed muscles bunched and slid under the skin stretched over the
bones. She had to look away.

The back bumper nudged the fourth man, a skinny kid with a notebook.
Isabel looked over his shoulder. He was mapping the garlic plots, marking
the names of the different varieties in tiny block letters: Polish White, Music,
Siberian, and Elephant. The drawing showed how each of the wedges curved
slightly, a path for the planters in between. He had been out first thing in the
frosty morning measuring, using string to mark the segments. Alejandro.

Jasmine nuzzled his neck. "Where do you want the straw, *mi amor*?"

"We have four types planted, each split between two plots." His pencil
tapped the drawing. "We'll mulch one of each, see if it makes a difference."

Isabel dumped two bales into the barrow and wheeled them toward the
centre of the circle. Splinters of eggshell and other compost fragments speckled the dark soil. She clipped the baling twine on the first bale. The straw

expanded with a sigh, like her breasts, she thought, when she unhooked her bra.

Frank and the others had moved into the old farm the winter after Janna had left home, the winter Isabel had given up booze. She'd also had to give up most of her friends. Watching videos night after night, she'd gotten bloated on popcorn and Pepsi, joined a choir, and tried quilting, but nothing really took. When spring came, she spent more and more time in her garden, trying to recreate memories of her mother. She planted all the old flowers the first settlers found could survive here: delphiniums, sweet William, lupines, yellow clematis, columbines, poppies, bleeding hearts, and forget-me-nots. Thyme, oregano, lavender, mint. And the ones they had to baby: roses, honeysuckle, and dahlias. Trying to create the possibility of another kind of life, the one she'd imagined for herself before her mom died.

It had been her mother's sister, Alice, who had suggested Frank ask Isabel to come out to see what was left of the huge rock garden that had been planted at the front of the house, to show them which of the plants were weeds and which were keepers. She had told them what she could and on later visits to help with the garden's reclamation, she told them more. Most gardening books weren't much use with the valley's confusing combination of a short growing season and long hours of summer daylight. Things that shouldn't grow did; others that should didn't.

The kids were mostly vegetarian and rarely drank. They were enthusiastic about her knowledge and she was grateful for the way they included her in spite of her age. They fed her strange food, which she came to like. They brought her heritage seeds and cookies. Their friends slept in Janna's empty room; some stayed on and made her evenings and weekends easier to struggle through, still sober. And Frank waited, his hair in some lights the same colour as rye whiskey.

When the planting was finished, Isabel stayed behind while the others piled into the pickup and bounced across the grass toward the old house straddling the top of a small rise. She shrugged on her jacket and felt for the bulbs in her pockets. She walked the curved pathways of the garlic bed, as if to instill their shape into her body's memory. Every few steps she paused and tucked a cluster of grape hyacinth bulbs into the dirt under the straw. In other spots, scilla. When they lifted off the mulch in April, they would find a curved path of colour and fragrance through the garlic shoots. That was the thing about gardening here. The winters were long enough that by the time the world had turned through a hundred changes and travelled halfway around the sun, you'd forgotten what you'd done in the fall. The spring always surprised you.

She hoed the fallow dirt in the centre of the plot and planted a circle of her own garlic, a stock that had been grown in the valley for over twenty years, around the edges. In a smaller ring inside, she crammed snowdrops and some tiny narcissus from the old railway restaurant plot.

She patted the ground down over the bulbs. She scooped out a six-inch hole in the centre of the ring, the soil now cold on her hands. It was almost dark. She pulled a peony root from her pocket, a root that had come from her grandmother's garden. Lily Thomas had reminded her of the bushes that drenched the back alley behind the grandmother's house with huge blowsy flowers every June.

Since the day Isabel found Lily's house gone, she'd taken to buying the old woman coffee at the A&W, a place she preferred to her tiny room in Pleasant Haven with its north window and a view of a car wash parking lot. They talked about gardening, about how the thirty-year lease the church had given Lily had expired last summer, about the priests she was convinced stole her flowers for their altar. They talked about the huge garden Isabel's grandmother had created around the house up on the hill above town where Isabel had played every Sunday summer afternoon of her childhood.

It must have changed hands a dozen times since the old folks had died, but daffodils still lined the front walk and the big linden tree bloomed every summer, its dense foliage muffling the crash of shunting trains at the foot of the mountain. Lily had taken her down the alley, pulled a sharp spade out of the pocket of her pink coat, and told Isabel where in the tangle of escaped raspberry canes to dig for the peony roots.

Isabel tucked the root into the ground. Before she covered it, she said a prayer for Janna, a prayer to overcome anger. Isabel had felt it in herself when she hugged Janna at her college graduation last spring. She'd felt it in her daughter, the way her pretty face pinched in resistance and her body became an awkward stick that Isabel wanted to shake. She covered the root and prayed that Janna would grow soft, would send out tender shoots, and that she would come home.

†

"We've found a roomer for you," Jasmine said, as they sat down to the Thanksgiving feast.

"Great." Janna's room had been empty since Amy had gone back to school and Isabel could use the cash. "Who is she?"

There was a pause. She looked around the kitchen where all the community members gathered to eat. Right now, they all looked like naughty kids with a secret. Except Frank. He shaking his head.

"Okay, okay. I give. What's the joke?"

They told her about Lance Everett, about his place half a mile back in the bush. No power. No road access in winter. He usually parked his truck at the ranch and snowshoed in and out. A couple of months ago, he'd been badly injured in a car accident. He was out of the hospital, but couldn't manage the bush.

"There's no way I'm having some guy hanging around the house feeling sorry for himself."

They said he had a job.

Isabel hadn't had the boys live with her for years and didn't miss the way they filled the house and left chaos behind. She wasn't going to let a man in to use the toilet while she had a bath and odds were they wouldn't be laughing together over some movie hunk's nice butt.

"Let me think about it."

That evening, before she'd even hung up her jacket, a girl taking a dental assistant program at the local college dropped by to see the room. She looked around Isabel's cluttered house with such barely concealed disdain that Isabel was suddenly tired. She was tired of being alone and tired of having strangers in her house. She had been hoping the girl would be right and she wouldn't have to say no to this Lance character, would make him a cup of tea and say the room was taken.

She hadn't decided what to do when he knocked at her front door. About forty, she figured as he stood on the top step, leaning on a cane. Fading red hair cut short and standing straight up. A gaunt face, clean-shaven skin pale, eyes tired. Too old to be living rough. He set a small pack down inside the door and unzipped his jacket. He was no bush bum. His clothes were clean, shirt tucked neatly into jeans, hiking boots scuffed but serviceable. Good quality too, better than anything he'd find at her store.

"I'll be honest," she said, plugging in the kettle. "I'm hesitant about having a man live here. Tell me why I shouldn't be."

He looked around her kitchen. The blue and yellow linoleum was worn almost white. The windowsills were piled with envelopes, seed catalogues, and salt-stained flowerpots. Dishes were stacked beside the sink, its old porcelain cracked. His voice was quiet.

"I have a friend in Terrace — she's helping me with this. And my son, he lives there with his mother. Most weekends I'll be there." He limped to the table, sat carefully down, and shook his head at her offer of tea. "I don't take up much room and I'm used to taking care of myself."

Isabel wasn't convinced. She imagined him hobbling in and out of the house. Uncomfortable silences. He leaned toward her and she could see, as his body shifted, the pain in his light grey eyes.

"I'm not begging for a place. I'm sure I can find something else. I'd rather not be here, thank you very much. But I find myself in a tight spot. I'll take the room if it's with the understanding that I can leave or be asked to leave on a week's notice. I don't want to be living in a place with silent tension. You'll hardly notice me but I won't be skulking around."

"Where do you work?"

"At the forestry office just down the road. I'm a plant biologist, a botanist."

Isabel felt a clutch of anxiety about her garden.

"I'm usually out in the field until the snow flies, but now they've got me sitting at a computer writing other people's reports." He shifted, uncomfortable in the hard chair. A glimmer of sweat appeared on his forehead. "I'm going to be needing daily physio to get in shape for next year's field season. It would be handy, being close to things."

He sat there with his hands resting on her kitchen table, his feet tidy under his chair, balancing against the pain. He occupied about as much space as Isabel did, but was stocky where she was thin. He held his body very still. It gave off no sparks in spite of the way his eyes held hers before looking away.

"Well, I guess we can give it a try. When do you want to move in?"

He gestured toward his pack. "Now? I have to be at work in the morning and it would save me a lot of hassle."

"What? You just walk upstairs with that pack and there you are?"

He grinned. "Well, I do have a couple of boxes in the truck. Small ones."

"You parked out front?"

He nodded.

"If you'll give me your keys, I'll drive the truck around the back and bring in the boxes for you."

He pushed himself out of the chair, shaking his head.

She held up her hand. "You don't have to worry about me fussing over you. It's not my style. But I don't see what's to be gained by you toiling out those crumbling front steps with your cane to wrestle in some boxes I can likely manage just fine seeing as I spend half my working life shifting boxes."

He handed her the keys.

"See how you manage the stairs; the sheets are in the hall closet. Your room is on the left."

He pulled out his wallet. The phone rang. She waved him away. "We can figure that out later. Go see if you like the room."

She picked up the phone.

"Hi, Mom." It was Trevor.

The relief she always felt to know he was alive. "Where are you?"

"Prince George. We were thinking of driving right through. We'd get in about two. Do you have room?"

She thought of Lance's quietness. He might as well get used to life on Railway Avenue.

"It'll be the couch."

"Ouch."

"I've got a new roomer."

"The couch it is."

"I'll make it up for you. Just keep quiet when you come in."

"Thanks."

"Love you, buddy."

"Me too."

She hung up. Only then did she realize he'd said, "we."

The boxes weren't heavy — mostly clothes and maybe a couple of books. A rattle of pills. She knocked on Lance's door. He'd found the sheets and made up the bed. A couple of shirts were folded neatly in an open drawer. She set the boxes on the desk and nodded to the posters Amy had left behind. Trees and clusters of people. Something in Spanish.

"I can get rid of those."

He shrugged. "They're okay."

"My son, Trevor, he'll be arriving in the night."

Lance's face, worried. "You'll be wanting the room."

"No, no. It's just for the night. He's got his own place up the Kispiox Valley. He's a driller and has driven through from somewhere in Mexico. He's crazy for driving. Anyway, not to worry. Just so you know what's happening if you hear them coming in. There's only the one bathroom."

He nodded.

She handed him the keys. "Your truck's out back. I locked it."

He thanked him and they stood there for a minute, silent. He seemed able to wait without expectations. Isabel felt herself relax. "Good night," she said.

She heard Trevor later — the quiet door and the squeak of the couch springs. She knew by the murmurs the other one was a woman. She cracked open her window to let in the outside sounds: the buzz of the halogen lights over at the train yard, the exhaust fan at the plywood factory. A car passed.

†

When she went downstairs the next morning, she was surprised to see a pot of coffee on and the dishes washed. She hadn't heard a thing. She looked out back; Lance's truck was gone. That was easy. She sat in her chair by the window that looked out onto the garden, warming her hands around the coffee cup, her feet cold in the draft. A grey garden, except for some purple oregano flowers and a splash of green where the little creeper, whose name no one seemed to know, covered one rock wall. The freshly turned vegetable bed's black soil glittered with frost. She was glad for the cold; it would do the peony no harm and would keep the garlic from a fall sprouting. A couple of years ago, a warm November, late rains, and a hard frost had killed most of her bulbs and half of her perennials.

She didn't keep records like Alejandro. She kept it all in her head, all the different years laid one over the other. She could remember when the beds were small, when the yard had been mostly lawn. There wasn't a bit of grass out there now.

A big raven landed in the mountain ash dangling its heavy crop of berries on either side of the fence. He hopped onto one of the outermost branches, bobbing and swaying as it dipped under his weight. There were berries all around him, but he inched out, his eyes fixed on a clump right at the tip of the branch. Frank, she thought, and laughed to see the bird take a berry in his beak and roll it back and forth before gulping it down. She'd be hearing from him soon. Asking about Lance, warning her about his bad habits.

It wasn't until she'd finished her coffee and was rounding up her purse and jacket, thinking she'd probably need a scarf and gloves because there was a wind bending the alders in the ditch, that Trevor stumbled out of the living room. A T-shirt and boxers. A new tattoo on his right arm, some kind of bird with a long tail. He hugged her, a smell like smoke, a bit of diesel, and something she didn't recognize. His face scratchy against her cheek. She was always surprised at how much her body missed her kids, even the sandwich hugs the boys would crush her in when they came home stinking and half drunk from a hunting or fishing trip.

"You still working at the store?" He'd been gone months now and Isabel had been thinking about quitting when he'd left.

She nodded.

He pulled out a chair and pushed her into it. "I'll drive you."

He refilled her cup and poured himself one, smiling sleepily across the table. She was always mad at him when he was away because she was frightened he would be hurt. The postcards a month out of date. But as soon as he was in the room with her, she was happy. Seeing his open face was like seeing her own best self reflected back. He embraced anyone who claimed relation to him, and there were dozens of folks who did; he welcomed them all into his house and didn't wonder or blame. He held no grudges. His morning hair, thick and bristly, reminded her of his father whose astonished joy had made him a generous lover. He'd held no grudges either. Unfortunately she'd been married at the time, Jason crying in his crib upstairs.

Trevor finished the coffee and stood, turning for the stairs. "Janna said to say hi."

The name clattered between them, like glass shattering on the floor. She waited, staring out the front window across to the railway tracks, while he climbed the stairs. Dead thistles in the ditch, their seed heads frosted silver. The sun was just beginning to hit the mountain. She wondered what it would feel like to be up there right now, shivering in the early light. There were people who'd pitch a tent up in the rocks like that and wake up in a sleeping bag, nothing but a thin skin of nylon between them and the sky. People like Jasmine and Frank. Probably Lance. Was that kind of life over for him? Would a cold morning freeze all the metal inside his body?

She was no camper and could no more imagine life in a tent than she could imagine Janna in her little room alone down in that huge city. She'd like a picture. She wondered if Trevor had any.

He came back downstairs, a wet splotch on the front of his T-shirt. He was a clean man with hardly any whiskers. It was the Gitxsan blood. He pulled on his jeans.

"How's she liking it?"

"She said the first couple of weeks were rough and she's not that fond of residence. They're all either hippies or geeks. But she's got her own room, she said. A little microwave, a fridge, her own bathroom."

Isabel nodded, unable to ask further.

"I took her out for coffee." He poured himself another cup. "Didn't have time for supper, she said." He fished a bright pouch out of his pocket and tossed it on the table.

"I know you worry about her and me and Jason. These are supposed to help."

Isabel pulled open the drawstring and spilled out a handful of tiny figures onto the table. Each one was dressed in bright clothes made by wrapping thread around their bodies. Black hair puffed out from their little heads, their faces sketched in with blotches of black ink.

"You tell them your worries and put them under your pillow — then they worry while you sleep."

"Seems unkind to dump all that on these blameless little creatures." She stroked one woman, her feet hidden under a long pink wrap.

"Believe me, Mom, they're better off here than down there."

"Then we all thank you, sweetheart." She was so happy to have him here, sitting at her kitchen table. She nodded toward the living room. "Who's the girl?"

"Soryada."

"Pardon."

"Soryada Verapaz." He enunciated the syllables. "She was cooking at the camp. Wanted to see snow, she said."

Another one of his girlfriends. Isabel would just get acquainted with one and he'd be on his own again.

"I should go, honey."

He ducked out back and started his pickup. A frightened face peered around the door of the living room. An Indian face. She could be one of Trevor's half-sisters.

"Soryada?" Isabel struggled with the name. Held out her hand. "I'm Isabel. Trevor's mother."

The girl nodded and pronounced "Hello" very carefully. She ran a hand through her hair. A long black swath that needed a wash and a brush. She wore one of Trevor's T-shirts pulled down over her panties. Trevor opened the door and spoke to her in Spanish. It sounded like a bark. She ducked back into the living room.

"Hey," said Isabel, "what was that about?"

"She shouldn't be coming out in her panties, like that. I told her to get dressed."

Poor kid must be scared half to death, she wanted to say, but she just pulled on her coat and walked out to the rumbling diesel. The bitter fall wind funnelled down the long straight stretch of Railway Avenue.

He dropped her off outside the back door of the store and waited to make sure she got the door open okay. She reminded herself of his kindness. She knew he would stop at her bank before he went home, put down a payment on her mortgage, a mortgage that was almost done. She was not going to start worrying about another woman's daughter, at least not yet. Once he got settled, he'd bring her back for a visit.

She shoved the door open and waved him away. As she stood in the dim glow of the night lights, feeling for the switch, the smell of cardboard and shoe glue settled in an ache behind her eyes. The fluorescent tubes flickered and hummed, lighting up the floor-to-ceiling boxes, plastic bags glinting where the cardboard had split. The path through the storeroom changed from week to week and she'd had more than one fitful night, dreaming herself trapped in a maze of boxes, the stacks tumbling all around her, cutting off the way out. Maybe the worry dolls would take away those dreams.

By the time she hung up her coat and turned up the furnace, the phone was ringing in the lunch room. She could barely get to it, the room was so stuffed with the last-minute cartons of Halloween specials that were supposed to have been put out over the weekend. There must have been some no shows, or maybe the new girl had quit. She was glad once again that she'd refused the answering service Jason wanted to buy for her. The manager couldn't track her down on her days off.

She picked up the phone. It was the new manager, ranting about the un-professional attitude of the sales associates. Maybe it was time for a change, Isabel thought as the woman talked about the new strategies she was going to implement. The colour-coded sales charts. The productive rivalry Isabel needed to work harder to instill in the staff. Isabel had seen a dozen managers come and go and none of them could sell clothes and keep the staff happy like she could. She didn't know if she felt like waiting around long enough for this one to figure that out and leave her in peace.

After she scoured the burnt coffee out of the pot and put on a fresh one, Isabel went out front. She liked the store's mystery, the way the mannequins blurred in the dimness at the back of the store, the way the darkness turned to colour and light up near the big front windows. She paused, alert to secret possibilities, and listened for any sound beyond the furnace's hum. She heard a car door slam shut. Before the back door opened and voices spilled into the silence, she flicked on the front lights and watched all the shadows slip away. And so, she thought, let it begin. Let it begin again.

5

Álvaro choked on mouthfuls of damp soil, stinking of rotten flesh. He clawed the dirt away from his face and his eyes. Tangled bones dug into his back as he struggled to dig his way out of the hole. He fell back again and again as they collapsed, clattering under his feet, falling away from his scrabbling hands. The slippery smoothness of femurs. The sandpaper joints. The splintered ribs gouging his back. Shoving himself finally into an unsteady crouch, he opened his eyes to light washing through white gauze curtains. A Madonna embroidered in dusty wool hung on the wall at the foot of what he slowly recognized to be his own bed. Untangling his legs from the sweat-soaked sheets, he heard Walter coughing in the kitchen. He placed his feet on the cool linoleum.

These were old acquaintances, these exhumation dreams. Bones pale against the grey dirt. Scraps of cloth and beads tangled in the vertebrae of a neck. Rubber boots rattling with the small bones of a foot. He had pressed the arch of his own foot to a shovel to help in their uncovering. He had prayed with the taste of dirt in his mouth, the taste they had died with. Dirt on their tongues, stones between their broken teeth. He had stood with the families as they received the bones from the forensic anthropologists and arranged them as best they could in the coffins. He had donned all the power of his regalia to bless the wooden boxes lined up in the long trenches, then, once again, set his foot to the shovel. He would awake from the dreams thinking he was receiving the gift of understanding.

He stroked the worn linoleum with the soles of his feet. They were ugly, his feet. Ragged nails on the end of the long toes, lumpy veins crisscrossing the tops. The left one sagged in the middle where it had been broken. Scars at the ankles where they'd tied him. He pulled on his socks and shoved his feet into the old moccasins Walter had given him.

Since they let him go, a heap on the side of the highway, he had tried not to look back. He had shoved every lie Vinicio told him deep inside and struggled to repair the ruptures in his body and build his muscles so they were strong enough to keep the lies buried. He had worked until exhaustion felled him into unconsciousness. He had looked away and away and away until Clara's whispered confession slit him open again. Sent stumbling north, he sought oblivion in the safety of distance. He lost track of the days he'd spent in Walter's garden and in the kitchen preparing the simple meals the others preferred. He read dozens of Walter's mysteries where the murders were quick and always solved.

He and George told Walter about their time in Winnipeg and the church where Álvaro had introduced the Spanish mass when hundreds of Central American refugees came to the city in the early eighties. He was even able to tell stories about his return to Guatemala with some of those same refugees a decade later. About the work after the peace accord and the exhumations. Guatemalan massacres dating back generations offered up a field school for forensic anthropology. Beatings, bullets, and machetes. Knowledge useful in other places: Rwanda, Bosnia, Chile.

But he could not talk about the chasm that had opened when he was thrown into the back of the blue van. When every simple certainty unravelled in a house of darkness. He could not tell Walter that it wasn't fear of damnation or the love of God that kept him from killing himself. It was his mother's Mayan stories about skulls whispering words of love into the ears of princesses, of the dead coming back to inhabit the living. Too many ghosts fluttered the nerves under his skin. He did not want to become one of them.

His mother. Walter's morning kitchen sounds — the water poured into a pot, the pot banging down on the burner, the cutlery rattling in the drawer — brought back some of his earliest memories of walking with his mother in the morning darkness up the rutted track to pass between the white gate posts into the green irrigated gardens of Mario Fortuny's ranch, *La Finca Libertad*, the sun touching the tops of the hills high above the pastures. Son of an Italian immigrant who had come to Guatemala in the late 1800s, Fortuny ruled his domain like a Medici prince. Or a Mafia don.

César López, a carpenter, and his young wife had been hired by Fortuny in the early fifties. When the workers occupied the plantation a few months later during the short-lived land reform years of President Árbenz, César told them it was of no use to anyone if they starved the cattle and burned the buildings, some of which he had worked hard to build. Listening to Walter prepare the oatmeal, Álvaro understood for the first time that during those months, his mother had lived in that house as its mistress. Held the keys to its cupboards and helped Cesár keep track of the money and the cattle. A pregnant Q'eqchi' woman married to an itinerant *Ladino* carpenter. Because they were outsiders, because Cesár knew something of the world beyond the hills that surrounded the plantation, the farm workers had looked to them for leadership.

After the Americans ousted Árbenz, and Fortuny returned from the capital with his own little army to kick out the *campesinos*, he was pleased with the excellent condition of his property. Instead of shooting Cesár, he offered him the position of manager. Knowing what was likely to come, Cesár had declined. Knowing there'd be plenty of work for carpenters rebuilding burned houses and repairing broken furniture. Piecing together from the scraps, coffins. A child of darkness he had called Álvaro, born into chaos of 1955 when thousands of the Guatemalans who had welcomed the Árbenz reforms were being arrested and murdered.

A good omen, Fortuny had said when he called Cesár to his office, shook his hand, and told him about the birth on the same day of his daughter, Clara. A twin to Álvaro. Here's to a return to good government and prosperity for both our families, Fortuny smiled, lighting their cigars. Cesár could stay in the village house, Fortuny offered, all jovial good spirits, and his wife could come up to the ranch and work in the kitchen. She could bring the baby with her. Cesár spitting out this story when he was drunk. Behind Fortuny a photo of President Eisenhower hung on the wall. Tucked into the frame a newspaper clipping showed the deposed Árbenz in his underwear boarding the plane to Sweden.

It must have been hard for his mother to return as a servant. Mornings, she carried the sleepy Álvaro along the rutted track between their house and the ranch. Dust in the dry season, slippery clay in the rain. She'd speak in her own language and tell him stories about her home where the people didn't gather in villages much, but were spread through the hills living on their own small plots of land. Where the men didn't need *el patron*'s permission to plant the corn. Where they were strict about the old ways. The community had a saint's name and a mountain god and she knew what prayers kept the spirits in balance.

At the ranch, they spoke Spanish. Fortuny's father — an Italian peasant, Cesár always said, a useless younger son with no land to farm — married a *Ladina*. So did the young Mario, leaving him with only a few words of Italian. His wife had none. When the family was in residence, Álvaro slid into the

Fortuny children's lives. Clara insisted that her twin, as she called him, must have his lessons with her and her older brother, Vinicio, in the dining room. At first the distant mother, reading to them in a bored voice. Later, as she came less and less often to the plantation, the children escaped a succession of tutors to play complicated games of hiding, sneaking, and dramatic rescue, Vinicio always pushing them.

Playing with Vinicio was, Álvaro came later to realize, like drinking with an alcoholic. It was almost impossible to resist the initial high-spirited invitation even if you knew, the worry niggling inside, that the fun was going to spiral out of control into something stupid, mean or terrifying. Daring Álvaro to ride through the young corn the villagers had planted. Repeating Fortuny's words about their stupidity, their ignorant ways. Idolatry. Devil worship.

The threesome: Clara refusing to kick up mud on the freshly laundered clothes spread on the bushes down by the river. Vinicio taunting Álvaro, calling him a chicken. Álvaro, distracting him, making him laugh at his imitations of the workers, his mother, even Fortuny. The sweeping gestures as he shaved, as he hitched up his trousers and adjusted his balls. The way he settled back in his chair to listen to scratchy opera recordings.

When Cesár was home, Álvaro's world was another way. His mother made tortillas instead of biscuits for their breakfast and he had hot milk instead of chocolate. They listened to his father's stories. He was a restless man, raised in a Catholic orphanage, taught his trade and released into an itinerant life, picking up jobs as he travelled through small towns and villages all the way down to the capital. He'd even been to the Atlantic coast where they grew bananas and the air was so wet it felt, he said, like you'd been caught in a magic rain that never fell, just hovered in the air. He spoke of a world not tied to the ranch and carved Álvaro a parrot which his mother painted blue and orange.

Álvaro had loved the magic of his father's saws. The lathe he lugged home on his back one day, treadling square blocks of wood into buttons, knobs, balls, spindles, the pale wooden heads for the dolls his mother decorated. She twisted together a paintbrush out of dog hair and drew delicate eyebrows, little red lips, and bright blue eyes onto the wooden heads, transforming them into people, some of them surprised, some laughing, some angry, and many quiet faces that gave nothing away. His mother's own.

The way she could keep things hidden, she should have been a priest. All through his childhood, she had prepared him well. How to behave at the ranch. How to behave around his father. In the village, where his father's *Ladino* background, his mother's different customs, and her work in *el patron*'s home separated him from the other children. Her eyes worried when he rode off with Vinicio, trailing his guilt and his longing. She had struggled to keep his divided spirit firmly attached to his body. Taking him down to the river, she'd light candles and incense and call his spirit back from wherever it was she thought it had gone. The relief when she finished and stood him between her knees to feed him pinches of egg and chicken, his spirit warming to the taste of hot food.

In the small room in the centre of the house on a quiet Vancouver side street that brought together a group of Oblate priests joined in their service to the misery that flourished just a couple of blocks away, Álvaro laughed at the thought of asking the priests who prayed for him every day if they knew of a nearby river. Of a Mayan spirit healer. The priests spread out each day, one to the mission, one to visit the prisons, one to counsel the drunks, each taking turns celebrating mass for the parishioners who trickled into the church next door. They were so few for the work that needed doing, he felt guilty: for the food going into his mouth, for the time he threw the lemon pie out the back door to splatter on Walter's wheelchair ramp, for the days he curled into a ball and spit out words. Get away. Get away. A part of him standing outside himself, hands hanging at his sides, aghast and helpless.

While the others muttered about his needing professional counselling, Walter was like a seminary soccer coach. Walk it off, he'd say if you twisted your ankle or doubted your faith. When Álvaro emerged from two days curled up in bed, his back to the door, Walter handed him a knife to chop onions. In the garden, he handed him the hoe. Root out that pigweed, he'd say. Now let us pray, he'd say and Álvaro would bow his head as if he were doing just that.

There were moments Álvaro felt as young and hopeful as he had twenty years earlier when he and Walter drove those highways another five hundred miles north of Vancouver, so empty between the mountains. The lightness of the air upon his skin up there was a memory he'd never lose. The flies drifting in the swirling currents above the creeks, fish rising to them. Walter would take Álvaro to the Indian fishing camps to say mass. He'd cast his hopeless line just downstream from the nets, always one old Indian giving him advice, the others shaking their heads, laughing as they plucked their nets clean of the big red salmon. They were as unlike the Indians of the movies as his own mother's people were.

But most of the time now he felt like one of those fish struggling under the surface of the water. Every shadow a threat, every kind word hiding a hook. Like Vinicio's voice — all lies, he told himself, his head buried under the pillow, his body clenched in a tight curve. Like his father's rage.

By 1965, Guatemala's turmoil had entered their home; his mother was learning to read from the catechists who had come to their village. A crucifix appeared on the household altar and a little radio hung on a nail in the kitchen. Vatican II had done its work and the priests were speaking to the poor. Their message of social change didn't go unnoticed by the Guatemalan army.

Cesár came home from his trips angry at all the coffins he was building. Not the ones for the women in childbirth, their tiny babies wrapped in their arms. Not the ones for those killed in the buses rolling over into the ravines. He knew the details of every death, he said, and it was once again as bad as the days after Árbenz. Mutilated bodies dumped beside the road, the families silent. He'd been as far as Mexico, he said to his wife. We should go now. These people here, he spit, some said she spied for *el patron*. Others said he spied for the guerrillas. If things get bad and I'm not here, you'd have no family to hide you, he told her.

If they left here, she'd say, there was only one direction she'd go and that was back to her village where she'd be welcomed but she wasn't so sure about him. Sometimes Cesár was drunk. Sometimes there'd be blows. Álvaro would go to the pile of lumber behind the small goat pen and sit there with his school books until it was quiet inside. He'd wish for the days with Clara at the ranch, his father back on the road. Wishes he could never reel back in.

On Cesár's last visit home, the guerrillas had stopped him on the road. They told him how the Americans were using the dupes in Guatemala to try to bring poor Castro down when all he was trying to do was feed his people. The guerrillas were honest soldiers, the liquor in him yelling now. Álvaro's mother hushed him, crying. Álvaro curled up on his mat in the corner and wished he was brave enough to sneak up the long track to Clara asleep in the deep softness of her bed.

The next morning, Álvaro had helped his father replaster the house. As they mixed the mud, his father warned him to not speak of anything he'd heard the night before. A talk, man to man. It could endanger any of them. It was time Álvaro came with him to see the world. Time to get him away from the sad little plantation village, those rich brats and their spoiled ways. Time to teach Álvaro his trade. Álvaro was packing the mud into the narrow gap that had formed around a window frame when Cesár stopped talking. Turning for another handful, Álvaro saw him staring at him, a frightening pain on his face. Álvaro stepped toward him, wiping his hands on his pants, reaching out, asking what's wrong? Are you hurt? The pain changed in a lightning strike to anger. Cesár shoved him away, yelling for him to stay back, *el bastardo.* Don't touch me!

Álvaro stood outside in the sun, the mud caking on his hands, listening to his father yelling at his mother. I have seen those hands before, he yelled. I have seen them closing in fists to bash some poor bugger whose cow stumbled into his pasture during the night. Álvaro's mother crying, sobbing, begging. His father whispering. I have seen them fluttering like *las mariposas* over the breasts of some little *puta* he has found in the fields. The boy looked down at his hands, the skin dried and wrinkled like that of an old man, and wondered why his father called him a bastard.

And then his father was gone, leaving the house half plastered and his tools hanging near the door. His mother refused to answer his questions. Don't speak of him, she said, her hands quick to strike. When the tools were sold and the lathe disappeared, something, he knew, was irrevocably broken.

Álvaro rubbed his face and scrubbed his hair with his hands. In the small chapel next to his bedroom, the other priests gathered to say morning prayers.

Lord, open my lips, and my mouth will proclaim your praise.

He waited, as he had every morning since his arrival. George's rich voice carried the hymn. *Time, like an ever-rolling stream, bears all its sons away; they fly forgotten, as a dream dies at the opening day.*

He had tried to join them. But he couldn't get through the prayers without weeping or raging. Lashing out. Everyone distressed. When he was ready, Walter had said, and they left him alone. But they knew he listened through the thin wall, sometimes with his head buried in the blankets, some mornings as he stretched. Did push-ups. Sit-ups. Squats until his knees swelled, the skin so tight it almost burst. Some mornings, quietly like this, sitting on the bed, his feet on the cool linoleum.

That morning he wondered if their prayers were getting through. The exhumation dreams were from a time when he was still intact. When the bones of his body, cushioned in muscle and sinew, connected with nerve and blood vessels, carried him, blind as he was, about his business in the world and in the spirit. The time when nightmares did dissolve upon waking and he could remember much of his childhood with fondness. When God was in the world with him.

At daybreak, be merciful to me, O Lord.

Prayer was what he missed the most. Collective prayer. The way it had first come alive when he was a novice, kneeling with the others and feeling its power as a physical presence, a flush of heat and exultation, the whole community of Oblates, of Catholics, of Christians praying around the world, one group picking up as another left off, as if their prayers and the turning of the world were one thing. But now there were places he could not bear to go and they were places that prayer took him.

George's voice hushed to a dramatic whisper. *For two days now I have experienced a great desire to be a martyr and to endure all the torments the martyrs suffered.*

Álvaro groaned as he realized what day it was. October 19. The celebration of Isaac Jogues and Jean de Brébeuf, martyrs. He covered his ears, but the words seeped through as George's voice rose in passion.

Let me so live that you may grant me the gift of such a happy death. In this way, my God and Saviour, I will take from your hand the cup of your sufferings and call on your name: Jesus, Jesus, Jesus!

Álvaro flung open his door and stood wild in the arched entrance to the sanctuary. The men sat in a semicircle, Walter with his eyes closed, his head tilted to catch the words.

My God, even if all the brutal tortures which prisoners in the region must endure should fall on me, I offer myself most willingly to them and I alone shall suffer them all.

George's joyful eyes met his. He thinks I'm responding to his little ministry, Álvaro raged, struggling not to speak his fury. George proceeded to the responsory.

Through faith the saints conquered kingdoms and did what was just. They secured promises and were strong in battle.

The others responded. *All of them have won approval for their witness to the faith.*

"God tried them," George began and Álvaro shouted the phrase's completion, making it a question. "And found them worthy of himself?" He flung his derision, an explosion, into the midst of their contemplation.

"Álvaro, you forget yourself!" Walter's voice was harsh. He struggled to his feet, clutching at the walker.

"You think torture is some kind of test? The fire that tempers the steel of your faith. If my faith was strong enough, I'd be the better for it. I'd show the bastards, wouldn't I? They'd want to eat my heart while it was still beating, wouldn't they? Grab hold of my strength."

Álvaro's anger was a powerful antidote to the hallucinations, but they were breaking through. His ears were filling with the ringing laughter of the dark house he tried to keep shut up inside himself. The smell of lemons and death filled the small room.

"You think you know anything of evil?" he yelled, feeling the contempt suffuse his body and swell the clanging in his ears. "You think God finds us worthy?" He could see George's lips moving but could hear nothing over the clamour inside his head.

George moved toward him, a hand reaching out. Álvaro twisted away, banging into the doorway. "Don't touch me," he cried. "Ever!" He lunged for the light coming through the barred window in the back door. He wrenched the door open and stumbled outside as angry voices rose behind him. George's cry chased him into the garden.

Through the darkness that always followed the ringing laughter, Álvaro found his way to the stool he'd placed behind the garden shed, a shadowed spot where he could sit out of sight of the house or the church or the back alley. He hunkered down while the pain and terror rolled through him, tumbling him like the earthquakes tumbled boulders, breaking him even as he broke everything he came in contact with.

†

It was the cold ground under his bare feet that brought him back to himself. They burned with an old pain that the gravel made worse. Beside them, his shoes and socks. Someone had placed his jacket over his shoulders. Their kindness suffocated him.

He lifted his feet, one at a time, and picked out the small stones embedded between the scars. He pulled on the shoes, his fury gone, leaving him as it always did, rubbed raw and tender. He put his arms inside the sleeves of the jacket. The air, smelling of the roses climbing over the peeling white fence that bordered the alley, felt like needles under his skin. Tall stalks of corn, heavy with ripening heads, turned yellow in Walter's garden. He walked into their midst and stood, head bowed, listening. He fingered his rosary. In the ways of their village, his mother's brothers had planted corn for him, preserved its seed to pass on. His mother fashioned the seed into a rosary to bless his priest-hood path. You never know, one uncle said, his mother's face reflected in the pattern of wrinkles, the shape of the teeth, smiling. It might grow yet. Álvaro's pale *Ladino* skin, blushing.

Her whole village was gone now. The earthquake had taken his mother; two years later, the civil war had taken his uncles. And his father? Vinicio's lies whispered in the wind as it sifted up through the side streets from the ocean, riffled through the narrow gaps between buildings, through holes in the boarded-up warehouses and into the leaves of the trees of Strathcona. It rustled in the stalks of golden corn and he felt as if his heart struggled to beat inside a crumpled wasp nest.

The summer after his father had disappeared, the rains were good. There was plenty of pasture for the cattle and Álvaro, now fourteen, stopped dream-ing of becoming a guerrilla or of finding his father. School was finished for him. Clara was rarely there, living mostly in the city with her mother. He rode with the foreman and came home to the ranch, to the small room off the kitch-en he shared with his mother. Fortuny had given their house to another family.

Vinicio will make you foreman, Clara whispered on one visit, pulling him aside. A graduate of military college, Vinicio had come home with his hair cut short, his posture stiff — as if he had been hurt somehow. Looked around his home as if he were a stranger to it.

The old man was proud and encouraged him to bark orders. Told Álvaro it was time he learned obedience. Guffawing, he sent them out to find girls, Álvaro delirious with the smell of Clara, their bodies smouldering with something neither of them yet recognized. Until the night in the barn, the rain pummelling the tin, the eaves gushing water into the rain barrels. Vinicio shoved one girl in his direction and took the other into an empty stall. Álvaro and the girl beside him listened through the rain to Vinicio's grunts. Álvaro stroking her hair and feeling her breasts through the stiff embroidery of her *huipil*. Afraid of her skin. Afraid of his mother discovering the wet stain on his pants where the girl had put her hand.

That rain was thirty years and thousands of miles away from the mist now drifting into Walter's corn. *Sprinkle me with clean water and cleanse me from all my impurities and my idols; Give me a new heart and place a new spirit within me. Take from my body my stony heart and give me a natural one.*

Álvaro stood in the garden, ashamed of his earlier outburst, ashamed of all his outbursts, and there was no way he could find to force himself back into the house to apologize. Over the past month his apologies had become meaningless. He zipped up his jacket and pulled on the toque someone had shoved into its pocket.

He slipped out the alley and walked toward the sound of traffic. Walter had kept him close to the priests' house for the past month. He wasn't ready, they thought, for the chaos of the streets. For the snapping electricity of the trolley buses and the police on the downtown east side. There was a crackdown on the dealers, Walter explained, and it was better to stay out of the way, especially if you didn't like uniforms. But it was to the streets Álvaro wanted to go now, the places that every city had somewhere and some cities had everywhere, where pain was made visible, literal.

Within a couple of tree-lined blocks, he saw the signs. Broken bottles. A needle. A pile of flattened cardboard at the base of a huge drooping conifer. Plastic bags rolled along the sidewalk. He picked one up, sniffed for glue, the desire for its oblivion a sudden explosion. A neurotoxin, the street worker had explained when he'd first started working in Guatemala City's *Zona Uno*. It's ideal for the kids, she'd said. It floods the frontal lobes where emotion resides. It floods them and disconnects them — no stress, no pain, and no fear. No memory. Nothing but the smell of plastic. He tried not to think of the yellow tube of glue in the kitchen drawer back at the community house. Glue he had stared at until someone asked him what he was looking for.

He turned a corner into a street blocked with cars. Beyond the choking traffic, the grey water of the harbour. The white froth on the waves made him thirsty, even though he knew it would be salt.

A bell rang at his heels and he jumped around, down in a crouch. A huge grey-haired man in a wheelchair held both hands up in a gesture of surrender. "Whoa! Sorry about that, man."

Álvaro stood up again as the man backed his chair away, his pitted face pinched in apology, his eyes watchful. His jacket was submerged beneath a welter of pins and ribbons and bows and his legs were covered in a plaid blanket. The wheelchair was festooned with bulging plastic bags — they were tied to the armrests, the backrest, and a rack behind his shoulders that looked as if it was rigged up just for the purpose. The bags were full of cans and bottles. Perched on the top of the whole contraption was a huge striped umbrella.

He bent his massive body sideways to fish in a pocket. He held out a coin, his fingers encased in translucent plastic gloves. "You need a couple of bucks to grab some breakfast?"

"I would very much like a drink of water."

The man pointed a couple of blocks down where people clustered around a van pulled up on the sidewalk. "They have juice."

Álvaro took the shiny gold and silver coin and looked at it carefully. The queen, he recognized. Flipping it over he read, "Canada. 2 Dollars. 2000."

"You just off some boat?"

Álvaro smiled. "I've been away for a long time."

The man's finger, ghostly under the glove, pointed at the polar bear on the coin. "I used to take my kids to see the bears at Stanley Park. Those are big buggers."

Álvaro welcomed the small details. The shape of money. The English name. Stanley. He thanked the man and walked toward the van.

In the cluster around the cart, people moved with the careful steps of the hungover, the still stoned, and the damaged. They didn't jostle one another; they formed a semicircle where they could all see each other. A woman who looked as rough as the rest of them served up coffee and pastry. She forced juice on some, chiding them about blood sugar. Some paid her in beer cans and empty whiskey bottles. For his two dollars, she handed Álvaro a plastic bottle of juice, a pastry, and a stick of gum. He thanked her and sat on the stone steps under a nearby awning to drink the welcome liquid.

A thin youth moved around the van like a broken bird — flapping, dipping, and turning. Stopping to nibble a bite of pastry, then revolving like a top, spinning and circling at once. Drivers' pale faces, sleepy in the red light, watched those on the sidewalk from behind locked doors and thick shields of glass. The boy staggered in widening circles around the pastry wagon and in between the cars, the drivers anxious for their paint jobs.

"I had a dog like that once," the big man said, parking his wheelchair beside Álvaro. "A retriever. If she couldn't find the bird you'd dropped, she'd start running in circles, getting wider and wider until her nose caught a whiff of blood, and then," his arm zapped out, "she'd take off straight to the bird."

As he spoke, the youth saw something down a side street and ran across the lanes of traffic, the broken bird and demented retriever in one body. Álvaro bent his head into his hands, dropped his elbows onto his knees, and watched the tears he could not stop drip down to splash on the speckled stone between his feet. Where he'd felt fury and fear before, he now let waves of despair wash over him. He was back in the morgue in Guatemala City, the attendant's gloved hands pulling another sheet off another body.

"They just let you out of somewhere?" The kindness in the man's voice broke through.

Álvaro looked up. "You could say that."

From under his blanket, the man pulled out a box of tissues. Álvaro took one and wiped his eyes.

"Where'd they have you?"

Álvaro thought of the small room, the curtains, the dusty Madonna. "A private place. Just a house, really."

"Family?"

Álvaro nodded. He held out a hand. "Name's Al," he said.

The other man shook it, his plastic glove sticky and warm. "Constantine." He shifted in his chair. "The folks inside the Carnegie here, they'll help you find a place. That is if you need one." He hurried on, anxious not to cause offence. "They don't ask a lot of questions."

The coffee wagon bumped off the sidewalk into the traffic. Buses passed, stopped, doors hissing as they opened and closed.

Constantine nodded to a clock at the intersection where time and temperature alternated in blue light. "The bottle depot's opening. Gotta go."

He wheeled off across the street and up toward the highrise office towers. Behind Álvaro, locks clicked back and doors swung open. A trim woman and a man in a suit, both Asian, scooted up the stairs and ducked inside. People drifted away from the curb and up the stairs. The cold stone seeped through his pants, chilling his back, and making his kidneys ache. Two cops walked by, yellow jackets saying Vancouver Police. They gave him a look. He flinched. They stopped.

"Your name, sir." A woman. Bulky. Her body padded with gear. His body spasmed into a fetal crouch. An arm under his. He screamed.

"Christ, we've got a live one here."

He heard raised voices, people gathering. People asking who he was. He called out a name. Clara. The metal gate squealing open. Clara, he screamed.

The woman bent again to ask his name, her hand on his shoulder. Clara. He would not go with them. Never again would he go with them. He lashed out, his fist hitting the padding on her chest, his hand yanking her hair.

He was face down on the steps faster than he could think, held there as the voices rose around him, the English suddenly the cackling of outraged chickens.

The woman hissed as she manacled his hands, and hauled him into the back of a wagon. There was no safe place. It was dark and he was inside another van, in another country, rolling on the metal ribs of the floor, banging into the wheel wells as the driver squealed around corners and accelerated for the speed bumps, the men cackling as they heard him cry out. He could not stop screaming.

And then he was strapped down in a pink room. George's face was pale against the pink wall. Álvaro closed his eyes. He sank down again, down into a room where screams ricocheted in bright colours off the filthy walls. When he awoke again, George was still there. The room was full of people in lab coats. A man released the restraints.

"Padre, you're a brave lad to take on the city's finest. Not good timing, though. Things are a little tense down there these days. Best to lie low."

What had they told him? Álvaro wondered when the doctor traced the scar on his eyebrow, along his chin. He lifted his hospital gown. Even through the sedation, Álvaro could sense the man's distaste at what looked like self-mutilation. A bizarre tattooing. Crude arrows pointing to his groin.

"A most extreme case," the doctor said. He pulled the gown back down and turned Álvaro over to open the back of his hospital gown. There was a collective gasp from the students gathered at the door. Letters carved to remind him. *Nuncas mas*. George cried out. The doctor's voice changed.

"What kind of monsters has he been mixed up with?" He parted the hair to trace the cross carved into Álvaro's scalp. He described the ruin of his feet.

"I think that's quite enough," George finally said. He pulled the curtains closed around the bed and Álvaro felt the air move across the skin he had kept so well hidden for the past month. For the past two years. On the other side of the curtains George spoke quietly to the doctor. Álvaro rolled over onto his back, raised his palms in front of his face. The lifeline on his left hand carved a path right around the base of his thumb clear to his wrist. The line on his right hand was broken, crosshatched into a hundred tiny scars where he'd put his hand out to stop his fall onto the shattered glass of the torture room.

George stood beside him, barely able to meet his eyes. "I don't think we realized," he stuttered. "We'll get you the help you need."

That's what Álvaro was afraid of as he stared out the window of the car that drove him through the shining stream of traffic on the clean streets of Vancouver. Through the towers glittering in the afternoon sun, across one of the bridges high above the boats sparkling on the water below, up the long straight street lined with trees, the big houses hidden behind high hedges, all sparkling clean.

Who here would understand anything of what he'd been through? In this city without razor wire or gates. No men with rifles. The car turned into lush green shade, circled and came to rest in front of a white building, a building that looked Spanish. Turquoise trim. George helped him out of the car. *Oblate House* it said on the door. *Welcome* on the mat. The last time he had been to the provincial house, the Oblate order's administrative centre for western Canada, the superior had been very cranky after hearing what had happened with Isabel. They'd kept him here until the transfer to Winnipeg had been arranged, a naïve young priest whose holy anguish barely disguised his fierce desire for one woman's flesh. A desire he thought would never dim.

The door opened and he walked across the cool floor, a thin, quiet woman drawing him inside.

"Eloise," he said. It had been twenty years, but he remembered. She had been plumper then. Now she was thin to the bones.

"Father Álvaro," she said. "It's been a long time. It will be good to have you here."

"The home for errant priests."

She giggled. "And you're the only one under seventy."

He followed her through the back door, across the lawn to another house. One he didn't recognize.

"The Oblate country club," she laughed as she led him past the swimming pool, the little grotto for the virgin, and under the second-floor balconies into the L-shaped house. "From the days when we needed more room, if

you can believe it." She showed him into a room — a single bed with a plaid
bedspread, a table, an embroidered wall hanging, a crucifix, a chair. A small
braided rug. A closet. She put his case on the table, turned back the covers,
and patted the pillow. She drew the curtains.

"You've had enough excitement for this week," she said. "Why don't you
rest? I'll send Andrew over — he's our one living breathing novice and the only
other resident under seventy — I'll send him over to fetch you for vespers."

He sat on the bed as she closed the door. A lawnmower hummed somewhere. The reflected light off the water in the swimming pool rippled across
the curtains. His left thumb traced the scars on his right hand. After a while
he wedged the chair under the doorknob and lay down on the floor. He began
to do sit-ups.

6

Amy found Janna in the library. Janna cleared her computer screen and sat back. Her report on the principles of partnership for her commercial law class was due tomorrow.

"It's too bad you left when you did," Amy said. "Just when our little costume party was getting revved up."

The international business seminar had featured a mining company executive with projects in Asia and Madagascar, the Canadian distributor for a clothing manufacturer with factories in Central America and the South Pacific, and a vice-president for a detergent company that sold its products worldwide. Three suits and a grad student moderator. Janna was wondering what it would be like to work in Madagascar when Amy, dressed in the consignment clothes, slipped in, a thirty-something man in tow. She winked at Janna, but didn't sit with her. She took careful notes during the presentations, and nodded as questions about Asian banking procedures and the culture of Nicaraguan contract negotiation were answered. When she stood to ask a question, the moderator didn't hesitate to acknowledge her.

She asked the mining company executive, very politely Janna was relieved to hear, how he dealt with conflicts over land acquisition in Indonesia where local indigenous people disputed ownership with the government. A little mutter went through the class as people tried to place her. The man tugged at the knot in his tie and leaned into the microphone. Spoke about the delicacies of doing business where there are internal politics that are really none of our business. But a good company working in places where the rule of law is not always followed needs to make alternate arrangements to protect its shareholders' investments. And to protect the jobs for those people who want to work.

"This is perhaps an accounting question then," Amy went on. "The two hundred and fifty thousand dollars a year you pay the security firm that has been implicated in the deaths of thirty-five villagers and the injuries of another two hundred. How would you enter that in the books? Would it be security or risk management? Public relations?"

The man leaned back in his chair, all jovial man of the world. "I'm an engineer," he said. "I leave the accounting to skilled people like yourselves."

Amy turned to the students and shrugged. "Beats me," she said. "I thought protection money was something you paid to the Mafia."

Some students snickered, but none made eye contact with her. Janna saw that the man she'd come with held a small video camera on his lap.

"I think it's someone else's turn now," the moderator said and pointed to a small dark woman standing at the back. She wore a navy belted dress.

She addressed her comments to the detergent manufacturer. "I'd like to begin by acknowledging your company's skill in maintaining its market diversification."

He nodded genially.

"Could you describe for us the strategies you used to circumvent the Costa Rican government's efforts to have you introduce mustard oil into your glue as an irritant so the street children of San José would not inhale it?"

As he pulled the microphone toward him, already speaking angrily, she held up her hand. "Sir," she said. "On behalf of *los resistoleros* of Central America, I am here to salute you for maintaining the approximately twenty-five million dollars in annual sales that glue sniffing brings into your coffers. You are providing these poor children with inexpensive peace of mind."

That was when the back door opened and a group of rough-looking kids fanned out in the audience to distribute little baggies that Janna found out later each contained a tablespoon of glue. Amy's friend was recording the whole fiasco when Janna slipped out a side door, afraid Amy would acknowledge her in some way. Dumb, dumb, dumb. What had she been thinking when she invited her? She met the security guards coming up the back steps and stepped aside to let them pass.

In the library, Amy sat across from Janna. "Wasn't Sister Amelia fabulous?"

"Who?"

"*La ángel de la guarda des resistoleros.*"

"She's a nun?" Janna had thought she looked like one of the accounting profs.

"Neat, eh? She said it was a wonderful way to celebrate Halloween."

"Don't you think glue was taking things a bit far? It grossed quite a few people out. I mean they don't mind questions about ethical practices — we do talk about that stuff in class. Codes of conduct, fair labour practices. But those kids. The little bags." Her nose wrinkled. "It was kind of sickening."

"Gross is the whole point," Amy said. "It's bad enough for the street kids here, but it's nothing like Guatemala City. They carry their little bags of solvent like your girlfriends carry their retro compacts to powder their perfect noses. Or stash their coke. Little sniffs whenever they get nervous."

"Exactly what girlfriends are you talking about?"

"The kids have cracks and sores around their mouths and noses where the fumes burn their skin. Black eyes and cracked jaws where the cops have kicked them for trying to sleep under their cardboard blankets."

Students looked their way as Amy's voice rose. "They stink of glue and dirt and the semen of the rats who fuck them." Amy was shaking with rage. "It is gross. And every asshole who owns one share in that company needs to know exactly where their dividends come from."

"I am right here," Janna whispered. "You don't have to yell."

"Fuck 'em," Amy said. "Researching essays on the romantic context in Yeats' late poetry or some such shit."

No wonder Isabel liked Amy, Janna thought as she packed up her computer. After her mother downed a couple of drinks, nothing bugged her more than people's efforts to calm her down, to keep her from saying or doing something embarrassing. Janna, always torn between wanting to be part of the fun and being afraid where the fun would end up.

"Where are we going?" Amy asked.

Amy's anger was gone, just like that. Like Isabel. A flash and it was over and the warmth returned. A warmth that had made Isabel's house a place Janna's friends wanted to stay, her brothers' friends, some of the cousins, uncles. There was never any fuss about who might say what, or who might kick over a can of Coke on the carpet. If a girlfriend needed a place to hide from her angry parents for a day or two. And, Janna had to admit, Isabel's boyfriends and the booze never came past the front door. She slung her pack over her shoulder and walked toward the elevator.

"Gotta catch a bus — meeting my brother downtown."

"No problem. I'll pop by later — show you another way to celebrate Halloween," Amy said and took off down the stairs.

Janna stared at the elevator doors and watched them open. A man looked out at her, one hand holding the door. No, she shook her head.

She wasn't going to meet Trevor. That had happened a few weeks earlier. He'd called her, said he was waiting outside. She'd run down to where his big diesel pickup idled at the curb, a new tattoo on the arm he reached across to pop open her door. A sports cap on backward, a hemp chain around his neck. Three earrings in one ear, four in the other. The hand on the steering wheel was scarred across the back, the fingers blackened with whatever it was he did on the drilling rigs.

Parking is hopeless here, he'd said, and taken her to a White Spot along Broadway. He'd never lived in Vancouver but seemed to know his way around. She'd sat with her hands wrapped around a coffee cup, watching him eat. Cutlery clanked and dishes rattled on the busboy's trolley. He was tired, she could tell, after driving for three days straight. Dark pouches under his eyes were a sure sign and the rough and red patches across his cheeks and his chin. He'd been gone since June, working long shifts in some dry hot mountains way out in the middle of a Mexican nowhere.

He pulled a flat package out of his pocket and handed it to her, telling her to stop staring at him and open it. She unwrapped a piece of cloth, woven in a copper and green pattern of birds and leaves. It's a special bird down there, a spirit guide for some of the locals, he'd told her. He showed her the new tattoo, the same green bird with a long tail and a flash of red at its chest. She rubbed the skin, still rough from the ink. His girlfriend could tell you more, he said. A quetzal. Not raven tricky, but more noble.

"We don't really have any of those kind of stories at home, but this bird, it tried to save some great Maya warrior. People down there think a lot of it."

"Girlfriend?"

She was visiting some nuns, he'd said. They're all Catholic down there and nuns raised her.

"Poor kid."

"Nah." He shook his head. "She liked them fine. She did okay."

Trevor would never listen to much in the way of complaints. When he came back from a drilling job and found her living with Jason and Cindy in

Prince George, she'd tried to explain. I'm not saying your leaving didn't make sense, he had said, and I'm glad Jason was here to take care of things. But there's nothing good going to come of you staying mad. He'd been the one to bring Isabel to her graduation, both of them as prickly as devil's club. But he'd got them through it.

"I knew you wouldn't like any of the really bright stuff they make down there," he said, "but this might give you a laugh."

He threw a gaudy drawstring bag onto her placemat. She opened it and shook out six tiny figures onto her hand. Each was dressed differently; some were men, some women. Black hair curled on their heads. Worry dolls, he'd said. You tell them your troubles and stick them under your pillow and let them do the worrying for you.

She'd reached up to scramble his hair, stiff with something trying to keep the cowlicks down. He'd be getting Isabel to cut it as soon as he hit Smithers, she'd said. He'd laughed. She seems to be taking care of herself, he'd said.

"It's her birthday in a few weeks. You want me to take something up for her?"

A birthday present for Isabel. She'd shaken her head and felt so lonesome when he drove off she wanted to call him back, climb into the truck, and drive home with him.

†

All Souls' Night at her sociology professor's, Amy told her as they walked through a jungle of untrimmed hedges around to the back door of a big house sprawling down the slope overlooking the ocean. She shuddered as the leaves brushed her face. The night *Latinos* usually visit the graves of their relatives and bring them food and drink. Skeletons dangled from the trees and skulls lit with little red light bulbs clacked in the wind blowing off the water. But these people's dead relatives are either buried in faraway places or missing in action. So, the Colemans put on a special party. Salsa music and smoke wafted out the open windows. And Spanish. Animated conversations, exclamations, and cries of appreciation. Oh great, Janna thought. Maybe she could sing *La Cucaracha*.

Amy led her through an entrance hall crowded with coats and shoes into a large living room. People clustered in front of the fireplace, under a huge window festooned with paper skeletons, and in the doorways leading to the rest of the house. Someone touched her arm and she turned to see a short man with thick glasses. He said something to her in Spanish. Janna looked for Amy but she was already across the room enveloped in a group hug. Janna pointed to Amy and shrugged her incomprehension at the man. She turned away, already regretting coming, already looking for an escape.

"Here I thought Amy had brought one of her little *Latina* refugees." He was the sociology professor, Thomas Coleman.

"Like Amy, I was actually born and raised right here in BC," she answered as he guided her toward a table at one end of the room.

"Ah, but you're the image of a little salsa dancer from Spanish school in Panajachel."

Janna had no idea what he was talking about.

"Wine, beer, tequila." He waved at the debris of bottles, glasses, melting bowls of ice, and scattered slivers of lime on a corner table. She poured herself a glass of wine.

"Is this your place?"

He laughed. "My wife's, really." He waved to a group of women, heads bent together over the pages of a small book, one of them moving a finger along a line of type. "Old money. I am merely a tenant."

Janna didn't know what to say.

"Let me show you around."

Janna liked to think of herself as wise to the ways of the world when it came to parties. When she was a kid there were the huge family gatherings out at the lake, gatherings where her mom often ended up drunk and leaving with someone else's boyfriend. She and her brothers would be tucked into a cousin's bunk beds for the night and taken home the next day. Her mother mowing the lawn as if nothing had happened.

Then there were the high school gravel pit parties. She'd spent most of those comforting distraught girlfriends and shaking boys out of alcoholic comas. Hiding car keys. At college it had just been more and harder drinking in chaotic dormitory rooms. Beer cans and pizza boxes stacked to the ceiling. Disgusting bathrooms. Her only party at UBC so far had been the wine and cheese reception welcoming the students in the CA stream. Accountants in suits, mostly men, and a couple of women with muscular arms and legs and gold chains around their necks.

None of her experiences prepared her for this Day of the Dead party. Coleman propelled her through the crowded rooms introducing her. In one, two short men who looked Indian were talking quietly in some language that seemed all clicks. In another, a big man, his belly swelling his T-shirt over the belt of his khaki pants, held what looked like an old rug on his knees, pointing at a bright figure woven into the design. He and the two women examining the cloth looked up through a fog of blue cigarette smoke. Smiled. Bent back to the cloth.

The kitchen was filled with people leaning against walls, perched on stools and preparing food around a long wooden table. Tiled counters and deep blue cupboards, some with red birds and yellow flowers painted around the handles, stretched along two walls. Plants lined the wide windowsills, their foliage cascading down to the red and white tiles on the floor. The fridge and gas range were bright red, and beside the back door an old cookstove shone with polished chrome. Old money indeed. Amy detached herself from the table, a plate of food in each hand. She was rattling away in Spanish to a kid who looked about sixteen. He was trying to take something off the plate. She danced sideways, out of his reach, and ploughed her way over to Janna.

"Follow me, *mi amiga,* and we'll find something for your undoubtedly starving tummy."

One platter was covered with little green packets. Cookies dusted with icing sugar and tiny sugary skulls were piled on the other.

"The tamales are pretty hot, but the cookies should be okay."

The boy's big hand snaked over Amy's shoulder and his fingers deftly lifted three skulls and dangled them over his open mouth. As Amy's elbow caught him in the ribs, he dropped them in and danced away, mouth bulging.

"Where's he going?"

"Up to his video games, no doubt. Little bugger."

Janna watched his big feet climb the stairs, the Nike slash on the heels, wishing she could escape the adults at this party. "He's related to that Coleman character?"

"Son of."

She was about to ask Amy who the mother was, but she was gone again, along with the food. Janna was alone with an empty wine glass. She refilled it and drank, feeling the warmth radiate through her otherwise empty stomach. The contract law report waiting patiently on her hibernating laptop in her empty room in residence needed, she thought, one more rewrite.

It was an unusually warm evening for November and windows were open. She pushed aside the empty glasses on a windowsill and leaned out into the darkness, feeling the warm air behind her, the cool air on her face. The leaves wreathing the window were hung with little skulls, their red eyes blinking. Beyond that, darkness.

She closed her eyes. Out of the rise and fall of voices, a little bell chimed, and as she listened, it rang again. And again. Every minute or two, the bell. It will ring all night, Professor Coleman had explained, to summon the dead. Maybe her father had died and was waiting out there in the darkness right now, waiting for her to recognize him. She used to open the old school atlas and pick towns from every province. Chicoutimi. Major. Bay Vert. Nanaimo. She'd dance around saying, Nanaimo, Nanaimo, and imagine she had knowledge of him embedded somewhere in her, knowledge just waiting for her recognition. For a while she'd thought he was maybe a trucker, one of those men with bellies falling over their belts and rolled-up sleeves too small to contain the huge forearms, powerful from slinging big chains and hauling freight. Arms that were always open from grasping the broad steering wheel and a big bull neck that rotated on massive shoulders as he turned to back his truck into tight alleys. When she'd started college in Prince George, she'd imagined him as a professor for a while but she had to admit none of her mother's boyfriends had been remotely professorial. He'd be some cowboy who'd hate this party, this cluttered house full of people from places that seemed like a dream of words and fragments. He'd probably tell her to lighten up, to come have a beer.

The flash of a camera from the darkness below the window startled her.

"You look vaguely familiar," a voice said, "but out of context."

Janna looked at the winking skulls. "I'd have to be Buffy the Vampire Slayer, maybe, to be in context?"

His laughter was way out of proportion for her joke, but she enjoyed it and was curious to see what he looked like. A boy, really, that twenty-something indeterminate age, walked blinking into the bright light of the living room, a brown paper bag in one hand and a small case in the other. He wore baggy boarder pants, a hooded sweatshirt, and a toque. With his goatee and the narrow black glass frames accentuating the slant of his eyes, he looked

Asian. When he set down his bottle and case and pulled his hoodie off, his T-shirt rode up revealing his boxers waistband a couple of inches above his buckle and his lean stomach.

She was suddenly shy and turned away. An older woman had come up beside her. "Boys never looked that good when I was your age," she said. "Or if they did, we were warned to stay away from them."

The boy offered his bag to Coleman, who had materialized out of the crowd and was already taking the hoodie. He was, Janna realized, a very attentive host.

"Professor Coleman," the boy said, offering his bag to the little man. "I tracked down some mescal if you can believe it."

Coleman was unscrewing the lid when the woman stepped up and relieved him of the bottle, one arm around his shoulder. "*Muchas gracias*, David, is it? My husband's been talking about you all day. Glad you could make it. Now, Thomas," she said the name with a Spanish inflection, "let the poor boy have a drink before you put him to work."

David looked over at Janna and shrugged helplessly as Coleman poured two tumblers full of amber liquid and took his arm. They disappeared upstairs. Janna was still trying to put it all together — this regal grey-haired woman dressed in a maroon dress flecked with deep blue, silver birds dangling from her ears, looked way too elegant to be married to the sticky Professor Coleman and way too old to be anything but that skull-eating kid's grandmother. And what work did, what was his name, David, have to do upstairs?

Amy reappeared, refilled Janna's glass, and introduced her to more people. There was a young woman who spent a year working on a coffee plantation in El Salvador, another woman who had accompanied refugees returning to Guatemala from Mexico. Two were doing research on the textile industry in Central America. Saying Liz Claiborne with disdain. Tommy Hilfiger. Janna dragged Amy out of that room when one girl started lifting people's hair and reading their shirt labels.

They stood for a moment looking out through the window at the smokers gathered on the big deck. Amy pointed out a woman who returned from university to find her family had disappeared.

Disappeared? thought Janna. Like the girls on the posters in the gas stations? The ones gone missing on Highway 16? Isabel and Trevor always on to her, not to hitchhike.

"And Ruben, there," Amy continued, "he watched them rape and kill his wife. Pregnant with their first kid. He was maybe nineteen. They threw him in the pile of bodies, covered him with dirt, but it was shallow. He got out."

He was laughing at some joke, his face unmarked by the horror he'd lived through. He looked like her brother. Broad cheeks, dark eyes, lips puffed out a little around his big white teeth. Scruffy hair standing up like Trevor's did.

Everything seemed to blur, the voices and music around her jumbled into a noise that overwhelmed her. She wanted nothing more than to be alone in her tidy little room. Her clear words organized on the computer screen in front of her. Music in her earphones. She slipped away from Amy and found herself in a line-up for the bathroom. She stared at a photograph of boys diving off a big stump into a lake, praying that whoever was in the bathroom would please hurry up, praying that no one would talk to her.

"It seems a bit clichéd at first, but the jagged branches on the snag make you wonder what kind of danger those boys are jumping into." The voice paused. She turned. It was the guy with the mescal, David. He looked very pleased with himself and a little bit drunk. "And the oblique angle of the light is very nice."

"Excuse me," she said and snatched her pack from a hook by the door. She was threading her way down a path toward Marine Drive when she heard feet running behind her. She stepped off the path into the underbrush. It was David, his face flickering in the light filtered through the trees as he passed her. His footsteps paused as he reached the street below. She waited until he had climbed back up the hill before extracting herself from the blackberry thorns. A few minutes later she was squatting in a flowerbed on the street's wide meridian, unable to hold back any longer.

Shifting awkwardly, trying not to splatter her shoes as her pee hit the ground, she dug her hands into the dirt to balance herself. Her fingers brushed something and she dug deeper until they were wrapped around a hard, smooth shape. She tugged harder and pulled up a bulb. She must have planted a thousand bulbs with Isabel over a dozen Octobers. She dug around and pulled up another, then more and more until the dirt was littered with their round bulges.

7

Isabel handed the parcel card to the postal clerk without thinking. He must have seen the alarm on her face when she recognized the tiny writing on the package.

"Bad news, Ms. Lee?"

The box rattled slightly as if filled with padded golf balls. "Just a surprise, that's all." She smiled at him and walked out into the bitter darkness. She was glad she'd worn a scarf and thick tights that morning. The wind found the seams in her coat as she walked down the back alley toward home. She clutched the parcel to her chest, the fingers in her thin gloves freezing into pain. Her back ached from a long day standing at the till and she was so Friday-tired she tried to hurry, half running and dodging the frozen puddles gleaming in the lights streaming out from all the warm houses full of kids and friends and families planning their weekends. Her purse kept slipping off her shoulder and banging against her thigh, the strap twisting and tangling in the ends of her scarf.

When she finally reached her back gate, she was locked in shivering spasms. One tug reminded her she'd latched it from the inside that morning. She stared between the high slats at her dark house. She'd been hoping for Lance. Hoping for the gate to be open, the lights on, the heat turned up, something cooking for dinner to distract her from whatever surprise Janna's package contained. She cut through the neighbour's yard and stumbled across the frozen ditch up onto the road by her front gate.

She stood for a minute to catch her breath. Through the side window of her dark house, she could see the pale glow of the microwave clock. The wind whistling along the straight swath of the railway tracks rattled the bare branches of the lilacs against the porch. She did not want to go in. She did not want to see the breakfast dishes she'd left on the table. She did not want to stand shivering while the furnace clunked on, rattling and banging until it warmed up. She wanted to throw Janna's package under a clump of tattered thistles and flag down one of the passing cars. She wanted to get a ride to the warmth, noise, and light of a Friday night bar. She watched headlights approach and pass, approach and pass, almost tasting the hot rum she would order.

A gust of wind full of grit snapped her out of her longing and up the steps to fumble with the front door lock. She was close to tears when she stepped inside, desperate now just to get warm. But before she could even close the door behind her, a small shape hurtled out of the darkness to throw itself against her legs, claws scrabbling at her tights.

Mercifully the lights flicked on and a loud "Surprise!" rang out before she booted what turned out to be a puppy down the hall. A jolt of pure rage coursed through her as she looked at the smiling faces of Trevor and Soryada, the staff from the store, Jasmine, Alejandro, and most of the other people from the farm. She blinked back her tears and fury, wondering who had thought this up. She looked across the living room to where Lance stood with her aunt, Alice. He shrugged and shook his head. Frank grinned from the back door.

"Gotcha!" he crowed. "Totally gotcha!"

"Frank, you do anything like this again and I'm going to compost you," she said, struggling to make it sound like a joke. She turned to hang her coat on a hook and tucked the parcel under a heap of mittens and scarves. She had no intention of opening it in front of an audience. She squeezed Alice's hand and wondered what they'd have done if she'd flagged down one of the passing cars. Wishing she had.

As if Alice knew what she was thinking, she pulled her close and whispered, "Now you behave yourself, young woman. You may be all of forty-nine, but I'm still keeping an eye on you."

After the standard Lee birthday dinner of hot dogs (with the addition of tofu wieners for the vegetarians), potato chips (organic), and salad, everyone crowded into the living room. Soryada carried in the cake, a huge tiered platform slathered with white frothy icing and lit with dozens of candles.

Isabel took her time, exclaiming over the decorations, counting and miscounting the candles. When she finally blew them out, three emerged from the smoke, still burning amidst a cacophony of whistles and claps.

"My three loves," she said simply, thinking of Janna. Wishing she was there beside her. Janna used to make her beautiful birthday cakes copied from glossy magazines. Cakes shaped and decorated to look like bouquets of flowers, one year a wheelbarrow full of paper daffodils, another time all silvered to look like a sheet of ice and decorated with a figure skater twirling a glittering skirt and a long head of red licorice hair.

"Thanks, Soryada," she said, slicing through the rich icing to release the smell of chocolate and cinnamon.

Trevor pulled his girlfriend under his arm, her head against his shoulder. "Just be glad we talked her out of another Mexican tradition," he said.

Soryada giggled and whispered.

"Tell us," Jasmine said.

Soryada moved to sit beside Isabel. She smiled at her, a beautiful smile in spite of slightly crooked teeth and a small scar whitening the corner of her upper lip.

"I would take your hair like this." She slid her hand under Isabel's bangs as if feeling for a fever and put the other hand on the back of her head.

Alejandro laughed and shouted something in Spanish.

Isabel cried out, struggling, as Soryada suddenly pushed her face toward the cake.

Alejandro shouted, "*Mordida, mordida*!" and translated as Soryada pushed Isabel down until her nose touched the icing. "Bite, bite!"

"At home," Soryada said, "we would push your face right into it!" But she released her, and, as Isabel spluttered upright, she reached out one finger and flicked the cream off the tip of Isabel's nose. She licked it and grinned.

Isabel looked into her brown eyes, the irises flecked with golden light, and was completely disarmed by the girl's merriment. She hugged her. "It's a good thing you stopped where you did," she said, "or I'd have had to eat the whole cake myself."

Lance brought in the presents as everyone chattered and ate. Isabel exclaimed over the gardening gloves, tools, and gift certificates. An answering machine from Jason. She shook her head at Frank's extravagant orchid shipped direct from a specialty store in Vancouver. As she sat back, someone released the puppy from wherever it had been hidden. It exploded into the pile of wrappings, chewing the paper, barking, and licking icing from sticky fingers. Its fur was a feathery mass of burnished red.

"Whose is he?" Isabel asked.

Trevor sat him up and waggled his paws. "Isabel, I'd like you to meet Perro. Perro, Isabel." He stretched one of the puppy's paws toward Isabel. "Your new momma."

The dog yipped.

Isabel stared at him. "What would I do with a dog, for heaven's sake? I'm at work all day. It'll pee in the hallway. It'll destroy the garden."

"We've trained him. If you give him his toys, he'll chew them instead of your plants. Try him out for a month and I promise if at Christmas you don't want him, we'll take him back."

The puppy's sharp little teeth nipped at her fingers. They were red and sore from the cold, but somehow the little teeth were welcome. Isabel felt something in her loosen, and she struggled not to cry.

"What's its name again? Perry?"

"Perrrro," Alejandro said. "It's Spanish for dog. But you have to roll the rrrs, or it means 'but.'"

"Pain in the butt," she nodded.

"No, no, but — as in the coordinating conjunction."

Jasmine groaned. "As in the exception. I like all my presents *pero* the dog."

"I love you, *pero* not your taste in sweaters."

"Your head is swollen, *pero* your dick is limp."

It degenerated, as it often did with the farm crew, into unfathomable hilarity. Perro bounced from one giggling group to another as they collapsed together onto the couch and carpet.

Alice handed Isabel a flat package. She gasped when she saw the advent calendar glittering with hundreds of tiny golden leaves and bell-like flowers. It promised to reveal the secrets of Christmas plants: poinsettia, holly, ivy, the small trees that produced frankincense and myrrh. Alice beamed across at her with such pleasure, Isabel almost cried again. Alice was the only one from either of her parents' big families who didn't judge Isabel for her failings. Alice was the one who kept her mother close.

By the time Isabel said goodbye to the poor sad store clerk tearful over the transfer of a promising boyfriend, Lance had gone to bed, and Soryada was making up the couch while Trevor took the dog outside for a last pee. Leaving her presents in a heap on the kitchen table, she climbed the stairs, reassured by the presence of warm bodies in the house, by the evidence of friendship.

It wasn't until she was lying in her bed, the lights from the railway yard orange beyond her curtains, that she remembered Janna's parcel tucked away downstairs. She thought about sneaking down to get it, but she could hear the quiet voices below her and she didn't want to explain. Waiting for the house to settle into silence, she wished her girl was home. Whenever Janna sensed that Isabel was upset, she'd come into bed with her to talk, and they'd often fall asleep together. Her smell of clean hair, what was the face cream she used then — something that smelled like peaches? She'd twitch in her sleep, yelping as her muscles jerked. Isabel would think about Álvaro at those times, remember the shape of his face, the sound of his voice, the way he was delighted with simple things: the little rose at the centre seam of her bra, the zippered compartments in her purse. After they had made love, if there was space and time, he would go through the papers, the makeup, and the loose coins to organize them. Make a tidy pile of the garbage. She would hide the orange candies he loved just so he could find them. He would reapply her lipstick for her and wipe off the smudges his fingers left on the golden tube. He would brush her hair and clean the brush, letting the strands of dark hair float away in the currents of air.

She remembered the way the river changed from swollen June brown to dappled green as the summer passed. The wild raspberries and saskatoon berries she fed him just before he disappeared. It was as if thinking about him with Janna dozing beside her would somehow make Janna know her father in the ways that really mattered. Because there seemed to be no way to talk out loud about their time together without making it sound pathetic. Or dirty. Father Walter's voice curdling in her ear. She still sometimes mourned Álvaro as the lost love of her life — until her anger forced her to deride herself for being such a fool.

Isabel finally fell asleep. She dreamed a long erotic dream, orgasming in a vague memory of breath in her ear and a mouth between her thighs. When she awoke in the early morning darkness, the wetness between her legs brought back the dream, but the pulse of release was not the climax she remembered. It was the beginning of her period. Periods that were becoming more and more haphazard. By the time she'd taken a shower, dressed, and gone downstairs, Lance was already lacing up his boots. The dog was at his feet. She'd forgotten the dog.

"I've already taken him out for his morning constitutional. He should be okay for a while."

"How do you feel about dogs?"

"Animals should not be given as gifts." He rummaged for his mitts through the pile scattered by the back door. "But if you decide to keep him, we'll have to move stuff like this out of his reach. Maybe build him a run. I'd be able to stop by at lunch since I'm so close, take him out for a quick walk."

Isabel had been looking forward to a quiet cup of coffee and maybe some birthday cake for breakfast. Not a puppy. "What should I feed him?"

"They brought food. I've already put out a bowl for him."

"Do you think he'd like a little trip to Terrace? Think how much Dustin would love him." Lance's relationship with his son was complicated. He had to walk a fine line with the boy's mother or she'd block his access. The visits had to be kept simple. If they had too much fun, Dustin paid for it in subtle ways, Lance said. He was twelve.

"A puppy would definitely be too much fun," he said.

She was surprised when he bent to give her a quick hug. "Happy birthday."

"Don't feel you have to stick around for that stuff," she said. "You're always welcome, but there's no obligation."

He had a way of receiving information, a kind of calm analysis that she still wasn't used to. He thought before he answered. "There's a certain pleasure in feeling obliged," he said, zipping up his jacket. "It's when others try to impose obligations where there are none that I get irritated." He pulled on a hat.

She held Perro back, both of them standing in the blast of frigid air that rolled in from the frozen morning. His truck was already running, boiling up great plumes of exhaust. She could see the stiffness in his walk, but he no longer used the cane. He didn't say much about his injuries. Time and physiotherapy seemed to be making him stronger, but with all that metal pinning him together, the cold had to be painful.

She switched off the back porch light and the dog followed her into the kitchen where Lance had already washed up. The puppy hunkered down over his bowl, his name tag clanking against the metal as he crunched on the food. Isabel looked out the side window across the dry stalks of the raspberries and the small patch of grass under the linden tree, her favourite spot to sit when the tree was in fragrant bloom and the evening sun stayed high long enough to make it all the way around to the low horizon northwest of the mountain.

Right now, the only light on the butterfly bracts and red stems came from the orange rail yard lights, but the morning sun lit the mountain's peak. The sky was clear and little wisps of snow trailed off the high windy pinnacle. Isabel swallowed a couple of aspirin to ease the menstrual cramps already spreading across her lower back, poured herself a cup of coffee, cut a piece of cake, and sat down to consider what to do with Janna's parcel.

When Janna drove off with her boyfriend, Isabel hadn't believed she'd be gone long. When Jason called to ask what the hell was going on and why had Janna decided to move in with them and finish her Grade 12 in Prince George, she still didn't think it was permanent. Several pleading phone calls later and a disastrous visit when she ended up screaming at Jason's wife on their doorstep for not letting her in to see Janna finally got the point across. Janna wasn't coming home. By Thanksgiving, Isabel had pulled herself together and given up booze for what she hoped was the last time. For a few months she wrote polite letters every month telling Janna what movies she'd seen, what clothes were in the store, about the lovely jackets Isabel's cousin had brought in to the fancy clothing store he ran on Main Street. Which of Janna's girlfriends had won track meets and what boys were in trouble. She sent her a subscription to the local newspaper and put together a box of Christmas treats for her. But when New Year's passed without any word, she stopped.

Trevor tried to set things straight when he returned from a long drilling job in Portugal. By the next Mother's Day, she received a polite card with irises on it. "Have a great day, Mom. Things are fine here." A scarf for her birthday and a basket of soap and hand cream at Christmas.

Isabel waffled between an almost overwhelming urge to stalk the hallways of the community college where Janna went after she finished high school and an angry determination to do nothing at all except get on with her own life. Still sober, she was surprised to find she was able to have fun. To laugh at jokes, to delight in gardening successes. To tell those who asked that Janna was doing well at school and enjoying life in Prince George. But when she finally got to see her at her graduation last spring, she felt as if she was standing on one side of the Bulkley River at Moricetown Canyon and the beautiful young stranger Janna had become was on the other, the big river chock full of snow melt rushing between them. In the old days, the only bridge across was a precarious jumble of driftwood lashed together with telegraph wire. Now it seemed like even that was gone.

Isabel examined the parcel. The girl was a perfectionist. The brown paper's tidy corners were fastened with neat squares of tape, the label perfectly centred, a band of clear plastic packing tape protecting it. No return address. She turned it over, running her fingers across the paper as if she would feel some warmth from her daughter's fingers transmitted to her hands. The sweetness of the chocolate cake curdled on her tongue and she tried to wash away the taste with coffee. Cramps crawled up her spine. She slid a fingernail under a flap and severed the tape. The paper lifted and she slit another piece of tape. She slid off the paper, spread it carefully, and looked for some clue to her daughter's life. Please recycle this bag. More tape. She used her icing-clogged knife to hack through it, already chafing at Janna's orderliness. She lifted the lid, and felt through the styrofoam chips to pull out four zip-lock bags each labelled with the names of tulips, each containing four bulbs, some with dirt still clinging to them. Geanka. Van Nelle. Purple Prince. Dark Secret.

Doesn't she know it's November? That the ground is usually frozen solid by now, usually covered with a foot of snow? Doesn't she remember where she comes from? The spurt of anger subsided when she saw the white envelope under the bulbs. Her name, Isabel, in the same tiny letters. The little drawing of a bell at the end — their joke. "My mom is a bell."

The card showed an English garden, a riot of colours tumbling over a stone wall, a cottage covered in roses. A figure with a straw hat bent over a hoe in a profusion of red and blue flowers, impossible to say what kind. *Happy birthday, Mom. Hope it's not too late for these — Amy sends her love. Janna.* Amy? How had they run into each other? She put her little finger on the period between love and Janna. She rubbed at it until it blurred into a purple smudge. The anger bubbled back up through the sorrow. This is ridiculous, she thought. This politeness. She didn't know where her daughter lived, didn't have her address or her phone number.

The puppy tumbled at her feet, chewing at the chips that had fallen to the floor. Still angry, she bent to his mouth and roughly scraped the fragments out from between his teeth. Scooping up the hot mess, she dropped it in the garbage. The puppy skipped along beside her, jumping up and barking. What was that thing with the knee Trevor had showed her — whump! Over went the dog, sliding on the clean linoleum and she was instantly remorseful. She bent to stroke his long silky red coat and noted the black lines around his eyes, how the ears had long tassels, and how the tail flopped on the floor. She put her face in his neck as he squirmed and wriggled under her grasp. Janna would love this dog. She would love the way he smelled of the outside, the frost sinking into the ground, the willow leaves blackening on the grass. She stroked the length of his back. When he wriggled himself right over, legs in the air, tail flopping, she reached down to scratch his pink belly with its dark spots, avoiding the little fur-covered sheath with the wisp of hair at the end and the tender flaps of skin at the junction of his hind legs and groin.

"If I'm going to plant those damn bulbs, we're going to have to dig to China to find a piece of ground that is not frozen," she said to the dog. "But we'll have to wait until the sun warms things up a bit. Now, can you help me put these dishes away?"

The dog wriggled happily.

†

Isabel was crouched in a flowerbed on the east side of the house, a trench already dug, when Soryada found her. The overturned dirt was pale with ice crystals, but a couple of inches deeper, it was still unfrozen. As if with some premonition of the cold snowless fall, Isabel had lifted all her dahlia tubers from this bed back in September and stored them with the remnants of Elly Thomas's garden. If the tulips actually survived, she didn't know where she'd put the dahlias — maybe right on top. The puppy, tethered to the fence a few yards away, yelped to see Soryada.

"Ah, *mi cachorro*," she said, tickling the dog.

"What's that you called him?"

"*El cachorro*. It's puppy in Spanish." She rolled out the rrrs. "*El cachorrrrro*." She brushed the willow leaves from his fur. "I'm going to miss him."

They'd found him tied to their mailbox, twenty miles up the Kispiox road, skinny like the dogs at home, she said. Soryada scratched and stroked the puppy until he settled down at her feet, eyes closed, ears flopped right back. Isabel set the bulbs deep into the trench in clusters of four.

"You must be a very special gardener to grow something now, in this cold," Soryada said. "I have never seen this before — the trees with no leaves, everything dead. Trevor has told me it all comes back." She paused. "But aren't you afraid?"

Isabel had never heard her say as much at one time. She tried to think of an answer as she filled in the trench. She looked around at the heavy mulches of fallen leaves she scrounged from all her neighbours' rakings, the straw piled on the asparagus bed, the grey dirt of the tilled vegetable plot, and the burlap around the little cypresses. The red berries of the mountain ash echoed the red leaves of the stonecrop over in the rockery. She saw it all as latent, expectant. A child tucked into a bed, the covers pulled up over her head. A pregnant woman. The winter, a time to rest and dream.

"It doesn't all come back. Some winters kill perennials that have thrived for years. But then again, some plants you don't hold out any hope for, things you planted on a whim, well, they surprise you. You just never know."

"It's not for selling, the things you grow? Or for eating?"

"I grow some food." Isabel paused, unable to explain why she grew such a big garden, why she wanted to make dahlias bloom in difficult places, why she struggled every year with her clematis, the Markham's Pink and the new breeds coming out of Poland, ones people said wouldn't survive more than a lucky season or two. It had something to do with her mother, she knew. And her bare feet in Mrs. Thomas's dahlias.

Stretching the stiffness out of her back and hips, she clipped the leash on Perro, and wrapped her scarf around her ears. "Let's take this boy to have a look around town," she said and led Soryada through the little trail across the alley to the town's perimeter trail. The bitter smell of ripe cranberries hung in the air, the leaves crispy underfoot. The dog was ecstatic.

"I hope you're here in the summer — you'll see how beautiful it is. Maybe then you'll understand."

Isabel regretted her words when she saw the shadow cross Soryada's face. Six months was all she legally had. After that, things got complicated. Friendship was something she guarded against with Trevor's girlfriends. They came and went between each drilling season. There hadn't been any so far who measured up to the expectations of his Gitxsan family. Or who wanted to try.

"I'm used to this," she said gesturing to the clumps of nettles and horsetails sagging along the edges of the path. "I can't imagine a place like Mexico. Is it green all the time?"

"In the rainy season, yes. Then in the dry season, it can get very brown. But the days don't get short like this, and it doesn't get cold."

There's something about walking conversations, Isabel thought. You say things you wouldn't say if you were looking at each other across a room. As they walked down to the river, they took turns with the leash and talked like two women who had known each other a long time.

"Your Trevor, he speaks pretty good, what we call cowboy Spanish. But I want to improve my English."

"It sounds good to me."

"We get lots of practice in the camps. Not many of the Canadians speak Spanish. Only enough to get a drink and a woman."

Soryada hesitated, waiting for a group of joggers to pass. Isabel nodded good morning.

"For many girls," Soryada continued, "the dream is to get an American to bring you north. Even if you don't get married, you want to see what it's like." Soryada hugged Isabel's arm. "I always said I didn't want that, that I wanted to get back to my country, not get further away from it. But Trevor, he looks like the men from my village. Something about the way he sits, with one foot always up on something. A log or a tire. His hat tipped a little bit sideways. Sometimes I look at him and I think I'm home." She laughed. "Until he opens his mouth and that big fat English comes out."

Isabel was still trying to make out what Soryada had said. "Back to your country?"

"I am from Guatemala."

Isabel nodded, unwilling to ask where exactly is Guatemala? The pause stretched into a companionable silence as the women and the dog walked down to the river. The surrounding mountains were holding back more and more water as the temperature dropped, and the river had shrunk into the centre of its bed. They walked across the big sandy flats the low water exposed, sand whose warmth Isabel remembered. She admitted to Soryada that as the year squeezed toward the wasp waist of December, in this time before the snow covered everything, it did get harder and harder to remember how green the land could be, how warm and welcoming the sand felt to bare feet in the summer.

As they came full circle to climb the hill back up from the river, Soryada spoke again, her voice quiet. She told Isabel what she could remember of her mother bundling up the tortillas still hot from the fire in her *tzute* and pushing her out the window as soldiers broke through the door. Her eyes, fierce and angry, her voice yelling to run, run. Her voice like a hand coming to strike her daughter, to force her to keep running even as she could hardly breathe for crying.

Soryada stopped on the sidewalk of one of the quiet streets of the subdivision with its pale houses, the neat lawns soft with melted frost, the shiny trucks parked under basketball hoops.

"In the middle of one word, her voice choked off, and I fell to the ground as if I had been choked too. I looked back. A man leaned out the window, his rifle aimed at me. He was laughing. I rolled under some bushes before he fired. As I ran down into a ravine, I was mad at my mother. She must have done something, I thought, to upset the soldiers."

Soryada's thick braid caught the sun as she crouched to pick up Perro. The dog snuggled into her shoulder as she told Isabel how she hid up in the hills, hearing the rifles and watching the smoke rise up from her village. She hid alone, crouched down in the bush. She ate the tortillas and wrapped herself in the *izute* that still smelled of her mother.

"Those hills," she said, "they were full of people. I hid three days until strangers found me asleep, all curled up like this tired puppy. They took me with them across the ridges to a place where they said the soldiers would not come. I didn't know we were in Mexico. The sisters came there and asked me if I'd like to go to school. I said yes and they took me to the orphanage where I learned to read and write. Spanish and English. And they taught us how to cook."

"Your mother?" Isabel was afraid of the answer.

Soryada sounded matter-of-fact. "If she was alive, she would have found me."

Isabel stood behind Soryada as they waited at the stoplight to cross the highway, stroking the dog's tired head where it rested on Soryada's shoulder, sleepy eyes looking back at her, nose nestled against Soryada's braid. "I'm so sorry," she whispered.

The light changed and the girl nodded, shifting the dog to her other shoulder. She carried him all the way to the back door of Isabel's house.

Trevor was in the kitchen, beating eggs.

"Breakfast?" he asked.

"Just coffee for me," Isabel answered as Soryada showed her how to rub the puppy down with a rag and helped her pick a spot for his basket and blanket. The dog slurped water from his bowl, splashing the floor and Isabel's leg, flopped into his basket, and fell asleep.

Soryada opened the drapes in the living room and stripped the pullout bed while Isabel rummaged in the cupboard under the TV. She brought an old school atlas into the kitchen and opened it on the table as Trevor ate his steady way through a huge breakfast. She found Mexico, a green tail on the big yellow United States.

"Show me where the camp was."

Trevor leaned over and pointed to a spot in the southwest part of Mexico. "About here."

"And where is Guatemala?"

Trevor pointed to the irregular block; it was blue, immediately south of Mexico. He peered closer. "We drove down here one weekend. One of the guys wanted to see the volcano. What was it, the highest in Central America? A Godawful highway."

"Tajumulco," Soryada said.

"Didn't see much. It was socked in."

"Covered in clouds," Isabel explained to Soryada. She traced her finger over the map. "I knew a man from somewhere down here once."

Trevor got up from the table and carried his plate to the sink. "Mom, you knew a man from just about everywhere, once."

"I can't remember which country. I think it ended in an a."

Soryada laughed, her finger tapping from north to south on the map's bright colours. "Guatemala, Honduras, Nicaragua, Costa Rica, Panama, Colombia!"

"Where is your village?"

"Was," said Soryada, peering over the map. She pointed. "Somewhere in here. I remember people talking about Nebaj," one finger pointed, "and Hue-huetenango." She looked up at Isabel. "But when I asked about going home, the nuns told me my village is gone. There's nothing to go back to. But I still want to go. There must be someone who knows me."

Trevor came up behind her and kissed the top of her head. Isabel slipped out of the room. She felt cold and went upstairs to see if she could find the sweater she wanted. It had been her mother's. A cardigan of dusty pink wool with white buttons shaped like little hens. The wool had lost its resilience, but the sweater was still in good shape. She pulled it on and slid each hen carefully through the embroidered buttonholes.

Isabel had aunts and uncles and cousins working in half the offices and stores in town. There were times when she would have happily drowned them all, just to get her mother back. Just to sit her down and make her a cup of tea. Ask her what to say when Janna's voice filled with the same longing Isabel had heard in Soryada's. There's got to be someone to tell me who my father is, Janna had said to Isabel, who'd already turned away from her questions. Turned away until Janna's longing turning to venom. Maybe she'd put an ad in the fucking paper asking all the likely prospects to volunteer for DNA testing, she'd said. Isabel had almost told her then. Probably should have. What a mess — one that grew and grew until it seemed that whatever she did would only make things worse.

Doors opened and closed downstairs. Water ran in the kitchen sink. Isabel sat in the rocking chair under the small bedroom window and watched the sun shine on the mountain. Its short November arc was more than halfway drawn and it would sink soon behind the south shoulder.

There were so many people in the world, so many places, she thought, why did it matter where any of us came from? Childhood friends didn't really know us any better than strangers did. No matter how much we joked with our uncles, tried on clothes for our aunties, played hide and seek on long summer evenings with our cousins, or whispered secrets into our lover's hair, we each came out of some dark unknowing that was never fully illuminated. Even our own children. Isabel imagined Trevor and Jason and Janna shining and turning like bubbles floating into sunlight. What recipe of genes and geography made up the sad residue that would be left when her own bubble burst? A little smear of liquid on the grass.

Isabel pushed herself out of the rocking chair, feeling the ache in her hips from the long walk. She started down the stairs. Before she lost her courage, she'd ask Trevor for Janna's phone number.

8

"Eloise says you've refused further counselling."

Álvaro swivelled his chair around. A tall woman, grey hair swept up under a bright woolen cap, toucan earrings dangling against a pale face, stood in the doorway of the tiny office, her arms piled with rolls of paper. Glasses dangled on her chest, tangled in a rosary of black jet. He struggled to place her.

"Margaret Coleman, Eloise's sister."

One of the main funders for his street kids project in Guatemala City. He faithfully sent photos of the kids at his school and asked for prayers on their behalf. Prayers for the ones who had died. She had written back words of encouragement and thanks. They'd never met. He rose to shake her hand.

"I'm so sorry about your troubles."

He tried not to squirm as she looked him over. He'd taken to wearing black T-shirts and jeans. Clothes that moved with his body, not ones that slid over his skin. His arms, bulked up from the gym, were unmarked, except for the remnant scars at his wrists. His watch covered one. On the other he wore a woven band, the quetzal picked out in tiny stitches.

"What do they have you doing here?"

"Translations. Stories for the website, the newsletters. Reports for the governments in the Latin countries where they have kids' shelters. Fundraising."

"Covenant House has always been very good at fundraising." She looked at the posters of black kids playing basketball and Indian girls bent over notebooks. "Eloise is worried about you out there in that gloomy house smelling of pot roast. All those old men, then coming down to these sad stories. Not to mention the rain we've been having." She shifted the rolls under one arm. "It's been seventeen days in a row, rain every day. The city feels like it's rotting."

"She worries too much."

One hand reached out to touch his hat. "These little watch caps are all the rage these days."

He couldn't control the flinch. She pretended not to notice even as she pulled back her hand. "I'll have to get one for my son."

She turned to go, fumbling with her papers. He jumped to catch the ones she dropped. Offered to help carry them upstairs. While they climbed, she told him who they'd found to take over his school in Guatemala City and that the children missed him and sent their best wishes. It wasn't until they were standing outside a door labelled Art Therapy that Álvaro guessed what she was up to.

He spoke to her back as she unlocked the door. "It's best for those kids that I'm far away from them. But talking about what happened isn't any good. I basically need to pound on something pretty much every day. Since the old men at the provincial house aren't really suitable targets and the furniture doesn't belong to me, I go to the gym."

She opened the door. "Who have you talked to?"

"They sent me to a psychiatrist who wrote some prescriptions. Then a post traumatic stress group." The room heavy with smoke, the walls covered with affirmation statements. The sad stories of car accidents, flesh sizzling in house fires, the rapist coming through the window. He had been unable to add his story to their misery.

He looked past her into the big room, full of watery afternoon light. "Have they sent you to convince me to try this?"

He was none of her business and the provincial superior had no right involving a woman they thought he'd feel an obligation to. But instead of walking away, he followed her inside to set down the paper on a big paint-stained table. Jars of brushes, dozens of pots of paint, and two easels holding big sheets of blank paper. The walls were covered in paintings. He wasn't prepared for them. Lots of black. Flashes of red. They hit him like a huge curling wave of heat. A giant blue couple standing with their backs to each other. A house with a sun rising overhead, trees, and a little family. A body dangling out of a shattered window. All of the emotion in the paintings funnelled into his body, standing the hair on his neck straight up.

"Have you talked to her?"

"Who?" He could barely hear what she was saying.

"The art therapist. Chris Mundy."

"I don't think so. If I have, I don't remember." Álvaro wanted to get out of the room.

"She runs groups for the kids here. She also works with torture survivors. War zones. Started with the Vietnamese years back, Cambodians. Central America in the eighties, when they were all coming through. Now I think it's Bosnians."

Álvaro stared at a painting of a figure wrapped in grey. A swarm of wasps darted in from every side, stinging the bits of exposed pinkness wherever the grey didn't cover it. Angry red welts were scribbled into the stung bits. Margaret came over to look, reached out one finger to touch a place on the thigh where the red scratches tore the paper.

"Don't!" Álvaro cried, swatting her hand away.

Her shock and the way she shrank from him, holding her hand, brought him back to her presence. Regret. He bent his head into his hands and rubbed his face, the scar throbbing. Even though all he expected now was pain, he was never ready. Even though he held himself in a permanent crouch of self-protection, his defences still crumbled.

He went and looked out the window at the leafless trees, the cars on the street below, and the ocean beyond. It was good there was this ocean here. A place where the water pooled and circled and swept everything away, brought it back reordered. Like prayer used to do for him.

He wished he could remember his priest's life. The combination of tedium and delirious conviction. His body tingling with the expectation of joy, knowing that the possibility of ecstasy waited in every moment. Every day, the transformation of communion, the cleansing, and the renewal. The felt presence as the whole world prayed together. *Give me a new heart and place a new spirit within me. Take from my body my stony heart and give me a natural one.*

He spoke to the tree trunk outside the window. "I'm sorry." He turned to see she had already absorbed the shock, and was worried instead about him. The red mark on the back of her hand where he had struck her would be a bruise. "I'm pretty much a lost cause."

"I'd like to give you a hug," Margaret sighed, "but it's probably not a good idea."

"No," he said, realizing how lonely his body was.

"Why don't you give her a try?"

"Who?"

"Chris. She's very good. These art therapists, they know there are some things you can't talk about. You can't think through. Things you can only feel." Margaret paused, touching the beads at her throat. "She'll be in Monday."

When Álvaro had walked away from the last counselling sessions, Walter had stood up for him. Oblates weren't made to sit around contemplating their navels, he'd said. Pry out the damn lint and get on with it. Leave the rest to God.

Covenant House had phoned the next day and asked if he could come in a couple of days a week and make some translations for them. They'd been very kind. Whatever he felt comfortable with, they'd said. After Margaret left, he bent once more over his desk, the chatter from the next office soothed him with its combination of the banal and the serious — anxiety about a weekend date, about some wedding, about one of the kids who'd run away, another who was making a home visit — and he realized how much he wanted to keep working here. It was a fragile link: the smell of good food cooking and the kids' voices, the same edgy laughter, the jabs of outrage at some unfairness. These Vancouver kids were bigger, though, and slower-moving than the ones he'd known in Guatemala City. The thousands of small dark shapes dodging through the rain-black streets of Guatemala City, flickering like fish under moving water. At least until the solvents kicked in.

In his last few months there, he'd buried himself in their chaotic lives. Their clustering on the cement doorstep of the little downtown school Margaret's money had paid for. The bodies pushing inside when the grill slid open in the mornings, shivering cold, coming down. Cleaning up their cuts and bruises. Chattering over loot they'd rustled from the cemetery where the graves were rented like rooms. If the rent wasn't paid, the bodies were thrown into *la baranca*. The kids scavenged whatever the workers missed. Rings rattling loose on finger bones. Lots of rosaries, the smell of death sometimes still on them. Bullets. All he could think to do was make them wash their hands and their treasures.

Juan Tzul collected bones, the tiny ones — the fingers and feet. Álvaro had tracked down an old anatomy book and turned it into a game. Trying to assemble an entire hand, for example. One time they'd found the skeleton of a baby inside the mother. They'd gathered the pieces together into a tiny cloth bag and buried it properly. What is the state of this baby's soul, Juan had asked? If it hasn't been blessed but hasn't been born? Will it be in hell? He wanted to be a priest. He muttered the act of contrition even as he stole food and sniffed gasoline. Álvaro blessed him every morning but refused him the last rites, saying he must not seek death.

He had tried to teach him to read. Juan would stare at the page and trace his fingers around the letters and say what they looked like, the shape of a word. *La casa* looked like a trolley car, he'd say. *La madre* like what? A house with a balcony. Or a church with two steeples. A refuge. The lines on the page were a secret code he could never decipher. How is *el perro* a dog, he'd ask. A dog has four legs — some have three, but there's no dog alive with one leg. And Álvaro would find himself drawing the words with cartoon appendages. Love, he'd think. How could he draw love for Juan, the bone collector? He had written *la niña* in fetal finger bones. *La preciosita*. The joy on the boy's battered face as he slipped into a coma, Álvaro's fingers glistening with holy oil, his lips moving in the final blessing.

†

All weekend, Álvaro expected a phone call from Covenant House. The last thing they needed was a crazy man upstairs who'd assaulted a woman who was undoubtedly one of their donors. He wondered who they would choose to initiate the quiet dismissal. He was shivering in a lawn chair beside the pool someone had emptied on Saturday when Walter found him on Sunday. After missing mass again.

"Why anyone chooses to live in Vancouver beats me," the old man said, lowering himself into the chair across from Álvaro. The rain had dropped almost an inch of new water into the pool. "Damn thing will be full again by next Sunday."

"You're not going to start in on the empty vessel metaphor, are you?"

Walter snorted. "I was thinking how at least up north you could, in winter, use the aforementioned receptacle for a skating rink. Where the cold does you some good."

Álvaro waited.

"There's a reserve at the end of a big lake up there, hell, half the reserves are at the end of big lakes up there." He laughed. "This one is a beauty.

Rough looking when the roads are mud and potholes and you can see all the junk piled up around the houses. But the snow comes and it's forty below and the church is blue and white like the sky and the snow. The graveyard goes back to the early eighteen-hundreds. You stand there at the altar with those graves behind you like an anchor. A strong anchor reminding you of why you're here celebrating with those good people who have come out to clear the snow off the steps and light the stove three, four hours before you get there, and the old timbers holding the place up are snapping and groaning in the cold. It is the greatest blessing to be there. It is what we were made for."

There were times Álvaro could not help but stick some of his pain into others. When Walter thought of priests and torture, he thought of Brébeuf and bravery. He didn't think of the inquisition, the priests whispering in the ears of their brothers, the ones they flayed, promising much if only they would give them names of the others, erections stiff under their black frocks, lips dry with excitement. All the eloquence of love, sympathy, and regret as they cut you open and sewed you back up filled with salted shards of glass.

"In the old Mayan stories," Álvaro said, "wood was what the gods first used to make men. It didn't work very well. Animals tore those first people apart."

"Clay's the thing," Walter said. "Easier to work with."

"The Mayan gods used clay too. The second time. But the people wouldn't hold together. There was no need of a catastrophe — they just dissolved. When they finally got it right and made the old Maya, they set in motion three thousand years of slaughter. And another five hundred of martyrdom at our hands."

Walter had leaned close to him, the mint strong on his old breath. "You know we're not called here as fixers, Álvaro. That's the oldest red herring in the book."

"But there was another effort they made," Álvaro said. "The gods made one very fine group of people. Unfortunately they made them too well. Their vision was too acute, too near to the vision of the gods themselves. And when the gods questioned them, when they led them in their catechism, they didn't answer properly. They were curious about the world and forgot to praise the gods for making them."

Álvaro drew his finger across his throat. "Pffft." He opened his hands. "Lord, open my lips and my mouth will proclaim your praise." He looked away from Walter. "All my torturer wanted, Walter, was for me to confess my sins and sing his praises." The voice was loud inside his head, the cajoling whisper. The hand holding the razor or the cigarette, the pain waiting in every nerve. "Right now, the language of prayer seems too much like I'm talking to him."

Walter's head bent and his hand came up to cross himself.

"You can see my problem? And talking to a psychiatrist doesn't seem any better."

The old head snapped up, his derision evident. He took Álvaro's hands in his and put them together palm to palm. "We need to find you something that uses your hands. Something active. Your hands and your heart. That translation stuff — it's all inside your head again, isn't it? Maybe we should change that."

"Hold on." Álvaro's stomach clenched. "I'd like to stick with that for a while if they'll let me. It's something."

A voice called them in for lunch and Álvaro helped Walter to his feet. On the slow walk to the dining room, Walter told him about an old Carrier Indian who thought the priest needed a little instruction about love in marriage. It comes, he said, and it goes. Like the creeks in high places. You're climbing right alongside one, drinking from it now and then, splashing it on your face to cool you down. Then it disappears. Where there was water, there's nothing but a little spill of rocks and maybe a trace of dried mud. Your dog, he's no help. He runs off whenever he sniffs out a patch of grass or snow to cool his feet. He probably knows exactly where that stream went, and he figures you do too. After all, you're the boss. So you keep going, not wanting your dog to catch on to your foolishness. Then, a few hundred yards further up, for no reason you can figure, there's water again and maybe a dipper. You take a drink and keep going."

"What if your love is truly gone? How long do you wait?"

"You don't wait. You keep going," Walter had said. "Find some form of prayer you can make use of, son. Find that prayer and stick to it. You're a priest and you always will be. There's no changing that."

†

Álvaro wanted nothing more than a prayer he could hold on to. On Monday, he rode the bus down Granville and across the bridge. He walked up the quiet street and rang the bell at Covenant House. If they let him in, he told himself. If they let him in, he would talk to her. Today. Now.

Hello, Father Al, they said, smiling. No averted eyes. No mention of Margaret. He climbed the stairs up past his office, up to the third floor, and knocked. A woman opened the door. She wore layers of clothing, bright colours, shawls, scarves, things in her hair, bracelets. Where the frame of her body was visible, it looked strong. A wide mouth between angular cheekbones. A nose stud.

"Margaret suggested I come to see you."

"Yes. She mentioned it."

She held herself very still.

"You sound hesitant." He was surprised at his disappointment. From where he stood, he could see out the window. No ground, no water, no sky. Just the trunks of trees. The walls were stripped of pictures.

"The pictures," he said. "They're very powerful."

"They're meant to be private. Margaret shouldn't have brought you in here." She turned away, walked into the room. "I don't often work with men anymore. Or priests."

"Are you Catholic?" he asked.

"Have been."

For some women, Álvaro knew, the church was not a friend.

"Do you believe God arranges the whole world to test your faith?" he asked.

"Often."

"So which of us is taking the exam here?"

Somewhere in that moment, she gave something up. He could feel a shift in the air pressure. She gestured him toward a collection of chairs. He chose a dark stool. The shelves on the walls beside him were filled with stones, beads, crystals, carved bowls, balls, statues, stuffed toys, and small pieces of gnarled wood. When he sat, she sat across from him and over to one side. He had to choose to look at her.

"Is it possible to do this without feeling like a child?" He nodded toward the shelves. The easels and pots of paint.

"What do you want?"

He thought. He wanted to feel focussed, directed anger. He wanted to sleep. He wanted to play soccer with a dozen novices. He wanted to feel the presence of God. He wanted everything. "I don't know what's possible."

"You were tortured?"

He flinched. Something about the sound of the word in English. Torch. So close to touch. Tear. The chchch sound of instruments hitting bare flesh. The grrrowl of pain. And satisfaction. *La tortura* was much more delicate. Oblique.

"I don't want to talk about that. I've tried. It doesn't help."

"Help what?"

He looked right at her. Her eyes were blue, the irises flecked with gray. She was, he saw, intelligent enough to be afraid. Afraid of his pain and of what it could carry for her. He looked away. "How do you counsel people to process evil?"

She sighed and got businesslike. "It depends. We can use whatever works. If you need to bring God into it, you can try to figure out what God is teaching you so you can better serve him. You can try to figure out what sins God is punishing you for. It gets harder if you feel you need to focus on Satan."

"Satan? No. I don't want to focus on Satan. Or God."

"If I have my facts straight, the actual torture took place a couple of years ago?"

"May I ask what facts you have?"

She watched him as she recited what Margaret must have told her. What Eloise must have told Margaret. "You returned to Guatemala in the late eighties. You helped gather testimony for the peace accords. Worked on the exhumations of mass graves. Accompanied peasants to the city to look for their missing children — in the orphanages, on the streets, and in the morgue. In nineteen ninety-eight, you were in Guatemala City working for the church's human rights commission. Just before their report was published, you were picked up, detained, and tortured. Upon your release, you received treatment for your substantial physical injuries but largely refused to talk about what had happened. Like everyone else, you were distraught about the murder of Bishop Gerardi and your difficulties, you said, seemed to be a case of mistaken identity. A matter of poor timing, unrelated to the bishop's death. You went back to work, focussing now on street children. You established a school for the least likely to survive kids, ran a fitness and self-defence program for them, and seemed to be functioning well enough, though your colleagues sensed a certain distance — which they respected — until one morning street workers found you unconscious in a basement. Stinking of glue and talking about death threats."

Álvaro tried to meet her eyes. "Margaret is frighteningly thorough."

"It was decided to get you out of the country, but they were nervous about getting you through airport security. You were indeed on someone's list."

He clenched and unclenched his fists. She continued.

"After a shaky beginning here, you appeared to be recuperating. Resting. Enjoying the quiet routine of life in the community house with only the occasional lapse. Then one day you experienced what appeared to be a psychotic episode and they took you to the even quieter provincial house. Sent you for counselling as the lapses continued. You wanted some work. They sent you here. You appear to be depressed. And in some doubt about your faith."

"Prozac will make me a believer again?" He laughed an abrupt laugh. "It's not depression. That would be easy. Peaceful even. It's rage. I bend to listen to one of the old priests at dinner and I want to sink my teeth into his ancient ear, an ear that has heard a hundred thousand tales of woe and still doesn't understand. I want to rip it right off his head. Margaret reaches out to touch a painting and I almost break her hand. I want to break everything."

"The men who tortured you?"

He stared through the trees, their individual trunks blending into a wall. But a wall that was cracked. There was light on the other side of those trunks; he could see it flickering as the wind moved through the few remaining leaves. He was exhausted. "Whatever it is we're going to do, I can't do it right now."

She stood and walked over to the window. "On the other side of the trees, across that road, there's the edge of the Pacific Ocean. Some quiet evenings I can hear the waves washing in and I wonder where they came from. Japan? Hawaii? Kamchatka? How long does it take a wave to cross the ocean?"

"Do they cross all that way?"

"In a river the water travels and the wave stands still. In the ocean the wave travels, but the water stays behind. God finds different ways to move us."

He retreated to the safety of politics. "The government used to quote Mao of all people — they'd say the *campesinos* of Guatemala were like the water the guerrillas swam in. To get the guerrillas, they said, we had to remove the water. Over two hundred thousand drops of water in the end. Dead."

She shrugged, bitter. "In the world's eyes, a mere cup or two."

He pushed himself up from the chair, feeling the tenderness that never left his knees. He could no longer run any distance. He could only press iron and punch the canvas bag.

He stood at the door. "Do you have children?"

"None of my own," she said. "But I am expecting a couple of the residents to show up right about now." She handed him a card. "Phone if you want to try this. My office isn't far from the provincial house."

He nodded and walked out the door, down the stairs and out into the street, into the weather of the world where the wind blew, rain fell, and birds lived and died. Something had been tossed to him and to her. A *milagro*, perhaps. A sliver of tin. She may not have noticed but he'd felt it slip between his ribs and lodge in the meat of his heart.

9

A guy sat on the floor, his back against the lockers lining the hallway. He grinned up at Janna as she slipped out the side door of the classroom. His dirty blond hair was cut medium short; his pale shirt hung out over tan pants. No socks in his running shoes. Either a thrift store dresser or grabbing whatever he found in the heap on his bedroom floor.

"Reviewing the inventory supply system not turning your crank?"

She'd seen him before, in earnest discussion with a couple of the profs. Gesturing wildly, but fixing their attention. Greg something. Some kind of math genius.

"I like systems, actually," she said, trying to shut him out. "So practical. Will the cloth arrive at the factory on time? Will the summer dresses be in the stores by February?" She swayed a little, one hand against the wall. "But there's something about the lights in there. The canned air. It's making me woozy."

He pulled his long legs out of her way. "End of term exhaustion. The synapses stretch. The connections get jittery."

She wasn't sure she heard him right. The ringing in her ears grew and he got further away, sliding down the wrong end of the binocular lenses, shrinking into a cartoon figure, mouth opening and closing. She had to get outside. She put one hand to the lockers and tried to walk in the direction of the stairs. Her hand hit the elevator buttons. She pressed them all and leaned against the wall. She slid down until she was sitting on the floor.

The next thing she knew Greg was in the elevator with her, one arm around her shoulders, a hand under her elbow. He smelled like an old hairbrush, like he didn't get his clothes all the way dry.

"Please get me outside," she whispered as the elevator door opened on the ground floor.

There was a bench in a sheltered alcove just outside the door. She watched her shoes shuffle through the leaves littering the grass. She sat down on the cold stone, welcoming the chill seeping up her spine, the icy air in her lungs. Greg sat beside her, uncertain. She leaned against him, feeling the warmth of his body. He turned her toward him and took her hands. He was asking where did she live, could he get her home, should he call security for help. She stared at his big hands with the blond hairs growing out of the knuckles. She looked down at the leaves around their feet. Some of them were slivered green around the base where the stem joined the leaf, green veins not yet submerged in red.

She bent, reaching for one of the leaves, wanting to feel its veins between her fingers. She remembered laying out leaves carefully on her mother's kitchen table and spreading a huge sheet of paper over them, the two of them working with charcoal to make rubbings. The outlines appeared, leaf by leaf, until perfect imprints from plants growing in Isabel's garden covered the paper. Together they labelled them: Golden Jubilee, Red Butterfly, Blue Angel, and Morning Glory. Nasturtium, lavatera, luneria, and Riviera rose. Isabel had taken Janna's hands in her own, turned them over and looked at the dark lines the charcoal had drawn in her palms. She'd traced a line running from the base of Janna's forefinger in a clear curve down and around the base of her thumb, telling her she knew she'd have at least one kid to take care of her in her old age.

Janna had tried to pull her hand away from the tickle in her palm, but Isabel held on. Now, on the bench outside UBC's business administration program building five hundred long miles south, Janna remembered her small hands resting inside her mother's, their shapes so different, and she could hear Isabel saying, "You've got your father's beautiful hands."

Janna leaned against this strange boy's chest, crumpled the leaf in her fingers, and sobbed.

†

When she woke up in her own bed, it was dark. Her shirt was twisted up under her arms. Her panties were still on, but her slacks were hanging over a chair, damp from her sitting on the cold bench. Her socks were tucked in the damp shoes beside the bed and her pack was on the desk. Vague memories of a slow walk to her residence and handing him the pack to find her key. Stumbling into the room, the blast of heat. Did she sleep with him? she wondered, feeling between her legs. Her thighs were chafed and sore. Surely she'd have remembered that. Then she did remember. She sat up, stiff and thirsty, reaching for the cup he must have left beside her bed. The chafing wasn't from him. It was from the other boy. David.

She gulped cold tea. A knock on the door brought her out of bed. The floor rep stuck her head in, saying her friend had asked her to check in. She'd been sick?

She'd just skipped lunch, Janna told her. After eating, she'd feel better. You know how it gets this time of year. She stood blocking the door, not wanting her to come in. The rep was already bored, turning away. Half the girls in residence were starving themselves.

Janna looked at her hands pushing the door closed, sliding across the brown paint and the semester timetable she'd taped there back in September. Her small brown hands with their slender fingers, the nail beds long and set deep. The skin puckered at the knuckles and stretched across the tendons and the wrist bones. She moved her fingers across the smooth wood, recalling the warm skin, a paler shade of brown, and the long angular body of the other boy. David Miro.

She had planned to spend the previous weekend studying, but found herself distracted by the sounds around her: the coughs, the doors opening and closing, the voices in the corridors. She usually loved this time of year. Printing out the crisp pages of final reports and reviewing computer screens of notes, distilled to the essence. Everything organized into desktop folders, carefully backed up on disks all lined up in their cases. Like having all her clothes pressed and organized in her closet — shirts, slacks, skirts — the shoes tidy below.

She'd been heading for the library when a downtown bus pulled up at the stop, blocking her path. She slung her bag over her shoulder and jumped on, wondering even as she did so, why? She claimed a single seat and leaned her face against the cool glass, staring out into the grey rain. The bus lurched and swished its way along the wet streets, past all the soggy gardens and empty afternoon houses, between the stores and cafés clustered around intersections, down the endless tedium of Fourth Avenue and finally across the bridge to the glass and glitter of downtown. Golden lights sparkled in the bare branches of delicate trees.

The bus stopped across from a big hospital. People waiting for the bus to come the other way all turned their heads in the same direction. Behind them, dwarfing them, a garish display of lights blinked and shivered on the front of the old building. A sign invited people to buy another light for the Festival of Lights, and a huge thermometer measured the amount of money raised so far.

People crowded onto her bus, their wet coats, packs, and shopping bags pushing against her as they forced their way down the aisle. One man breathed noisily, a tube coming from a pack on his back to a little butterfly taped under his nose. Another wore a bandage around his neck, the front yellow with ooze. As the bus pulled away, she saw, through a break in the traffic, two little blue elasticized hospital slippers set neatly in front of the bench inside the bus shelter. They sat there as if someone had just stepped out of them, perhaps climbed on a bus and disappeared.

The bus rounded a corner and stopped across from a building with columns like a Greek temple. A big vertical banner flapped outside. Totem poles. Emily Carr, she read. At the art gallery. She struggled to her feet and pushed through the raincoats and rolled umbrellas.

She walked up the steps under the columns, looking for the way in. Three wet teenagers, their feral faces grinning at her mistake, asked for money. For smokes. One pointed around the corner to the gallery entrance. Once inside the echoing grey foyer, she hesitated again. Two lean and elegant women came out of a back room and pushed through the doors that led to the exhibits. She went to follow them but was stopped by a man in a blue jacket, asking to see her membership card. Explaining the entrance fee. School trips to the tiny art gallery at home had been free and Janna hadn't been inside one since. This had better be good, she thought, stuffing the pamphlet he gave her in a pocket.

She immediately got lost in a maze of rooms hung with Japanese prints. *Ruptures in the Floating World* the sign said. Whatever that meant. They were like storybook drawings or weird superhero comics full of men in armour and swords with bulging calves and thin pigtails. She leaned closer to look at a flute player, his cape blowing around him, bare feet firmly planted in sand. There was no water, but she knew it was just beyond the low mound of the dune. She could imagine the sound of the waves rising and falling behind the music of the flute and the wind rustling through the grass at his feet. The blues of the sky changed as night descended. Another man crouched in the grass behind him, a huge sword in his hand. Was he a menace or was he hiding from the flute player? The music would tell and she could hear the music. Not the individual notes but the idea of the music, and if she looked at the picture long enough she would be able to hum the melody and she would creep under his wind-filled cape to lean against him; she would place herself between him and the swordsman and let the sword cut into the soft muscle of her shoulder just so she could listen to the music he was playing even as the blood leaked out of her veins.

She didn't realize she'd put out her hand to touch it until a guard cleared his throat and touched her in that same spot on her shoulder.

"Please don't touch the prints, Miss." A tall guy, probably in his forties. Thin red hair. Blue eyes. Something wrong with his skin. He got to stand here all day and look.

"How much would this cost?" she asked, peering once again at the brush-stroke outlining the thigh, the way the wind bent the grass.

"I don't think any of these are for sale," he laughed.

He waited beside her while she bent to read the name: *Fujiwara no Yasumasa Playing the Flute by Moonlight.* She wrote it on the palm of her hand.

She made a further fool of herself by asking him where the totem poles were. Paintings of totem poles, he said, looking at her with the same pity as the kids outside. He pointed to a huge flight of stone stairs. An old woman hobbled down, one hand on the banister, the other holding a purse firmly to her hip. Janna climbed past her, climbed and turned, climbed and turned, until she saw the name: Emily Carr. She caught her breath at the paintings. Here they were, the poles she'd played among down by the Skeena River, the old wood warm under her hands. The Kispiox River in flood. She looked at them until the greens, dark reds, and browns were blurring along the wall, until another guard told her they were closing in five minutes. He led her outside and opened the door into the December darkness, the rain sweeping the streets. She stood on the wide steps and closed her eyes. But the poles were already fading, the northern rivers' roar lost in the sound of tires on the wet streets. And she was going to get soaked.

"Hey," called a voice behind her.

She turned. It was the boy from that party Amy had dragged her to. David Miro.

"Did you like the show?"

"The show?"

"The Japanese prints."

She nodded, and showed him the lettering on her hand.

He was impressed and she suddenly wished she wasn't wearing old fleece sweats and a Prince George Cougars sweatshirt under her jacket.

"That Coleman guy is quite the collector," he said. The prints were mostly his, he explained. It had taken him a long time to talk him into lending them to the gallery.

"You work there?"

"It's a co-op job. In collections." He started to explain the difference between permanent and collections and loans, between the work that was hung and the work that was stored, and Janna wondered if there was anything in this city she wasn't ignorant of. Standing on the art gallery steps, the blurred lights spidering out along the diverging streets, she felt an unexpected longing for home, for the small collection of roads and houses and stores where people she knew lived and worked. From the ski hill you could see the whole town: the houses and schools, the sawmills, the railway tracks, the highway, and the river coiling under the bridge and through the nearby farms. You could see the mountains beyond the town, marking its boundaries. No one lived up there in the bush, no one who knew any secrets she wanted hold of.

But even from there, she couldn't see her father. That was a lesson she could find no way of learning, no matter how she studied it. Jason and Trevor each had his own father and, when she was little, she understood it to mean a man who took you special weekend and summer places, places Isabel didn't go. It meant going for rides, because Isabel didn't have a car. It meant coming home with a new bicycle or dirty from fishing. It was who came to pick you up when your mom was sick. For a while, Janna thought maybe only boys had them. Then Jason took to saying hers was the man in the long coat and leather hat who walked by their house on his way to the liquor store every Saturday morning. He lived in some shack between the sawmills, worked as night watchman all week and drank all weekend. His stride was already loopy by the time he walked back the other way. Jason would push her toward the road, urging her to call him dad. "How about a kiss for your little girl?" he'd sing out, the man never looking in their direction, his whole concentration bent on his destination.

When Isabel overheard Jason, her anger was terrifying. The house felt like a cartoon drawing the way it bulged with her fury. When this happened the kids knew to keep quiet. To wait it out. But Jason said something at school about the bruises on his arm and he was gone and there were strangers at the house, Isabel white and rigid at the kitchen table. Trevor's dad came in his big pickup and hoisted Janna up to sit between him and Trevor, her little backpack clutched to her stomach.

When they were allowed back home, none of them spoke of Janna's dad. Not in Isabel's hearing. She'd cleaned up her act for a couple of years after that. Janna couldn't remember what set her off the next time.

Snapping open his umbrella, David Miro interrupted her reverie. "Can I buy you a coffee?"

She nodded, realizing how hungry she was. She never ate breakfast and had skipped lunch. And now it was dark again. She ducked under his umbrella and followed him through a maze of stairs and shrubs, past fountains of water running down stairways. A huge glass building rose from the darkness, bright and empty inside, full of padded benches and closed doors.

"Where are we going?"

He took her hand and led her onto a quiet street and into a small coffee bar tucked into the corner of a huge office tower. It wasn't fancy; its little glass case of picked-over pastries had a bedraggled look. The newspapers were strewn over the six or seven little tables and a few napkins were crumpled on the floor. But what a perfect location, she thought. Thousands of coffee addicts within a few vertical metres. After they ordered, they went back outside to sit at the one table under a glowing brazier. He lit a cigarette, some kind of dark thing that smelled like pipe tobacco. The street was blocked off and no traffic crawled along in the rain. She warmed her hands on her coffee and burnt her mouth trying to get past the foaming milk.

"That's where else I've seen you," he exclaimed. "At UBC. You're a business student?"

She nodded and sipped again, feeling the coffee burn down her throat.

He explained his program — a hybrid arts administration graduate diploma that included some business courses. "I have a couple of seminars and then I work at the gallery. I am going to advise the rich on their art collections." He leaned back and blew smoke into the night. "Have my own gallery, if I can raise the capital."

ert

She asked him questions about the art business, how much commission galleries charged, how much people paid for Japanese prints. How they decided what to buy. The returns on investments. She listened and rearranged her plans for the apartment she wanted when she landed that job in the accounting firm where she could crunch the numbers and bill big hours.

She would come home to quirky lamps, a good stereo, and a clean kitchen. Chrome. A little Honda. Clean like all the cars in Vancouver were clean. She'd jog along the beach every morning. And it was definitely possible that she'd be able to hang at least one flute player on the wall. Sit on her beautiful couch, feet tucked under her, listening to the flute and the wind rustling the grass, the waves on the sand. She laughed out loud, wondering when she was going to start worrying about exams.

"What's the joke?"

Janna shrugged. "The whole idea of art, really. It's like any other business. Some guy working for almost nothing to make something rich people pay a lot of money for. Something that's maybe beautiful, but its resale value is determined by whim."

She pushed back her chair, thinking Amy's politics were messing with her head. That and the coffee buzzing through her system like electric currents, the coffee and her hunger. None of the pastries had looked edible. David stood, the red glow of the brazier lighting his face. "It's more than whim."

"Is it?" she said, looking him over as if she was still in the gallery and he was a statue. She tilted her head, first to one side and then to the other, the way she'd seen people do in front of a picture. His face was slightly freckled, and she stepped sideways so she could look at his ear and the way his neck rose out of his jacket. She walked around him, not caring what he thought. She put out a hand, touched his shoulder to keep him from turning and walked right around him, pausing to note where the hem of his pants was trodden at the heels, the highlights in his gel-streaked hair, the blush rising right into his ears as he realized what she was doing. She felt dreamy as she walked her fingers down his back feeling for the vertebrae beneath the jacket. She came round the front and stared at him, feeling an arousal that startled her. One she didn't care if he saw.

"What do you have against whim?" she said. She shivered at what she felt was power.

"I live just a couple of blocks from here." He tried to keep it light but his voice was hoarse. "You're getting cold."

She shrugged again and turned, felt his hand land lightly on her shoulder, guiding her through the rain, the umbrella forgotten. She felt like she was underwater: the rain on her head, the pressure of his hand like the pressure of water against her body when she swam, a pressure she could feel against all her limbs. As she followed him up the stairs to his place above the Asian import shop, she took off her wet jacket trying to relieve that pressure. His key so quick in the lock she barely had time to pause and think before she was lost in the taste of smoke in his mouth, the skin, and the urgency. But there was a moment when she thought of Isabel and about how these things happened. And then didn't think of her or anything else.

†

She was half-asleep in a tangle of sheets when David raised her hand and kissed the writing blurred on her palm. When he tried to get her to talk about why she liked it so much, she ignored him, looking around the big bedroom. Two ornate dressers, the dark wood intricately carved, the knobs filigreed ivory balls. Clothes spilled off a big table under a big window draped with dozens of patterned scarves. The walls were covered, every inch, with posters of art exhibits and the ceiling slanting over the bed had hundreds of coins pressed into the plaster. She could hardly breathe in the dim perfumed air. She climbed down off the bed as he said something about cultural connotation and went looking for the bathroom. She didn't want to analyze her feelings about the flute player. She wanted a weekend off from being a student.

When he followed her right into the bathtub to ask her what she thought about the contaminating effect of western cultural imperialism, she turned him around and asked about the line of thumbprints tattooed down his spine. It was a first-year art project, he said. Before he could explain further, she nipped the top print with her teeth, wondering whose thumb it was. They alternated, left thumb, right thumb, left thumb, right thumb, all the way down to the crack in his butt. Her mouth still at his neck, she walked her fingers down the prints until her hands were in the water and he stopped talking about art. It had turned out to be exactly the kind of weekend she wanted.

†

By Monday afternoon, she was having doubts. Papers spilled out across the floor, where she'd dropped her bag when she crept in sometime around four that morning. Her weekend clothes, still in a heap on the bathmat, smelled of smoke and sex. Thank God she'd managed to have a shower before she went to class, shuddering to think of Greg taking off her pants. She had a vague memory of a girl helping him. A real gentleman. She tried to reassure herself about the weekend. She'd been working too hard and needed a break. She'd had that. She needed sex. She'd had that. She still needed food. She had hardly eaten all weekend. David had cooked something, but it had been too spicy. And late on Sunday they'd smoked a joint that she was sure was spiked with something else the way she could still feel it curving all the straight edges in her room. Like she told the rep, if she ate something, she'd be fine.

She pulled on some clothes and ran down to the vending machines in the basement. She bought chocolate bars, chips, a packet of cheese and crackers. A couple of Cokes. Back in her room, she flipped open her laptop, turned it on, and popped in a CD, hoping the techno buzz and Cokes would be enough to power her up to tackle some of the work she'd planned to do over the weekend. There was no way she was going to be able to finish the statistical analysis, but she might be able to do a draft of her final report for international studies. As she stared at the neat lines of text appearing on the screen and felt the sugar jolt through her system, she began to think she just might pull it off.

10

Álvaro's suitcase, still streaked with the dust of Guatemala City and smeared with Vancouver rain, lay open on his bed in the provincial house. He'd stripped the sheets, spread the blanket back over the mattress, and laid out his few possessions. His clothes. His Oblate cross tucked between his socks. The blue tin cup that had stood, full of forgotten water, on the table while his uncle's small house crumbled around it, a single roof beam crushing his mother in her bed. February 4, 1976, when he was a novice in Mexico City.

He tucked the cup in a corner of the case and, between the folds of his one white shirt, he slipped the creased postcard of the Virgin of Guadalupe. After visiting her shrine, he'd sent the card to his mother to celebrate a day of pure feeling with the spirit alive in every nerve. Once he became a novitiate, his mother had returned to her village and been welcomed home. She was a respected healer and a midwife, the uncles said later. Things she'd never told him. They had taken a photo of her in her coffin for him. She wore the carefully preserved *huipil* of her youth with its lightning zigzags and coiled around her beautiful silver hair, the red coral snake *tzute*, cloth he remembered from the time before his father disappeared. Another mystery he'd thought back then he would never unravel. He'd spoken to the carpenter who had built her coffin, a young man uncertain how this pale *Ladino* was connected to the village and why he wanted to know where he'd learned his trade and how busy he'd been after the earthquake.

The uncles told him they'd found the postcard propped up against the cup, the stars in the Virgin's robe the same blue. If only she'd had it with her, they said. The Virgin's grace wasted on a cup. These men he was meeting for the first time lit candles and fed him liquor. They told him about the mountain's saint name. Gave him the rosary in its little pouch. He was a pure and fiery Catholic then, washing himself clean of the old ways and the rituals his mother performed in quiet corners. Rituals he and Vinicio had trampled as they rode Fortuny's horses through the planted ground.

It was to the Virgin of Guadalupe, Álvaro thought, he should go for guidance now. He would ask her for a sign as clear as Juan Diego's roses in winter to see if he was, at last, on a path that would make him whole again.

The first thing he had drawn for Chris Mundy was a *milagro* of the heart. He'd sketched dozens of them in the week before his first appointment. The four lines of a square. The soft curves of a heart and the shading to show its volume. He was bursting with its urgency, jiggling his knee impatiently as she explained the process. How they would begin slowly. Find out how much energy he had for this and how far he wanted to go.

He wanted to begin by drawing something for her. A gift. He started to explain *milagros*. How they offer protection. We'll talk later, she said, and sat him down at a table with paint, brushes, pencils, and crayons lined up around the edge. Dozens of colours. She spread a big sheet of paper in front of him and sat down, off to one side. His certainty vanished in the face of the blank paper. He brushed his open hands across it several times, feeling its texture. His breath caught in his chest as he struggled to choose. He felt like he was choking as his right hand moved of its own accord over to the thick crayons.

Silver for the square of tin. Four grey slashes, forming a square as wide as the paper itself. The pain in his chest became acute as his fingers hovered over the reds, the pain so palpable it was as if his heart itself was crying out for the right colour, and leapt, joyous, when his fingers figured it out and chose three. The joy turned to despair at the clumsy lump cross-hatched with scribbles. He had made the heart too big.

He looked across at her, desperate. It has to be smooth, he'd said, and she showed him how to use his fingers to spread the colour. Many people are surprised by what happens when they draw, she told him. They are surprised at what comes, how quickly they are engulfed. He struggled to catch his breath, to find words to tell her about the heart. He bent to ease the constriction in his throat, bent close, and rubbed the harsh burgundy, orange, and scarlet scrawls until the paper glowed as red as the sacred heart on the crucifix in *la finca's* kitchen. The constriction grew and grew until he bent to kiss the heart as his mother had him do each morning when he ran into the kitchen, still warm from his bed. He was panting, exhausted from the effort.

Chris said something about establishing a sanctuary, a place he could visualize if things got too upsetting. Perhaps a place he had loved as a child, a place where he felt safe. He thought of Clara saying her first prayer of the day, then sitting at his feet while he brushed her hair and his mother prepared them each a cup of chocolate.

"Keep hold of that image," Chris said. "Tell me what you're seeing."

He told her about the wood crackling in the stove, the metal creaking as it warmed up. Herbs hanging from the ceiling, the smell of coffee, and the sticky skin of milk on the surface of the cocoa. But he relaxed too far into his own story and was smiling at Chris across the table from his silly heart when he heard the click of riding boots on tiles. Vinicio calling the dog. Calling Álvaro. Chris's studio filled with the smell of lemons and the voice, a soft hiss. *El pobrecito*, he heard. The boot on the spade, the spade cutting into the crumbling dirt, and the yellow bones. Finger bones reaching out to pull him in. He tried to push them away and was surprised to find that his own hands were not strapped down. Stained from the drawing, they scrabbled at the crayons on the table.

"Father Álvaro." Chris's voice was a thin thread flung from a great distance. "Father Álvaro, there's no one else here. You're safe, Father." She was close to him and he smelled her shampoo, something apple. The lemon vanished and he slumped back in the chair, his body trembling. He lay his head down on his arms and sobbed.

He didn't know how long he cried before Chris touched his arm and handed him a box of tissues. As he lifted his head, the smeared red of the heart glowed on the paper. He took a tissue and wiped his face. His shoulders relaxed. He took another and blew his nose. His stomach unclenched. She handed him a glass of water, gathered up the soggy tissues, and tossed them in a wastebasket. Gave him a few minutes to stare out one of the high windows at the bare branches of the trees outside.

"Can you tell me what happened?"

He felt the rosary in his pocket.

"Why don't you bring it out?" she asked.

He pulled out the chain of corn, the kernels forming a rosary, the cross woven of corn husks. Each seed's centre was punctured by the threading of the string. He wrapped it around one hand. He wondered as he always did if it could still germinate.

Chris waited.

He unwrapped it and spread it out across the heart. There was no refuge

for him in the kitchen of his childhood. No refuge in his memories of Clara.
No refuge in his mother's love. And even as he struggled to speak, the smell
of lemons again wafted through the room. The fear returned and clenched
every muscle in his body. Fear and enormous fatigue. He was so tired of being
afraid. He was so tired of trying not to be afraid.

"What do you smell?"

Her attentiveness gave Álvaro an understanding then of last chances. He
had to try. "Lemons," he said, his jaw clenched around the word.

"Tell me about the lemons."

"He uses lemon juice for an aftershave. He has a lemon tree beside his
house, and like his father did, he goes out in the morning and picks a lemon.
Slices it and rubs the cut surface over his face. Then he squeezes out the juice
and drinks it. His body's bullet-proof vest, he says."

"He?"

Álvaro reached out and picked up a small pot of paint. He unscrewed
the lid, poured thick black drops down the length of the rosary, and smeared
them across the heart. His skin seemed to shrink and tighten across the scars
on his face and skull. "Ms. Mundy, may I introduce Vinicio Fortuny. My con-
stant companion."

†

And so the therapy began. Saying the man's name out loud unstopped something in Álvaro and he had not been able to stop drawing since. But each
drawing left him more exposed. Stumbling in, exhausted after that first session,
he tried to retreat to his room. He was called to come to dinner and meet with
old friends from Winnipeg. After the second, he was asked if he would help
translate for a delegation from Costa Rica. After the third, he was asked to sit
with Father Donald who was swelling up with fluid, his heart unable to pump
the blood away from his lungs. He said yes to every request, each so small, so
well intentioned. He felt guilty about the shrinking energy of his community,
of the men who had been everything to him after he had lost his mother,
who had helped him transform the loss of Isabel into compassion, who had
let him go back to Guatemala when he could no longer bear listening to the
refugees' stories he was asked to translate as they tried to make a life in Winnipeg. Whose warnings he had ignored as he tried to lose himself in the debris
washed up in the streets of Guatemala City. Who were paying for his sessions
with Chris.

He had taken to sneaking in to his room, hoarding the time it took to draw the images that kept coming. Every handprint on the floor, every fence and tombstone, every chicken bleeding in the dirt was something made bearable. Diving deep into his own dark house with a crayon to light the way, terrified and exhilarated. A knock on the door asking if he would walk with Father James who was in the restless throes of early dementia. He said yes to everything and failed everywhere. Hiding in a hedge with the old priest for an hour, half a block from the house because a hydro truck with its man in a hardhat and the orange traffic markers represented indecipherable threats. James, incontinent, wet, cold, yelling and hitting at Álvaro until a neighbour called the police.

Clearly the provincial house was not suitable. Perhaps he needed a residential facility — there was one on Vancouver Island they could send him to. But he wanted to keep working with Chris. She was called in to consult with the superior. With her, she brought Margaret Coleman's invitation for Álvaro to move into a quiet upstairs room in her house. She had taken in many refugees, Chris said, some who had been tortured. She would provide a quiet place with no obligations. The superior, not waiting to see Álvaro's response, simply nodded in thanks. Margaret would pick him up the next day.

Álvaro closed his suitcase and looked around the small bedroom. One of so many rooms he had shut the door on. So little to carry, really. He walked across to the main building. None of us really knows how much weight another carries. Or why some of us keep it all while others can let it float away. Like Walter. He heard his voice before he saw him, standing in an office doorway, talking to someone about the previous night's hockey game.

Álvaro paused, waiting for the inevitable. Walter turned toward him, his walker filling the hall.

"You ever play hockey in Winnipeg?" He didn't wait for an answer. "That's what you need. A good hockey brawl with young players, ones who can knock the stuffing out of you."

"I do better at soccer."

"It's because we're all old men in this town. You're damn near one yourself but around us you act like one of the young roosters, voice still breaking halfway through a squawk."

Álvaro set his case down. His cardboard tube of drawings.

"If I was ten years younger, I'd do it myself, like I did the first time you ran off the rails."

That was another bedroom, the one they'd shared for his short time in the north. The summer of Isabel.

When Álvaro first turned to the church it was not for the love of God. It was to escape the chasm that had opened up beneath him when Clara was sent to school in Los Angeles. Forever, it seemed, she had opened her door to him. Her twin. As the house subsided into sleep, he would sneak down the hallway, his bare feet certain of every step, his hands sure on the latch. At first they were just children cuddled together for comfort. But that changed and the hands set out on different journeys under the covers, under the clothes, all their attention focused on each other's skin. Endless kisses in the damp darkness. The little gasps as they found new places. Their whimpers as he travelled a little distance into her, stopping before he hurt her, his fumbling ejaculations.

Then one night, Clara's door had been locked and he heard his mother's voice inside. The next day Clara was gone. Their secret, his mother's now. If they find out, she told him, dying would be the least of your worries. When he opened his mouth to protest, she slapped him. Do as I tell you, she'd said. One of the catechists ducked under a roof in the village, the water spouting out of the gutters, the streets streaming. Yelling an invitation to a seminar in the next town. When? Now. The truck idling, the faces watching. A couple of young men from the village and a couple of strangers, all of them nervous. The man holding out a bundle of clothes his mother had wrapped for him. Tortillas still warm in the middle. He was fifteen. He'd gone.

The seminar led to the seminary and somewhere in that first year, he had ignited. He had burned through school, burned through his mother's awkward visits, burned right through his farewell visit to the plantation two years later — Fortuny's pistol on the table as he paid the men lined up outside the back door of the main house, Vinicio standing behind him in his army uniform. Clara's debutante portrait hung in the dining room, all satin and ruffles showcasing her pale shoulders and neck. Her eyebrows arched, eyes looking over the photographer's shoulder. It's not a good place for you, his mother told him. Don't go there anymore. The discipline of his studies had been a luxurious freedom. A call to leave his past behind, his desire sublimated. Or so he thought. In Smithers, everything was new, his parishioners a confusing mixture of Carrier, Dutch, Italian, Irish, and Canadian. And there was Isabel. Her little boys like puppies. His body in flames.

He spoke to Walter. "You still think I'm worth a thousand Isabels?"

Walter's face crumpled into a laugh. "I do. And you're at least as much trouble." He gestured toward Álvaro's tube of drawings. "All these females. Eloise, the Coleman woman, this therapist. It's not good for a priest. They don't understand the mental toughness you need to do this job."

Álvaro picked up his case and his drawings and walked with Walter down to the dining room, goaded by Walter's predictable response. On the way he began to tell him about a woman from a small village in the north of Guatemala. About mental toughness. How it began, often, with fear. When the soldiers came, she hid, but she could see everything. The people were herded into the church, with kicks and rifle butts. Children were thrown inside, thumping to the floor. A soldier dragged a screaming woman from a nearby house. He grabbed the little girl clinging to her legs, and sliced the cloth that tied the baby to her back. He swung them like rags and the hidden woman covered her eyes thinking he was going to crack their heads against the tree shading the church steps. When she looked again another soldier was holding the children, one in each arm, laughing as the others threw the mother to the ground and took turns raping her. Sometimes two on her at once. Their rifles inside her. When they were done, they threw her limp body into the church, slammed the door, and hammered it shut. They poured gasoline on the wooden porch and tossed a match.

Álvaro set down his case and pushed open the dining room door. Walter bent over his walker, not moving.

"The woman could not stop watching the terrified girl and the crying infant. She prayed to the Virgin of Guadalupe for their souls and thanked her for one small miracle when the man threw them, still alive, into the back of the truck with the other soldiers. The truck drove around and around the church until the screams stopped and even the tree outside the door was burning. They finally drove away with the boy and the girl, her nephew and niece. The woman they raped was her sister."

Walter stood in the doorway as Álvaro poured them each a cup of tea from the huge brown pot that stood wrapped in a cozy on the sideboard. He spooned in sugar, poured milk, and set out the cups on the worn lace tablecloth.

Walter spoke. "Álvaro, I know that women suffer."

"As she breathed in that smoke," Álvaro continued, relentless, "she smelled the roasting flesh of the rest of her family. She took them all in, she said.

Made a place for them in her body. Sometimes — this was years later — she could feel the whole village inside her, especially when she was afraid. They would jostle for room under her rib cage, in her heart and her lungs, and in her trembling bowels. She gathered courage from their tumult and tried to calm them."

Walter's fingers made the cross. Álvaro finally looked away, his tongue awkward, Ana Elisabeth's story in his mouth.

"She hid for a while in the hills and then made her way to a village on the other side of the mountains. People knew better than to ask questions. She helped with the crops, and married a man whose wife had died in childbirth. She cared for his children but had none of her own. The clamouring in her belly would not let her rest. She wanted her sister's children."

Walter came through the door, sat down and took the warm cup in his hands. Drank. Álvaro told him how the priests were back in Quiché by then, some of them gathering testimony for Bishop Gerardi's report. The exhumations had begun. People were speaking out.

"She came to me." His bitterness and regret were bones in his throat.

"We went to Guatemala City and inquired at the orphanages. We asked a hundred useless questions. One day we came out of an office to see the Army Day floats passing in the street. There were hundreds on the streets, rows and rows of khaki and camouflage. When the red berets of the *kaibiles*, their faces and arms streaked with black, passed us, I could hear her stomach churning. She had a way of looking soldiers in the eye, always looking for her sister's murderers. And then she saw them."

"The soldiers?"

"The children. Dressed like a little prince and princess, waving from an army float. The girl, who was about twelve, looked around when her aunt called out her name. Looked around and burst into tears."

Walter's face was full of hope, ready for a happy ending.

"They were finer featured and lighter skinned than most Indians and could pass for *Ladino*. Their adopted mother, a good Catholic, was moderately wealthy. Reports said they were happy children, well behaved, attentive. Going to a good school."

"What did you do?"

"That's my question to you. The aunt lived in a shack with a tin roof and a dirt floor. She wove a few things to sell, planted a garden, and tended some chickens and a cow. Her husband planted corn and beans and picked up labouring jobs where he could. His children went to school when they weren't needed to work."

Álvaro looked at Walter across the table. The kitchen help had been in and out, setting for lunch; there was a fresh pot of tea.

"Here is a woman who has risked her life to find her sister's children. She is willing to take them in, feed them, clothe them, and try to send them to school. By doing so, she is endangering not only herself, but also her husband's family. The entire village. She asks me what to do."

"The adopted mother's Catholic, you say?"

"Probably more devout than the aunt."

Walter shifted uncomfortably. "Could she not be introduced as the aunt?"

Álvaro did not answer.

"She would not have to lie. She is the aunt." Walter was practical. His hands expressive. "She could tell the mother. They could plan together."

"Aside from the problem caused by the aunt's very Mayan features, I thought the same. I arranged a meeting with the children's adopted uncle, a man I knew."

Álvaro met Vinicio in the small restaurant just off Central Square, a place they'd met two or three times before to sort out a difficult situation between the church and the military. If these particular inquiries are dropped, Vinicio would suggest, perhaps these other questions will be answered. Inviting him to visit *la finca* where his father still ruled supreme. More dairy now than cattle. Cheese even, if you can believe that, he'd laughed. Álvaro always noncommittal. Polite in his questions. The mother an American citizen now who never set foot in Guatemala. Clara a devout housewife in a villa near the new cemetery. Split her time between her children and charitable works.

"My mother worked for his family," he explained to Walter. "I amused him. I was a fool, he thought, for choosing the priesthood. And then leaving a comfortable life in Canada and returning to Guatemala. But I was useful. No matter how well established, how wealthy, people always find information valuable in a political situation as fluid, shall we say, as Guatemala's."

Turn it into a story, Chris had suggested. Give the events a framework. Contain them. Create distance from what your body is experiencing now.

A past and a habitable present.

He was a powerful, urbane man, Álvaro told Walter, sitting there with an amused smile on his face. Álvaro asked after the sister, Clara. The smile had flickered when Álvaro enquired more closely about Clara's children. Disappeared when he told him about the aunt, an odd coincidence, he suggested, saying nothing about the months of searching. Nothing about the testimony Ana Elisabeth had sworn. Perhaps a visit to put her mind at peace about their welfare? Would Clara be interested?

Vinicio had been adamant; Clara was a fragile woman, just finding her way to happiness with these children. There would be absolutely no contact. It was a clear warning. Vinicio was stubbing out his cigarette, rising to leave when Ana Elisabeth walked into the restaurant as they'd arranged so that Vinicio could meet her and be reassured by her calmness. On his way out the door, Vinicio walked right past her.

What Álvaro didn't tell Walter was that while Ana Elisabeth stood, adrift in the room full of *Ladino* bank clerks and civil servants, the strip of bright cloth bound up in her braided and coiled hair as a token of resistance, Álvaro's concern had been all for Clara. Fragility? Finding her way to happiness? He found he wanted to see her, to comfort her if he could. Ana Elisabeth had shaken his arm to get his attention. You didn't tell him about me, she begged. Say you didn't tell him. She was terrified.

He told Walter about Ana Elisabeth's fear. He'd pulled her into the chair, hushing her. He's their uncle, he said. I'd hoped he would help. He's not a bad man, he said, and saw her face close against him. The teeth clenched behind the lips.

"What was it?" Walter asked.

Álvaro told him where she'd seen Vinicio.

Walter's face spasmed. "And so was complicit in the rest?"

"In command."

"Is this what got you into trouble down there?"

Álvaro took off his watch cap and rubbed it across his eyes. His hair stood awry.

"She was a very simple woman," he said. "No education to speak of. Very little religious training — the catechists in Quiché were always being killed. But she understood the dilemma as well as we do. And she was more willing to trust God than I was. Than I am."

"What happened?"

Álvaro's voice was harsh. "The family in her belly would not give those children up. The children had lost their spirits, the voices told her, and they would sicken and die if she did not help them. She felt compelled to do as they requested. She approached the woman. But she never made it inside the door."

"She changed her mind? Probably for the best."

"I don't think so." Álvaro pushed his cup aside. "She's dead."

Walter's hand crept across the table to cover Álvaro's. The veins showed blue through the mottled skin, the knuckles swollen and arthritic. "We are born into suffering," he said. "We need to trust in his wisdom."

Álvaro's hand clenched. Everything he had told Walter was water swirling down a drain. He could not trust himself to speak.

"Open yourself to his mercy." Walter's hands squeezed his own.

I am wide open, that's my trouble, Álvaro thought. I am punctured. Gales howl through my openings. And when the voices come, they are not the voices of God.

He finally spoke. "Don't preach Job to me, Walter. I have not said no to God, but I can't bring myself, right now, to say yes. I need to disentangle the lies in me from the truth. If God wants me back, he knows where to find me."

Walter opened his mouth to speak again. Álvaro struggled to keep his voice down. "My mother was stronger than any man I have known. Ana Elisabeth's faith was a thousand times stronger than yours or mine. I could name dozens more. I don't know what has become of Isabel, but I do know that I'm not worth a hundred cockroaches, much less a thousand women."

Álvaro didn't understand then why the fight fizzled out of Walter. He saw the usual impatience. The underlying compassion. But not the anger he expected. There was something else. A wariness. Maybe it was Margaret appearing in the doorway, her arms full of roses. She laid them on the table, pulled small scissors out of a pocket and began snipping off the ends and arranging the flowers in the water pitcher.

"Can you still cast a fly, Father Walter?" she asked.

Walter coughed in surprise. "There's not many fish in Vancouver's storm sewers."

"There are still Oblates up north, aren't there? You and Álvaro should plan a trip there next summer. Isn't there a pilgrimage on the shores of some big lake?"

The old man's face filled with longing. "Rose Prince of the Carrier Nation," Walter whispered. "She was one of those women, Álvaro. She found her place in the church in spite of her afflictions. Prayer was her therapy."

"Lucky girl," Margaret said, clearing up the rose clippings and wrapping them in one of the napkins from the dispenser on the table. And Margaret is one of those women, Álvaro thought, who knew how to handle priests like Walter, and priests like Álvaro. He wondered if she had plans for him.

"Is that all your luggage?" she asked as she went out the door into the hallway, carrying the pitcher of roses. Álvaro followed her, nodding. He bent to lift the case, but paused, uncertain, as she walked down the hall, genuflected at the chapel door, and went inside. She came back out, empty-handed.

"The roses," he stammered. "They're lovely. It's very kind of you."

"They're for the Virgin," she said.

"The Virgin?" Walter asked from the doorway.

"The Virgin of Guadalupe." She looked from one man to the other. "It's her feast day."

11

Greg had taken to bringing Janna a smoothie and energy bar most mornings as she wrote her last papers. Walking her to class and sitting with her in the cafeteria. When one of her stats classmates said something about how lucky she was to be hooked up with him, she realized they were seen as an item. She wondered if that was why she hadn't heard from David. If he'd asked around, he'd have been told. Greg was, she came to realize, a big and awkward deal in the business school. Each night she was sleeping less, lying awake, wondering what to do about him. Talking to her worry dolls, lining them up and asking them when he would make a move. How he would go about it. Why he hadn't already. So she could tell him no thanks.

The campus emptied as she knocked off her exams, one by one. Financial Accounting — easy. Income Taxation — not too bad. By then the smokers outside the social work building were gone and she'd pretty much given up on David. Logistics and Operations Management — in spite of missing that last class, she squeaked through. International Marketing — she prayed Amy would never see her answer to the question on strategies to develop and protect international branding. And now she wrestled with Stats, distracted by the heating system's knocks and bangs, the only noise in the all but deserted residence. Sleep had become impossible. She talked to one or two listless students who weren't going anywhere for Christmas. She half hoped she'd hear from Isabel, that maybe Trevor had passed on her phone number, but there'd been nothing. She was briefly tempted by Amy's offer of a ride to Smithers, but the timing was off.

The day before the exam, Greg knocked on her door, his pack over one shoulder, his duffel coat unzipped. She asked him for help with a stats problem. He talked for twenty minutes about the history of the problem, the development of the formula, and how a statistician in Sri Lanka was working on a new analysis. He leaned against her desk, holding his pale hands cupped in front of him as if he were showing her an invisible ball, twisting and turning it so she could see it from every direction.

She excused herself to go into the bathroom. The facecloth, wadded into a stiff clump, stank of mildew. She threw it into the corner with the rising pile of dirty clothes and scrubbed her face with her hands. Her red-rimmed eyes stared back at her from the streaked mirror. What gives with you, girl? Where'd this inner pig come from? She brushed her teeth.

Greg was flopped on her bed, reading a book outlining new community development economics. She started on another problem. Around noon, he opened his pack and brought out buns and a squat Mason jar of soup to microwave. Apple slices and carrot sticks. When she thanked him, he brushed her words away. He thought there should be more contact between economics and commerce students, he said. It made her feel like a science project.

They wolfed the food in a silence she found more and more tense. Waiting for him to do something. She finally invented a study group that met at one. He plunked his feet on the floor, gathered up his food containers, pulled his jacket off the hook on the back of her door, and disappeared. As soon as he was gone, she was lonely. She checked her email again. Gave up on stats and burrowed into her sheets. Dozing, she recalled random details of David's body. The dark nipples. The fine line of black hair leading from his navel to his thick pubic hair. His pale penis bobbing as he pulled the condom over its length. She touched herself as she lay there, her fingers slow and tender until she fell asleep with both David and Greg mixed up in her dreams. She couldn't get Greg's musty smell out of her nostrils, it was everywhere and she was thrashing her head around trying to make it go away but then it was David who shrank into a child, a child calling to her across a field of broken glass, calling her to help, please help and as she stood there, her feet bare, she felt a pulse in her vagina and an old-fashioned Coke bottle fell out and shattered, the noise bringing her awake and afraid in the mid-afternoon gloom. A glass had fallen and broken on the floor. She barely moved until morning.

"What are you doing for Christmas?" Greg asked her as they walked to her last exam. How pathetic, she thought. This geeky guy was feeling sorry for her, was going to ask her to go home with him for Christmas. He'd told her a bit about his father, a research chemist on long-term disability because of some kind of dementia, the mother dithering and feeding them all the time. Their old house crumbling, his word, in the middle of an upmarket Shaughnessy neighbourhood. What fun that would be.

"My family is Buddhist," she said. "We don't do Christmas."

"Oh, what practice do you follow? Theravada? Vajrayana?"

She ignored him and swung her bag over her shoulder. She held out a hand. He looked at it. She grabbed his, shook it. "Thanks," she said. "Thanks for everything. Have a good Christmas."

In the echoing clatter of the cavernous exam hall, she showed her ID and held out for inspection her flat of gum, can of Coke, and pencils. She was led to her place, a small desk attached to a green metal chair. The scooped-out seat was cold against her fleece pants. She shivered, the nerves flickering up from her stomach and travelling along her arms, little zaps as she drummed her fingers against the desk. Two minutes until she could open the white sheet on the desk in front of her. She wrote her name and her student number on the exam booklet. Her course and section. She could feel herself beginning to detach as the lines of the desk wobbled. She held on to the edges as if she were on a boat, rocking in an eddy, the river rushing by. Afraid.

A bell chimed. She opened the page and blanked at the first question. And the second. And the third. She didn't know what they meant. She looked at the title at the top of the page, checking to see it was the right exam. She looked around to see if anyone else was puzzled. All the bent heads, the pencils flicking. Some chemistry students pulled out little coloured balls and squares on wires. They clicked them together, linking them in the contorted shapes of babies' rattles. They looked down at their papers, scribbled, clicked and reshaped the toys, their pencils between their teeth. When she saw a proc-tor frowning at her, she put her head down on the desk and closed her eyes. All around her the balls snapped and clicked.

When the proctor shook her to say she could leave if she was done, she real-ized she'd fallen asleep. The panic rose like a great wave and she could barely breathe. No, she said, she'd keep going. She stuffed gum into her mouth and went back to the first question. She selected an answer. Then the next one. A, B, C, D, she shaded in the little squares. Sometimes E. When the exam ended, she set down her pencil, feeling as if something was gnawing a semicircular opening under the curve of her ribs. Her mouth was raw from the gum. She wondered if there was anything else left in the world but the crying girl rushing past the squat, grey-haired man showing a smiling young woman a configuration on the model. The haggard, the hollow-eyed, the red-rimmed messes. The happy chatterers. She felt as if she'd landed in the aftermath of a battle, the victors cheerful, the wounded and dying dragging themselves away from the scene of their defeat.

Outside she waited in the cold air, trying to figure out what had happened. Goosebumps rose on her arms, but she didn't think to put on her coat until she was shaking, her jaw clenched. She hugged her pack close, tucking her hands under her arms, and ran. Her cellphone pulsed against her ribs. Greg ·probably, finding out how she did. She ignored it and ducked into an alley, a shortcut to residence.

"Whoa!"

She looked up just in time to literally bump into David. His hands were held out to catch her. He was wearing a black wool coat down to his calves, a long scarf, and gloves. His hair stood up in little licks, gold-tipped black as if he'd been dipped in gilt. A surge of adrenaline made her giddy.

"I just bombed my last exam," she said.

He grinned, not believing. He opened his coat and wrapped it around them both. His heat startled her. He smelled wonderful. She didn't. Nose against a down vest, she mumbled. "You're dressed for the Arctic here."

He spoke to the top of her head. "I have a ticket to an outdoor concert at the Nitobe Gardens."

She welcomed the pressure of his hands against her body and his face against her hair. She drew back, reluctantly, still standing in the circle of his arms, under the wings of his coat.

"I've got some time," he said. "Do you want lunch?"

She shook her head. "I'm beat. I'm going to jump in the shower and then crash for a few hours."

He walked with her down the stairs toward the House of Learning. Ice crystals formed at the edge of the waterfall, streaks where the spray fell and froze before it was washed away. She stopped as she always did, to listen to the water's conversation, the way it whispered songs to the world even as it froze. Hush, it said. Hush. She gasped when David's gloved hands found their way under her clothes, the leather warm on her rib cage, his thumbs seeking out her nipples.

She was glad of the chaos of her room because it hid how little was there besides a calendar, stats graphs, and a couple of mountain posters. Trevor's wall hanging was the only beautiful thing really. She tried not to notice how carefully David draped his coat and folded his vest over the one chair. Slipping into the bathroom, she threw her dirty clothes into the cupboard under the sink and stepped into the shower, opening her mouth to flood the tender interior and wash away the mustiness of the last two weeks. The shower door slid open and he was with her, his hands sliding over her slippery skin. More water, more cavities, more unspoken conversations. She managed to forget about her exam. Fifty percent of her final mark, a big zero.

"The music is about to begin," David said later. She got out of bed and opened her window. It looked out onto the high wall surrounding the gardens. A faint sound of flutes floated along the cold afternoon air. She felt lightheaded. He came and stood beside her, listened, and named the music. She looked at their bodies, side by side in the pale winter light. His skin had an amber cast to it, the pale yellow of old ivory. Hers was browner. But the colour was close, a colour that lacked entirely the pinkness of her mother's skin. She used to wonder what colour her father was. Her skin darker than Jason's, but paler than Trevor's. Somewhere in between the two men who came on weekends to take the boys to hockey tournaments. The white car salesman and the Gitxsan fisherman. She used to examine every man who knocked on the door, asking for Isabel. Every man who hovered at the edge of their world, trucks sending out clouds of exhaust on the street in front of their house, men asking where her mother was. The ones her mother never let set foot inside.

She ran her hand across David's chest and decided her father had not been Asian. David came from culture, from class. From people who went to symphonies and had memberships in art galleries. From people with expensive prints on their walls. Her grandmother had that kind of class. Her mother didn't and here she was, a northern bush chick with worry dolls tucked under her pillow. He closed the window. "It's too late now. I'm going to hear about it though — that ticket was very hard to get and my friends will be pissed."

"Is that a problem?"

He laughed. "You're in business school — don't they teach you about networking?"

He picked up his clothes, checked for God knows what. Lice? He buttoned up his faded pink shirt, made sure his pants hung below the waistband of his boxers. Janna felt suspended — he was suddenly an irritant, but she didn't want to be alone. She did not want to think about the exam, about how soon it would be Christmas. He held up his vest, restless and uncertain. He pulled it on, zipped it up. "Why don't we get some food?"

"Sure." She picked up some of her own scattered clothes, guessing which were the least dirty. Black stretch pants that were almost baggy, she'd lost so much weight in the last couple of weeks in spite of Greg's attention. Little folds of material across her pelvic bones, the stomach concave between them. A midriff top and then a big sweater. And the leather jacket, the one she had spotted that day Amy bought the clothes. The one she'd saved for.

In the graduate student lounge, over congealed sushi, he told her he'd taken down the exhibit at the art gallery that morning. "That beautiful print you liked. The flute player. Soon it will be locked up in a drawer in Coleman's file cabinet."

"Sounds like residence," she said. "Don't you hate the end of term feeling? All that intensity and then, whoosh, like a bubble popping."

"There are remedies for such feelings." He pulled out his wallet, poked a finger into a slit, and fished out a small fold of cellophane enclosing five tiny yellow pills. He laid one on a fingertip and held it toward her.

She shook her head.

"Sure?" He dropped it into his own mouth, and offered her another.

Her tongue slid slowly out. He waited, eyebrows raised. She nodded and he dropped the pill onto its tip. She pulled her tongue in and swallowed. They went outside into the late afternoon dusk. He asked her if she had a car. "Not here," she said. She was already inventing another life for herself, imagining spending Christmas in his apartment.

As the bus accelerated to cross the bridge, she began to hum a Christmas carol — *God rest ye merry gentlemen, let nothing you dismay* — and giggle. They sat at the back of the bus. As it filled, she was pressed up against the outside wall and David sat half-sideways, his back to the man wedged in beside him. Two big women filled the seat in front of them, their backs as solid as a wall between her and the other passengers. David wrapped his arm and his coat around her, his hand on her breast, one finger circling the nipple. The bright lights wobbled as the bus lurched from stop to stop. Under the cover of his coat, David slid his cold hand down under her sweater. She shifted slightly to give him easier access, hooking one foot over his boots. She stared at the boots, the way they were so firmly planted, feeling at the same time his fingers searching. Long fibres of sensation descended from her crotch, descended into the boots, roots descending into the grey mat on the floor of the bus, into the dirt in her mother's garden. It wasn't until he pulled her up at their stop that she realized how stoned she was. The stairs to his apartment slid into each other, the rail twisted and bulged under her hand.

He turned the key in the locks, one, two, three, and led her into the dark living room; all the Christmas lights from the stores across the way lit up the walls with red and golden light. Huge shadows advanced and receded across the ceiling as traffic moved along the street below. The light seemed to respond to the sounds, swelling and exploding in big sunbursts, then subsiding into washes of colour.

"What did I eat back there?"

"Two C-B." He giggled. "It's like Ecstasy only sexier."

He was right about that. She took off her jacket, and as its weight left her shoulders her whole body responded to the lightness. She kicked off her shoes and twirled a slow motion spiral around the room's hardwood floor. She remembered the bed and the scarves and the postcards. She wanted to see the light playing across the objects on the walls. His hand covered hers before she could open the door and a large uneasy moment filled the room. He didn't want her in there.

She swayed, suspended, as he brought out candles, which he lit and set out on the ledge that ran along two walls. He pulled the futon off the couch onto the floor and tossed some cushions around. He flipped through a huge basket of CDs. She stared at the light pinpointed in the shining doorknob of the bedroom. Then the music began — a single flute — and she was transfixed. The notes entered her body: bubbles of sensation in her crotch rose in a line through her midriff and forked to her nipples. Wanting to remove the layers between the music and her skin, she peeled off her clothes, undulating to the notes as if they were fingers. She barely noticed when the light and music turned into David's hands; time stretched into one long nerve bundle of sensation.

She vaguely remembered looking out a window sometime in the night, her thighs warm against the radiator, snowflakes falling into the space between the buildings, blurring the lights into shimmering waves. David stood behind her, slowly moving inside her, his hands on her breasts, between her legs. She had opened the window and let the outside air swirl across her, feeling the snowflakes like other hands on her body. It seemed as if they moved there for hours; when she finally came, Janna felt her whole body break into flakes of light, flakes of light with huge empty spaces between each glittering prism.

She awoke to the sound of David's voice, far away, talking. On the telephone, she hoped, covering her head with a quilt he'd thrown over them sometime in the early morning. She hunkered down, wishing he'd come back to cuddle her warm. She was light-headed and shivery, her throat raw. Outside, car tires swished through puddles. The snow had turned to rain.

She pulled the quilt off her head and heard David laugh. A satisfied ugly little laugh that made her realize she didn't know him at all. Not in any way that really mattered. His words carried clearly through a pause in the traffic. The one I told you about, he said, and something about one last young fuck before the return of the bitch. It shouldn't be a problem, he said after a minute. A knot formed in Janna's stomach and she felt as grey and washed out as the light falling across the dishevelled bed on the living room floor.

The kitchen door opened and he came out with a steaming cup and set it on the floor beside her. He was polished and gleaming, dressed as if for the symphony or a waitering job, a white open-collared shirt, black pants, black carved beads around his neck, an earring shining discreetly above his collar. His hair was gelled back into golden Christmas pine cone tips. Behind him, she could see dishes washed and set out to drain. A bag of garbage tied and set by the door, his suitcase beside it. He wasn't coming back to bed. He had one more thing to tidy up. Her. Her anger surprised her. Gave her energy.

"I'll go out and pick us up something for breakfast," he said. "Any requests?"

"Whatever," she said, shoving aside the covers.

"Friends are coming to pick me up in a while…" the words trailed off into an awkward pause as she stood naked in front of him. "We'd give you a ride home, but we're going up to Whistler." He stared at the bruises the radiator had left on her thighs. She forced herself to stretch, unconcerned. She scratched her head.

"I don't feel I can ask them to drive back the other way when the traffic's like it is."

The room was freezing but she refused to shiver. She picked up the cup. "I'll just grab a quick bath."

He nodded as she sipped the tea. It felt good sliding down her throat. She walked to the bathroom, knowing he was watching her.

"Janna?" She liked the uncertainty that had entered his voice, such a change from the boy brute telephone persona. He was trying to figure out if she was going to berate him, or cling and whimper. She liked him anxious. But he wasn't anxious enough. She wanted to see his composure vanish. She turned, rubbed one breast.

"If the phone rings, let the machine pick it up," he said.

She just turned and went into the bathroom. In his medicine chest she found some cold pills and took two. While her bath ran, she found a thermostat and turned the heat up. She gathered her clothes. Outside, the rain was a grey wall of water.

She sank into the hot water and let its warmth seep into her. Dangling her arm out of the water, she inspected her clothes: panties, socks, tights, and T-shirt. She grimaced and dropped each one into the water. She didn't care what kind of hurry he was in. She was not going to put those clothes back on. She soaped them up, rinsed them, squeezed as much water out as she could and draped them on the clanking radiators.

After her bath, she went into the bedroom looking for something clean to wear. Compared to the chaos of her previous visit, it was spotless. The bed was neatly made, the tables and dressers polished, the surfaces cleared of everything but a couple of photographs of Asian temples and a big carving of a bulbous woman in spotted stone. She pulled open a drawer and looked into a tangle of bra straps, thongs, silvery belts, and scarves. Messy, but very nice lingerie. Silk. She balked at putting on another woman's underwear, but in the next drawer found a black chenille sweater that looked warm. In another she found a nice little kilt, Christ she'd look like a schoolgirl, and big red wool socks. She ran and slid across the long living room floor right up to the closed door of the other room. She opened it to see a computer, bookshelves, desk, and swivel chair.

David had told her he was house-sitting for a prof on a year's sabbatical in Thailand. Well, the sabbatical part may have been true, but the implied distance in their relationship was not. A series of photographs hung around the room. David's spine. They'd been taken in the bed he hadn't let her into last night. In each picture, the photographer reached out a hand, extended a thumb and placed it on one of his vertebrae as if laying down a fingerprint. In the first picture, the thumb was on the top vertebra. In the next, the top vertebra was tattooed and the thumb pressed on the second. In each picture, the thumbs descended the vertebrae, one by one, until the entire column was tattooed. The tattoos he'd said were part of a first-year art project. In the final photograph, a handprint appeared on each buttock. He must have drawn the line there because his butt was untouched. Or maybe that was next. Looking closer, Janna saw that in the first photograph, the photographer's wrist was tattooed with one petal-like flame. In each subsequent photograph, an additional flame was added until flames encircled the wrist.

She found the woman in another photograph. Probably in her mid-thirties, she had short spiky hair and a long face, her mouth an almost invisible line. Standing very pale against bright green shrubbery, she wore a shirt with a high standing collar. Janna recognized her by the hand held up to what looked like another tattoo around her neck. Flames encircled her wrist. The knot tightened inside Janna's empty stomach.

The phone rang. After two rings, the answering machine clicked on and a woman's voice called over the message. "David, David, pick up the damn phone will you?"

She heard the downstairs door open, and without thinking, picked up the phone, as ordered. "David, David," the voice continued, angry now. She put down the receiver as the key turned in the lock. She smiled at the fear on his face when he saw she was wearing his girlfriend's clothes. He looked like he might be sick when she explained how her clothes fell into the bathtub and she had to find something to wear. She praised the very interesting underwear this woman had.

"Don't worry. I didn't take any," she said and flipped up the kilt to show him.

"Very funny," he groaned. "She's not my girlfriend, she's my prof. And she's coming back to reclaim her apartment later today. Hence the cleanup and my imminent departure."

She took the bag of pastries from his hand and set it on the table. She pulled off his coat and pushed him into a chair.

"Relax. She has so many clothes, she won't even notice these are gone."

What a sap, she thought, as she climbed onto his lap and fed him bits of biscotti dipped in takeout lattes. She was determined to mess up his clothes and rumple more than his hair. The forked nature of man. While a thousand worries crossed his face — the friends, the girlfriend, his clothes, the girlfriend's clothes, her wet undies on the radiator, his hair — his dick didn't have a care in the world. It wanted to get unzipped and take a closer look at what was under the kilt. It didn't care whose twat was up there as long as it was warm and wet. It didn't care if it was wearing its own little raincoat either, and she ignored David's protestations to slide down over his unprotected penis with such sudden intensity that all his anxiety was swallowed in the laughable single-mindedness of his dick. She controlled his pleasure, prolonged it, waited until his face blurred and slackened and then rose off him just as he came, just in time to get semen all over his nice black pants and the girlfriend's kilt. It was all she could do not to laugh. But her own anger returned when an expression that could have been fury began to build in his face, something close to hate.

The moment lengthened and stretched between them. She was climbing off his lap when the phone rang. She reached over, picked it up, said hi, and passed it to him. By the time he hung up, he was all hurried business and she was pulling on her boots.

"We're leaving in five," he said, like he was some kind of gangster, and ducked into the bathroom, slamming the door behind him. Janna opened his wallet. About fifty bucks in cash. A couple of credit cards. A gas card. She slid her little finger into the crack and extracted the pills. Three left. She unwrapped them and rolled them around in her palm. She wrapped one back up and dropped it into her purse. She dropped the other two pills into a teaspoon and ground them up with the back of another spoon. She added some sugar, mixed it with her finger, and stirred into his coffee.

A car honked. He downed his coffee. She pulled on her jacket over the woman's clothes and followed him out the door, leaving her own behind. On the street, she kissed him, tasting the coffee still on his lips. She waved at the faces peering out the window of the nice little BMW. Merry Christmas.

That night in her small room in the empty residence, she wondered how his holiday was going. She hoped he was struggling through some complicated dining protocol at the house of rich, what did he call them? Patrons? Or listening to his mother chatter about his career prospects, suggesting women he should mate with. She wished she could have been there when the girlfriend returned to find another woman's clothes drying on the radiator.

She dug out her cellphone to call Jason. Maybe Trevor. She needed to talk to someone real, someone who knew her. Her smugness vanished when she saw Isabel's name appear. Trevor must have given her the number. She paced the room while she listened to her message.

"Hi, sweetheart." A pause. The voice deflated. "I wanted to thank you for the bulbs you sent. I managed to get them planted even though it was so late. I don't know how they'll do. They're probably used to that soft life down there." A little laugh. "I know it's short notice, but I've just talked to the airline. There's a seat left on tonight's plane and I've booked it. All you have to do is be at the airport by six-thirty." A man said something in the background and impatience crept into Isabel's voice. Impatience Janna knew all too well.

"Well, goodbye then. I'll meet the plane." Distracted by something in pants.

Janna leaned her hot cheek against the cool window, wondering how hard she'd have to press to send cracks shooting through the glass, to shatter it into a hundred lethal pieces and fall with it onto the ground below. She stood there for a long time before she realized how hot she was. How she couldn't stand without leaning. She wanted to be curled up in her own little bed, her quilt tucked around her, her mom coming up the stairs with apple juice. She wondered if it hadn't been a very, very bad idea to take the last pill. She slumped on the bed and phoned Greg, not sure what she was going to ask. For a bowl of soup? A ride to the airport? The phone rang and rang; when an old man answered, she'd almost forgotten who she'd dialled.

"Who is this," he said. "Who is this? Who is this?"

It must be Greg's father.

"Have you got my car ready?" he said.

"Your car?"

"When will it be ready?"

"Not yet," she said. "Not yet. But soon." She hung up.

She felt all the places on her body where it hurt: her bruised thighs, the chafing between her legs, the fingernail marks on her buttocks, the whisker burn on her face and breasts. Her tender nipples. She closed her eyes against her thoughts of the woodstove in the tiny living room at home, the flame dancing behind the glass and the pot of spiced apple juice simmering on top, its cinnamon smell filling the house. She sat down on her grubby bed and pulled out her worry dolls. You're the mother, she told one and you're the father, she told another. And let's have a granny and two boys. She propped them up on her pillow. That leaves you, she said, holding up a little girl doll dressed in a long green skirt and red top. The Christmas girl. She tossed her up in the air and caught her. What will we do with you?

12

Álvaro waited outside the open bathroom door for his turn. Margaret's son, Joseph, bent to wash his face, his shoulder blades moving like wings under his pale skin. Álvaro was reminded of the grave where the victims had been forced to lie face down, shoulder to shoulder in a tidy row and then been shot, one, two, three, four, five, six, seven, eight. Shortest to tallest. As if some demented artist had been arranging a show, an artist who could well have been in the group that gathered with him and the surviving villagers to gaze at eight pairs of scapula, heavy wings pressing what had once been frightened flesh deep into the crumbling dirt.

Joseph straightened and scrubbed himself dry, tossing the towel over his shoulder and banishing the memory.

"All yours, Father Al." He grinned and jogged down the hallway to his room, jumping in little zigs and zags, practising his surfing moves. His family was going to spend Christmas week at their cabin at Tofino and this time of year the waves were, he said, great.

The boy had been unperturbed by Álvaro's arrival. He'd shared this bathroom with dozens of Margaret's strays, Álvaro figured. The family's easy familiarity made him feel like a novice again, a novice in charge of his own education. He and Chris had fit in four more sessions and he'd been free to think them through. To continue making pictures upstairs in his small room, finding stories in the chaos of sensation. No difficult questions, no how are you doings, no questions beyond did he think it was ever going to stop raining?

The Christmas dinner at the provincial house had clarified his choice, a sign, he thought, from whatever spirits were watching over him. The old men around the table washing down turkey with wine. A forced joviality. George on one side and Walter on the other, visiting from the downtown house. Walter taking him aside, encouraging him to make a confession so he could take communion at the midnight mass. Father John, he said, had worked many years in South America. He was willing. English or Spanish.

"The release after a good confession, one where you really get things sorted out and you know God is welcoming you to begin again." The old man smiled. "You've forgotten," he said. "How long has it been?"

Álvaro stared past Walter at John, who looked like a dozing turtle, his nose a beak, his head all polished wrinkles bobbing in and out of his collar with each slow breath. His parish had been a few hours east of Walter's and they'd often met midweek to prepare a meal together. To discuss parishioners over a poker game. He'd practised his stumbling Spanish with Álvaro.

Álvaro laughed. Walter was, as usual, partly right. In spite of the pain he experienced in his sessions with Chris Mundy, he was beginning to make confession. Finally a good confession.

Walter spoke through a mouthful of shortbread. "Altogether too long, I'd bet."

Álvaro had wished only that he smoked, so he could step outside without giving offence and look at the night sky.

When he helped stuff the last bag into the Coleman's car, slammed the door, and waved them off, his whole body relaxed. He raised his face to the light rain and let the drops gather in his open mouth. He swallowed, tracing the water's descent. He couldn't remember when he had last been alone and unguarded.

An hour later, he stood in the bright kitchen, the long wooden table scrubbed, the counters cleared, and the floor swept. He set out water, paint, and brushes. Pencils and felt pens. Paper. He pressed his hands flat upon the rough paper, closed his eyes, and breathed deeply as Chris had suggested. He thought about the roots and trunk and leaves this paper had once been — the soil and water and sunlight, the birds that had nested in its branches. He drew strength from understanding that the molecules that spun together his body with all its shattered nerves were no different than the molecules that made up the fly's wing trapped somewhere in the fibre of this paper. He waited.

Words floated into his head. *How beautiful upon the mountains are the feet of him who brings glad tidings.* He wrote them in green paint across the page and waited again, letting the memories come.

He had told Chris about the sudden hands upon him as he stood outside Clara's gate in Guatemala City and pressed the buzzer. It was a quiet neighbourhood. Birds chattered in the huge trees shading the gardens behind the high white wall. He had phoned and she was expecting him. A cautious invitation. Her voice uncertain, curious. Children's voices floated up and through the razor wire coiled along the top of the bricks. There were no other sounds but the grunts of the men who clamped his mouth and wrestled him into the back of a blue van, blindfolded him, and tied his hands and feet. Birds he heard, birds and children's voices and just before the door slammed shut, he thought Clara called his name. Álvaro?

He'd shredded his lips against his own teeth trying to answer until the man covering his mouth threw him down and kicked his cries into whimpers. Even though you've seen the bodies, he told Chris, the cuts and the burns and the parts cut off, you can't, when you're there, imagine anything worse than this simple pain of rolling around on the metal floor in the back of a van, banging into sharp corners. There are speed bumps everywhere in Guatemala, Álvaro told her, and these men hit them fast, laughing as he ricocheted off the walls, searching for a posture that eased the pain.

He had painted the door in Clara's wall bright red. The children's voices rose as butterflies; Clara became a small frog perched amidst the coils of razor wire, a bright-eyed frog looking down at the supplicant, the one on the outside. Everything on the outside of the wall was grey and streaked with rust from the iron spikes, and he was just a smudge at the red gate.

What happens if you open that door, Chris had asked, and go inside?

He explained that no one on the outside got to open that particular door. An invitation was required.

"Did you have one?"

His finger traced the coils, the dried paint rough against his skin.

"I thought I did." He had filled his brush with red and painted himself out of the picture.

At first he was sure he'd been picked up by mistake. The Peace Accords had been signed, and most of the kidnappings were economic, not political. Some gang had grabbed him thinking he was the kind of rich man who lived on that kind of street. As soon as they realized he was a priest, he thought, they'd toss him out beside the road. Even as the van laboured up the steep climb into the hills north of the city, he hoped. But then he lost track of everything but the pain.

When the van finally stopped and the doors opened, the cold rain of the altiplano washed over him. He was hauled inside a courtyard, the kidnappers laughing as they rolled him under the rain spouting off the roof tiles. To clean up his stink, they said. When he tried to speak, a boot came out of the darkness, rolled him into a corner.

He had drawn dozens of pictures of this place, the curling up and cowering. The fear all black with streaks of purple. Purple when another breach was opened in the body. Tell me what you can, Chris said. And he had, to a certain point. Nothing subtle. Fists and boots. Cigarettes. Filth in the drinking water. But there were some things he did not tell.

The next morning, a woman had been thrown beside him. Álvaro could smell her hair in his face and for a moment was soothed by its clean fragrance. She rolled over and he felt her breasts against his cheek. He tried to turn away, but hands held his head. The guards were forcing them into this posture. Fingers scrabbled at the buttons on her blouse and the breasts, stripped bare, were shoved in his face. A voice laughed, have a taste of these, Father.

All awareness of her body and concern for her safety vanished. His fear was now all for himself. Father, they'd said. They knew who he was and someone wanted him here. The woman screamed, twisting and cursing until a blow cut off her voice. She went limp and was lifted away. A voice in his ear, if she's not fond of priests, we'll give her the real thing. He lay very still, listening to the men taking turns with her. Their grunts and her whimpers of pain. Again and again and again.

Afterwards the guards sat under the courtyard's roof, flicking their burning cigarettes into the wet huddle Álvaro made. They laughed at the way he jerked as the butts hissed on wet skin. The fear that kept him silent during the long hours turned on itself and blossomed into shame. Shame at how the woman's body had aroused his. At how he'd been glad they took her and not him. The first interrogations had been, almost, a relief. Punishment he deserved. He never did know who the woman was or why she was there.

He looked again at the words he had painted. *How beautiful upon the mountains are the feet of him who brings glad tidings.* After a week of questions about how many children he'd kidnapped, how many babies he'd sold to Canadians, and what orphanages he was in league with — all this he told Chris about — they'd put him in a truck and taken him back to the city. He'd not been able to keep himself from hoping as they lurched through the traffic — horns, brakes, and the stink of diesel. They'd taken him into a building, down hallways, removed his blindfold, and thrown him onto the floor. The room was an office. A desk with stacks of papers. A grey filing cabinet. Through an open door, a bathroom. Tub, sink, and toilet.

When he saw the brown leather shoes, the pressed khaki slacks, and smelled the lemon, he'd thanked God even before he felt the hand on his shoulder and the voice in his ear. Vinicio. Even knowing what Elisabeth had seen Vinicio do, he felt same flood of relief he'd felt as a child, mixed with the same fear. If he had displeased Vinicio, he'd be punished, but he'd finally haul him up on the horse and take him back to the ranch to get cleaned up, his wounds tended by his mother, his pride soothed by Clara's indignant defence.

Vinicio might be angry that he'd approached Clara, but he didn't know about Ana Elisabeth. He couldn't know that Álvaro knew where those children came from. Álvaro had been taught a lesson and now he'd be given a warning and released.

Vinicio made no greeting. His dark blue eyes slid over Álvaro without any acknowledgement. Clean him up, he told the men. The chiding voice, the what kind of nonsense have you gotten yourself into this time Álvaro, was absent. Protecting them both, Álvaro told himself. Pretending indifference. Vinicio watched a guard dunk Álvaro in the bathtub, the hot water stinging the burns, the bruises livid in the bright light.

Barely able to stand as he crawled out of the tub, Álvaro had wiped himself with a towel and apologized for staining it with his blood. He tried to joke about his swollen and bloody testicles, saying he didn't need them much anyway, all things considered. He didn't understand the signal Vinicio made to the guard until the man's boot connected with his groin, dropping him in agony onto the tiles. When he regained consciousness, the toe of Vinicio's shiny shoe was lifting his cheek off the floor. He'd bent close and whispered, "This is no joke, Álvaro."

And Álvaro knew then what his body had already understood.

In the bright kitchen in Point Grey, he stared at the words on the paper. He finally reached for a paintbrush, dipped it in the glass of water, and stirred it into the paint. Two ovals of brown appeared under the words. Then he flipped the paper around so the words were upside down at the bottom of the page and the shoes were standing on top of them. He was aware of his testicles hanging loose in his sweatpants, cowering in there as if Vinicio's shoes were in the room with them. No jokes, he whispered and climbed the two flights of stairs to his room to change into snug jockey shorts and jeans.

Back downstairs, he stood in the doorway of the kitchen staring at the paper, his heart pounding with the same terror it felt when he realized Vinicio would not save him. Two brown ovals. The chasm opening.

The phone startled him and for the first ring he thought it was Vinicio's cellphone ringing in the torture room, Clara telling her brother she'd heard at last from the Oblates, that Álvaro had been needed in the north. For a funeral. Vinicio had repeated her words out loud, nodding his head and smiling at Álvaro slumped against the wall. Knowing one source of hope was gone.

"It was from you he learned his kindness," Vinicio had said to her. "The church is lucky to have him."

When the second ring sounded, Álvaro remembered where he was. He picked up the phone and looked out into Margaret's winter garden. Orange berries and dripping green foliage. A girl asked for Joseph. Out of town, he said.

He'd just turned back to look at his painting when it rang again. Did he know when Joseph would be back? He explained and then unplugged the phone. He set aside the words and the shoes and pulled out another piece of paper, the girl's voice still reverberating in his head. So young and breathless with the expectation of Joseph. Crushed at his absence. He thought of the boy surfing, a child really, unaware of the full power of the water bearing him aloft. Álvaro wanted to be able to ride the turbulence of his own childhood, a turbulence that linked him to the turmoil that rolled like great waves through Guatemala. A turbulence that reached back, if Vinicio spoke the truth, even before his birth and contaminated everything.

Álvaro's brush moved softly across the paper. He was a small smudge of brown where the red curve for the road ran into the green he painted across the top of the page. The green of *la finca*'s grass when everything else was rustling in the dryness of November. The daily walks when he told himself hero stories about his father. His mother's hand raised to silence him. He dipped the brush in purple.

Vinicio's voice in his ear. It was with the image of Joseph on a wave that Álvaro decided to try to ride this wave of emotion, the anguish entering his body and taking him once again into that office, the roof a huge drum pounded by the million-handed rain and Vinicio waiting and waiting until the rain was loud enough to drown the screams. In between the incandescent pain, his voice, reeling Álvaro back to consciousness, spoke of their childhood. How sad he had been to see Álvaro so upset at Cesár's departure. How he'd sworn to his father not to speak the truth. It was that dry time of year when the corn was almost finished and the leaves rasped together in the breeze. Remember, Álvaro, he said. And as Álvaro turned his head away, the teeth in his earlobe, ripping.

"When I ask you a question, answer." The voice husky, the hand turning his head back. "Look at me and answer." The two of them, alone in the room.

Those eyes, Clara's eyes, opening wells of pain. "Say, yes, Señor Fortuny." His hand on the switch.

Álvaro stood over the painting, pools of smeared water now where he'd let the forgotten brush drip, Setting it down, he turned to rummage in the cupboards. He mixed flour and water into a bowl and added paint powder to tint the paste the pale yellow of his childhood home. He plunged his hands in and pulled them out to smear paste across the blurred paint. His hands moved as if they belonged to someone else, hands older now than his father's ever were, hands that had forgotten how to hold a machete, how to swing it through the underbrush to clear a path. How to cut the corn. How to plaster a house. He slopped on more paste and planted his hands again, leaving handprints layered across every inch of the big rectangle of paper.

He paced the kitchen, letting the anger build. The skin drying under the flour tightened just as it had that day his father called him a bastard and turned away. He opened a jar of chili powder and sprinkled it across his drying handprints.

"Yes, Señor Fortuny." Álvaro had rumbled the syllables out of some place at the back of his throat, looking into Vinicio's eyes as he told him how Cesár, the man Álvaro had thought was his father, had shown up at la finca waving a machete.

"I loved you like the brother you are, Álvaro, but Cesár, he would not stop talking. Perhaps you are his son after all. Not knowing when to keep your mouth shut."

Álvaro threw the bowl of paste across the room, shattering it on Margaret's bright tiles. He grabbed a knife and slit open one of the palm prints hardening in the paste on the paper. He had tried to break the ropes that tied him. He had struggled to shut his ears. Vinicio's voice relentless.

"Even idiots knew better than to complain when my father fucked their women. Papa took his machete easily and pinned him down. He told him about all the times. While Cesár was building the new barn. While Cesár was chasing parrots in the jungle. While Cesár was building coffins."

Álvaro slashed at the hands.

"At the end of each story, he cut off one of his carpenter fingers."

He took one of Álvaro's hands in his, caressing it. "He was dead before ten stories were up."

"Liar," Álvaro spat, clenching his hand into a fist.

"I could take you right to the place we dumped him. You could collect his bones for evidence. Count where the fingers were cut."

Vinicio's arm chopped up and down and Margaret's kitchen filled with the smell of lemons. The rain streaked the windows, and the lights of the city blurred across the water. Álvaro looked at the knife and the shredded paper. All that remained of his handprints were tattered ribbons and the grey day had become night.

"But you, Álvaro, you," Vinicio had said, peeling open each finger from Álvaro's fist. "You have our father's hands."

"Liar," he whispered into the empty house. They always lie, others told him. The ones who studied these things. Never believe what they say.

He lifted the knife and drew it slowly across the scar the ropes had made on his wrist until a thin line of blood leaked out. The pain brought him back and then rolled him over again. Choking, he painted a huge red circle right onto the table. He stared at it for a long time. He ran his hand across his own cheeks, feeling the whiskers rasping, bending.

He once thought becoming a priest would give him solace. But Vinicio had destroyed that too.

"The morning prayer, Álvaro. *Lord, open my lips.* Say it, Álvaro."

For how many years, every morning, had he begun his day with those words? With what hope! He took a pencil and bent close to the red circle, one cheek resting on the table, his eyes just inches away. His pencil started moving.

"Open up, Álvaro. Come into the Lord's presence singing for joy," Vinicio teased, sounding just as he had when they were both children. "Say it, Álvaro."

And he finally did. He always did. If he resisted they'd simply clamp his nostrils shut and hurt him somewhere. When he parted his frightened lips, anything could happen. A spoonful of sugar, a spadeful of shit. Every morning for how many days? A splinter of ice, a cup of scalding coffee. A cattle prod and the explosion of pain.

He drew a hundred trembling sperm in the centre of the circle, his tears pooling on the wood, smearing the paint. He drew two children, a girl and a boy. Clara and Vinicio. Two more. Clara and Álvaro. The pale faces and the black hair. Two more. Ana Elisabeth's niece and nephew.

"You don't want to destroy your sister's peace of mind, do you?" Vinicio had said.

No, he shook his head.

"Clara is a good Catholic mother, Álvaro. Taking care of children abandoned by neglectful parents. We don't want to disturb that, do we?"

No, he shook his head.

"Promise?"

"Yes," he nodded. "I promise."

And he was gone, leaving Álvaro in the small room they'd made his cell, the graffiti on the plastered wall, handprints of blood. The festering graffiti on his body, a brand. Vinicio inside his head. He tumbled through layers of pain and fever. Layers of shame. Rage. Hate. He stopped eating. He refused to drink. He had already stopped praying. At first, his guards ignored him; he curled up as still as his body's tremors would let him lie, and he waited to die. Floating between pain and unconsciousness, the quiet voice of his mother urging him to call back his spirit. He was a little boy again, one who hadn't heard Vinicio's words, who wouldn't believe them if he had, and he was happy to open his mouth to receive the little piece of chicken she placed between his lips. Waking, he looked with such love upon the young soldier urging him to eat that the boy's impatience turned to confusion.

You think you are saved. Álvaro spoke to the figure of Ana Elisabeth he'd painted on the table, outlining her in yellow. You think you finally understand and then, the joke is on you. He smeared the paint across the little figure.

The young soldier washed and shaved Álvaro, the blade across his face scraping at the whiskers still pushing through the split skin. Álvaro thought he no longer cared what happened. Then Vinicio was in the room, half a lemon in his hand. He rubbed it over Álvaro's face, this small pain as huge as anything that had come before. The anger radiated off Vinicio's crisp uniform like waves of heat. His eyes were burning.

"You are such a little fish." Vinicio swept dishes aside to shatter on the floor and tossed a newspaper on the table. Bishop Gerardi, the headlines said. Murdered. A colour photograph of the body sprawled face down on the garage floor, a pool of blood. Álvaro breathed in and out like a tired dog.

Another lie, he told himself. It was not possible. Not now.

"You priests," Vinicio said. "You profess your faith to the ignorant, then pray for a martyr's death and leave them to suffer their own stupidity. Your little informer, ringing at Clara's gate, saying you'd asked to meet her there. She had a gift, she said, for the children."

Clara knows, Álvaro thought. We are all safe if Clara knows.

"Luckily I was there," Vinicio said, and Álvaro's hope vanished. "I took her little package, thinking her fear was for my uniform. Then I saw what was in the package. The *huipil* and sash from her village, the stupid cow. She had recognized me. A pity. You see, Álvaro, everything you do to help them only makes it worse. They would all have been better off if you had stayed inside the churches where you belong. You stir these people up. You get them into trouble. And then you abandon them."

Two soldiers brought her in. Even though her face was bruised and swollen, one eye completely shut, he recognized her. Ana Elisabeth. Her right arm had been pulled out of the socket and made an ugly bulge under her torn blouse. Her skirt was clotted with blood and feces. When she saw Álvaro, she went rigid, her moaning silenced. They stared at each other. She spoke first.

"You," she hissed. "You hear his confession and give him forgiveness."

"No," Álvaro cried. "He's lying."

She pulled herself away from the men and leapt toward Álvaro. He heard her shoulder bones grind as he caught her, gagging at the sound, at her stink. Shards of glass sliced her bare feet. The pain stopped her and she looked down at her arm, not understanding what was wrong. Her mouth opened and closed. Opened and closed. He pushed her toward Vinicio, who sidestepped neatly. She swayed there in the middle of the room, the men ranged around her, waiting. Her mouth opened again and words came out like angry wasps, a swarm of high sharp noises, voices quarrelling with each other, pleas for help, names, no, no, no. The terrified guards backed toward the door; one crossed himself. It was her village, Álvaro realized. The villagers who lived inside her.

Álvaro had forced himself to walk across the broken glass toward her, his eyes seeking hers. Holes into blackness. Her screams became the cries of people burning. Álvaro heard the flames and smelled the smoke, the burning flesh. He lifted his hands to his ears and she spat in his face. He staggered back and, for that moment, felt as one with Vinicio and the guards. She terrified him and he hated her. He hated her for bringing him to this place, for her peasant stubbornness, for the human stink of her fear. He hated her for all the reasons the others hated her and he was as relieved as they were when Vinicio pulled out a pistol and shot her, a small hole in the centre of her forehead. The noise stopped and Ana Elisabeth Yax dropped like a stone, the air whooshing out as she hit the floor. The soft thump of a body falling to the ground, the crunch of glass.

Álvaro tried to paint that thump; he made little mounds along the edges of the table, little mounds with twists of cloth, a leg, and a bare foot. When he saw that he'd painted the foot broken, the bones tearing through the skin, a detail he didn't remember until now, he dropped his head onto his arms and slept. Outside the drawn curtains, it was still raining.

When he woke up it was midday. The rain had stopped. The wind had stopped. The fridge hummed in the big house and the furnace rumbled.

He left the mess and went upstairs to stand in the shower. He bundled his dirty clothes into the washing machine. He dressed quickly, hating the sight of his body. The scars and the flush of blood just under the skin. He tried but could not shave, could not stand the sound of the razor scraping the whiskers. He was afraid of the tree branches scratching against the bathroom window, the radiators popping and groaning. He checked all the doors and rattled the window latches.

He lay back on his bed, remembering Walter driving him north through the mountains still topped with snow. His introduction to Canada. The great empty highways, the fresh green of spring. And the light. The gift of beautiful light that never seemed to end. He'd liked to drive in the pale twilight, down the back roads and through the quiet little towns, looking at the farms and the roadsides white with blossoms. Walter telling him until you've lived through a winter here you won't truly understand the light's magic.

He always thought of Isabel in that summer light, Isabel as a young woman, her body so alive and responsive. He had tried not to think of her often, not allowing himself the pleasurable pain. But she snuck in when he felt most unworthy. He thought of her with her two young boys attaching themselves to her with the openness and familiarity that he longed for — her sitting on a chair and one of the boys standing behind her, leaning over her, arms dangling over her shoulders, face turned to tell her a story, mouth right against her ear. One with a head in her lap, playing with her fingers. The young one in her arms, head on her shoulder, eyes closing in sleep. Leaning up against her, one arm around her legs, head against her hip. He thought of what he had given up and congratulated himself for his strength, his faith. Told himself they were all better off without him.

He slept again and awoke, thirsty. He drank two glasses of cold water standing at the bathroom sink. It slid down, cold, into his stomach. He poured a third and went down to the library to find Margaret's brandy. He dumped a big splash into his glass and sat in one of the chairs. Isabel. He sipped his drink, the brandy burning its way down. Isabel, with her ear to his chest, giggling as she listened to the noises of his body. Holding his arms while mosquitoes bit him so he'd think of her every time his clothes moved across his itchy skin. As if he'd needed reminding.

In a slow dream, he returned to the kitchen, retrieving a paintbrush from the litter on the table, and laid a clean sheet of paper on the counter. Half-asleep, he outlined the lobe of her ear, the brush tracing the delicate passage inside. His tongue remembered. Sheet after sheet he painted, her breasts, her thighs, her mouth, the wisps of hair on the back of her neck. The imprint of her feet upon the soles of the red sandals. He had found a safe place at last, a place where Vinicio had never been.

Fatigue dropped on him like a blanket but he could not leave Isabel behind. He dragged in a rug and spread it out under the table. He set his glass of brandy beside one table leg, curled up on the rug and covered himself with an old sweater. He fell asleep remembering the last time he was with Isabel, her face above him in the dim light of the bedroom, the curtains moving in the breeze from the half-open window.

†

A key in the door brought him, panicking, awake. A voice calling his name sent him back into his dream, and for just a moment, his body moved as easily and quickly as it had moved to lift Isabel off him and scramble for his clothes. Then he struck his head on the table and got tangled in the table legs. Walter and George stood in the doorway looking at him in dismay as the brandy glass slid across the floor and shattered. He felt as frantic, as half-dressed as he had that other time.

"I'd say he's been on a three-day toot by the looks of him," Walter said, a derisive smirk on his old face. Álvaro lunged at him, yelling for him to get out, get out, get out, but George was already between them, leading Walter away, sitting him down in the living room before turning to Álvaro. He approached him with the delicacy he'd use to approach a jumper standing on the guard-rail of a bridge. One hand out. The eyes demanding contact. Álvaro did not want those eyes looking at his paintings. His body blocked the door to the kitchen; he spread his shoulders and held his arms out like a goalie filling the net. Seeing his distress, George backed away, explaining how they'd phoned several times knowing he was alone. How they left a dozen messages.

"I insisted we come." Walter's voice was flat, drained. He wasn't going to wrestle Álvaro to the floor this time. "I thought you'd killed yourself. I didn't want the family to find you. Now that I can see you haven't, can you tell me where the toilet is?"

Álvaro pointed down the hall and waited until Walter shuffled out of the room to sit down himself. George perched on the arm of a chair beside the Christmas tree, his long body agitated, folded in awkward lines. Álvaro closed his eyes.

"You've been making pictures?" George's voice was careful. A tremor of something like awe underneath.

Álvaro nodded.

"How are you feeling?"

"I'm not sure. You startled me." He breathed in and out, the only noise in the quiet house. The toilet flushed.

"He was terribly worried," George said.

"If I die in a state of mortal sin, he'll take it as a personal failure."

"You know we're all worried about you."

"It helps to know that one day I'll be dead. I saw a woman shot once." He made a gun of his finger. "Poof! All her pain and anger vanished. It was," he paused, "a relief."

"You must promise that you're not planning anything."

He stared at George for a long time without speaking. His face was framed by the fir boughs behind him.

"Don't," George said.

The bathroom door opened.

Something about his insistence angered Álvaro. His conviction that if you decided not to do something, you wouldn't do it.

"You must promise," he said again.

Álvaro's voice was a hiss. "The last time I promised anything was when my torturer said to me *Nuncas mas*. 'Never again, right, Álvaro?' I had promised to behave because I thought I was going to be killed at last. He carved it into my back to seal the bargain and I was still alive when they dumped me beside the road."

Vinicio had said Álvaro didn't deserve a martyr's death. It would be much better if he lived, knowing what he had brought about. If he lived to see the ruin of all their priestly dreams, their communist plans. Never again, he hissed.

He scrubbed at his hair. "I don't make promises anymore. But I'm not planning to kill myself."

When he saw the relief on Walter's grey face, what was left of Álvaro's anger vanished. He jumped up to help him into a chair. The old man crumpled into it, barely denting the cushions, and closed his eyes.

"I'll make some tea," Álvaro offered, waving away George's offer of help. He groaned when he saw the kitchen. The broken glass, the table smeared with paint. The rumpled sweater on the floor and the whiskey smell. His crude drawings of Isabel's breasts and thighs. Later, he told himself, and plugged in the kettle.

When he brought the tea and poured the hot liquid into the mugs, he felt lighter somehow. Unburdened. He spooned sugar into all three mugs and, as soon as he tasted its sweetness, he realized he was starving. He reached for the cookies he'd put on a plate.

Walter's hand shook as he brought his cup to his mouth. He set it down again. "Forgive us," he said.

George opened his mouth to protest, but Álvaro spoke first. "For all your noise, old man, it's better than the way the others tiptoe around me. Gentle requests. Sideways looks. Wondering when I'm going to explode." Álvaro sighed. "There's always a chasm between us."

"Unbridgeable?"

Álvaro shrugged.

Walter bent his head for a moment and when he lifted it again there were tears in his eyes.

Álvaro gestured toward the kitchen. "I know it looks bad in there, but this is helping me. I don't know why, but it's different than talking. It's different even than thinking. It isn't faith or philosophy. It's physical action. And you know us Oblates, we're men of action."

Walter tried to smile.

Álvaro bent to slide a finger into the Christmas tree stand. Dry. Needles were scattered on the rug among the few remnant scraps of wrapping paper he'd meant to clean up. What was it, two, three days ago?

"There is something you can do for me," he said, head down, hands busy with the tree.

"Anything."

The women in his life. His mother's suffering, because of him. Clara. Ana Elisabeth. He had to hope there was one woman to whom he could make reparations.

"It's Isabel. Can you find out where she is? How she's doing?"

"Isabel?" George asked.

Walter looked at Álvaro for a long time. He finally nodded. "I'll do what I can."

13

Isabel stood at Alice's back door, afraid to knock. She gazed out across the brown fields, frozen hard and mean. It was a strange winter. After a few December flurries, the snow had all blown away leaving the whole valley stunned by the first green Christmas in memory. Except it wasn't green. It was eight-hour days of brown and grey and sixteen-hour cloudy starless nights. It was going to be hell on her perennials.

The wind finally drove her inside. She opened the door and called out. A muffled hello came from the kitchen. Isabel shook off her jacket in a heap on the bench in the mudroom, stepped out of her boots, and drew a deep breath before opening that door. She was terrified.

Isabel Lee didn't believe in New Year's resolutions. The New Year's Eve her mother died, Isabel had been at a teenage party, a staggering drunk sixteen-year-old. When they called her to the hospital, she was afraid to go near her mother for fear she'd smell the booze. Afraid to say goodbye and then it was too late. The next year, married and pregnant with Jason, Isabel had sent her teenage husband out to party while she sat in the living room of their tiny apartment and talked to the photo of her mom hung on the kitchen wall. Told her what a fool her daughter was for getting into this pickle.

Instead of getting dressed up and drinking, she cleaned up and stayed sober. No matter what. She'd sit the kids down on New Year's Eve day and they'd sort out their unfinished business before the new year began. Quiet apologies, lies confessed, projects finished or officially abandoned. The neighbourhood dogs did well with the freezer-burnt fish and the neighbourhood kids got outgrown toys. They'd clean the house and take down the Christmas tree. They'd cook hot dogs over the bonfire they made of it in the backyard, Isabel would cut their hair and they'd end the year bathed, brushed, and clear-eyed. As the clock ticked toward midnight, they'd talk to Grandma's picture, telling her about the fish they'd caught or the races they'd won. The new friend at school. Janna drew pictures and tacked them to the wall beside the photo. The grandmother who was younger when she died than Isabel was now.

"Isabel!" Alice stood in the open door, hair tied back and hands white with flour. The front of her Christmas apron was dusted white. "How'd you get here?"

Her stomach churning, Isabel grasped her aunt by the shoulders and kissed her once on each cheek. "Alejandro lent me his car," she said, shivering. "Its heater isn't working very well."

Clucking like a banty hen, Alice pulled her into the kitchen where a kettle steamed on the big old wood range and the south window caught the faint glow of sun behind the high clouds. She sat her at the table and prattled on about how she was finishing up some last pies for the New Year's dance at the community hall while she made a pot of tea and set out the cups, the honey and milk, and Christmas cookies. She knew something was up. Isabel rarely drove, and never in winter.

Isabel could not get started. She was afraid this might be the last time Alice would welcome her into her home. She was afraid of losing her. She had taken a taxi out to the airport on Christmas Eve, hearing the cheers go up as the plane landed in spite of the freezing rain pelting the runway. Waiting for the last person to struggle across the slippery tarmac into the warm arrival lounge. No Janna. No phone call. Nothing. She'd called Trevor in tears and he'd come to take her to his place for a few days. Isabel and Soryada both lonely in the midst of his big family. Until one uncle clapped Trevor on the shoulder and announced that the clan would fund a trip to see if he and Soryada could find any of her family down there in Guatemala. Since it looks like you two are going to stick it out, he said.

When she saw the hope in Soryada's eyes, Isabel made a decision. If Janna didn't want contact, Isabel was going to have to figure out how to live with that. But she was going to track down Álvaro and, finally, tell Janna who he was. Where he was. Let her decide.

Teeth still chattering, Isabel blurted it all out. How she had to set things right with Janna. How she needed to find her father before she told her and that Alice could maybe help her. Alice didn't falter until Isabel said Álvaro's name.

She stared at her niece as if she were a stranger and turned to put wood into the firebox. Ramming a piece through the smoke that billowed out into the room, she swore and rattled the poker. The metal door banged shut and she opened a window, flapping the smoke out with a tea towel.

"Isabel, sometimes." Alice was furious. She slammed the window shut.

"Dad had just died," Isabel said, desperate. "I'd been ploughing through the mess he left behind and found Mom's dresses. They made me crazy, like a thirteen-year-old with new breasts."

"You're going to blame a dress? Doesn't that take the cake?" Alice stood with one hand on the window frame, as if she was evaluating its possibility as an exit. Her mouth was a thin line, the tendons in her neck rigid. "The poor kid. I remember him. He's about two months ordained, just moved from Mexico City to this completely unfamiliar place, trying to make sense of us all. And here comes sweet little Isabel, ready for redemption."

"Do you have any idea how many priests screw around?" Isabel cried. "I've made a study of it. Thousands of them. All those housekeepers. All those altar boys. Single mothers in need of counselling."

"Stop it."

Isabel struggled to explain. How he was like nobody she'd ever met. How she really thought it could work. She was ready to leave town, move to some place where no one knew them. "The boys loved him," she said.

"He came to your house?" Alice was appalled.

"He coached soccer, remember? All the kids loved him."

"And more than a few of their mothers, if I recall." Alice's laugh was bitter. "I can't believe none of them noticed."

"Me neither, to tell you the truth. We were lucky."

Alice snorted. The pale light streaming in the window behind her revealed streaks of grey in her short hair, the fine network of wrinkles crumpling the skin around her eyes. Her anger fizzled into disappointment. "So he finds you're pregnant and runs away?" She slumped into her chair. "I admired him for going to Winnipeg, to the inner city. Even more when I heard he'd returned to Guatemala with the refugees. It's hard to think of him as a coward."

Isabel shrugged, her own anger building. "He was gone. Just like that," she snapped her fingers. "Before I even knew. I thought of an abortion, I was so mad."

"Before you knew? You never told him?"

"How could I? The other priest wasn't handing out a forwarding address." She poured the tea.

"So why did he leave?"

Isabel left out the part about her shoes in the bedroom. Just said the old priest found out. She never heard anything from Álvaro after that day.

"Are you sure he knows about Janna?"

"The pregnancy was no secret. I told Father Walter whose baby it was." Isabel sipped her tea. Some kind of mint.

Alice's face flushed a deep pink. "So he knew that whole time I took Janna to church? How could you let me do that?"

"Going to church was all Janna's idea and so was stopping. She came down one Sunday morning in her sweatpants and T-shirt and said she was going fishing with Trevor. It took me a while to get it out of her — I guess the good father had been praising the sanctity of the virgin birth to these little ten-year-old girls." Isabel shook her head. "Janna'd said something about her being like Jesus because she didn't have a father either and he set her straight in no uncertain terms."

"I was afraid to ask." Alice took a paper napkin from a big stack on the table and folded it in half. She pushed some toward Isabel.

"It's him that was the big chicken," Isabel said. "There was this little girl, the church's daughter, you could say. He should be rejoicing. One of the flock returned. Even if she was a bastard, she was one of their little bastards. When she just stopped coming, did he have the balls to find out what happened? Didn't he care about her immortal soul? Or was he more worried about being embarrassed?" Isabel's voice shook as she concentrated on the napkins. "How could I tell Janna one of those assholes was her father?"

Alice protested. "It would have hurt him very much. He would have felt at fault himself for the younger priest's…" Alice paused, looking for the right word, "…lapse. He was fond of Álvaro, I remember."

"A jealous old queer, probably."

"Isabel!" Alice was angry again. "Not everything is about sex."

Isabel started on another pile of napkins. "Not everything, maybe. But damn near."

Alice looked out the window at the slate grey fields and the brown pasture. Four horses, their heads down, were looking for the green frozen at the roots. "No one forces them to take those vows."

Isabel was sorry. She knew Alice's marriage wasn't happy and that she had long ago given up hoping for children of her own. That the church meant everything to her, which was probably why she was folding napkins and baking pies for the big dance at the community hall where she and other Catholic women would bring in the new year serving food to drunks.

"I hope whatever it is you're doing to stay away from drinking sticks because you're going to need your wits about you if you really want to sort this out with Janna. What is it, three years now?"

Isabel nodded. She raised her cup to her mouth, but it was empty. She set it down again, the cup rattling in the saucer.

"Why didn't you tell her?" Alice grinned. "It's not like it would have caused much more fuss than Trevor's arrival did."

Isabel groaned. "I couldn't have kept that secret if I tried — there was no telling Jason's dad that this little Indian baby I'd just popped out was his."

When word had reached Trevor's father, he snuck into the hospital when she was alone, asking a nurse to keep a lookout for visitors. He'd had a good look at the baby, sticking his face up close and whispering some Gitxsan words into the open mouth and kissed him. Said he wanted his name on the birth certificate. She'd written "unknown" on Janna's.

"I tried to tell her a few times, but I chickened out. I kept thinking that maybe one day he'd show up and tell her himself. When that didn't happen I made up my mind to confront Father Walter. Enough, I thought. At least I can talk to Álvaro. Send him a picture, maybe. But I showed up at the rectory and they told me Father Walter wasn't there. When will he be back, I asked. He won't, they said. A woman, you know who I mean, always hanging around the place. She was very pleased to see my shock when she told me he was gone for good. Retired. I was angry enough to kill someone. That's when I really went for a loop. Almost lost the kids. "

The tears rising in Isabel's eyes infuriated her. Álvaro's disappearance had defeated her in some significant way. And after Walter was gone, she stopped pretending to herself that she'd pull herself together and make big changes. She was left with only the small ones, the weeks and months she struggled to stay sober, then the failures, the blackouts, the coming home to find messages from the kids saying which father they were with. The kids always uncomfortable when she made promises. New Year's the only one she'd never blown.

Alice took the folded napkins and tucked them into a plastic bin. She set out another stack. "Why now?"

Isabel's voice shrank. "She doesn't know that I really have stopped drinking this time and there's no reason for her to believe it if she did know. But maybe if I get up the courage to tell her about her father, she'll at least talk to me."

"You still don't hear from her?"

"Do you?"

Alice shook her head. "Cards, that's all."

"Having her mad at me would be better than this nothing."

"I'd better find out where he is," Alice said.

Jumping up from the table to hug her aunt, Isabel swallowed the lump in her throat. Alice squeezed her tight before pushing her away.

"If he's still alive."

"Still alive?"

"People die, Isabel. People die all the time."

Isabel wondered if Alice was sick. Who would she tell if she was? Not that husband of hers. If she collapsed on the kitchen floor, he'd just wander through asking if she'd ironed his blue shirt.

"Last I heard he was in some kind of trouble in Guatemala. We were asked to pray for him."

"What kind of trouble?"

"Guatemala is a very bad place to be a priest. People who try to help the Indians there, they get grabbed, tortured, even killed." Alice pushed back her chair, all business. "I'll see what I can find out. Now you better get out of here. I have things to do."

When she sat to pull on her boots, Isabel picked up the phone lying on the bench at Alice's back door. As she had done every day since Christmas, she dialled Janna's number. Maybe if she thought Alice was calling, she'd answer. The same message. The cellular phone customer is either out of range or not answering the phone — please try your call again later.

Isabel drove Alejandro's car too fast along the road twisting between Alice's fields of frozen sod. As she gained on the only other car on the road, its exhaust a faint whisper of white against the faded asphalt, she was angry again. What she had done with Álvaro back there under the green willows beside the river had been the most serious she'd ever been. And in spite of the way he had disappeared, in spite of the other priest's disapproval, she refused to feel shame. Especially not after she told Father Walter Prytuluk she was pregnant. The screen between them so she didn't have to see his face as she braced herself to ask where she could reach Álvaro. Is it money you want, he'd said, the disgust bending the word. How do you even know it's his? Her promiscuous behaviour was common knowledge, he'd said.

The brake lights flashed on and off ahead of her and the little car fish-tailed past the stop sign and out onto the highway. It slid across both lanes of traffic, between an approaching logging truck in one lane and a minivan in the other, coming to a miraculous stop at the edge of the river bank. Isabel tapped the brakes until she inched to a stop. She looked across to where the other driver bent his head into his hands. A small figure stood up behind his seat, a comforting hand on his shoulder. Beyond them the bank dropped down to the half-frozen river, steaming between the chunks of ice. Isabel waited for her heart to slow.

The only shame she felt, she'd spat out to Father Walter, was for the church. For its cowardice. When she spoke about abortion, his silence told her all she needed to know. She still wondered sometimes if she'd gone ahead with the pregnancy just to spite the old man.

Across the highway, the driver settled back into his seat, flashed his signal, and pulled out. A plane appeared out of the clouds to the southeast and banked low over the river on its way to the airport. Isabel turned onto the highway and followed it toward town. Toward her little house and the little party she had planned.

When Isabel opened her back gate, the preparations were well under way. Brush was piled high in the centre of the vegetable plot. On the picnic table, a red and green cloth fluttered in the frigid air, anchored by dishes, cutlery, and a big vat steaming on a Coleman stove. Two stacks of white plastic chairs waited for their occupants to choose a spot to sit upwind of the fire to be lit as soon as it was dark. The barbecue had been wheeled down beside the table; the escaping smoke smelled of wood chips and slow-cooking pork — Frank's specialty. He, Jasmine, Alejandro, and three or four other friends were sitting on the back deck trying on skates from a tangled pile.

The back door opened and Jason stepped outside, a Tim Hortons coffee cup in his hand. A tall, skinny man wearing khaki pants and a pale pink shirt, the tan tie pulled loose from his neck, he'd come straight from his dad's car lot and wasn't dressed for the outdoors. He struggled to smile. He'd never been comfortable with Isabel's friends and was, she knew, always worried she was going to embarrass him yet again. She grinned at him, happy that he had made the effort to show up. Glad there was no sign of his wife.

Trevor took immediate charge. "Go and show Soryada what good skating looks like, Ma. Jason and I'll mix up the hot chocolate and get the fire going hot enough to warm you up when you get back."

Perro jumped ecstatic circles around Soryada as they tramped through the afternoon dusk toward the small lake on the other side of the rail yards. They jumped the tracks and climbed through the railcars in the sidings as Isabel knew her kids had done, as she and her friends had done when they were kids. Soryada shivered in the cold, but her eyes were bright. She whispered to Isabel that she had once been taken to an ice show in Mexico City, how it was wonderful.

The skaters broke out of the dismal alders, dead leaves still clinging to the branches, into the clearing the lake made. There was a bench, a smoking firepit, and not a flake of snow on the ice. A cleft in the mountain opened the way for a shaft of sunlight to shine through a gap in the clouds at the horizon.

Alejandro was the first laced up and he skated straight to it, twirling in the light like a golden thing. He was a beautiful skater, light and delicate. Frank was next and he whooped as he hit the sunlight, executing a big jump. Men who grew up with skates on their feet. Soryada watched, mesmerized, until Alejandro skated back, took her hands, and backed away, pulling her, sliding on her boots across to the golden band of sunlight.

He pointed down. When Isabel skated over she could see, under the ice, small trout swimming slowly in the cold water. It was a miracle to be standing on top of the water and to see to the bottom, the trout quivering and the small plants waving in liquid tremors. Soryada was half afraid. She chattered to Alejandro, and Isabel saw another woman emerge, a kind of emotion and intelligence that didn't always come through in her careful English.

Alejandro was a different person in Spanish as well. He started to sing and Soryada joined in. It was some silly thing and soon Alejandro was salsa dancing with her, as graceful on skates as he would be in shiny black dancing shoes. Soryada, too, could dance beautifully. Isabel wondered if Trevor knew this about Soryada. If he would be jealous to see her like this. If he should be.

Frank came up behind Isabel, reached around behind her to grab her right hand and across her belly to take her left. "Come on," he said and tugged her away to skate around the lake. It felt wonderful as they moved back and forth in unison across the perfect ice. Perro jumped and barked all around them, sliding in surprise as he tried to stop. She enjoyed the warm blood flowing down to her toes, into her hands, warm in Frank's, and wondered if maybe she'd finally figured out how to be friends with men.

"What a funny old fellow you are sometimes," she said. "My dad used to skate with me like this."

"I don't know that I like you to think of me as your father." The flush in his cheeks was from more than the cold.

"Why not? When he wasn't drunk, he was just about my favourite man. I'd forgotten what a great skater he was. A good dancer too."

Frank tightened his grip and began with "Speaking of drunks," and went on to tell her that Lance was sleeping one off upstairs, right now. Though you never knew. He might have woken up and started all over again. He used to drink a lot. That's why he and his wife split up and she had custody of the kid. The boy isn't happy with the wife's new boyfriend but there's nothing Lance can do. Frank telling her all this while they're skating.

Isabel knew Lance had been worried about the Christmas visit and had hoped to bring Dustin back to go skiing. She'd been looking forward to meeting the little guy, to see if she could make him laugh. He was awfully serious, Lance had said.

"You might want to stay out of his way," Frank continued. "He's looking pretty hard to get laid."

Isabel ducked out of his grasp and scooped up Perro, Frank's hot breath on her cheek, in her ear, unbearable. "Enough already."

Frank shrugged. "He said some things."

"I'll bet he said some things, some really stupid things. Like we all do when we're sloshed. I'll bet he thought he was talking to a friend. Someone who wouldn't go around telling his other friends things they'd rather not hear." Even as she spoke, she knew she was crossing a line. "I'll bet both of us thought you were a friend."

He stared at her, breathing hard. His face hardened into a mask of indifference, mouth a straight line, eyes slitted. She'd tried to tell him a dozen times she wasn't interested in him as a lover. Not now. Not ever. Maybe now he would believe her.

He shrugged again and skated away, joining the others. The light faded as the sun snagged on the mountain and dipped behind it. All her pleasure disappeared with it. In spite of what she'd told Frank, she was shaken. Just what she needed. A live-in drunk.

Back at the house, Trevor had put Jason in charge of the fire. Other arrivals had laid the picnic table with marshmallows, buns, wieners, and salsa and chilies for the hot dogs. A big pot of hot chocolate. Another of apple cider. Trevor had already poured out Lance's flask of vodka, sat him down in one of the chairs, and was talking quietly to him. Lance kept nodding his head. A goofy grin slid off his face, leaving desolation in its wake, only to reappear. He raised one hand when he saw Isabel, but then it flopped back down as if he didn't quite know what it was doing.

Isabel stayed away from them, knowing Frank was hoping for all hell to break loose. Knowing Jason was expecting something unpleasant to happen, already planning his escape. Once the wiener roast was well under way, she put him in a chair at the backside of the fire and draped the plastic cape around his shoulders. He didn't protest; it was part of the ritual. The clearing away for the new year. She snugged it up tight under his chin and bent to ask if he'd heard from his sister.

He shrugged, uncomfortable and Isabel wished she'd just kissed him instead. She didn't know how much Janna had told him when she ran away, but he'd only once asked Isabel for money to help out. Couldn't you at least get something out of her old man, he'd snapped when she said all she could manage was the family allowance. She'd hung up the phone and it had been months before they'd spoken again.

His hair was the same golden brown his father's had been and it was already thinning in the same places. As she trimmed the ends curling on his slender neck, she told him about the close call on the highway and he told her about a little Subaru four-wheel drive station wagon he had on the lot. She should think about it.

"You were right about that answering machine," she said. "It comes in handy. Just don't you ever use it as an excuse not to call back."

She blew the hair off his collar and flipped off the cape. "Happy New Year, my first love," she said, kissing him goodbye. He had a party at Cindy's folks, he said.

She watched him and Trevor give each other backslapping hugs, thanking her lucky stars for the solid creature Trevor was, the one against whom all the family tumult crashed and broke, to subside into something navigable. They loved each other, those two, in spite of their different temperaments. From when he was a toddler, Trevor had been able to deflect Jason's jealousy simply by adoring him. Both fathers included both boys whenever they could — Trevor's because that's what families did, and Jason's because Jason was always better behaved when he was with Trevor. She hoped he could talk to Trevor now, unload when Cindy got too nasty, spent too much money, ate too many doughnuts, refused to even speak to Isabel. Just handed over the phone to Jason when Isabel called. Or hung up without a word. Jason saying it would be easier if he called her. And he did, dutifully, once a week.

As Jason opened the back gate to leave, Isabel saw Frank sitting in his truck, the engine idling. He was talking on his phone, nodding, yes, yes. By the time Jason closed the gate, Frank was pulling away. Sorrow and relief for both departures. Some things couldn't be fixed.

"That Lance giving you trouble?" Trevor asked as he took his turn in the barber's chair.

Isabel looked through the smoke. Lance had a girl on his lap now but there was still that long distance pain, the look she'd thought had to do with his car accident. Now she wondered. He met her eyes across the tousled head pressed giggling into his shoulder. He put his hand up to the girl's hair, stroking it as if it were something precious.

"Not so far," she said, struggling with Trevor's cowlicks. Bending to give the swirl at the crown of his head a kiss. "Is he going to be okay?"

"I think so. He doesn't have any more booze and he's not driving. His truck's somewhere else."

"Thanks."

When Soryada told her she wanted her hair cut short, Isabel protested that she wasn't really a hairdresser. Soryada insisted and they both laughed at the shock on Trevor's face as it fell in coils at her feet. Whoops went up as the remaining hair, relieved of its own weight, sprang up around her laughing face and Isabel was finally fully present at her own party, feeling in her fingers, in Soryada's pleasure, the presence of her daughter. Janna would love her, she thought. She should be here.

Everyone cheered again when Trevor picked up Soryada, his nose and mouth snuffling around her head like an eager puppy. Isabel gathered up the cloth under the chair and flipped the hair into the fire, the acrid smell of its burning billowing up into the night sky. To Isabel its stink was the smell of cleansing. They all stood and watched it rise, the old year vanishing in smoke and vapour.

At first they all thought it was ash drifting down onto their upturned faces, but then one by one they held out their hands like children do. Flakes landed everywhere, some tangling themselves in the fuzz of mittens, others white against black leather. Some glistened for an instant and then coalesced to a drop of water on warm skin. They held their hands out and turned, offering the evidence to each other. A collective sigh and then cheers as the few flakes gathered themselves into a flurry and everyone whirled around and around, arms out, welcoming the snow. At last, the snow they'd all been waiting for.

Part II

14

The small window that opened at the foot of Álvaro's bed swirled with white light, light that filtered under the curtain and spread across the quilt. His still half-asleep brain struggled to decipher the mound on his feet. He wiggled his toes and watched the white lump fracture and slide. Snow drifting in through the open window. He wiggled his toes again. He had slept dreamlessly and awoken to nothing more than snow and the pleasant feeling of being warm and dry.

Make a note of it, Chris had suggested when he told her about the lightness he felt, spreading his pictures on the table between them. This happened and then this happened and it was awful. The pictures, paper and paint. Flour and chili powder. It wasn't everything, but it was something. No God anywhere in it. Lightness or emptiness?

Lots of people live without anything they'd call faith, she said. Day by day. Assuming they'll be free-floating molecules at the end of it.

"Floating or falling?" He'd drawn three little Mayan figures, the first tipping over, the second upside down, the third turning back upright.

Chris had looked at the picture for such a long time he almost dozed off in the afternoon twilight. She cleared her throat to bring him back. "This upsets you?"

"I don't know."

"We used to jump off things all the time when we were kids. Snow banks and sand cliffs."

"But landing?"

She pointed to the space beneath the last figure. It was empty. "Isn't that what we're doing all the time?" she asked. "Falling toward the centre of the earth, falling toward the sun, falling into the universe? Maybe there is no bottom. Maybe there is just the falling."

He stared at the white paper. Inside his body, somewhere between his heart and stomach, something flipped. He leaned back, holding on to the arms of his chair.

"Maybe we have to get used to it. Come, somehow, to enjoy it."

His sudden laughter, a child's gleeful explosion of pleasure, startled him into memory. He and Clara riding a log over a small waterfall, splashing into the pool where women were washing clothes. The women screeching at them, angry and afraid for their spirits. Water was dangerous. Water and blissful abandon were deadly. Forgetting yourself. His mother, burning endless cleansing copra to assuage the mountain god she thought was determined to steal Álvaro's spirit.

Álvaro brushed the snow back out the window. Every time you wake up peacefully, Chris had said yesterday, every time you smell the rain and are glad, every time the food simply slides down your throat into your welcoming stomach, make a note. You are alive. You are alive and welcome.

Through the big slow flakes, he could see down to the waves carving a grey curve where the snow hit the tide line. Snowflakes merged into a blur of pale, shifting fog. A small prayer formed. *Lord, take away my heart of stone.*

Downstairs he found Margaret standing on a chair chalking the Magi's initials above the front door. It was the feast day of the Epiphany. The Spanish words for the blessing of the house slid as easily from his mouth as it had in hundreds of Guatemalan homes. Margaret was delighted.

It must be the snow, he thought as he sat down to breakfast, the lightness tingling through him. It changed everyone. Here was Joseph, usually on his way to school by now. Here was Thomas, who never appeared before ten, wearing a thick sweater with reindeer circling his chest. Between bites of egg and sips of tea, he tried on gloves from a stack on the chair beside him.

"Will you need help shovelling?" Álvaro asked.

Thomas looked at him and down at the puffy blue glove on his hand.

"It's done," Joseph answered, his mouth crammed with a muffin. He reached for a mango. "Today's his first snowboarding lesson. My Christmas present. First snowfall after Christmas I told him."

"Isn't it a school day?"

Joseph swallowed. "It's snowing in Vancouver. That is enough to stop the world. The snow will be beautiful. Light enough for turning, but a soft landing."

He turned to his father, his fingers deftly wielding the knife that peeled the mango. "You're going to love it." He licked his fingers and spread out his arms at shoulder height, fingers spread. "Cast off the tyranny of poles and float free."

Thomas pointed a mitten at Álvaro. "Why doesn't he join us? All that working out he does, he should put those muscles to some use. You could teach two as well as one."

Joseph shrugged, sure. "But I know you're just hoping he falls more than you do."

"Go, Álvaro, go," Margaret said, appearing from the basement, still in her housecoat, her hair uncombed. "There are four boxes down there," she said to Joseph before the phone interrupted her.

"Lord," she said, "they're in a panic already." She took the phone out into the hall.

"What is it?" Álvaro asked.

"Warmth for the homeless," Thomas explained. "Hats, mittens, socks, fuzzy blankets, and mugs of hot tea. Margaret is the campaign coordinator and her troops despair without her commanding presence."

"Oh shut up, Thomas," she said, coming back into the kitchen. She hung up the phone and sat down with a cup of tea. "Drat that Amy."

"What's up?" Joseph asked.

"She's got this friend, a student, who got sick and didn't have a clue how to take care of herself. The most basic things like drinking plenty of water when you have a fever. How complicated is that?"

Thomas and Joseph concentrated on their juice glasses.

"Where are her parents? Leaving the girl alone all through Christmas. Do they think giving birth and buying them cellphones and designer jeans is what being a parent means? Leave it to strangers to take her in?"

Thomas looked up. "She's coming here?"

"Just for a day or two. Until Amy can figure out what's really wrong with her. I guess it's complicated."

Joseph pushed back his chair. "Gentlemen, daylight is wasting."

Álvaro hesitated. "Shouldn't I be helping downtown?"

Margaret plopped a couple of pieces of bread in the toaster. "Nothing like snow to bring out the do-gooders. There'll be plenty of help. Just drop off the boxes on your way across town." She yanked open the dishwasher and rooted around in the cutlery tray.

Before Álvaro could protest, Joseph dragged him downstairs to rummage through the boxes for the homeless. He pulled out jackets and toques, handing them to Álvaro to try. A vest, a fleece, a red anorak, and a toque with earflaps and ties. Snow pants.

When they opened the basement door, the snow and cold air floated in. Thomas had already shovelled a neat path to the garage where the car sent out great feathery plumes of exhaust. Joseph shoved two boxes into Álvaro's arms and they piled everything in and strapped Joseph's snowboard to the roof.

As they drove through the snarl of downtown traffic to deliver the clothes and then across the big bridge thrust out into the white swirling air, no land or water visible beneath them, past all the cars driving into the city, Álvaro felt as if he'd left himself somewhere behind. He had nothing with him but the unfamiliar clothes on his body and he was travelling to a place he'd seen only as lights blinking high above the city.

It wasn't until they were standing in the lineup waiting for the gondola that fear returned. They were herded into the car, a forest of skis and poles and snowboards and sleepy faces shivering in the unheated metal and glass cage. When the doors were drawn shut, the gondola swung into the air. Álvaro sucked in his breath as the car swooped up toward the trees looming on the steep hillside in front of them. Thomas stood close, one hand on his arm, explaining. Reassuring. The gondola jerked up above the trees just before clipping them. Álvaro stared at the logo on Joseph's snowboard, a large black arrow curling in on itself, for the long minutes as they rumbled up the cable, the trees and cliffs appearing and disappearing through the snow. Finally a pause, a bump, and the gondola stopped in its metal berth, disgorging them into a gloomy cave of a room and then back outside into snow, bright clothes, and children calling back and forth.

Joseph lowered his board to the snow and dropped to one knee, saying he needed to take one run to settle his blood before the lesson. He snapped the clasps on his boot and the sound of shackles spiked through Álvaro, a sound repeated around him as skiers bent to their boots and bindings. Snap. Snap. Snap. He hunkered down into a squat and covered his ears with the big mitts Joseph had given him, waiting for Vinicio's orders. People swirled around, laughing and calling. But it was Thomas's hand on his shoulder, Thomas's voice that spoke.

"If you need to leave, say the word."

Álvaro looked up. The glasses were fogged around the rims, but Thomas's eyes were visible. It was those eyes that Margaret must love. The wise child's unblinking attention. Álvaro scooped up snow to rub on his face, hoping the cold would bring him back. Thomas stood, one hand still on his shoulder, talking about when he used to come up here with his own father. The rope tow and wooden skis. Girls in those tight wool pants. The old French priest who claimed it was the closest he expected to get to heaven. The body wanting nothing more than to fly, he'd said, and what could be wrong with that?

Álvaro unbent his knees and followed Thomas over to rent a snowboard. By the time they'd been outfitted, the snow had slowed and Joseph was waiting for them. He led them to a gentle open slope out of the way of the crowds, the snow lightly packed.

Now, come, he said, and Álvaro held his breath and strapped himself in. Joseph took his hands and raised his arms to shoulder height. Facing him the whole time, his grip firm and reassuring, Joseph talked him through his first attempts. Try this, he said. No, this. Keep your weight centred. Lift your toes. Now your heels. His hands knew when to grab hold, knew when to loosen up. When to let go.

Half a painful hour later, Álvaro and Thomas could sideslip down the hill frontward and backward. Álvaro was getting used to the feel of the ground dropping away beneath him, but his knees and thighs ached and he shivered in the wind that spun little twisters in the snow. He looked longingly at the lodge beyond the trees.

"No way," Joseph said. "No breaks until you carve at least a couple of turns." He showed Álvaro how to shift his weight. How not to overcompensate when he picked up speed.

"Remember, it's counterintuitive. When you speed up, you want to throw yourself back to slow it down. Don't. You'll catch an edge and smash your head. Lean into the speed and you'll come right around and slow down again."

"Counterintuitive!" Thomas roared from the snowdrift he'd fallen in. "It's insane. Why didn't I bring my skis, dammit!"

Joseph spoke to Álvaro. "Don't be afraid of the speed. Let your body do the thinking." He gave him a little push.

Caught off guard, Álvaro went and, just for a minute, his body did figure it out. He felt his weight shift on the board, put pressure down on the back leg, and pivoted to the right, the speed, pure feeling. He stayed with it, completed the turn, caught his breath, and dug into a turn to the left. And there he was, riding down the slope toward Thomas who was scrambling to get out of his way.

"Yahoo!" Joseph hollered. "The father flies."

The snowboard slowed as the hill flattened and Álvaro miraculously remained upright until he stopped. Again, he thought, like a two-year-old wanting to be thrown into the air. Again.

On the drive home, Joseph slept in the back seat, the car steaming with the warm stink of sweat and wet wool. By the time they got down into the city, the snow had mostly melted, and the cars sent wet spray into the pedestrians cramming the sidewalks. Exhilaration slumped into exhaustion as they unpacked the car, shuddering in the wind coming off the inlet.

Joseph jumped into the shower stall in the basement; Thomas and Álvaro crept upstairs, groaning.

"Father Al!" A girl called to him from the bright kitchen. Her hair was vampire black and the fingers tearing salad into a bowl were tipped with green nails. Metal glinted from her nose and one eyebrow. She wiped her hands on Margaret's quetzal apron and came toward him, arms outstretched. "*Como esta?*" The voice was gravelly, familiar. She stopped when she saw he didn't recognize her.

"I beg your pardon," he said, this wonderful English phrase that covered so many awkward moments.

She drooped, her hair a little black shoe rag, her lips pouting. The mouth did it, a fat little mouth that had chattered in terrible Spanish.

"*El banano sano,*" he said, and she laughed.

The kids had hidden him behind a broken-down bus to watch her street theatre in the centre of Guatemala City, giggling as she taught them about safe sex with an erotic display consisting of bananas, ketchup, condoms, and the kids' own mouths. She waggled her tongue, wiggled her hips, and wielded bananas with clear intent. Pointing to the cracks around the kids' mouths, she told them death enters here. She pointed to their groins, and their bums. Death enters here too.

When Juan Tzul opened his mouth to suck heartily on a ketchup-smeared, condom-covered banana, Álvaro had moved to stop it. Armand pulled him back into the shadows. It's just pretend, he whispered. But see. His mouth is clean.

"Amy," he said, forcing himself to smile back as she clasped his hands, saying something about how much she missed Guatemala. How much she missed the kids. Especially the ones who had been lost. She nodded toward the small shrine just off the kitchen, the one Margaret had made with the photos he'd sent her. Juan Tzul. Moises. Armand. Emilia. Marta.

"What the fuck madness is this?" she'd screamed after Marta had been killed. Gone all tight and hard when she'd seen the body. The nipples cut off. The genitals shredded. The mouth, a gash. "Just plain dead isn't good enough," she'd cried out in the morgue. "They want you still breathing while they fuck you, but they want their fucking to kill you and their own dicks are too limp to do the job."

She'd been out of control, in danger herself, when they got word her mother had died. Álvaro had struggled to break through her shrug of indifference and get her safely home. All the people in Guatemala, he told her, who risk their lives to find out if their relatives are dead or alive, to find out where their bodies were thrown — she owed it to them to treat her own mother's death with respect. He'd driven her to the airport, put her on the plane, and gone back to fooling himself that Vinicio had made him strong. He would go to the bottom of *los barrancas* to get a kid back. To the police station. To the morgue. A certain kind of suicidal longing.

"I hear you're still rescuing kids," he said.

Amy nodded, pointing to the ceiling. "She's been taken in hand. And you? Margaret says you're in some kind of recovery."

He shrugged. Recovery? Able to survive a day on Grouse Mountain. Just barely. He'd be as crazy as she'd been if he ever set foot on a Guatemala City street again. As soon as he saw the mounds of orange rinds beside the juice vendors and smelled the leather of the policemen's boots. As soon as he saw one desperate child ducking into the shadows with a *Norte Americano* in a white shirt and jeans. He shivered and Amy shooed him upstairs to change. He longed for a bath, but the door was closed on a murmur of female voices.

In his room, he pulled off his clothes. He opened the window and scooped up the remnant snow, gasping as the cold electrified his body. His scrubbing raised his scars to bright red welts and he apologized, not for the first time, to the little girl in the painting at the foot of his bed. She looked blue and cold herself as she teetered on the edge of a bathtub, peering out at him as if to decipher the strange calligraphy of his body. He'd liked it, he told her. The snowboarding. For at least an hour he'd liked it very much and hadn't thought about his body except to send it urgent pleas to stay upright. Now he was tired and wanted to sleep.

When Joseph called, he forced himself downstairs to a thrown-together meal, the mood dismal. Thomas's age showed in the bright light, the red marks where his skin cracked from the day out in the cold. Joseph ate without looking up. Amy pouted and Margaret was angry.

She put down her fork and sat back. "This is ridiculous. Amy, you've got to contact this girl's parents. I don't mind taking her in, but her family needs to know she's not well."

Amy's fork stopped halfway to her mouth. "You're speaking to the converted. Her mother would be here in a flash if she knew she'd been sick. But Janna refuses to tell her. Or to let me tell her."

"What's the problem at home?" Margaret paused, suddenly delicate. "Abuse?"

"No, no, nothing like that. Her mom's great."

"Her dad?"

Amy shrugged. "Don't know. Isabel never talks about him, that's for sure."

"Isabel's the mother?"

"Yeah. I roomed with her when I went home to Smithers this past summer."

Álvaro was in a narrow tunnel, noise and darkness closing in to obliterate what the women were saying. But not before he heard Amy mention the little house down by the railway tracks. The two older brothers. And the town. His food filled his throat. He spit it back onto his fork and deposited it carefully on the plate where blue fish swam around the edges, each one's mouth biting at the next one's tail. They were all within a millimetre of becoming someone's dinner. What kind of mind would paint this in such bright cheerful colours? He looked underneath. Guatemala.

He heard the name again. Isabel. Amy was talking about how word was she'd had quite a few boyfriends, not always good choices. Maybe Janna's dad was someone she'd be better off not knowing about. Álvaro had tucked her away deep inside him, safe from any inspection but his own. He hadn't even mentioned her to Chris. But here she was, present in the room, scrutinized and found wanting.

After a long silence, Thomas spoke up. "Sometimes children are born out of rape. It's very hard for the mother. She loves the child but hates what the child represents. Who the child represents."

Joseph clattered his cutlery down and blurted out his distress. "How would you like to hear your old man raped your mother? Talk about messing with your head."

"I don't think so," Amy said. "It just doesn't feel like that's what happened."

"Maybe that's why she won't call her mom," Margaret said.

A car honked outside. They looked at each other.

A quiet voice spoke from the doorway. "I'm sorry for all the trouble I've put you to, Amy. Mrs. Coleman."

The manners were exquisite, the voice perfectly controlled. Everyone at the table knew she'd overheard and even Thomas Coleman blushed.

"I won't be imposing my complex family problems on you anymore."

She nodded to the shocked faces all turned to look at her, picked up a small plastic bag, and walked out the front door.

"Janna!" Amy ran after her.

Álvaro was still struggling to understand what she'd said, so surprised had he been to hear English coming from her mouth. Before she'd spoken, when he'd seen her standing there listening to them, he thought he was hallucinating, so much was it like his dreams on the bus coming to Canada. Clara talking to him, the words a blur. Clara turning away in sorrow. Clara's face clenched in fury. He pushed back his chair, stumbled to the door, and saw Amy watching a taxi pull away from the curb. The dreamy free falling he'd talked to Chris about was all a joke. He was plummeting down a mine shaft and the air was getting hotter and hotter. His lungs were full of fire.

Margaret snapped orders to Amy, the two of them driving off into the night to find her. Álvaro left Joseph and Thomas to clean up the kitchen and dragged himself up to the bathroom where he threw up, the food still virtually intact, floating in the toilet. He looked at it as if he could find some kind of explanation there. But he didn't need anyone to explain, he told himself as he flopped on the bed he'd woken so happily in that morning. He stared at the little girl. She stared back, waiting for him to say something.

"My name is Álvaro," he said out loud. "I am your father."

It felt as if the fish on the plate had been let loose in his bloodstream. Doors slammed. He was back in the torture room. He could smell Vinicio. Feel the sting as the lemon bit into the cuts on his face. "*Hermanito*," Vinicio saying. "Little brother. And your mother, such an accommodating little whore."

The vomit came too fast this time and splattered the floor beside his bed. He retched and retched as Vinicio tut-tutted in the background. Clara's hair in his face as he rode behind her on her horse. Clara pale and sleepy, pushing him out of her bed. Her drowsy insistence. Clara in her debutante dress, her hair piled up on her head. Her anger.

The mess drove him to action. He cleaned up as best he could with his dirty clothes and opened the window wide to let in the cold wind driving what was now rain through the rustling branches of the trees. Bundling up the mess, he crept downstairs and threw it all in the washing machine. He stuck his head under the kitchen tap, swilling out the taste of vomit. TV sounds came from behind the family room door. The men were battened down. He found a scrap of paper beside the phone. A UBC residence. His heart pounded. He was terrified they'd bring her back and hoped they would. That he would see her again. When Margaret came in, he slid the paper into his pocket.

He waited, one hand crushing it.

"She wouldn't let us in at first, but we contacted the floor supervisor and she took Amy up." Margaret's face was the colour of ash. "I am too old for this. I am too old to be rescuing college students from their own stupidity. I am too old to have a fifteen-year-old son. I can't remember being that young anymore. I can't remember it being fun. It seems such a waste of energy."

Álvaro's skin fluttered like a freshly killed goat hung up for gutting, the surface of its body twitching with electric currents. He stepped aside to let her pass.

"And what you need is peace and quiet, not histrionics. We should never have brought her here."

Did he wish he didn't know? He couldn't think that clearly. He plugged in the kettle, but forgot to fill it with water. Margaret took it from him.

"Is she going to be okay?" he finally croaked.

"If she doesn't slit her wrists."

Álvaro's heart lurched in sudden fury as she slammed around the kitchen, putting away pots left in the dish drainer. Opening the dishwasher, rearranging the dishes, adding soap. He wanted to strike her.

"If she doesn't want help, what do we do? Leave her alone in her little room to waste away to a skeleton? It's hopeless. Her mother needs to know. Someone needs to have a talk with her."

Those words. Álvaro's anger surged. I'll have a talk with her, son, Walter had said. Leave it to me. He would have watched Isabel get big, heard the news of the birth. Walter had known all along.

He wanted to tear the night apart, rip the noise out of the air. Margaret's voice. Vinicio laughing in his ear. The breath, entering. Spermatozoa, he'd said. Whipping their tails out through the world, trailing their slime behind them. And he'd drawn a line of the viscous liquid under Álvaro's nose, smeared it on his mouth. The smell, the taste so strong in the kitchen, he wiped at his face with his sleeve. It was as if Vinicio, too, had known everything after all.

"I'm not bound by any privacy rules," Margaret said, handing him a cup of tea. "What's the last name again? She must have a phone." She rummaged for a pen, a scrap of paper. "Isabel."

"Lee," Álvaro spoke without thinking. He listed the number he had called maybe ten times, more than twenty years ago.

Margaret looked up, startled.

Álvaro decided he wasn't going to lie about this. "Isabel Lee on Railway Avenue. A little house right across from the rail yard. The whole ground would shake every time a train went by."

He could feel Margaret's gaze upon his face. He felt the scar, as if it conducted electricity up from his pulsing throat into his mouth. More words. "And, if I'm not mistaken, that girl is my daughter." His teacup shattered in his hand, the scalding liquid spilling over his hands.

He heard Clara's voice calling his name as his captors held him in the shadows, a hand over his mouth. "Get inside," he wanted to scream, "Don't open the gate." His teeth shredding his lips as they moved against the crushing pressure of the hand. She'd been expecting him. She'd wanted to see him. The earth filled his mouth, Juan Tzul's small bones rattled in his pocket. He wanted to do divination, to throw the bones to read their prophecies. He knew he could do this now. The power flowed through him and he could look on the bones and see the future and not flinch. There were no surprises left in the world, Clara. There's nothing you can do to surprise me. I can see you as a whore on the street, a nun smiling from a website, a *Zona 7* matron shopping for a new dress, bored, smoking, drugged with some tranquilizer. The crone in the morgue laying him open, raising the blade and bringing it down to whisper across his throat, his nipples, his terrified testicles. Nothing, Clara, will ever surprise me again. Here you are come back to me. Here you are to prove all of Vinicio's lies, truth.

Thomas Coleman appeared in the doorway, rumpled in pajamas, skin flaky, hair awry. He held out one arm toward Margaret, supporting the wrist with his other hand. He hadn't wanted to bother her earlier, he said, but he thinks he's maybe broken something. The whole hand was blue and swollen, streaks of red going up the arm.

Álvaro's rage flamed. He bent to pick up the curved shards still rocking on the tiles. He wanted to lay Thomas's arm down on the table and slice it into rags. To slit Margaret's throat and still her tired laugh.

"Thomas Coleman, don't you just take the cake."

As she reached once more for her coat, Álvaro clenched his fist around the broken porcelain.

15

Janna's first mistake had been to write Amy's mother's name on her university application form as her emergency contact.

"What was that all about?" Amy had asked in the hospital room where Janna was hooked up to an IV line — for rehydration, they'd said. Amy was doing an agitated little two-step, bracelets jangling and beads clacking. It was making Janna dizzy. That and whatever else they'd injected into her IV line.

"I get this call from my mom's business partner wondering what the hell Isabel Lee's daughter is doing putting my mother down as her next of kin."

"I always liked your mom," Janna said. "Maybe we could trade." She'd do better, she thought, with the pleasant accountant who came to high school careers day wearing very nice clothes, talking about how she'd started out training to be secretary, and now she had her own secretary and a little BMW.

"Janna, my mother is dead."

Janna hadn't known that. She must have actually had breast cancer when she'd modelled clothes in the breast cancer fashion show Isabel helped organize every year. What Isabel's mother had died of.

"She had cancer forever. Always making these miraculous recoveries. You kind of stop believing it after a while," Amy said. "I was in Guatemala. When I came home for the funeral, my dad looked like shit. He tells me his liver's buggered and could I stick around until it's over."

Janna didn't know that part either.

"You've got at least one perfectly good parent," Amy had said. "Figure it out."

The second mistake was thinking Greg might be just the ticket to rescue her from Amy. As soon as they met, they joined forces and his vaguely threatening explanation of how Janna's illness had gone completely unnoticed for almost ten days until he'd insisted a janitor let him into her room added weight to Amy's work. She had talked Janna's program advisor into letting her repeat her statistics course, start her financial audit course two weeks late, and still keep her scholarship.

Her third mistake was agreeing to stay with the Colemans while she regained her strength. They were in the business of rescuing waifs, Amy said, and Janna fit the bill. Overhearing Amy talk about Isabel brought back all the memories of the aunties cluck-clucking over her poor kids. How she just couldn't seem to keep her panties on. Janna had wanted a grenade to flip into the middle of that dinnertime conversation. Until Thomas Coleman lobbed in his own explosive. Rape.

It would explain so much. Isabel's patience when Janna asked and asked and asked. Her lectures to the boys about respecting women. Even when they don't respect themselves. Even when they're nasty. You never know, she'd say, what else is going on in their lives. Leave if you want, but don't ever, ever, ever hit them. But how could she look at Janna and not hate her?

"Did she tell you that?" Amy said it right out.

"No." Janna was trying to force down a bagel Amy had heated in her microwave.

"So why the big breakup?"

"None of your business."

"I don't think it's what happened," Amy insisted. "She'd have done something about it."

"Abort me?" As soon as the words were out, Amy looked ready to slap her. She started talking about what an idiot Janna was and she was damned if she was going to hang around and listen to her badmouth a friend who had taken her in when her parents had both died, for Christ's sake, was worried about her daughter, had stopped drinking as far as she could tell.

Janna watched Amy's pudgy little mouth moving. Even when she stopped talking to breathe, it still hung open. How could her trim and gracious mother have given birth to someone like Amy? Dying all that time and still elegant.

It wasn't until Amy had stomped off that Janna heard the words about Isabel having stopped drinking. She went to the window, but stepped back when she saw Greg leaning against the next building looking up at her. He raised an arm. His head turned and he smiled at Amy coming out the downstairs door. A gust of wind blew through the ragged square and Amy shivered and struggled with the buttons on her jacket. Greg bent to help her, unwrapped his scarf, and wound it around her head. Then, in an awkward shuffle, he took Amy's face in his hands and kissed her. She wriggled against him like a walrus pup, took his hips, and shook into a little dance step. They leaned together, arms around each other, and walked away.

Where was it, Janna wondered as jealousy prickled through her, where was it you thought other people went when they went away? What was it you thought they did? When Greg wasn't home on Christmas Eve, did she think he'd been waiting sorrowfully for her to call? And Amy? She'd never seen Amy's place. Who she lived with. Did she and Greg lie in bed together, Greg's deranged father bleating at the door, and laugh at pathetic little Janna?

Even as she tidied her room and emailed a stats assignment to her professor, she felt once more adrift. Adrift somewhere between the blue plastic chair and the sad little bed, her feet cold on the linoleum.

She dressed and walked to class, eyes closed against the slanting rain. In her financial auditing class, the professor explained how every transaction should be traceable back to a real exchange between humans. Goods or a service and some form of cash. Hours worked. Vacation taken. A complex genealogy. An unbroken line from conception to the grave. The marker on the grave where, if you dug, you would find evidence.

If there was a gap in the life history of a transaction, the professor went on, it could mean several things: ignorance, carelessness, incompetence, or intent. And if it was intent, then there was usually something to hide: tax evasion, fraud, embezzlement.

It wasn't ignorance. Her mother knew who her father was. She stretched her hands out on the keyboard of her laptop and looked at them, searching for his signature. It couldn't have been rape. When her mother spoke about her father's beautiful hands, there'd been powerful emotion in her voice. Sorrow. Love, perhaps. Janna typed a few more notes, the fingers automatic on the keys, turning the professor's moving lips into something for later retrieval. She felt relief wash through her, relief for both her mother and herself. Eyes closed, she typed and typed until the man's voice stopped and the students around her were gathering their coats and pushing past her. She followed them outside, around the corner and through the doors of the café into a lineup. She needed to eat, to speak to someone and enter into a monetary transaction.

Even before the man in front of her started to turn, she realized it was David. Just what she didn't need. As she stumbled back, trying to get away, the colour rose up from under his collar and flushed his face with venom. He made an ugly sound, cunt, he said, fucking cunt, and his friends turned to see what was happening. He twisted up his hand to give her the finger, a gesture that carried a clear threat. She turned and fled, bumping into a man holding the door open for her, his dark eyes full of concern. As she pushed past him, she thought she'd seen him somewhere before. But she wanted to get away from all those people in there, turning to look, to wonder what she'd done to make that guy so mad.

Back in her room, she dumped her coat on her bed and stared at the tapestry she'd hung on the wall at the foot of her bed. Trevor, she thought. She could put his name down on the school form. And Jason. Remembering calmed her. Reattached her to her body. She sat down in the chair and stared at the birds sitting so calmly on the branch, one, two, three in a row. Three eyes looking her way. She lifted her hair off the back of her neck. She had planned to go to the gym but could not imagine walking into the clanking weights and hum of track machines. She took a deep breath, pulled on her jacket, her running shoes, and a scarf. She was not going to be afraid.

16

Margaret had called Chris Mundy from the emergency room that night. Thomas waiting for a cast, Álvaro getting his hand stitched up. Making him promise not to hurt himself again. Or anyone else, she'd added, her face so white, the exhaustion so etched into the skin around her eyes and mouth, the nurse brought her a pillow. And then she'd left him to it, her withdrawal as clear as her determination to continue to support him. He'd seen her kneeling one evening, a crack in the door to the bedroom, a candle flickering, her spine straight in its white nightgown, her hair braided down her back. The dim light turned the grey to a vague shadowed lightness, turned the tired woman into a young girl at her devotions. A flush of shame sent him back to Chris.

He had already told her about Ana Elisabeth and Vinicio, about the torture and her death. He had told her what Vinicio had said about his mother. How he thought he'd never know if it was true, but he would not judge his mother for what happened.

He hadn't told her everything about Clara. And he hadn't told her about Isabel. His new-found sanctuary.

We think there's a kind of nobility in carrying the burden of painful secrets, Chris said when he told her about Janna and what it meant, not just the fact of her, but the fact of his own father. He had taken his place in her familiar room, amidst the paints and clay and bright toys in the sand tray only to find he couldn't draw one thing. The crayon dangled loose in his fingers.

Why didn't Isabel tell me, he raged. What right did she have?

"Don't priests keep secrets all the time?" she countered.

"Walter, too. He'd have known," he said. He flung the crayon down on the table, remembering Walter's hesitation when he asked him to find out how Isabel was doing.

"When I left Smithers, I'd asked Walter to explain. To give her my apology. To ask for forgiveness. When I phoned and asked about it, he told me she already had another boyfriend."

"Maybe she did."

Not so soon, he insisted. They'd been talking about making a life together. She'd felt just as much as he did, he was certain. And Walter knew that.

"I made a good confession," he said bitterly. "I doubt if he did."

It's what priests do all the time, she said, her hands rearranging a shawl full of sparkling fibre. She was watching him carefully, that clinical attentiveness. You know so much, and never tell. There's power in that knowledge. Keeping secrets. Hiding babies. Protecting others.

"If I'd known," he began and then stopped. If he'd known, what would have changed? Would he have left the priesthood? Would he be a happily married schoolteacher in Smithers with four or five kids? Would he be a divorced drug counsellor in Vancouver? His knowing wouldn't have kept Vinicio from burning the people in that village, from stealing those children, it wouldn't have stopped Clara's pain, it wouldn't have kept the beasts from snarling in Ana Elisabeth's stomach. It wouldn't have kept Juan Tzul alive.

"What do you tell? What do you leave unspoken? When do you lie outright?" Chris poured them each a cup of tea. It was cool in her office, and water condensed on the outside of the glass. "We are crowded with stories," she said, "some truth, some lies, many of them not our own. I've begun to believe the body — and maybe the spirit your mother's Mayan practice was so anxious to keep intact — knows the truth anyway. Unconsciously. It's like the forest. All those plants and flowers and birds singing. We walk through it every day and think we know it well. But most action is taking place underground, the hundreds of little creatures living a complex life out of our sight. And we are all rooted in that."

He left Chris's office with a plan that began with Walter. Álvaro's anger faltered when George brought him into the old man's darkened bedroom. The skin had collapsed into the hollow cheeks and his frail body barely displaced the blanket. Álvaro was able to bend to him, kiss his cheek, and take his hand. The anger returned as he told him about Janna.

"Are you certain?" Walter asked. "She was known for her…" he paused, "…willingness."

"The girl is my sister's twin," Álvaro said. "You must have known."

"Your sister?" Walter pushed himself up on his elbow, the red flaming in his cheeks. "What sister? You never talked about a sister."

George opened the door, reminding Walter to stay calm. His pale eyes flickered between the men.

"Get out," Walter said. "This is none of your business."

"I don't care who knows," Álvaro said, his voice rising. "I am an illegitimate bastard, I have a half-sister and brother by a man who probably raped my mother, and I apparently have a little bastard child of my own. One you've known about all along."

George hovered in the doorway, his long fingers plucking at the T-shirt stretched over his small paunch.

"We'd have lost you if we told you," Walter whispered. "We needed you more than she did. She always found someone else."

Álvaro's anger shifted again, shifted into something cold and implacable. As if Vinicio was in the room with him. The ways in which someone can say what happened and still be lying. There was no we. Walter did this all by himself. Not wanting the other priests to know what he'd let happen with the young man he'd been so eager to initiate into the full wonder and mystery of the vocation.

"The decision wasn't yours to make," Álvaro said.

The old man sipped water through a straw. The flush in his cheeks had faded leaving only the reddened splotches of broken capillaries. George had slipped away. Doors opened and closed. Low voices spoke urgently and the television in the priests' living room was turned down.

"The power God gives us moves in mystery, Álvaro, but to pretend we don't have it is a great lie. I used what was given me in the way that seemed truest to his will. And I don't regret it. Whatever nonsense people spout now, a child is a woman's place. That care is her great gift. You were made for other things."

"How can you say that without choking?" Álvaro spit out. "I have a daughter. It changes everything."

"You're a priest," the old man said. "There's no changing that. Leave the girl to her mother."

Álvaro could not speak. Walter's hands were swollen, the blood, George had told him, backing up from his heart. Álvaro looked out the window at Walter's winter garden. The few withered corn leaves were half covered by the turned earth. The outer leaves of the winter kale were frozen stiff. Prickly rose vines splayed like hairy insect legs across the back fence. The silence stretched so long, Walter's eyes closed, and his breath caught in a little rasp at the back of his throat.

George reappeared in the doorway, his green winter parka zipped up, black gloves in one hand, the other hand jiggling keys in a pocket. Another man stood behind him, like a bouncer ready to enforce the orders. Álvaro stood to leave.

"Do you remember learning how to float?"

They turned to look back at Walter, his voice clear and low. He was staring at the Oblate cross hanging on the wall beside his bed.

"I'll never forget the day I leaned back into the water and trusted it to hold me up. It's a miracle that we float, Álvaro. The water our Lord walked on, it holds us up too. You just lie back and trust it and there you are. It can hold up the whole damn world. This dying is a funny business. It's almost like falling into the water.

"And soon, I'll be right in the middle of it, breathing it in and out, not just bobbing along on top."

Álvaro gave up, for the moment, his anger. "It's no wonder you like fishing, old man."

†

A couple of days later he met with the provincial superior in the warm study, a fire in the grate, Eloise anxious at the desk outside. The spectre of administrative and legal ramifications battled with the man's genuine concern for Álvaro. Was it essential the girl be told at all? Álvaro thought for a long moment about Ana Elisabeth before he said yes. But it's complicated, he said. She's vulnerable right now.

"As are you," the superior said, taking off his glasses and rubbing his eyes. "You'll want to have some clarity yourself so we can respond appropriately. Tell me how you were doing before you got this news. Did you feel yourself on the way to some determination about your vocation?"

The wording of the question puzzled Álvaro. Like a job interview. "Right now, I can't think of myself as anything but her father."

The superior's bark of laughter surprised him. "What fools we've been. If Walter wasn't so fragile himself, I'd be tempted to teach him a lesson out in a back alley somewhere. I'd hoped even the older ones knew we can't get away with these secrets anymore. Our Lord may forgive us, but while we're in this flesh, the repercussions are endless and mostly profane."

Eloise put her head around the door, reminding them that mass was about to begin. The superior's arm insistent around Álvaro's shoulders, leading him to the chapel and the surprise of an Ash Wednesday service. The realization that he had forgotten about Lent left Álvaro shaken. How far away from all that he'd travelled and in how little time.

Last year in Guatemala he'd shown the kids the way Canadians make pancakes to use up all the butter and eggs on the Tuesday before Lent. Then together they'd burned the palm fronds, saved from the previous year's Palm Sunday. They clamoured for ash as a promise on their foreheads. The children understood perfectly the wild hope of Palm Sunday and loved to shout the hosannas. Like the Mayan brothers Hunahpu and Xbalanque, he told them, Christ went down into the dark house, into the cold house, into all the places of fear, and like the brothers, he came up again. They believed in the resurrection for as long as it took the wafer to dissolve on their tongue. Then it was back to normal; another mutilated corpse.

How could he ask them to give anything up for that? But like the poorest people everywhere, they were the most generous. Armand stopped trying to score goals. He would only pass the ball, he said, and let others make the point. Juan Tzul requested a funeral service for the finger bones he'd carried everywhere, jiggling them in his pockets like lucky dice. Emilia dabbed her makeup on the little ones playing dress-up, leaving her own face bare. He would, he told himself, for forty days, give up anger.

How can I ever get through until Easter, Moises had wailed as they passed the shoemaker's gluepots. It took your mother forty weeks to grow you, he'd told the jittery boy. Give our beloved Mother Mary Immaculate forty days. One at a time.

In the chapel, a priest he didn't know read the harsh warnings of the prophet, Joel. Locusts turning Eden into desolation. They closed his heart again, the conditional promises too much like the language of the pimps and police. Of Vinicio. Eloise, looking across to him, read St. Paul's call for reconciliation. He held up his hand to refuse communion. But the superior's thumb smeared ashes on his forehead and spoke the words Álvaro had said to the children, the man's voice transfused with the same love he had felt flowing directly from the mystery of transformation into the children's open hearts: "Lord, bless all who receive these ashes."

His longing for Janna had little of this sanctity. It was formless desire, a thin veneer over his emptiness. As such, it would do her no good. A week later, he listened dully to the superior's plan to involve Walter. An advocate for the girl and a lawyer who specializes in these cases. This involves all of us, he'd said when Álvaro protested. An Oblate never acts alone, no matter how much he might wish he could. The lawyer is there to protect us all, the girl included. To answer any unexpected questions. In the meantime, it might be best if Álvaro moved back home.

It was not a suggestion, Álvaro realized on the bus ride back to the Colemans'. It was an order. The damage control was about to begin. It was out of his hands and he felt like an old man when he clambered off the bus into the drizzle to make the transfer, waiting in the doorway of a coffee shop for the next number ten heading west, deeper into the riches of Point Grey. Those who wanted a cup of coffee murmured politely as they pushed their way past the wet travellers, shrinking away from the soaked raincoats, ducking under the dripping umbrellas. Álvaro's bus splashed up. He found an empty seat beside a grey-haired woman, her purse firmly held on her lap. After they talked about the weather and the way the crocuses were showing nicely in spite of it, she asked him where he was going.

His answer surprised him. "Out to the university. To see my daughter."

"A student?"

"Yes. She's studying business." His pride was inordinate. "She won a big scholarship."

"You must be very proud of her."

"Yes. She works hard." He didn't know why he was saying this. "But the rest of the family…it's never enough." He shrugged.

"Uh oh," the woman said.

Álvaro nodded. "I'm trying to patch things up, but they're all stubborn."

Her little snort of derision startled him. She snapped the clasp on her purse open and shut several times. She reached for the cord to signal the driver to stop. As the bus slowed, she took his arm. Her eyes were milky. "Don't get caught in the middle," she said.

He stood and helped her up as the bus pulled into her stop.

"She's your daughter. You're her father. That's between the two of you and nobody else's business." She spoke as if from her own experience, her own regret.

"Thank you," he said to her coat of turquoise wool. "Thank you."

He leaned against the window as the bus lurched back out into the traffic. The houses along Tenth Avenue were all clearly delineated behind the bare branches of ornamental trees, the tidy patches of lawn and black dirt showing splashes of colour where bulbs poked through.

By the time the bus arrived at the university, the wind had blown the rain away. The students moved fast, huddled down into their soaked sweatshirts and flimsy windbreakers. Damp air seeped through his jacket and chilled his shoulders. He shifted them, longing for the warmth of Guatemala City, its crowded streets, the bodies close and jostling, people yelling back and forth. He stood under the shelter, undecided. The possibilities opened before him: he could turn and leave and he might bump into her; he could knock on her door and she might not be there. Or she might be there with a lover and his stomach clenched at the thought. He might have a heart attack and die right here. How complicated this was going to be. He was living an elaborate fantasy. Like the street kids stoned and jittery, waiting for the raised eyebrow, the nod from the cruising johns. Or hoping for the rescue van sliding open the door to refuge. Or burrowing their faces in the little bag of glue.

The place he went after his body betrayed him. After the pain that was nothing like illness or injury, nothing like the crawl of death up the nerve endings of the body, nothing like these because it was pain that could be stopped in a second at the will of another person. A finger raised and it ended. A slow afternoon, a fly floating in the boredom of a cup of coffee and it began. The place where he inhaled the glue to erase the touch of Vinicio's razor along his jawbone. The sight of Clara's loathing. The knowledge of his own complicity.

17

Janna stopped at the crosswalk, waiting for the traffic to thin, dancing from one foot to another, trying to keep warm. The rain had let up, but the wind was still blowing. She followed three women through the opening in the trees, happy to get off the pavement and feel the leaf litter cushioning her feet. She'd forgotten how beautiful the trails were, how the trees buffered the noise of the cars and the bite of the wind. Her weeks of studying and illness had drained her strength and the women soon outpaced her. She kept going, nodding at people coming the other way, moving over as others passed her. She followed two men for a while as they discussed the best kind of process for suturing head wounds, an exchange as relaxed and amicable as if they were discussing movies. She kept running through the dizziness and the uncertainty, waiting for the fatigue and despair to pass, waiting for the place where you forgot you were running, forgot you were tired and were just present in the thwack thwack of your feet hitting the wet leaves, watching for roots and puddles, but it just wasn't happening and it was getting darker and darker and she was suddenly aware of how alone she was. No one had passed for several minutes. And David's words came slithering back, the viciousness of his thrusting finger.

Isabel, she thought, must have danced on the edge of danger all the time. There'd been bruises sometimes, and scrapes. She'd found her once on the back deck, slumped in a chair and wrapped in a blanket. Not wanting to come in, she said, until she felt human. Not wanting to pollute the house. Outside air always helped cure a hangover.

Janna forced herself to slow down and finally stop at the next trail junction. She was no longer sure which way to turn — the wind was still blowing in off the water and the treetops were bending and whispering like the white noise traffic makes in the distance. The staccato footsteps of a lone runner came up behind her, a man in shorts and T-shirt, sweatband around his head, thick curls poofing out around it. She asked him for directions and he pointed;

she nodded and watched him run off deeper into the trees, the gloom gathering him in until his movement became vague shifting shadows and he faded into the darkness. She turned and before long could see headlights in the distance and the opening in the trees that would take her out into that stream of light, of people, of music playing, news reports, cellphone conversations, back seat squabbles, and the general substance of being that she was not part of, knowing how blind they were to everything outside the beam of their headlights, outside the roadway. Blind to the possibility of the moose on the side of the highways up north, ready to step out into the road and explode your world into shattering glass and crumpled metal.

She picked up her speed and ran down the tunnel of trees, out onto the sidewalk, breaking through at last into that comforting exhilaration of a body doing what it's meant to do, running, running, and she crossed the road and ducked into the shortcut along the Japanese garden wall and the open square in front of her residence. And there he was, David and his two friends, waiting by her door. She stopped, still in the shadow, heart pounding, pleasure draining out of her body and leaving her limp and terrified. She put a hand in her pocket, feeling for her cell. Instead she found the little bag of worry dolls. Little Christmas girl in there with her adopted family, trying to get along. Refusing to take any shit. Fuck this, she thought and walked toward them. David, she called out, businesslike, calm. I owe you an apology.

Even before they grabbed her and backed her into the darkness, she knew she'd made a mistake. Her stupid little trick had started something she had no way of getting hold of. She was in a black tangle of venom, of hands twisting her arms, another reaching inside her jacket, grabbing her breast and yanking. David, backing away as the others shoved her along, kneeing her in the groin, spitting in her face, snarling out words she'd never heard and others she had. Hick bitch. Squaw whore. Skank. The pain scoured her. She tried to scream but a hand came around and covered her mouth, smashing her lips against her teeth. She was being attacked in full view of the lit rooms of dozens of students; the speed with which they did their damage showed they knew what they were about. It was only then she started to fight and it was useless. The pain was everywhere.

"Help," someone called out, running toward them. "Let her go!"

And suddenly she was flung against a tree and fell face down in the dirt. "We'll be back, bitch," David hissed and she heard footsteps pounding away.

She slumped there, trying to spit out the dirt in her mouth. She closed her eyes against the roar rising in her ears and placed her forehead against the rough bark of the tree. Saliva pooled in her mouth and she was stumbling through her mother's backyard in darkness, dirt on her hands, dirt itching around the roots of her hair, looking for her mother. Looking and crying, in some terrifying aloneness. The moon finally finding her and finding Isabel at the same time. Her naked body splayed in the dirt, her breathing hoarse and ragged. Janna tugged at her arms, calling at her to get up, get up, until her eyes finally fluttered open and she knew where she was.

She was still crying when she became aware of an urgent voice, anguished, some accent she couldn't identify. He reached out hands to help her up and she sank against him for a minute, feeling his solid bulk, his hands gentle on her body.

She'd twisted her ankle, and something wrong with her ribs made every breath a sharp jab. She stumbled with him back along the path but she did not want to go into the light. She tied her scarf around her head and hunched her neck into her jacket, hiding. She wanted to go to her room, but she was afraid of being alone. She was afraid of being alone, but she didn't want this man to see her. To know her.

"We need to call security," he said. "You need to see a doctor."

"No," she said quickly. "They're gone, aren't they?" She looked around wildly, afraid of the light, afraid of the dark. "I'll be okay. I just need to lie down."

He spoke to her quietly and walked with her through the pools of light and darkness to her door. He waited while she scrambled for the keys. He asked again who he could call, but she left him there, watching through the glass until the elevator door slid shut.

She rode it up, trying not to breathe, pushing past the group of students talking in the hall outside her door. She wondered what showed on her face as she slipped between them, into her room. If they even noticed the scrapes. She stood in the dark, her back against the door until they wandered away. She felt her way into the bathroom, stripped off her clothes, and turned on the shower. The water stung as it hit the scratches fingernails had made on her breasts. The scrape on her face when she'd fallen, her split lip. As she stood under the hot water, she cried, hearing again the contempt in David's voice. The names. She cried and cried even as she turned off the water, dried herself, put on her pajamas, and crept into bed.

The shadows of trees moving across the streetlight blurred in her tears. There was another world out there, one a thin crack away, violence buzzing under a skin so thin you could see right through it. Isabel had somehow made Janna believe it was a world she chose, one she liked. And everything she saw that night she left home confirmed that. Sitting there in her boyfriend's car waiting for him to come out of the pub with a case of beer, Janna saw a man and woman stumbling outside, his hands all over her. Shoving her into the shadow of a garbage bin, the laughing woman half pushing him away as he unzipped his pants and lifted her skirt, fucking her up against the brick wall of the pub. Janna had been close enough to see the way her mother's eyes changed when she saw someone watching her. She'd liked it. That had only changed when she realized the watcher was her daughter. That was the moment when Janna stopped making excuses for Isabel. The moment she made her boyfriend take her home to pack two cardboard boxes of clothes while Isabel circled her, drunk and blubbering, saying she was sorry, it wouldn't happen again.

Janna had stepped around her, tucking a stuffed lamb from Trevor, a picture of her brothers, and a small case of jewellery into one of the boxes. Isabel drunk and shouting at her as she carried her boxes to the car. Isabel throwing shoes and jackets onto the hood of the car, go, Janna's cold order, go, and the boy driving her away, the tires bumping over the only thing Janna regretted, the new runners Isabel had bought her when she finally made the track team.

But now she could not get the taste of dirt out of her mouth, the memory of her mother's body gasping for breath, lying in the dirt of her own garden.

18

He'd better do something, Margaret told Álvaro when she found him standing, soaked and distraught, in the alcove off the kitchen. He was reciting the
names of the lost children as if by doing so he could bring them back to life.
He recited all the ways he'd failed them. Not found them the help, the homes
they needed. Teased them when he should have been tough. Tough when he
should have been tender. He told her about watching outside Janna's building
all night. Her mother needs to know, she'd insisted. That girl needs her family.

"I am her family," he said.

A flicker of contempt thinned her lips. "Be that as it may," she said, "but
she doesn't know you from Adam. You can't just jump in unannounced."

Álvaro had a desperate thought — maybe she did know about him and
didn't want anything to do with him. Maybe she'd known all along. Just
another, what did they call them, deadbeat dad?

Margaret held out the phone.

Still he hesitated. Janna's resemblance to Clara had sidetracked him,
really. He had been thinking all along, he realized, as if Janna was something
between him and Clara. Since he'd seen her, he hadn't been thinking about
Isabel at all. And she exploded back into his memory. The way she'd laugh
as she tickled one of the boys, her pleasure in their helpless giggles and wrig-
gling joy. In his own. He hadn't heard Janna laugh. Maybe she laughed like
her mother.

"Maybe Isabel's not the person to tell. There must be a reason Janna
doesn't call her. And if she wanted to talk to me, she would have, long ago."

Margaret shook her head in exasperation, the little silver crosses of her
earrings slapping her cheeks. "Has no one told you? She's looking for you."

Timid Eloise, always turning away when Margaret fumed about the old
boys' club of the church, was as impatient as Margaret with this one. A friend

of Isabel's — an aunt? She'd been asking questions about him, but the superior was stalling.

"The girl doesn't know about you. Her mother wants to know where you are and what you're doing before she tells her."

Álvaro took a deep breath and dialled the number, his heart pounding. He got a man's voice on Isabel's answering machine and couldn't bring himself to leave a message. He hung up in distaste. All those men, Walter had said. There was always someone. But no one for Janna. No one she could call. This city, her *baranca*. Some kids were discarded and some, he knew, threw themselves away.

"You need to see her for yourself before you make that judgment," Margaret insisted. "It's not something you can do over the phone. I'll contact the aunt. It seems she knows you."

Thomas drove him to the bus depot, the rain sluicing the streets, the wind whipping up False Creek in great gusts. As the bus rumbled out of the sodden city, the familiar wire of dread reverberated across the hollowness in his stomach and the old buzz crackled in his ears. As the Fraser Canyon rose steeply around him, the snow heavy on the cedars, he held himself with the same careful balance he had learned in the darkness of the prison cell after his torturers slammed the door and left him alone. Before their footsteps died away, he was preparing himself for their return.

During the long bus trip through the dreary winter towns, Álvaro tried to convince himself he was a different man than he'd been six months earlier on the journey from Guatemala to Vancouver. He was not afraid of the driver's uniform anymore. When the bus picked up a basketball team in Williams Lake, he was not afraid of the wires trailing out from the earphones hidden under the boys' toques. When a man near the front of the bus reached across the aisle to take a wailing infant, Álvaro was only momentarily afraid for the baby's life.

You've done well, Chris had told him at the end of his last visit. You're stronger than you were last fall. Now take a break from Guatemala. Do what you have to do here.

As the bus lumbered through Fort Fraser and west toward Fraser Lake, twenty uncomfortable hours north of Vancouver, Álvaro saw the sign advertising the Rose Prince pilgrimage at the site of the old LeJac residential school. Walter had promised to take him that summer so many years ago. Show him a couple of good fishing spots. Not likely now. Not likely at all.

As he crossed the bridge spanning the ice-choked Bulkley River, he let himself finally think of Isabel and all the ways he'd travelled since he left here so long ago. The years etched in his body. He had no idea what to expect. When he stumbled off the bus into the dirty parking lot in Smithers, the cold made him gasp. The wind blew swirls of sand off the icy roads into his face, the tears from his watering eyes freezing to his lashes. A woman standing beside an idling car said his name. A slender woman, her scarf framing a smooth face, laugh lines deeply incised around the dark eyes, she waited, hands in her pockets, watching him through the billowing cloud of exhaust. There was something of Isabel in her smile.

She saw his confusion and quickly introduced herself. Isabel's aunt, Alice. More memories and more shame. Alice Black. That summer she'd left the Montreal convent to rethink her vocation before taking vows. They'd had long talks. His passion for Isabel had heightened his passion for everything and his faith had burned right through all the contradictions. Until he realized she was Isabel's aunt. Until he waved at her one day on his way to meet Isabel. She'd been sitting on a bench on Main Street, the boys with her, all three licking ice cream cones. Babysitting while Isabel walked down to the willows beside the river.

He refused her offer of breakfast, a shower, maybe a rest. These women, he thought. Why do they suffer us?

"I'm not sure this is such a good idea," she said driving him through a town he barely recognized. He had never seen it in winter, its squat homes hunkered down between snow-laden hedges. Clouds hung low over the mountain and blowing snow almost obscured the train yards where boxcars clanged and squealed in a haze of orange light. Alice parked the car. Across the road, smoke rose out of Isabel's chimney. A narrow path between clipped grey shrubs led to the neatly shovelled stairs. The porch windows were frosted white.

"She doesn't know I'm here?"

Alice shook her head. "I wasn't sure. I wanted to talk to you first."

Álvaro shook his head. "Please," he whispered. "I need to get this done."

†

On Sundays in winter, Isabel lit the wood stove. It took the chill off the house in a way the oil furnace never did, especially when it was twenty below and the wind whistled through the gaps around the old window frames. She sat back on her heels to watch the fire take hold. As the draft roared up the chimney pipe and the stove heated up, the metal creaked and crackled. Perro lay beside her, chewing on a stick of kindling.

Last night Trevor and Soryada had taken her out to dinner at the only restaurant in town where people dressed up. The one up on the highway in the hotel that belonged to her aunt's family. Lance had been spoiling her she'd realized as she choked down the ham steak special. He was always bringing home wild food from friends' freezers — huckleberries, salmon steaks, a venison roast — and he knew how to cook.

Not wanting to disappoint Trevor, she'd sawed and chewed and listened to his excited plans for the spring. Soryada, head down, mashed her food together and sculpted it into different shapes. The fork never rose to her mouth. Isabel had finally shoved her own plate aside. She'd leaned across the table. "When is it due?"

When they told her the date, she laughed and said New Year's Eve. She asked Soryada how she was feeling, told her how she shouldn't drink any alcohol even though she didn't really drink at all anyway, how she had to eat properly, get enough rest, but be sure to get exercise too. The same way she talked to all the girls she worked with, first time pregnant. And then it struck her. She was going to be a grandmother. A line of blood, a direct link with the baby growing inside the girl across the table, a girl who grew up in a place Isabel couldn't even imagine.

"Will my grandchild speak Spanish?"

Soryada spoke a soft phrase. "It's grandmother in my mother's language," she said. "I'll teach the child to say it. In Spanish also."

"*Abuelita*," Trevor said. He leaned back in his chair, his shirt straining across his chest. They'd be getting married, he said.

Isabel had smiled back against the thickening in her throat and, appointing herself the honorary mother of the bride as well as the groom, pulled Soryada into a hug. Part of her longed to tell them about Álvaro, wondering when she was going to hear from him, or about him. She tried to place him in a family portrait — standing behind Janna, a hand on her shoulder, Isabel on the other side. Speaking Spanish with Trevor and Soryada and her grandchild. She still saw herself in that portrait as a young woman, and Álvaro was a young man.

The fire finally got going and Isabel slipped upstairs to get dressed. Perro's claws clicked on the linoleum as he went into the kitchen where Lance was making a fancy breakfast to celebrate the news. She'd told him last night. He only went to Terrace every other weekend now, his access to Dustin restricted. In his quiet formal way, he'd apologized for his New Year's Eve behaviour.

She asked him if his drinking had anything to do with restricted access. Cause or effect. He'd hesitated until she told him a little about her own drinking. About Janna's anger and distrust. You do the one thing that makes sure you can't have what you want most, she said. They say it's the booze you want most, but it isn't that exactly.

He nodded. But she wasn't going to tell him that it was the man on the other side of the barroom table or beside her in the truck cab. There'd always been a man to drink with. And since Álvaro, there'd never been a man without the drink.

He didn't expect her to believe him, he'd said, but he'd never been what you'd call a drinker. He didn't really like what it did. His wife thought that was funny. She and her crew would return from a shift on the railroad and he'd come home to a party, Dustin pouring the beer. His anger and his fear for the boy an unwelcome rebuke. He still didn't really know how it happened, but she had friends who swore he was unfit. He didn't have many friends of his own. And once word gets out that you're a drunk, everything that happens has an explanation. Even his car accident. A moose on the road is always a good excuse, people say, and by the time they found him he'd have sobered up anyway. It's not that I don't ever drink, he'd said. But I'm not very good at it when I do. As she had seen. He'd leave at once if she wanted.

Instead, she'd offered to have his boy come — I'm used to boys, she said. It would be fun to have one around. He said he'd see what he could do. It was complicated at the other end.

It wasn't until Isabel stood looking at herself brushing up her hair into a twist, her mother's locket gleaming in the V of her new shirt that she realized he was courting her. And that she was interested. She smelled the eggs and toast with great pleasure. She hadn't felt this kind of anticipation since waiting for Álvaro's phone calls and twenty-two years is a long time.

Janna's birthday was in a month, she told Lance as she swallowed the eggs. She'd be twenty-one and most of the way through school on her way to some kind of a life. By the time Isabel was twenty-one, she was divorced with two kids and back home living with her dad. Maybe if she wrote her a letter, telling her about the baby and the wedding, she'd come home. For Trevor's sake at least.

She hadn't told Lance much about Janna. That's what she liked about him. He didn't pry. She hadn't told anyone about Alice looking for Álvaro. The way the church seemed to be stonewalling her. She was just wondering out loud how Jason would react to Trevor's news when someone knocked at the front door. Opening it to a blast of snow, she was surprised to see Alice. She'd usually be at mass this time on a Sunday. She was even more surprised to see someone behind her, a man wearing an old navy pea jacket like she hadn't seen since she was a kid, a black toque pulled down low. With the scar along his chin and another one splitting one eyebrow, he looked like a cross between a reformed junkie and a wrestler. Some Indian, maybe, on a wrestling-for-God mission.

She welcomed them into the crowded hallway.

"Just wait until you hear my news," she crowed, tucking Alice's scarf inside the sleeve of her coat and hanging both on a hook she'd cleared off. Turning to take the man's jacket, she waited while he pulled off his toque. His short hair stuck up in a mess of cowlicks. It would be a bugger to cut, she thought and even as she thought that, the man looked back at Isabel, his dark eyes alight, his mouth turning up into a tentative smile. Isabel stepped back, looking from him to Alice for confirmation of what she was already beginning to guess. They froze there, Alice and her friend, waiting. Isabel was waiting too, waiting for the emotion she could feel coming, she could almost hear its roar rising like trains did at night sometimes, roaring down the long straight stretch through town without slowing, coming closer and closer, a great thundering shudder that set the swampy ground trembling and rattled her old house so hard dishes fell and shattered.

She backed away from the concern on her aunt's face into the tangle of coats hanging on the hooks behind her and cried out with the same anger and loss she'd felt when the priest told her that young Father Álvaro had gone to Winnipeg where he was sorely needed and no he hadn't left her any messages. No messages for twenty-two years and now, without warning, this battered man.

Perro came scrabbling in, barking and jumping up to lick Álvaro's hands. He set the dog's paws down gently on the tumble of boots and coats. "Forgive me, Isabel. Alice tried to talk me out of appearing like this, but I insisted."

Isabel heard his voice, how the accent was almost gone. He looked from face to face. "Seeing Janna has made me impatient." He reached a hand toward her.

She jerked back and turned to Alice. "Did I hear that right? He's met her?"

Alice sighed and nodded.

"You can imagine my surprise." He tried to laugh.

Lance was standing in the doorway. He called the dog and squatted beside him, settling him with gentle strokes. "Do you need me, Isabel?"

She turned toward him and shook her head. She put a hand on each shoulder and turned him gently around, leaning her head onto his back and pushing him into the kitchen saying, "This is family stuff." They stood like that for a minute and then he was gone out the back door with the dog. Turning to invite the others in, she felt the draft on her back as if her skin had been laid bare. She wanted him back. She wanted to start the morning all over again, to retrieve the feeling of quiet possibility. She wanted his hand on her somewhere, the way he put it on the dog. She wanted him to still the anger bubbling up.

Álvaro followed her into the kitchen. "Isabel, Isabel, why didn't you tell me?"

"Oh, for heaven's sake," Alice said. "Give her a minute, Father." She pushed him into one of the chairs, the cooling cups of coffee and the half-eaten toast still littering the table. The open jar of gooseberry jam Alice had made.

"I don't know if I'm ready for this," Isabel said. She stared at him, sitting there in her kitchen, in the same chair she'd placed right there when she first moved into the house. Black circles of fatigue ringed his eyes and grey stubble speckled the dark skin. The scar on his chin ran down his throat and under the neck of his black T-shirt; his shoulders and arms strained its seams. He had bulked up since he was a young man. On one wrist a watch, on the other a woven bracelet. His fingers brushed at the crumbs on the table, pushing them into little piles.

"Still tidying things up, I see," she laughed and threw him a dishcloth. Alice filled the kettle and plugged it in. She pushed Isabel into the other chair and set about making toast and coffee.

Catching the wet cloth Álvaro felt a kind of vertigo, a frightening buzz of interference between him and his body sitting at this table, between himself and Isabel's stare. Remembering what Chris had taught him, he struggled to ground himself. He catalogued the things in Isabel's kitchen. A calendar picture of cows grazing in a golden field, snow on the high mountain beyond. A refrigerator covered with photographs. A poster of bright flowers. Beside each flower, shrivelled bulbs that looked dead. Dirt still clung to the roots and for a minute he saw the brittle hair of corpses.

He forced himself to look at her, but could not raise his eyes above the golden crucifix resting in the V of her shirt. It was a locket, he remembered, with someone's hair inside. Her mother's? All that remained of the figure carved upon it were thorns on the head and the nailed feet. Everything in between was smooth. Her hand came up to take hold of it, two fingers rubbing it. The skin on the hand was reddened, loose over the tendons. The polish on the fingernails was chipped. How could these be the fingers he had so joyfully taken into his mouth? He looked up at her mouth saying his name. He looked away, remembering where that mouth had been.

"Well," she said, grinning. "Here you are."

His mouth opened and closed. Why, he wanted to ask again, hadn't she told him? The two plates littered with scraps of toast, the man with the dog. It seemed an explanation. He spoke. "She doesn't really look like me, does she? I guess you couldn't be sure she was mine."

Alice groaned.

"And you are?" Isabel's smile disappeared, her voice cold.

"I have a sister," Álvaro said, stumbling over the words. "She looks exactly like her."

Isabel picked up a lid from the table and screwed it onto the jar. "Lots of girls look like Janna. You go out to the reserves and you see all these pretty little part-Indian girls, the slim ones, they look just like her."

"There's this patch of white hair." Álvaro's hand touched his right ear. "Just here."

She picked at something stuck to the outside of the jar, her eyes down. "So what does she say?"

"She doesn't know."

Isabel looked from Álvaro to Alice. "Could someone please tell me what's going on?"

Alice told her how Álvaro had been staying with a Catholic family near the university, people who also happened to know her friend, Amy Myerson. How she'd met Janna at school and brought her there. Álvaro had seen her, had heard that Isabel was her mother. He'd figured it out, but hadn't known what to do.

Isabel slumped in her chair and covered her face. "My God, what a mess."

"Why a mess?" asked Alice. "Isn't this what you wanted? Here he is. It's no coincidence. It's meant to be. Now figure it out."

They both stared at her.

"Oh, I get it," Isabel said. "The God thing." She shook her head. "No offence, Alice, but I don't see God in much, much less this. I'll leave that to you two."

Álvaro said nothing, the buzzing in his ears growing louder. He hadn't thought of God for what seemed like months now. When he prayed it was to something else altogether, something he'd have to think about when his feet were back on the ground, when he wasn't in free fall. He pushed back his chair.

"Where are you going?"

He pointed upstairs.

"Oh. Yes. I guess you know where it is."

They both listened to him slowly climb the stairs, his tread that of an old man.

"Isabel?" Alice hesitated. Isabel looked at her.

"What?"

"What did happen between you and Janna?" Alice was determined. "One day you're friends, the next day she's moved out."

Isabel pushed back her chair and stacked up the magazines sliding off the end of the table. She was not going to tell her about the night her careful defences had crumbled. The night outside the bar, that boozy excitement against that brick wall, still warm from the day's sun, a yes, yes, yes, heightened by the fear of discovery that always gave it the edge she liked. The pub doors opening and closing. The headlights just missing them. The eyes watching from the parked car. The terrible moment she'd realized it was Janna.

She stood with her back to her aunt, aligning the photos on the fridge. "Alice, I don't need anyone's help to hurt my children. I'd hoped that finding Álvaro might go some way to making amends for some of my screw-ups with Janna, but now when he's right here, I don't see how. We might need her, but she doesn't seem to need either of us."

"I guess she's maybe not doing as well as you thought."

Isabel's stomach flipped. She turned, one hand full of magnets, the other holding photographs. "What?"

Alice looked away. She told her about the hospital calling Amy Myerson, how she'd failed one of her exams, and how she'd dropped some classes after she'd been in the hospital.

"The hospital? What happened?" The magnets and photographs fell in a heap on the table.

"She's not talking much, I guess."

"Except to Amy? Why her? Janna never even liked her. And the boys? Isn't she talking to them?"

"One of your boyfriends, right?" Álvaro was standing in the doorway. "Or maybe one of the brothers." He'd seen it a hundred times, seen the children on the streets because they were safer there than in their homes. "One of them tried something with her, didn't he? That's why she doesn't come home."

The jar of gooseberry jam flew before he could duck. It glanced off his shoulder and crashed into the sink full of dishes beside him. Splinters hit his cheek. The coffeepot fell off the counter and shattered on the floor.

"You filthy-mouthed pig," she said. "Don't you dare go near my daughter."

He backed away, glass crunching under his boots. "They were right."

"They?" Isabel turned to her aunt frozen by the back door, one hand covering her mouth. "And who might they be? What might they be right about?" She screamed, "What aren't you telling me? What's happened to Janna?"

Álvaro's outrage almost carried him through. But the terror in her voice cut open the air and darkness leaked in. He looked down at the leather of his boots, dark against the blue and yellow squares of linoleum, wondering why the crunching fragments of glass didn't cut his feet. He felt something at his thighs and put out one hand to hold the table. He struggled to come back, back into the understandable anger in the ordinary kitchen where the windowsills were piled with envelopes and gardening magazines and striped leaves trailed from a salt-stained pot. But a fragment of a broken cup, gold shining on the curve of its rim, was lodged in the dusty foliage and he was gone again, gone to the place they'd dumped him, kicking him off the road into the garbage-filled ditch.

When a hand reached out for him, he scuttled under the table and curled up as small as he could. Lord, open my lips, he said, waiting for the cup. Lord, open my lips, he said, waiting for the cattle prod. Lord, open my lips, he cried, the Spanish bile in his mouth.

†

It was Thomas Coleman who knocked on Janna's door and took her away from the room she'd spent two days cleaning, forcing herself down on her hands and knees to wash the floor, forcing herself to stretch to reach the corners of the high window, the broom searching the ceiling for cobwebs that weren't there. Taking a shower every couple of hours with the lights off so she couldn't see the bruises. Wearing long sleeves and a scarf, a towel hung over the big mirror beside the door so she didn't surprise herself. Telling herself that she wasn't really hurt, this was how a rugby player felt after a rough game. But she had to struggle not to cry when she opened the door to Thomas Coleman's big grey eyes blinking behind his thick lenses.

He opened her closet door, handed her a sweater, her scarf, and her jacket and took her away from the smell of bleach. She'd told herself she wasn't hungry and believed it until he sat her on a bench in the pale February sunshine and gave her a slice of cheese, crackers, and half a pear. A flask of strong coffee. While she ate and drank, he explained that he'd very much appreciate it if she could come to some accommodation with her family and friends because his house had become the conduit for communications about her state of mental and physical health and he preferred people to have data to support their speculations. Apparently she'd upset Amy somehow and his wife was muttering that it was none of their business, but damned if they weren't all yammering away about her and disturbing his peace. And here he finds her limping around with a split lip.

She found herself telling him some of what had happened. He gave her a large handkerchief and when she was finished crying took her to the campus rape crisis centre. He was gone when she came out into the quiet reception area and stared, bereft, at a poster describing the symptoms of STDs. She wanted to talk to him, to get away from the doctor with her warm hands and kindness, the suggestion that she fill out a police report, the request for names and addresses of family and friends. Could she put down his name on the forms, she wanted to ask. But he was gone and she was left with prescriptions for painkillers and tranquilizers with a promise of antidepressants if she wasn't feeling better in a couple of weeks. The door opened, the poster disappeared, and there was Amy. Her hair was tied up in little pigtails, her ears, eyebrow, and nose glittered with silver rings. She wore a bright vest over a heavy wool dress hanging down to her knees, high wool socks, and hiking boots, and drew Janna into an embrace that dug loops of orange and red prayer beads into her bruised breasts.

"Stupid twat," Amy said, "you need Friendship 101 for Christ's sake." She drove her to the high-ceilinged house she shared with three artists, the entrance half-blocked by blue recycling bins and dozens of shoes and jackets, the big front rooms empty of everything but a couple of benches and huge fabric hangings. She sat Janna down in the kitchen clutter, heated a bowl of thick soup, and waited while she slurped down its strong tastes of curry and cilantro. Even as she opened her mouth to speak, Janna realized that she hadn't cried in front of anyone since she'd left home promising herself never to look or sound like her wailing, angry mother. Until today. And now, for the third time.

She told Amy about David, Professor Coleman's nice little protégé, about how she'd spiked his coffee.

"You moron," Amy said.

"I'm not a very good judge of character, I guess." She tried to joke. "Look at my friends."

"I must have missed him." Amy said. "Thank God. He sounds like a dangerous creep." She'd ask around about him, she said. He needed to be stopped.

"I think he's had his fun. I don't want him coming back at me." Janna didn't want to talk about how afraid she still was, how she didn't want to go outside. She didn't want to turn a corner and run into the immaculately dressed David Miro and see his venom.

"Yes," Amy said, "you'll have to be careful. We can keep you here. Or you can stay at Greg's. It's closer to the campus. And we can doctor you up a bit."

Two minutes into Amy's description of a Mayan healing ritual, a sudden yawn split the cut on Janna's lip and she couldn't stop yawning even as she dabbed at the blood with a tissue. Amy took her upstairs to a small room and a futon heaped with blankets. Janna burrowed under the covers into the warmth of her exhaustion, an exhaustion and release so profound it rocked her with the movement of a boat on a calm lake, the faint motion nudging her in and out of consciousness even as she sank deeper and deeper into a sleep peopled with the sound of voices, footsteps, doors, and running water. Somewhere at the bottom of the night, she dreamt she was in her bedroom in Smithers, the house shaking as a train rumbled past. The squeal of metal wheels slowing on the metal tracks and the final whoosh of the train's stopping. She woke to find herself standing in the doorway to Amy's room, Amy propped up on one elbow in her bed, blinking at her.

"The trains," she said.

Amy yawned. "The tracks are just out back. Bastards are supposed to be quiet at night."

"Back home, when the trains woke me up, I'd crawl in with my mom."

Amy threw back the covers." First good idea you've had in ages," she said.

"I miss her," Janna said, sliding in, the tears coming again.

"Of course you do," Amy said, wiping Janna's eyes with the long sleeve of her nightshirt. "We all do. Now go to sleep."

†

Isabel swept the shards and puddling coffee into the dustpan, wondering what Alice and Álvaro had expected. What she had expected. Falling into each other's arms? She swept and mopped, focussing on the broken glass. The open jar of peanut butter, the can of coffee, and the unbuttered toast, all went into the garbage. The litre of milk went down the drain. Every unbroken dish needed washing. Wiping and rinsing, wiping and rinsing, she ran the water hot and fast, trying to drown out the sound of Alice's voice and Álvaro's weeping in the living room. The dishcloth glittered and her fingers were speckled with little cuts. She rinsed out the kettle twice, filled it, plugged it in, and was making tea when Alice returned.

"He's asleep," she said. "He'll be all right."

"Thank God." Isabel swirled the teapot, anxious for the drink's warmth. Outside the snow had stopped falling.

"I tried to talk him out of that entrance," Alice said.

Isabel nodded. Sunlight slipped through a crack in the clouds and the smashed glass glittered in the sink, on the counter, on the floor, even a sliver in Alice's hair. When Isabel moved to flick it away, she flinched. Isabel dropped her hand to her side. She refused to apologize. Everything he'd said since he walked in that door had been an insult. Her anger made some kind of sense. But not his response. "Is he mentally ill?"

Alice tried to explain what Eloise had told her about the torture, the flashbacks.

"Why didn't he go to the police?" Isabel finally asked.

"It's the police who do it. The police and the army. People up here have no idea." Her face was old and tired, her voice weary. All those church conferences she went to, Isabel thought. All those bulletins she photocopied. Stacks of them at her house, in her car. Isabel oblivious. The whole world oblivious.

"Hundreds of thousands of people have been murdered in Guatemala — it's as if half of the people north of Kamloops tortured, shot, or hacked to death the other half, one subdivision at a time. Children. Babies. Pregnant women."

Isabel felt cold on the back of her neck, as if someone dead was standing behind her, breathing. "Is that what happened to Soryada's family?"

"Yes. If she'd stayed, she'd have been killed. Or worse."

It was as if a needle was passing through Isabel's skin, an umbilical cord of pain connecting her to the baby inside Soryada. "But that's terrible," she cried. "Why don't they do something about it?"

Alice poured them each a cup of tea. "They do do something about it. Father Álvaro was part of the group investigating the massacres. That's why he was so badly hurt. So he'd stop."

"And he has stopped?"

"Yes, I guess you could say he has. It made him ill. Something triggers it and he relives it. It's like he's there again. Not just remembering it, but there, getting tortured."

Isabel closed her eyes: the yelling, the broken glass.

"He's been getting treatment. It was going well, I guess, but then Janna walked into the house where he was staying. She looks exactly like his sister."

"You don't think of a priest having a family, but, Alice, are they all tangled up with this?"

Alice shrugged. "I don't really know. He doesn't talk about them."

Isabel had often imagined another life for Janna, one in which her mom and dad were together. Never here, in this house though. It was always somewhere else, away from all the small town talk. But she'd never had one thought for Álvaro's family. Not one. Janna could have been down there with them. She could be dead.

"Alice," she said, near panic again. "What has happened to Janna?"

†

Álvaro woke out of a dream of *la finca's* kitchen, of his mother putting wood into the firebox, the sparks bright in the dark afternoon, the rain clouds heavy over the mountains. Keeping all her secrets. She had been happy, they had told him when he went to her village after she died. She was very proud of her son. The fire in Isabel's stove flickered behind the smoky glass. On the wall, a row of photographs, Isabel's three children in each of them. The young boys holding Janna as a baby, the teenagers lounging at the imperious ten-year-old's feet, the still older boys bending to help her blow out a dozen birthday candles. Then they were young men holding her, laughing, stretched out in their arms. One tall, pale, and angular. The younger one darker, stocky, his Indian nose flattened against his cheeks. And always placed clearly at the centre of their world, Janna, a cloud of dark hair around the face that was also Clara's, the white streak above her ear.

He had no rights. None at all. He knocked on the closed kitchen door. Chairs scraped the floor and Alice opened the door. Isabel turned from the sink, the water rushing down the drain with a great swooshing sound.

"At least there's one thing around here that works," she said.

"I'm sorry for what I said," he wanted to get it out before he lost his nerve. "I had no right. I have seen too many damaged children and I'm afraid I've come to assume the worst."

"Well, from what Alice has told me, you've been damaged yourself."

He pulled out a chair and sat down. "Janna has no idea who I am, but you need to know what happened." And he told her about the attack. About her refusal to go to a doctor. To go to the police. "These men, she seemed to know them. I didn't understand it."

Hope drained out of Isabel and an emotion she could only identify as anguish constricted her heart.

"I'm so sorry," Álvaro said again. "Everything I tell you makes it worse. But I don't know what to do. If I was just a stranger, I could help. But with this secret, I am terrified."

"You're terrified? I left her a dozen messages. I bought her a plane ticket she never used. Half of Vancouver knows she's in trouble but no one will tell her mother. No wonder you all think I pimped her out to my boyfriends or something, for her to treat me like that."

She grabbed a jacket from the hallway, stepped into some shoes, and opened the door. "What I want to do is park myself on her doorstep until she lets me in. But I tried that once before and it wasn't very pleasant. Maybe you should do it. There's probably a seat on the afternoon plane."

"You can go too," Alice said. "I can buy your ticket."

Isabel shook her head. "I need some time to think this through. Right now it just seems I'll screw things up more."

She walked out into the cold sunshine.

†

Janna woke to the smell of coffee and toasted bread and a house empty of people. The kitchen was sticky with the remnants of several breakfasts and she filled the sink with soap and water and dirty dishes. As she washed and wiped and tidied, she looked out the window through a dusty jungle of leaves into a backyard of knee-high grass and stalks of dead-looking vegetation coated with sparkling frost. Small brown birds scavenged at their roots, rising and falling in little waves. A crumbling cement path led to a sagging back gate that opened into a jumble of rusted metal and dead grass, a high chain-link fence topped by razor wire and the train yards beyond. Scattered throughout the brown and tangled mess, clumps of daffodils, their stalks hidden, poked yellow trumpets into the sunlight. She wanted to tidy up the kitchen counters, sort out the clutter on the back steps, and take a machete out into that wasteland. She wanted to phone her mother and ask her to come help clear away the weeds choking the flowers. She imagined Isabel at work, picking up the ringing phone from the square pillar behind the store's cash registers and saying, "How can I help you?"

A door banged open and Amy was there with bags, books, Greg, and a plan.

"I was just going to phone Isabel," Janna said.

Amy stared at her. "Wow."

†

That afternoon Isabel stood outside watching the snow freeze on the linden bracts. She reached up a finger and flicked a silver drop off the branch. It tinkled into the frozen compost. She did not want to go back into the house. Lance's unasked questions. His tender distance.

She'd already pretty much lost Jason. And now it seemed she'd lost Janna too. And her half-remembered dream of Álvaro. Tucked away somewhere, under all the anger, her one true love. Isabel almost laughed, trying to imagine all of them sitting on couches somewhere, around a coffee table, passing a plate of sandwiches. She flicked another drop off the branch, then another. She hadn't told Alice about Trevor and Soryada's baby. The good news. Alice would be thrilled. A grandchild from two parents who loved each other, who seemed to know what they were getting into. She couldn't imagine dropping her own little bombshell into the midst of that happiness.

The back door opened and Perro ran to dance around her. Behind her, she felt Lance's attention like the press of air against her back. She did not know if she liked the feeling or not. She wished it was morning again, that she was just setting the match to the fire. Before she realized Lance was courting her. Before Álvaro. Lance put a jacket over her shoulders.

"Janna always wanted a dog," she said. "I told her they were too much trouble. That I'd just be fighting with her to clean up after it." She shivered now, finally feeling the cold. "She saw a man at the bus depot once, when we were picking up Trevor from some job, and this man had a dog hidden away in his shirt pocket. It was that tiny. A pink nose, whiskers, ears, and eyes poking out. A big man, loose-boned, you know, the way his shirt hung off his shoulders, a fisherman, I think, on his way to Rupert, and she just reached up and patted that dog, talking a mile a minute to it, asking it how it liked the bus trip and if it was hungry or needed a pee, just chatting away, she must have been about ten, her hair pulled back in barrettes, a little pink T-shirt that had a sparkly heart on it, pink shorts, and little silver thongs with a pink heart at each big toe, she'd flick those toes up and down to make the sparkles in the heart catch the light, and she was as happy to see that man and dog as if she was there to pick up her very own dad from the bus."

Isabel let the tears run. From behind, Lance put his arms around her. She stiffened at the strangeness of it, his height hers exactly, his body warm against hers. He held himself very still, just heat against her back and finally she said, "Where did she go? Where did that little girl go?"

Behind them, in the house, the phone rang and rang. Neither one of them moved. A wind whistled through the electric wires strung along the alley. More frozen drops tinkled down to the ice below.

"Now come inside," he said, squeezing her once before letting her go.

She turned and followed him up the three stairs to the back deck and into the house.

†

When the man's voice invited her to leave a message, Janna snapped her phone shut.

"No one there?"

"Some man asking me to leave a message. Has she got a live-in boy-friend now?"

"She's just renting out your room," Amy said. "Some guy with a girlfriend in Terrace. I met him at Christmas. You can try later. Now let's go get your spirit back."

Greg dropped them at the path to her residence. The leaves were pat-terned with frost, and the girls' breath hung in small white clouds. Janna's running shoes were wet, her feet cold.

"About here," she said, pointing to the bare patch of ground running beside a hedge. Wooden fence posts stuck out of the foliage every few yards.

A scruffy little path littered with cigarette butts, invisible to most of the residence windows. Under Amy's directions, she built a small ring of stones around two large flat ones Amy produced from her shoulder bag. Amy crouched and opened her bag, pulling out sticks of kindling, a knife, dried grass, a packet of red powder, a small flask of clear liquid, and matches. Janna spread out the cedar fronds Amy had instructed her to break off on the way to the path.

"It's like church," Janna said. Her voice was strained, almost a giggle. "Or like playing make-believe."

"Don't you start," Amy warned her. "Any kind of cleansing starts with intention and then incorporates smoke from sacred plants — we've got sage, sweet grass, copal, and the cedar. That ought to get things going."

Amy threw the match on the pyramid of herbs and wood. The liquor exploded into flame and thick smoke billowed up. Janna moved into its path as instructed and unzipped her jacket, letting the smoke drift across her body and up into her face. Keeping her back to the buildings, she unbuttoned her shirt and felt the cold air sting her nipples. Swearing when she saw the bruises, Amy fanned the smoke in her direction, saying her name over and over. Janna Catherine Lee. Janna Catherine Lee. Janna Catherine Lee.

The fragrant smoke brushed like soft feathers across her skin and something sweet and strong slipped in through her nostrils, tightening her throat and sinking deep inside her lungs, her blood, and out into the nerves and muscles of her arms and legs. She looked down at the body she had kept so carefully covered, at the pale patches between the mottled purples and reds, the bruised nipples, the ribs jutting out. The fingerprints encircling her wrists reminded her of David's tattoos, of his girlfriend's neck and wrists; goosebumps prickled every hair.

She closed her eyes and listened to Amy say her name until it blended with the sounds of the traffic on the road and the voices of students passing just a few yards away. She wondered if anything had changed.

"Any brilliant illuminations?" Amy finally asked.

"What exactly would that feel like?"

"Point taken."

"I do feel better. Not so afraid."

"Might have worked better if we'd thrown on a couple of fat weenies," Amy said.

Janna burst out laughing. "A wiener roast. Come to think of it, I am hungry."

"Well, that's another first."

As they emerged from the evening darkness into the orange illumination of the courtyard in front of Janna's residence, Amy called out to a man walking their way. She pulled Janna toward him. Janna stared at him. It was the man who'd rescued her. He was wearing the same thick navy wool jacket and black toque. Black jeans and running shoes.

"You remember Janna, Father Al. You were there when she made that memorable exit from Coleman's."

That was where she'd seen those eyes before — looking up from his plate, horrified as she listened to Thomas Coleman talking about rape. When he refused Amy's invitation to coffee, ducked his head, and walked away, he said nothing about rescuing her. Why was she relieved? She tried to keep her voice disinterested. "I've seen him around. Is he taking courses?"

"He went through some bad shit in Guatemala. Those scars are from torture. He's having some crisis of faith, I think. Seeing a counsellor, trying to decide what to do with his life."

"He's a priest?"

Amy shrugged. "Who knows anymore? He may be on his way out. He doesn't seem to be doing much of anything right now. He was great with the street kids down there. He'd go anywhere to haul one out of trouble, but he wouldn't take any crap from them either."

Janna wondered what you did if you'd been a priest all your life and then wanted to stop.

"He told me that once you're a priest, well, you're pretty much always a priest, even if you quit. You take this perpetual vow and in God's eyes, you're always one of his. Even the ones who've gone and gotten married. Crazy, eh?"

Janna claimed exhaustion and hugged Amy. Thanks, she said and promised to try Isabel again.

When the elevator door closed, Janna hugged herself, as if the smoke on her clothes and in her hair would keep her safe. Her room smelled of bleach. She opened the window until it touched one of the branches of the skeletal trees lining the walkways leading away from her residence. Under the shelter of an awning on the adjoining building, two people stood, smoking. The fear prickled through her. She'd seen the priest there at least twice. He'd been watching her even before David grabbed her.

She pulled the bottle of painkillers out of her bag. The blister pack of tranquilizers. Set them on the counter beside her computer. She was not over-reacting, she told herself. She did not need a pill. He'd been kind, but there was something screwy about him. He was not, she told herself, dangerous. That didn't mean he wasn't creepy.

What does a sane girl do when she's worried, she asked herself, looking at the tranquilizers. She doesn't take a pill. She pulled Christmas girl from her pocket and sat her on her pillow. Then she pulled her phone out of its little plastic pocket on the strap of her pack, took a deep breath, and dialled Isabel. Holding that breath through the message, she wasn't sure if she wanted some-one to pick up or not. She spoke to the machine. Can we talk, she said, and left her number.

19

Álvaro spent the flight wondering how he could make it up to Isabel. To Alice, who'd paid for his ticket. How could he ever repay everyone? Get a job pumping gas? Translating tractor manuals? He could do that. Levers and pistons. Tires and transmissions. His future felt like a shrinking tunnel, the walls moving closer and closer together, his Catholic god shrivelling to a cartoon head bobbing on a dashboard, voice rising, speeding up into gibberish, a frenetic babbling. Isabel had joined the ranks of so many women he'd misjudged, his fears and fantasies punctured by the photos on the mantelpiece of her tiny living room. She was not what he thought she might be. She was not his. She was not Janna's. She was inside her own complicated skin. The only thing left was Janna. Isabel had given him that. He'd asked the taxi to drop him at the university.

His courage faltered when he saw her with Amy. They stood there through her awkward introductions, neither of them knowing where to look as Amy babbled about spirit cures and the benefits of copra. He had to remind himself that the young woman standing dishevelled and flustered, the cold bringing colour to her cheeks, was Isabel's daughter. His and Isabel's. She was not Clara, nor was she Clara's even though she had the same smell of smoke Clara often had when they were children. There was always something burning in Guatemala.

Still a priest, Amy had laughed when he warned her against dabbling in things she didn't understand. The light-heartedness of her dismissal and Janna's embarrassed refusal to acknowledge him quelled the vague fantasy he'd begun to build about slowly getting to know her, and discovering the truth together. A moment of shocked realization followed by sweet reconciliation. It was all he could do not to shout it out right then and there.

Later, he wished he had. He was putting away the breakfast dishes at the Colemans' when Margaret handed him the phone, her eyebrows raised in a question. Isabel. A different Isabel. A giddy rush.

"She phones me last night all shy and sniffly and I'm thinking, man, you move quickly and this is going to be easy, why did I wait so long when I realize she doesn't know. Some bad date has reminded her of her mother's several dozen bad dates and she thinks maybe I'm human after all." Isabel's words tumbled out louder and louder and Álvaro took the phone into the library, wandering around staring at the Aztec rugs hanging on the walls, barely hearing what she said, his heart thumping.

Could he maybe hold off talking to her? I'm coming down in a few weeks, she said, and we're going to get together and maybe I should be the one after all to tell her. He should understand her difficulty — all those years of hearing nothing, assuming he knew about Janna and didn't care, and then he shows up. He must understand, he must give them a little time. Her voice that of a parishioner trying to make a salvation deal with her priest.

"I asked her about the hospital and everything and she says she's doing okay now. Amy and a friend have been taking care of her. She's doing well in her classes, she's going to be fine."

Álvaro was suddenly tired of all the things in the Colemans' house. He was tired of paintings, of statues, of rugs, of masks, of vases of dead grass and huge pots of living plants. He thought longingly of the small room he'd been given at the provincial house. Sometime today, he'd pack his small suitcase once again and move back. Maybe he'd take one of the pills the psychiatrist had given him.

"Thanks for calling," he said, the priest's polite response. "I did you a disservice, appearing like that. Let's just keep talking. See how things go."

When he handed the phone back to Margaret, he turned away from her questions. He grabbed his jacket and walked out into the bright morning. A flock of small dark birds chattered and twittered in a tree drenched in shrivelled red berries. He stared at them for a moment, trying to see some pattern in the rise and fall of their movement. When they rose in one huge swirling streamer, he followed them down to the water and turned his feet toward the university.

20

JANNA RAN ON THE TREADMILL, wishing the bruises had faded enough for shorts and a T-shirt. Next week. She sweated through the stiffness in her calves and the tightness in her chest. But she was here and she was going to keep coming. She was going to again feel as good as she'd felt when she was on the high school track team. When the exercise increased her energy until she could do everything — work part-time, ace her school work, and go shopping with her mom. Even statistics would stick.

Through the window in front of her machine, she could see down to the bottom of the climbing wall and up to where it rose to the ceiling high above her head. Two people in helmets, tights, and T-shirts were roping up. She might sign up for lessons once she'd got everything sorted. She'd laughed at herself when she'd finished talking to her mom and sat down to make a list. Welcome back, Janna, she'd said.

The treadmill's timer beeped and she started her cool down. Maybe she could leave some flowers at Professor Coleman's office, thanking him for whatever it was he'd done to warn David off. No, she'd have them sent. She didn't know how much Amy had told him and didn't want to.

Below her, one of the climbers moved toward the wall. Then a figure spidered up from the other side; he was wet from the pool and barefoot, his big hands clamping onto the rocks like thinking creatures, his feet feeling and testing for holds. She held her breath as he paused right across from her, twenty feet off the floor where there were now four people yelling up at him. The long muscles threw lines of shadow along his arms; the curve of his buttocks showed through the wet shorts and his calves bunched and relaxed then bunched again as he pushed off and angled away from her, still climbing. He reached out and slapped the ceiling, then closed his eyes to let his feet feel their way down across the whole width of the wall until he was at the opposite floor shrugging his way through the little band collected at the door. Janna's treadmill beeped again, signalling the end of her session. She laughed with a kind of crazy joy, the zap of a kind of energy she hadn't felt for a long time. As she showered, she sizzled with it.

She didn't falter even when she saw Amy's friend, Father Al, standing bareheaded and windblown at the entrance to her residence. She'd been half expecting him. He wasn't anything to be afraid of, she told herself, glad to see the warmth in his eyes. He'd helped her, he'd saved her, really. When he asked if he could speak to her in private, she invited him upstairs.

He hovered in her doorway as she hung up her coat and pulled the chair out from her desk. Chattering to fill his silence, she set him on the seat, poured him a glass of ginger ale, and offered him a granola bar. She was going to move out next semester, she thought. This was ridiculous, this cramped little room with the bed, the clothes, her Tampax box on the counter. Everything on display.

The man's awkward silence reminded her of Greg. The pressure building. Why had he come? She thanked him again for his help and asked for contact information should she need him as a witness. She didn't plan to press charges, but just in case. Otherwise, she was quite all right. He sat down, holding the slip of paper and pen she'd handed him.

He opened his mouth, about to speak, but she kept going. "Amy tells me you're thinking of leaving the priesthood. That must be a difficult transition."

He set down the pen and paper. Then he reached up and took her hand and pulled her down to sit in the chair across from him. He took both her hands in his and ran his thumbs across her knuckles, across each one of her fingernails, smoothing back her cuticles. One finger brushed the shadowed bruises still on her wrists. The warmth of his hands, their roughness, unnerved her. She tugged lightly, but he held on.

"Look," she said, pulling harder. "You're making me very uncomfortable here. You're going to have to let go."

He finally looked up at her. "I'm really here to talk about your mother." His voice cracked.

"My mother?" Janna blinked. "You know Isabel?"

"I think you could say that," he began.

She remembered Amy's story of the priest at her door in Guatemala. This same priest, telling her that her mother had died. Oh no. Not Isabel. Not now. "What's happened to her?" She clutched at him.

His hands were still stroking hers, soothing, like she was a child. She stared at them in terror, the thumbnail suddenly in perspective. The way it curved around the finger, deeply embedded with perfect cuticles.

"No, she's fine. It's not that."

She turned her own hands over, turning his with them and looked at his fingernails.

"We've both been trying to figure out the best way to tell you…" he broke off, uncertain.

Roaring, everything roaring. She looked at their hands tangled up together and struggled to extract her fingers from his grasp, from the fists they'd formed. She and Trevor used to play this game when they were little, her little fingers trying to pry open his fist to see what treat he held inside. She saw her mother's hand reaching down to take hers as they walked home from school, home from buying an ice cream cone, as they crossed the railway tracks coming home from the lake. She saw that same hand turn hers over and trace the lifeline in her palm. Her father's hands, Isabel had said. She had her father's hands. She flung Álvaro's hands away and jumped to her feet.

"You sneaky bastard," she hissed, shoving him toward the door. "Following me around like some pathetic pervert. And Isabel. All sweetness and apology. What a pair of cowards." She pushed him out into the hallway, glad for the anguish on his face. Doors opened and a few kids stuck their heads out.

"Why don't you both just die," she cried out. "Just fucking die!"

Part III

21

ISABEL WOKE UP IN THE BACK SEAT of Trevor's crew cab, eight hours into the drive to Vancouver. They'd finally left the remnant snow behind, snow that had come late and piled up so deep it was still blanketing the shaded corners of her garden. But there was heat in the sun now, and the bulbs she had planted at the ranch would be poking up under the snow-covered straw and her mother's peony would be stirring into tender red-stemmed life.

The rising sun cast long shadows through the pine trees and sagebrush scattered across the scoured hills of the southern Cariboo. She sat quietly, not wanting to interrupt the quiet music of Trevor and Soryada's Spanish.

When she was a little girl, it took three days to make this trip from Smithers — one day east on the gravel road to Prince George and then another two south on the narrow band of miraculous asphalt that led to Vancouver. Her dad would stop to talk business along the way: the smell of fresh-cut pine at a small sawmill, the fishing camp down on the Fraser flats, the horses at the ranch just south of 100 Mile. She'd wander with her mother through the herds of range animals, restless after being cooped up all winter.

Now, as they sped past all the little towns and ranches, she was still that girl wearing her new summer outfit — blue and yellow checked shorts and a white sleeveless shirt trimmed with matching checked collar and pockets. Her legs sticking to the white leather seat of the 1959 New Yorker, she'd sat between her mom and dad snapping her yellow flip-flops and pink bubble gum until her dad threatened to throw them out the window. She was still the teenager wearing her boyfriend's sweater, so long it almost covered her miniskirt, leaning back against the passenger door and stretching her legs across the seat of his graduation present, the 1968 Mustang, her white boots restless and teasing in his lap, her white lipstick leaving marks on each cigarette's golden filter. She'd egged him on to pass every car whose bumper they rode, Jason already flipping around inside her. And then Jason himself driving the 1987 Cadillac

De Ville to Vancouver for his dad, sneaking her and Trevor and Janna along so they could see, what was it, the Abbotsford air show?

All those girls flickered through her, images with no more substance than the glimpses of flattened grass around the boarded-up summer resorts and abandoned gas stations Trevor's truck flew past. She was speeding toward Janna and Álvaro, toward some reconciliation, she hoped. Or some further breaking apart. Whatever happened, on the other side of it, they would all be changed. This Isabel wearing a new pair of stretch jeans, a red cotton sweater, and a plaid fleece vest, half asleep in the back seat of her son's new Ford 350, was going to join all those other girls inside her.

A logging truck passed them going north, its tires catching the gravel on the shoulder and sending up a cloud of dust, an explosion of scattered light in the sun now clearing the eastern hills. She pulled her brush out of her purse and ran it through her hair. Trevor grinned at her in the rear-view mirror.

"Morning, Mom."

"Any more coffee in that Thermos?" she asked, a yawn cracking her jaw.

He shook his head. "We'll stop soon. Soryada needs to use the bathroom anyway."

Isabel leaned forward. "How's your tummy?"

Soryada turned to Isabel and shrugged. She never complained about the nausea but all she ate were crackers. The shadows around her eyes were dark splotches. Isabel reached out and pushed her forward so she could brush her hair. Soryada closed her eyes and bent her head against the tug of the brush.

"Any day now and you'll be feeling better," Isabel said. "Then we'll fatten up you and the baby both."

By the time they drove into Cache Creek, Soryada was asleep on the back seat. Trevor asked Isabel what exactly was going to happen in Vancouver.

"Janna's birthday party is still on, according to Amy. At some fancy house out near the university."

A road sign directed traffic east to Kamloops and the Trans-Canada. Trevor drove past it.

"Janna's going along with this?"

"It was her idea — she didn't want to see either of us alone."

"She wants an audience for some big scene?"

"Heaven help us."

They both burst out laughing, then choked it back, not wanting to wake Soryada.

"You still like this guy?"

She had tried to remember what it was about Álvaro she'd been so drawn to. Not just his beautiful voice with its exotic accent. His agility with a soccer ball enchanted boys and girls alike, and she hadn't been the only woman to notice the muscles under his sweat-soaked T-shirt. He'd been enthusiastic about sex too, as if by close attention, he could, in her body, decipher God's intent. She had felt holy, radiated with passion by a kind of language the men of the Bulkley Valley did not speak.

"There's nothing like anger to keep your feelings alive for someone. I mostly hated his oh-so-holy guts every time Janna asked me about him."

She wasn't sure what she felt now. "Do you remember him?"

Trevor shook his head and accelerated to pass a tanker truck. "Maybe I'll recognize him."

"Not likely. He looks nothing like he used to."

In her lowest moments, she'd imagined Álvaro a smooth talker cutting through the women in the Winnipeg parishes like a mower moving through the hay, leaving them strewn on the ground smelling sweet in the heat of summer. Whether or not he'd known about Janna, he was a coward for running away, the church like some rich parent saving its precious son from the trampy girlfriend. At other times, she had still dreamed of some kind of rescue. But the sight of his body crumpled and whimpering under her kitchen table had changed everything. She squirmed at the memory, at the way it diminished him. He had, she figured, suffered enough punishment for just about any sins he might have committed.

Trevor dodged through Cache Creek's light morning traffic, fiddling with the radio, looking for a sports report. He'd bought tickets to a Canucks game, extras for Isabel and Janna. It had seemed like a good idea when Isabel and Janna had their first careful phone call, planning the visit before she knew about Álvaro. Before Trevor knew.

Isabel had come home from work a couple of days after that phone call to find Lance spreading out maps on the kitchen table to show her where he'd gone on his first trip back in the field, a snowshoe hike to survey some slide damage on the Skeena. He'd been telling her how good it felt to be in the bush again. One arm rested on the table, his finger tracing his route on the map, his body tired and relaxed, his hair still wet from the shower. She'd envied the snow itself then, because she'd never seen him so engaged, his eyes clear and happy. When he asked about his son coming to stay over for the spring break, she'd said of course and pressed the play button on the answering machine. Trevor saying, what was this he heard about Janna's father? Amy saying, I've always said you were an amazing woman, Isabel Lee, but I am surprised at this one. But nothing like Janna is surprised. Don't worry, I'm right on it, even though it's probably going to get worse before it gets better. And then Janna on the last message, the flat voice of her worst anger saying please don't call because she did not want to waste the money it cost her to retrieve Isabel's messages and there was nothing she could possibly have to say that Janna wanted to hear.

Lance had poured her a glass of juice as she paced the house raging into the telephone, Perro following her, yelping when her angry feet shoved him out of the way. By the time she'd finished talking to Trevor, Lance had rolled up his maps and taken the dog for a walk. When Álvaro phoned to apologize, she was glad she could look through the window and see Lance turning the compost in the fading light, the sight of his body a charm against the anguish in Álvaro's voice. Against her own guilty relief that she hadn't been the one after all.

Someone else had broken the news and others worked hard to bring about a reconciliation. All she had to do was show up, she told herself as she'd cleaned the house and bought taco chips and pop for Dustin. He liked amphibians and computer games, Lance told her. And basketball. And as much as she found herself charmed by Dustin's unselfconscious questions about everything in her house — the photographs, the seedlings, the old-fashioned light switches — she was happy, she told herself, when Trevor picked her up that night, happy to put at least one entanglement behind her.

But once on the road, she realized with a hunger that could still surprise her, what she really wanted was to buy a mickey of whiskey and go for a ride in Lance's truck to some little lake in the bush where the ice had melted around the shore leaving an opening just big enough for a couple of ducks to paddle in. To park the truck and sip whiskey until the warmth ran from her belly down into what her mother called her girl parts, and fuck that man's body until all the metal they'd put in him heated up so he was as flexible as he must have once been. Melt the stiffness right out of his bones and make them both forget they had children tethering them.

Soryada rose up groaning from the back seat. Trevor pulled over and held her as she retched into the ditch. A few half-hearted flakes of snow drifted down from a cloud snagged on one of the canyon peaks. Isabel poured water for Soryada, worried for her and the baby. Snow swirled off the tires of the big tanker wheeling by, the whole pickup shuddering on the trembling ground.

This was shaking them all up, Isabel thought. They could all be broken by what came next, broken even more than they already were, even Dustin with his computer set up in her living room, his salamander in its cage on the mantel beside the photographs of her kids. He watched her with his father's eyes, trying to decipher where he might fit into this household. Whether she and Lance were lovers, knowing as well as she did all the possibilities of pain in forging these new links. Lance tried to reassure them both by acting as if everything was fine. Snowboard lessons up the hill. Videos. Dinner at friends of his ex's with kids Dustin knew. And somewhere in Vancouver, Álvaro and Janna.

She climbed down from the truck to give Soryada the front seat.

"Right about now, I'm tempted to cross the highway, stick out my thumb, and head out across Canada," she said to Trevor.

He opened the back door, his laughter a balm. "Not on your life." He lifted her inside, tickling her until she was laughing too.

"We're going to get this sorted," he said as the road dipped down beside the river, brown in its first flood. "No more sneaking around, no more secrets. We're going to all be in a room together and we're going to figure out how to get along. I'm going to tell Dad's family and, if you've got the brains I think you have, you're going to tell all your friends because once the moccasin telegraph is activated, word will spread fast."

Isabel tried to think it through. Alice knew and she'd know how to tell the rest of the family. Isabel would tell Jasmine and Alejandro when they got back from Costa Rica. Jasmine would tell Frank, wherever he was. As if he'd care. She wondered if Janna was in touch with any of her high school friends, if they'd already been told. "Oh God," she said. "What am I going to say to the women at work?"

"Maybe we should just put an ad in the paper," Trevor said. "Somewhere between the wedding announcements and the obituaries."

"The store should give me a raise. It'll be great for business."

Soryada spoke. "I have been reading the places where they say who has had a baby." She held up the Smithers newspaper, folded open to the classified section. "Maybe you could do that."

"Isabel Lee and Father Álvaro Ruiz would like to announce, belatedly, the birth of their daughter, Janna Catherine Lee-Ruiz," Trevor started.

Jason, Isabel thought. The last time she'd seen him was at New Year's. His silky hair under her fingers. "What about Jason?"

"I phoned him."

"You had no right."

"I had every right." Trevor was angry.

Soryada said something in Spanish. Trevor continued. "Janna's crying, asking me did we know all along? Were we laughing at her all those years?"

Trevor flipped his finger at a truck driver who passed him on the right, and accelerated past him again.

"The first thing I'm going to do when I meet the man is shake his hand and tell him thank God somebody finally let it out 'cause sure as hell you never were."

"I was getting ready to tell her."

"Bullshit," Trevor said, slapping the steering wheel.

Soryada put one hand on Trevor's arm, pointing to a rest stop. He shook her off and sped past it. She spoke up, insistent. The tension finally slackened in his shoulders. She touched him again and he flipped on the signal, nodding. They pulled off to the ragged edge of the asphalt under the pillars of a huge sign advertising a water slide. Trevor turned off the truck and spoke without looking at her.

"Jason asked me to tell you not to bother to call."

Isabel gulped.

"He said some things it will take a while to put right."

"I'm sorry," she said.

His T-shirt stretched over the broad back and a line of paler skin showed on his neck where she'd trimmed his hair. On one ear, the studs they'd teased him about when he first got them, glittered. Years ago now. Janna still living at home, happy when her brothers dropped by, all of them friends. Trevor and Jason swapping music, talking cars, electronics. Going fishing. She looked up at the cliffs rising on the other side of the river and tried to imagine herself a mountain sheep on the tiny paths Trevor had pointed out to her. If a sheep could keep an eye on her kids in that terrain, she ought to be able to negotiate her way through the next few days.

Trevor started the truck. "We'll just keep going for now and do what we can about Jason later."

Isabel's skin tingled with a thousand barbs. She wanted to jump out of the truck, cross the highway, and stick out her thumb. There'd be someone who would pick her up. At the very moment she most wanted to shake free of all her obligations, she also longed to feel a proprietary hand on her body.

The truck shuddered as a convoy of semis roared by.

†

Janna arrived first. It would be easier, she had told Amy, if she didn't have to make an entrance. As soon as she pushed open the back door, her anxiety diminished. The air smelled of fresh bread and furniture polish. Of emptiness. In the kitchen, the counters were covered in platters, bright cloths mounded over the heaping dishes for what Greg had taken to calling The Reunification Party. She trailed a hand along them on her way to the living room. Masks on the wall, plants, and a couple of couches arranged to face a fireplace. Logs ready to light. She moved into the hallway to the photograph of the two boys flinging themselves into the air. They're having fun, she told herself, trying to forget David Miro's voice pointing out the possible danger lurking under the water.

She pushed aside a bead curtain and looked into a small alcove at the end of the hall. A candle flickered under a crucifix. *El Colegio del Corazón Valiente* and *In Memoriam* were spelled out above it. Photographs of kids hung on either side — one with black eyes, a girl with a bruised face, a skinny little boy dancing ecstatically in water spraying from a hose, a bigger boy holding a soccer ball. Moises Osorio †1999. Juan Tzul †2000. Armand Guzman †1998. Emilia Estuardo †2000. Marta Barillas †2000. Three frames held flowers pressed under glass. Ana Elisabeth Yax †1998. Lucía Madriela †2000. *La niña* †1970.

Corazón Valiente. That was the name of his school in Guatemala City. A whirlpool swirled down into her stomach as she realized these children were all dead. She put one hand against the wall to steady herself. She tried to pronounce the names, wanting to hear them spoken out loud. They were all dead and the man who was her father would have known them. Talked to them, played with them, prayed with them, and fed them all while she imagined him driving a truck, or riding a bus on those empty northern roads. Baling hay or falling trees. All that time not knowing about her. The fact of Álvaro López Ruiz lodged in her throat and she couldn't force it back up or swallow it. Her father. How is it you could create a child and not know? What lunatic would devise such a system?

Janna had slammed the door in her face. She thought Amy had known he was her father and had been setting up their meetings, telling stories about what a great guy he was down there in Guatemala City.

"It's me or the goon squad," Amy had shouted through the door.

Janna ranted on the other side about how she'd lived her whole life politely answering women who kept asking her how old she was, when her birthday was, and watching them count backwards trying to figure out who had knocked up Isabel. Some of them must have known. That old priest telling her she was not a result of immaculate conception, and besides remember God made sure Mary had a husband when she had the baby Jesus, and there were some things best left unspoken, and he'd probably known himself, known and what? Laughed?

By this time, she'd opened her door and seen the fear on Amy's face, fear about Janna's sanity. When she'd told her that Father Álvaro Ruiz was her very own long-lost daddy, thank you very much, well, no actor could have faked that stunned disbelief.

"You're not the only one who feels stupid," Amy had said. "Talk about a cluster fuck."

Janna had refused to be babied. The anger scoured her into clarity. A haphazard DNA cocktail was not going to dictate her destiny. She went to class and went to the gym, Greg throwing exam questions at her as they rode gym bikes together. She sent the flowers to Thomas Coleman's office. She signed up for the intersession courses she needed to get back on track with school. She'd said she didn't want to talk to either Álvaro or Isabel and neither of them tried to contact her.

It was when she phoned Trevor, left a message, and didn't hear from him for a week that her anger shifted into uncertainty. Into fear. He had been a shield from Isabel all these years, but also a link. Assuming the door would be open whenever she chose to return. If she lost Trevor, she didn't know what she'd do. When she phoned him again, she could hear the weariness in his voice. Other voices were raised in the background. And she realized his fatigue might be coming from places that had nothing to do with her. That he might well have his own problems.

"I wouldn't mind getting out of here," he said, "and I don't want to waste those hockey tickets. What do you think?"

"Come," she'd said. "Come. And bring Mom. We'll get this sorted, somehow or other." And she hung up before she started crying, crying in big shuddering sobs that scared her. She was so tired of pretending she was fine. She was so tired of feeling, period. She was so tired. She hoped that if she saw Álvaro and Isabel in a room full of people, she might get used to it. If she overheard them talking, saw the way he put food on his plate, forked it into his mouth. The ways you get to know a stranger. Strangers.

Janna drifted up the stairs and looked into a bathroom still damp from a shower, steam on the mirror. Toothbrushes spilled from a cup beside the sink and thick towels were crammed onto the towel racks. Then the room where she'd been put to bed back in January. Where all the kitchen sounds came up through the heating vent. She crossed the hall to the master bedroom with its double bed neatly covered with a bright blanket. Under an ornate crucifix in dark wood, another candle burned. Janna stopped in front of the big window looking through bare branches over the tops of the houses to the water below, and ran her fingers across the dusty top of the ornate chest set under the window. It was decorated with painted carvings of the slender leaves and creamy calla lilies her mother was always trying to bring into bloom. On the top, a series of photographs of the boy, Joseph. A lock of hair curled up inside the frame.

A mother cherishing a child, she thought, and remembered the line of photos on the mantel in her mother's house. From somewhere, the air from an open window lifted the hair on her neck. She followed it to the room across the landing, to the single bed with its one white pillow, a colourful blanket, and the edge of a white sheet folded over. Over the bed, the open window. Outside, a tree's new leaves were unfurling. She knelt on the bed and reached for one, wanting to feel its veins beneath her fingers. She remembered again her hands in her mother's.

"I hope you have a good life," she'd said to Janna, "because it looks like you're going to live a long time."

The young leaf was smooth, its veins mere promises under the translucent green. Janna lay back, her head on the pillow, and twirled the leaf between her fingers. She tried to imagine what was coming after this moment, what kind of life. She'd been reading about Guatemala. She was terrified of what she read, but she couldn't stop. It was everything Amy ranted about, and more. It was heartbreaking. Good people tortured, murdered. Lies about everything. People she was related to lived there, negotiated their way through the chaos and violence. Or didn't.

Far below, a phone rang. Three times, and it stopped, the silence spreading back through the house. It was then she noticed the painting at the foot of the bed.

Oh, she thought. It was as if something alive was in the room with her. A pale girl standing on the rim of a bathtub dressed in summer shorts and a T-shirt looked out of the picture. In the blue behind her, a fish and a bird, upside down. The girl held her hands out for balance and Janna felt herself teetering, the porcelain cold against the arches of her own feet, feet that were big and clumsy. Here I am, the girl seemed to be saying with her hands and feet and hair, her eyes and mouth. Here I am. What do you see?

Janna wanted to cry because the girl was somehow not put together right. Her head was too big and her skin was so blue and cold, Janna wanted to take her jogging in the sunshine until the sweat shone on her collarbones and a flush came to her cheeks. It's what she should be doing, Janna thought. She should be running while she still had the chance, running until she heated up into something real, something alive.

Instead, she settled herself down to wait for the others to arrive.

†

Álvaro slid down to sit on the top stair and watched Janna sleeping. She was what he'd given up for Lent. Promised to keep his distance until the appointed hour. He could hardly breathe. In her face he saw all the girls he'd gone to identify at the morgue. He saw the fragility of the cheekbones, the narrow bridge of the nose, and the smooth line of the jaw and knew exactly how they could be shattered, knew how easily the slender cord stringing the knuckled vertebrae in the young necks could be snapped.

He'd listened to their stories come out in scattered bursts and jangled laughter, in threats of revenge and promises of good behaviour. Orphans, many of them, their parents dead in *la violencia*. Others were runaways, some with stories of abuse that had stranded them in jagged indifference, legs jittering, elbows and knees scabbed, and fingers picking at tufts of hair, scratching at sores. Stories that left him raging at the indifferent politicians, at the bored policemen, and, often, at the parents. He'd prayed for them, days and weeks and months of prayer. All offered up for those children and none for his own. In all those years, not one.

Clara at the morgue, her voice in his ear, "How do you confess a sin if you don't even know you've committed it?" It was seeing her face so clearly in Janna's that made him realize how deeply his transgressions were embedded in his own ignorance. The way the puff of white hair feathered around her ear, the deep indentation of the lobe, the gold stud.

If Janna woke up and looked over her shoulder at him, he would see Clara's debutante portrait, the one he'd seen the day he left for the novitiate in Mexico City, steadfast in his dutiful sense of giving her up, a novice in the first flush of faith. If Janna spoke, he would hear Clara's voice, the way it sounded when he phoned her to ask if he could visit and congratulate her on the children she'd so kindly adopted. How fierce she'd sounded about those children. How determined to prevail over what he pitied as her barrenness. His sense, even stronger after the torture, of holding truth as a grenade. Three grenades. The truth about the children; the truth about Vinicio; the truth about himself. Not knowing she had a secret of her own stitched up in her scarred uterus.

He had finally seen her. Just a year ago, he realized, stunned at the distance he had travelled since that meeting. It was unexpected, a week or two after the chaos of the Easter celebrations when Emilia went missing. He'd heard they had an unidentified female at the central morgue, a very young one found in one of the ravines. He draped his stole over his shoulders as the drawer was pulled out, averting his eyes until the body was made decent. He was ashamed at his relief when he saw she wasn't Emilia. She was a child, no more than thirteen, with gracefully plucked eyebrows and the remnants of mascara on the thick lashes resting on the cheekbones. Her face was unmarked but the hair was scorched right back to the skin. The attendant stroked the eyes open and the wide-eyed stare triggered some memory. As he struggled to place her, he said the prayers, knowing everyone within hearing was taking them in for themselves. Their daily bread, the city's death.

He made the sign of the cross on her forehead and ran his hand down over her eyes to close them once again, letting his palm rest over her nose and mouth, feeling for some memory of breath. He wanted the reminder of the cold skin to fuel his anger, his two years of push-ups, chin-ups, and punching bags in rage for the street children of Guatemala City.

When a woman called out his name, uncertain, in the dank low-ceilinged corridor, he barely recognized her. It had been thirty years and there she was, a thin *Ladina* matron leaning on her husband's arm. The grey streaked her black hair like ashes and what must have been slender elegance had been ravaged. His heart broke for her obvious misery even as he felt sudden joy; maybe Vinicio was here somewhere, another slab of flesh on a metal tray. But then he realized who the girl was. He'd only seen her the one time, dressed up on the float, but it was her.

Clara saw the recognition and cried out. It was a cry there was no defence against; it ripped something apart inside him. Ana Elisabeth's ghosts crowded in to fill the space between his ribs.

"Where is she?" Clara whispered.

Álvaro nodded to the attendant and waited in a small office for them to come out, wondering at whatever it was that was implacable in the universe. Whatever it was that had brought them both to this place. He nodded when the husband, his face full of fear and disgust, asked him to stay with Clara while he went to get the car.

As she sobbed in his arms, he looked over her bowed head to the diagram on the wall showing the muscles of the heart, how they are damaged by different kinds of trauma. Blood vessels drawn in pink and blue. Coming and going. The lungs, great pink sponges. This stranger who was Clara told him how Lucía Madriela, for that was the name they'd given her, had started wearing tight clothes, lots of makeup until she looked like a hooker. Just teenage rebellion, they thought, until the nightmares started. One night, she lit her hair on fire.

Vinicio tried to help, she told him, and Álvaro held himself very still. He'd found her a good therapist and even took her there himself. Adoption has its problems, he'd explained. But then Lucía refused to go. They had no choice but to hospitalize her, Clara cried, no choice. She kept lighting fires. Vinicio was taking her to the clinic when she opened the car door and jumped out and was gone. Vinicio looked everywhere for her, she told him. But it was no use.

"I have prayed a hundred million novenas asking forgiveness for what we did," she said, reaching up to touch the scar on his chin. "But it seems we are both still being punished."

What did she know? What did she think they were being punished for? What kind of God did she believe in?

"Clara," he'd said, "we were children. We loved each other sincerely. We stopped. No one was harmed."

"Your mother never told you?"

His heart jumped. "Never told me what?"

She shifted in the metal chair as if it hurt her bones. "How do you confess a sin if you don't even know you've committed it?"

"Never told me what, Clara?"

"She gave me something that killed the baby." She clutched him, her fingers bruising his arms. "I had to do it, don't you see? They would have killed you."

He sat back. Thought back. The memories emerged, faint at first, a young boy's petulance. Clara had stayed at home while the others went to a party on a nearby plantation. His mother had sent him on a dozen errands and when he'd tried to sneak into Clara's room, the door was locked. His mother, inside, told him to go away. When she finally left the room, he was afraid to try the handle. Afraid of some woman trouble he had no business with. Instead he'd followed her out into the early morning dimness to a place where there was a rock and a smear of ashes. A place even Vinicio didn't know about. Flower petals and candle wax. She dug under the flat altar stone and then pulled out a dark package from under her shawl. She placed it in the dirt, covered it, and tipped the rock back in place. She lit candles and sprinkled whiskey into the flames.

Black circles around Clara's eyes and then she was gone with her mother to Los Angeles. A good school there, Vinicio said. And no more words between them. He and his mother, the two people Clara had trusted most in the world, had done this to her. And she had no one to tell but a succession of priests, none of them knowing her lover was also her brother. He wanted to tell her everything. To take her with him deeper into the dark house.

But the door had opened and Vinicio was there. He gathered Clara into his arms, his dark blue eyes challenging Álvaro. Álvaro stared back, Ana Elisabeth's whole village fluttering between his ribs. Like some demented village dog indifferent to the boot, he barked out his warning.

"Clara?"

She turned, her face as pale as the tiles on the floor.

"Vinicio knows why Lucía lit all those fires. Ask him what she saw that day her mother died. Ask him what he did to her aunt."

Her face crumpled through confusion into loathing. Vinicio just shook his head as he turned with her to walk away. He knew he had nothing to fear. And now that Álvaro had broken his silence, he had made himself one of the dead. When Clara turned back to hiss at him, to curse him and his mother, he was left with her loathing and the knowledge that everything that had happened to him was deserved. Every single flick of Vinicio's razor had been triggered by the evil inside himself, his spirit long stolen by the mountain gods. He had wished then that he had died in the torture chamber, died without knowing.

It was from that knowledge that he'd fled. The sight of another life broken through his bungling. The sight of Clara's hate. It finally cut him loose and sent him down into the place where loud music drowned out some of the chattering ghosts, where the kids took him to a basement so he could let every nerve jangle with electric pain until they shared their little bags with him and the world went numb at last.

Janna stirred and rolled over, her back to him now, her ear poking up through a tangle of hair. Despair flashed briefly as he realized how inextricably she linked him to the Fortunys. She was evidence of their claim upon him, and he would happily shoot either Vinicio or the old man if they ever came into her presence. And yet he also wanted Clara to know about her; it was as if the child who had been laid beneath the stone had come back to them, cleansed of the double taint of their blood. He wished his mother were still alive because she would know what to do. More than any of them, she was able to live with what was outside her and what was inside her. She would come to this girl and take her hands and pull her into an embrace. The smell of smoke on her blouse and in her hair, the smell of smoke and tortillas and coffee.

He listened to Janna breathe. He found himself breathing in as she breathed out, as if her exhaled air was entering his lungs, spreading through his chest and down his arms into his hands until it was all he could do not to touch her. But he remembered what had happened the last time he had reached out to her.

A door opened downstairs and he heard Joseph's voice. Joseph, who hovered on the edge of complication. He put on some music in his bedroom just below. Janna stirred again. Álvaro pushed himself to his feet and went downstairs. He was not going to be the one to wake her up.

†

As Trevor parked his dusty pickup on the small street thick with blossoming cherry trees, Isabel was prepared to dislike every Coleman she met. The house was set back behind a tall hedge and cedar fences intertwined with vines Isabel didn't know the names of..

Trevor whistled. "Christ almighty, these places must be worth millions." He turned to Amy, who they'd picked up on their way through town. "They going to let us in?"

Amy told him that his Gitxsan blood was very high style in these parts and that Soryada would feel right at home, but the rest of them might have to go around to the back door. "You could maybe get taken on as a gardener," she teased Isabel.

"Look at these plants. I only ever see them in gardening magazines and they're growing here like the bloody nettles and thistles grow at home." Isabel glared at them all. "I hate Vancouver. It's just so moist and bursting with vegetation. So clean."

They all laughed except Soryada. She walked over to an evergreen shrub, its leaves threaded with white veins. She didn't know what it was called, she said, but she remembered it from when she was a little girl. "It's like me." She said a word in Spanish.

"A transplant," Amy said.

A car turned onto the street, a black sports car, the little cat leaping on the hood. They all watched it pass, the driver invisible behind tinted windows. No one moved until Isabel snorted. "The way that Janna has always been able to get everyone so they're stepping carefully. Tiptoeing around her moods. Bringing us all here to meet in front of perfect strangers. Does she think we'll behave better if there are witnesses to our idiocy?"

"Mom." Trevor's voice held a warning.

Isabel heaved two big shopping bags out of the truck. "This should sweeten her up. There'll be something in this pile of prezzies she likes and even if she doesn't, she damn well better fake it."

The others trooped behind her up the stairs. She knocked on the front door. There was the crash of feet running down stairs and then a boy as tall as Trevor at the door.

"Hey," he cried joyfully, ushering them into the hallway. "Let the wild rumpus start!"

†

The house was alive now; voices drifted up the stairs. A laugh that could only be Trevor's spiralled through the house, and Janna sat up, happy. Thomas Coleman stood at the open door.

"Professor Coleman," she said, blinking back at him.

"You slept well?" he asked, all courtesy.

"Yes," she answered. "This room is very peaceful." She gestured at the painting at the foot of the bed. "You feel that your presence somehow comforts her."

He nodded.

"Is she yours?"

He nodded again.

"It's very beautiful."

"Yes. Your father is very fond of it."

For some reason, those words made the fact of Álvaro easier. She nodded. Swallowed.

"Now," he said, "in honour of this special occasion, we have set out a large amount of very tasty food. Would you accompany me downstairs before that charming brother of yours and my cavernous son demolish everything?"

†

Isabel had tucked herself into a chair in the corner of the living room, wishing she had a glass of rye and soda in her hand instead of iced tea. Joseph had already taken Trevor upstairs to show him a new computer gadget. Amy and Soryada were helping Margaret Coleman in the kitchen. Thomas Coleman had lit the fire and disappeared. Music trickled in from hidden speakers, some gypsy guitar.

Someone came down the stairs, the slow heavy steps of an old man. Álvaro. He paused in the doorway, his eyes shadowed, and looked at Isabel as if she might have an explanation. Janna, she thought at once. Something's happened.

Álvaro pulled a chair up to sit near her, their knees almost touching. He was wearing a white shirt, open-necked, and black jeans. Black running shoes. His hair stood awry, flattened in some spots and sticking up in others.

She touched it lightly. "Young men spend quite a bit of time and gel to get their hair to look like yours."

"They do?" He scrubbed his head with his hands.

She ran her finger down the scar splitting his eyebrow. He shivered and drew back.

"There's nerve damage," he said. "Sometimes I feel nothing and other times it's all a jangle." He rubbed a spot above his ear. "I'm always hitting my head. My brain doesn't seem to know where my head is located."

"Where is she?"

"Upstairs."

Isabel had to force herself to stay seated, to not go to her and lay her hands upon the girl's body.

"What's she up to?"

"Collecting her courage, I suspect."

"I'm not so sure this is a good idea."

Álvaro shifted in his chair to ease the ache gathering in his knees. "This must be hard," he said. "It's been how long since you've seen her?"

"None of your business," she said.

Álvaro put his hands up to ward her off.

"Listen to me," Isabel laughed. "That girl makes me crazy and the closer I get to her, the madder I get. No matter how hard I try, we're going to have to have a fight before we can have any fun. Maybe I should just go up and get it over with."

Álvaro told her about how his father was away for weeks and months at a time. When they got word that he was on his way home, usually when a neighbour's kid was sent running to tell them he'd like a chicken killed for his dinner, his mother would pick up the machete with such irritation that Álvaro hid until the yelling was over.

Isabel was laughing with him when they heard from upstairs a whoop and a scream. Álvaro jumped to his feet, one hand on Isabel's shoulder. Trevor, his muscled bulk distorting the words on his T-shirt, burst into the room, carrying Janna under one arm, her knees hammering his back, her fists on his chest. He stood her up and pushed her gently toward Isabel.

"Here she is, Mom."

Álvaro hovered beside her, his hands looking for a place to settle, one of them curled in a fist. Janna looked from him to Isabel and squawked out a laugh. She flopped into a chair. "Hello, everyone."

Isabel wanted to touch her, to run her hands down the thin, muscular arms, tell her how good she looked in the sleeveless blouse, that pale yellow so nice against her dark skin, how the beige bell-bottoms were a bit long but that was probably because she was barefoot, her toes just peeking out. She wanted to get rid of the bobby pins holding the hair behind her ears in those silly clumps, brush it out. Cut it maybe.

She bent to the shopping bags full of presents and pulled out a box. She took it over to Janna and kissed her on the cheek. Peaches. She still smelled of peaches. She brushed a wisp of hair off her cheek.

"I love your shirt," she said, straightening the corner of the collar. "Try these. They'll be perfect with it."

Janna held the box.

"Go on."

Janna unwrapped the platform sandals, a ribbon of yellow threaded into the dark leather straps. "Hey," she said. "Thanks, Ma. Where'd you find them?"

"I've been getting secret shopping tips from the Queen of Bargains herself. Lily Thomas."

"Who?"

"The old lady who used to live across from..." Isabel stopped. "She had a beautiful garden."

Janna dangled the shoes from her fingers.

"She used to have a classy ladies clothing store. When I was a little girl, your grandmother bought me dress-up clothes there." Her hands slipping across the rustling, silken, and glittering racks of dresses while women talked above her head. "They tore down her house."

"Lily Thomas." Álvaro's voice seemed to come from far away. "The one who lived beside the rectory?"

Isabel looked at him then and knew from the way the scar along his chin turned red that he was back there with her in that creaking bed, the curtain blowing in the open window, trying to keep quiet as they struggled against each other, the key turning in the locked door, the voice booming hello from the front room, and the intensity of that moment as they both came, together, in terror.

She blushed too as the kids looked back and forth between them. Trevor started to speak and Janna thumped him hard.

"Don't," she said.

He giggled. "It does take a little getting used to."

Álvaro ignored them. "She would throw all the weeds from her garden onto the lawn. Walter would throw them right back. We were talking about her just the other day."

"Father Walter?" Janna's voice flattened.

Álvaro nodded.

"You mean the old bastard's still alive?"

Álvaro snapped his mouth shut.

Janna turned to Isabel. "Did he know about him? When I was going to catechism?"

"Yes, he did," Isabel said. "He most certainly did."

She waved a sandal at Isabel. "How could you let me go to those classes? Were you trying to piss him off? Or hoping he'd let something slip and get you off the hook?"

"I tried to talk you out of it. Several times."

"But he never told you about me?" Janna directed this question to Álvaro.

Trevor took the sandals from her hands. "Maybe we shouldn't go into all this right now." He squatted at her feet. "Let's see if the shoes fit you, Cinderella, and magically turn you into a lovely princess."

"No," Álvaro said. "He never did. I asked after your mother several times and he assured me all was," he paused, "all was well with her. In fact, I was a little bit hurt by that."

Isabel snorted.

"I know," Álvaro said. "It's embarrassing." He paused. "It's more than embarrassing. It's terrible." He stared at the sandals Trevor was lacing on, the same kind of sandals he had fit onto Isabel's feet so many times. He wondered what had happened to those sandals and looked up to see Isabel watching him. Smiling.

Trevor's warm hands on her feet calmed Janna down. She wished all hands could be like her brother's. Deft and protective. She remembered the way he'd hold her on his lap to keep her from squirming while he pulled out a sliver or the careful tissue nudging dirt out of her weeping eye.

Trevor pulled her upright and pushed her to stand between Isabel and Álvaro, Isabel's arm tentative around her waist, Álvaro's hand on her shoulder, the three of them awkward together like mismatched puzzle pieces.

"Soryada," he called. "Do you have the camera?"

A wave of shrieks and giggling broke in the kitchen. Soryada, her face buried in her hands, was gently pushed into the living room by Amy and Margaret. They prodded her until she dropped her hands and stood upright. She wore a dark striped skirt gathered at the waist, a brilliant embroidered blouse, and a red cloth coiled around her head. Her feet were bare. When she looked up, her smile was beautiful.

Trevor whistled. "My own Mayan princess."

"Isn't she lovely?" Margaret beamed. "The clothes are from a village near Cobán."

Álvaro recognized the red headdress from the pictures of his mother dressed for burial. The coral snake. This is what she might have looked like when Cesár López came to her village to build a coffin for her grandfather and, instead of money, took her away. The glory days of Árbenz, when change was good. When good was possible. He greeted the young woman in

Q'eqchi'. She shook her head and giggled.

He switched to Spanish and she told him she wasn't sure exactly where she was from but she thought near Nebaj. She had her mother's *tzute* though. Would that tell? She knew only a few phrases. She spoke them.

"Ixil," he said. "It's where I grew up."

"Are you Mayan?" Trevor asked.

Álvaro paused. "Half," he said. "My mother."

"She should wear it for the wedding," Margaret said, patting Soryada's stomach. "It's expandable."

Soryada twisted away, shy in front of Álvaro and Janna.

"Do you know how happy my aunties are to know that you have Indian blood?" Trevor laughed. "And you too, Janna. All that time you were trying to be an Indian, you were right on. But working with the wrong fish — I don't think there's many salmon in Guatemala."

"A wedding?" Janna said, staring at Soryada. "Expandable?"

"How kind of you to ask," Trevor replied. He bowed to Soryada. "Allow me to introduce my fiancée and the mother of my child."

"Another little secret everybody knows but me?"

Trevor scanned the room. "Have we told Professor Coleman? I'm not sure." And he yelled his name, grabbing the foot Janna had lifted to kick him. "What do you say, Soryada? We could make Janna the maid of honour — get her some duds like these. My little Guatemalan family. Mrs. Coleman, do you have another outfit we could try on my sister."

"No," Janna snapped.

Trevor ignored her. "Álvaro, maybe you could perform the service."

Before he could answer, Janna interrupted. "Oh, won't that get the town buzzing. All our dirty laundry flapping on the line."

When he'd seen those three men grab her, Álvaro had been sick with fear, flushed with fury. When he saw her sleeping, he'd been suffused with love. Now dislike curled in his stomach.

Trevor opened his arms in a gesture that took in all the uncomfortable witnesses. His voice became formal. The voice of the Gitxsan feast hall.

"You are no one's dirty little secret," he said.

Janna shrank back.

"And if you have any dirty little secrets of your own, no one here is one of them." He pointed to Isabel. "You're her daughter. Have you asked how she's doing? What it's like to meet this guy here again after twenty years?"

It's like the beginning of the corn vigil, Álvaro thought. The settling of business so the men would be in the right frame of mind for the slow sweet pleasure of the planting.

Trevor turned to Margaret. "You're her guest. She's been taking care of your dad, giving him a place to stay while he tries to get past whatever hell he went through."

A nod to Álvaro. "You're his daughter. The last thing he needs is some pissy little chick holding him to account for something he didn't even know about."

"So he says," Janna whispered.

"You had all of us. You had a home, you had all Mom's relatives, my family too, for Chrissakes. Have you talked to my dad in all the time you've been away? Asked him how his heart bypass went? How his feet are rotting with the diabetes?"

"Just a minute," Álvaro started, one hand on Trevor's shoulder.

Trevor, his eyes still on Janna, took Álvaro's hand and lifted it off his shoulder and tucked it under his arm. His voice was quiet now.

"We need you, Janna. And you need us. Maybe you've got a hundred aunts and uncles and cousins in Guatemala just dying to meet you. Folks who, from the sounds of things down there, might need your help."

Álvaro pulled his hand free and shoved it deep into the pocket of his jeans. His hands that needed somewhere to go. Somewhere that would not do damage.

Janna was desperate to get away from Trevor's voice, the stern warnings of the feast hall. She was desperate to get away from the masks looking down from the walls and the smell of salmon baking. She rose to go, but Thomas Coleman was hovering in the doorway. She glared at him, daring him to stop her. He did not move, nor did he look away. His squashed and wrinkled face was a question, his look one of intense curiosity and great sympathy. As she approached the doorway, he merely opened his arms and took her in.

"That's enough, Trevor," he said as she struggled to keep from crying. "Everyone. This is what comes of low blood sugar. Margaret, could we please eat now?" He brought out a big handkerchief, wiped Janna's eyes, and led her into the kitchen to sit between him and Joseph. Isabel slid in beside Soryada, reassuring her that she was not the cause of the angry words. Amy leaned between them with a bottle of wine.

"Me and Soryada, we're on the wagon," Isabel said, taking the bottle and reaching across to pour Álvaro a brimming glass. He looked at her as if he didn't know her, with the distant eyes she remembered from that day in her kitchen when her anger sent him to some terrible place.

Cutlery clattered against plates and Margaret scrabbled in a drawer for another serving spoon. Isabel was afraid for Álvaro. She returned the wine to Amy before she gave in to the temptation to lick the red drop about to roll down from the bottle's green lip.

Álvaro floated adrift even as he helped himself to the bright food Margaret and Thomas had so carefully prepared for these people they barely knew. For him. He floated alone, all sound muted around him. He wasn't afraid of Vinicio's voice and he didn't feel Ana Elisabeth jostling his heart. He felt nothing at all. When Isabel had filled his wine glass it was as if she'd poured him out of himself and into the narrow gold-rimmed glass etched with the small scallops. He watched his hand reach for it and pause.

Margaret nudged him to take the bowl she was passing. He stared at the lemon wedges and took the bowl instead of the wine glass.

Just keep going, Walter had said. The creek will reappear. He wanted to talk to Walter. He wanted tell him about his mother. How his mother had slept with Fortuny to save his father's life, only his father wasn't his father. About how he had made a young boy's fumbling love to Clara, who turned out to be his sister. How his mother, trying to save his life, had killed their baby. He wanted to tell Walter because he could not see his way to telling those stories to anyone sitting with him at this table. The lemons shimmered in the bowl. He set them down and waited while the eating and passing went on around him. Isabel leaned across and touched his hand. Trevor was speaking to him.

"Do you want to come to the Canucks game tomorrow? Soryada's beginning to get the hang of it and I might as well teach two at once."

"Hockey?" Álvaro used to play in Winnipeg. "I'd forgotten about hockey," he said.

"Do you like to fish, too?" Janna called down the table.

"Fish?"

"Trevor and Jason's dads were always taking them to hockey games. And fishing," she said. "So I figure we could start with a hockey game and maybe later a fishing trip."

"Are there fish in Vancouver?"

Isabel tried to damp down the hope that leapt inside her. "Maybe you could both come up north. There's plenty there."

"And be a happy little family after all?" Disdain crept into Janna's voice and ruptured the sense of possibility that had been growing.

Álvaro felt something move in him, something that needed to present itself. He spoke directly to her. "In some Protestant churches, parishioners stand up, proclaim their sin, and ask forgiveness of the congregation. Is that what you want?" His voice was not penitent, nor was it angry. It was the voice of a father speaking to his child.

Janna stared at him, some kind of recognition slipping in between her ribs.

Margaret rose. "I am going to be the one to ask to be excused. You have many difficult matters to discuss. Thomas, Amy, Joseph, let's leave these people some privacy."

In the embarrassed silence that followed their departure, Janna looked at her hands on the table. A fork in one. A glass of wine in the other. She set them down and pushed back her chair.

"Don't," Trevor said, already on his feet.

She looked around the table, at her mother's hand on Soryada's arm, comforting her. At Álvaro watching her, waiting. Trevor, ready to pounce. A family cobbled together with scraps of waste wood and crooked nails. She slipped one hand into the pocket where she kept Christmas girl and gripped her tightly. She'd never felt more alone.

"I don't want it to be about me," she said finally. "I don't want all these expectations and explanations. It doesn't mean anything. It's just some story we tell each other. I want to feel normal and I don't know how to make that happen. I've never known how to make that happen. Look at us."

Soryada looked around, bewildered. "Trevor, what is this normal?"

Álvaro felt his whole body stir, all the spirits of Ana Elisabeth, all the children he'd despaired for, prayed for, all the bones tumbled in the graves, his mother, even the great spirit of Bishop Gerardi himself, rumbling inside him. It took him a frightening moment to realize it was laughter shaking him, laughter and tears streaming down his face.

"Oh, *mi corazón*," he said to his daughter, "look at us." His arms spread out, his hands reaching for those beside him. "Look at the threads that connect us, look how far they spread out into the world. We never know what pain our best intentions will bring, what joy our mistakes." He reached across to Soryada. "There is no such thing as normal." And his laughter spilled over and was, for the moment, a contagion they all welcomed.

†

Álvaro and Isabel finished drying the dishes while Janna played Speed with Trevor in the living room. Her victorious cackle was followed by Trevor's groan of defeat. She insisted on another game.

"She's stubborn," Isabel said. "She'd never come when I called her — only when she thought the time was right. It's really a miracle that she's here today at all."

The others had returned. Amy was outside talking to Soryada, their faint Spanish rising and falling as she readjusted Soryada's clothes. Margaret crouched to pull something from a flowerbed in the bottom of the garden. Thomas looked where she was pointing. As she stood, he put an arm around her waist to pull her up and kept her hugged tightly to his side for a moment, his hand on her hip. Isabel turned away.

Álvaro stood with a dripping plate, listening to Janna tease her brother. She did laugh like Isabel. The times he'd seen her at the university, she'd been distraught or afraid. Or very angry. This was a girl who didn't need rescuing. She looked so much like Clara did when she used to play cards with Vinicio, her dark hair with its slash of white pushed behind her ears, her cheeks flushed with the pleasure of winning. Clara's hair now entirely grey, her Lucía Madriela in the big cemetery.

Isabel took the plate from his hand.

"Aren't you afraid all the time?" he asked.

"No," she said. "Not all the time."

Trevor had refused the game and Janna jumped up from her chair to stand in the doorway. She surveyed the kitchen, its bright colours all revealed as the plates and pots and trays were put away. Evening sun splashed long

lines of light along the big table, into corners and sparkled off the beads hanging in the room with the photographs. Isabel slipped cutlery into a drawer.

"I don't know what to call you," Janna said to Álvaro. She leaned one hip
against the counter. Her face was rounder than Clara's, her eyebrows lighter.
She brought a finger up to her mouth and nibbled on the nail.

Álvaro swallowed hard. "What do you call your brothers' fathers?"

"Just their names."

"Why don't you start there? Álvaro."

She tried it, stumbled and tried again, all the time staring at the sparkling
beads.

"Yes," he said. "That's very good."

She said his name and pointed to the alcove. "Can you tell me about those
children?"

He carefully hung up the dishtowel he'd been holding. The face he turned
to her and Isabel was frighteningly bleak. His arms dangled at his side, as if
he was about to be led away.

"I've been reading about Guatemala," she said. "It sounds pretty rough."

Isabel put a hand on her arm. "Maybe another time." She did not want
Janna to see him as she had. She did not want to see that again herself.

His voice was a monotone. "Some of them were children who came to my
school. It wasn't an orphanage or a shelter, it was a school. So I closed the door
every day at five and returned to the house where I lived with other priests."

"Where did they go?" Janna whispered.

"They had places — a couple even had families. But for most of them, it
was a cardboard box in an alley or a blanket and a piece of tin."

"Did they all die?"

He barked out a laugh that sounded like metal breaking. "No, no. There
were twenty or thirty at any one time and they were tough. We'd find some of
them homes or places in boarding schools. But every morning when I went to
the school to unlock the gates, I'd wonder who would be there. Who wouldn't."

"Couldn't they have come here?" Isabel asked.

He struggled to explain the uproar about adoption in Guatemala, about the
orphanage industry. About children being bought and sold. "Some," he said,

"are adopted by the very people responsible for the deaths of their parents."

Janna had parted the beads and looked through to the pictures.

"Is your family in danger? Our family?"

"No," Álvaro said. "No, they're not in danger, the ones that are left."

"Will you tell me about them?"

Somewhere upstairs, a phone rang. They waited, but it didn't ring again. Álvaro had made a vow not to lie. But he wasn't ready for this.

Joseph came down the stairs. "Father Al," he said, holding out the phone. "It's the hospital. Father Walter."

†

Isabel perched on the arm of the chair Janna was sitting in, the clothes Isabel had brought heaped on the floor around them. They had all been tried on and modelled for Amy and Soryada, comments exchanged, decisions made. The men were upstairs. Margaret had taken Álvaro to the hospital. The fire had sunk to embers and the curtains were pulled against the darkness.

"He told me a bit about his mother, back when we were together. She was killed in a big earthquake. But he didn't talk about the rest of his family. Nothing about this sister you look so much like."

"I think it's a sad story," Janna said, "and not one he wants to tell, if that look on his face was anything to go by."

"I still don't know what would have been the right time to tell you about him," Isabel said. "I've always hated secrets and the way they have of getting out of hand."

"If he hadn't found me, would you have told me?"

"I like to think so." Isabel shrugged. "But I honestly don't know. Finding out about his own troubles made it complicated."

"He's still cute," Janna said. "He looks more French Canadian than *Latino* with that curl in his hair and he's a bit battered. But I can see where you might have been interested."

"He was cute all right. He was so," Isabel searched for the right word, "enthusiastic."

Janna leaned her head back, uncomfortable with the word. Isabel's hand rested against her hair, and she forced herself not to pull away. "Do you still like him?"

Isabel's hand stroked her hair, lightly. "After I stopped wanting to kill him when he showed up out of the blue, I mostly felt sorry for him. I don't want to go to bed with him, if that's what you mean."

"Do you get them mixed up after a while?"

Isabel's hand lifted away and Janna wished she hadn't asked.

But Isabel was thinking of Lance. Only yesterday. The boy, Dustin, downstairs. Lance was leaning toward the bathroom mirror, shaving. The towel around his waist stretched tight across his butt and his back was pink from the shower. One hand holding the razor, the other tightening the skin on his face. The tuft of hair in his armpit had sent a spasm of desire in a vertical line from her diaphragm to her groin and she must have made a noise. His eyes met hers in the mirror. She had watched — Trevor and Soryada waiting outside in the truck for her to come down with the magazines she'd forgotten — as he finished shaving and turned toward her, pulling off the towel to wipe the remnant shaving cream from his face, his eyes never leaving her face. She looked down at the scar encircling one knee and the long purple welt curling up his thigh, disappearing in his pubic hair.

The door had opened downstairs, Trevor and Dustin talking. Before she could turn away, Lance had pulled her to him, his penis hardening against her stomach, his hands on each side of her face. His lips barely touched her mouth, but his eyes held hers. Light grey eyes like a creek bed under clear water. When Dustin set foot on the bottom stair, Isabel pulled away and ran down, the magazines she'd held clutched to her chest wrinkled and damp.

Isabel was lonely. Her body was lonely.

"No, I don't get them mixed up. I never have." Her voice was sad. "I've done lots of stupid things, but I like men. I like being with them. That doesn't make me some kind of..."

Janna interrupted. "Were you ever scared?"

Her mother picked up Janna's hand and squeezed it. "Tell me what happened."

Janna did just that. She told her about David and her feeling of power, of vengeance after he'd spoken of her to his friends as if she was a piece of trash. And then the pain and fear. The shame.

Isabel slipped down to squeeze into the chair beside her, to hold her while she cried.

"I ran into a few bozos in my time but never a creep who'd bring his buddies to help him beat up a girl." She fished a tissue out of her pocket and handed it to Janna. "You've got to pick them better than that."

Janna looked up at her. "Like you do?"

Isabel blinked at the sudden anger. "You know that's not what I meant."

"While I had my face down in the dirt there, I remembered something. I don't know how old I was, maybe three or four? It must have been in April or May, this time of year. The garden was turned but there wasn't anything growing in it. Something bad had happened and I'd been hiding. I just remember the dirt. Dirt in my hair, in my eyes, on my hands, and you passed out in the dirt. I was out there alone, trying to wake you up. I was so afraid."

Isabel's face had lost all colour, the lines around her open mouth deep gashes. Janna popped out of the chair and started shoving clothes into one of the bags.

"One of your expert choices? Some fun guy you had a good time with?"

Isabel whispered. "He never hurt you. I know that."

"How can you know that? You were unconscious."

"Believe me, I knew. I told you it was a bad dream. That we all have bad dreams and not to worry. To just scoot across the hall and climb in with me if you had another one."

Janna squeezed Christmas girl. "And did I?"

"Yes, for a while. And then they stopped."

Janna waited, the bulging shopping bag looped over her wrist.

Isabel sighed. "I could give you the whole sad story, but I don't really want to." How she was so short of money she thought she'd lose the house. The loans manager, one of her father's so-called friends, offering to help out. Dropping by the house, playing with the kids. Always bringing a bottle, the drinking getting harder and harder. When she finally figured out what he was trying, it was almost too late. Janna in her underpants standing on the toilet, him in there unbuckling his belt. Isabel had been so out of it, she could barely stand, but the rage jolted her upright and sent her after him, screaming, and telling Janna to run, run, run. He knocked her around pretty bad, but her hollering must have scared him off. She'd staggered outside after him, throwing stones at his car as it pulled away, calling Janna, Janna, until she passed out. The sight of her girl's dirty face, hearing her calling her, shaking her awake, the worst and best thing.

"Secrets," Janna said.

"I guess," Isabel said, taking the bag from Janna and hugging it to her chest. "I'll tell you another secret though. The creep who scared you was an upstanding member of the church. I went to Father Walter and told him that if he didn't get that guy out of town, I was going to sue the church for child support. You should have seen his face. It confirmed everything he already thought about me."

"The creep?"

"Oh, he left all right. But I found out where he went and sent an anonymous letter to the Catholic Women's League there. I'd have turned him in if I thought there was any chance of getting him arrested, but I knew it wasn't going to happen. It did straighten me out though. For quite a while."

"Not forever."

"No," Isabel said. "Not forever. But I never brought any of them home after that."

"Not even after I left?"

"Janna, I haven't had a drink for three years now and I haven't been with a man since you saw me that night. Not once. That look on your face. I think it's called aversion therapy."

Janna was afraid to hope. There had been so many times when Isabel had straightened out. Even tonight, she'd wondered when Isabel would take the first sip. She'd seen the way she watched that wine pour into Alvaro's glass. "What about the guy living there now?"

"What is this, the Spanish Inquisition?"

"It must be the Guatemalan in me," Janna said.

Isabel stared at her and burst into laughter. "I guess I'd better get used to it."

†

The laughter died when Álvaro pushed open the door to Walter's hospital room. George stood by the window, the provincial superior leaned his chair against the back wall, and two men Álvaro didn't recognize at first sat up close to Walter, one at least as old as Walter, his head settled down low in between his shoulders. He'd been the one telling the joke. Two priests from the north, George said, introducing them, and he remembered Father John. Walter lay stripped to the waist, the grey hair curling on his chest, stippled with stains from swabs and tape. A bandage crossed the back of each hand, bruises seeping out around the edges. One hand lifted in greeting. Álvaro bent to kiss him and saw the oil glistening on his forehead and chest.

"How's the birthday party going?" he rasped out.

The silence stretched as Álvaro looked around the room. John blinked and the younger man looked genuinely interested. The superior dropped the front legs of his chair to the floor.

"Yes, tell us." George seemed eager for gossip.

"It's very strange," Álvaro finally said.

Walter coughed as he laughed. "I'll bet it is," he wheezed.

"Do you have a picture?" John asked.

And the difficulty passed. He told them about her, asked their advice on how to proceed within the community. It is a hard thing, John said. So often the circumstances are painful, but surely the fact of the child is a joy. And it was. But he could not help wondering how they'd feel if she was standing in front of them. Not a child. Not such a simple joy.

After a while, Walter dozed off. Or lapsed into unconsciousness. It was not clear. The others bent, one at a time, to kiss him, to give their blessings, and to leave. Álvaro wanted to stay.

"You won't be going back?" George asked.

"I'm going to a hockey game with them tomorrow. I'll stay here for now."

Soon after the door closed, Walter's eyes flicked open. "Now come on, boy. Tell me."

After protesting that now was not the time, that Walter had his own passage to prepare for, Álvaro told Walter everything. About his mother, about Clara, about Vinicio. Álvaro bent his mouth to Walter's ear. He murmured words about Ana Elisabeth and Lucía Madriela. About Janna.

"She doesn't like me."

"No," Álvaro agreed.

"When she came to catechism, my struggle was not to blame her. The sins of the father…"

"…who was busy saving himself?" Álvaro paced the room. "You said it, Walter. We are not sent here as fixers. If we do have faith, and I'm not sure I do, we have to give it room."

"It's hard to give up that power. To lean back and let the water carry you. There's always one more secret to keep, one more problem to manage." Walter's voice faded. "Forgive me."

Álvaro gathered the old bones in his arms.

"I wish you could have baptized her," Walter said.

"Isabel brought her to you?"

"The aunt did. You know that moment when the infant is so serious, so concentrated. When you touch the water to their heads, they startle up, disturbed at your temerity. Angry that you're distracting them from their conversation with God."

All the babies Álvaro had blessed. All the springing bodies, the furious ones, the heat of the limp ones, the ones already gone. None of them his. The first never breathing, buried alone in the dark. The other, no matter how they grew to know each other, would never give her body up to his in the loving and unconscious way children do with the people they've grown up leaning against, they've grown up trusting.

"She'll be okay," Walter said. "That mother of hers went pretty wild for a while, but she was fierce about her kids. Still is."

They both sat in silence, listening to the night sounds of the hospital. Quiet voices in the hall, a door opening, a telephone.

Walter whispered, "When the salmon start running up the Nechako River — the Indians will tell you when that is — I want you to do me a favour. Before they bury my ashes, I want you to sneak a good handful."

Álvaro stared at him in surprise. Cremation? A handful of ashes?

"I know, I know," Walter said. "They balked at the cremation, let me tell you. That was as far as I got. They want me in the ground. But I want this too, Álvaro." He paused and took a breath. "It's an offering of sorts. Please?"

Álvaro nodded.

"Take them to the place where the river drains Fraser Lake. They call it the Nautley River there. A little nothing of a river, but beautiful. It drains some of the sorrow out of that big lake, all the things that happened to those children at the school there. LeJac. Do you know how far those big spring salmon have come? Hundreds of miles, fighting the current every fin stroke. Put my ashes there and let all of this float away with them, let it all float back down, past those big spruce and pine trees, past the little towns, and the aspens all nice and freshly green, past all the kids swimming in the back eddies of the river, down, down right to the river's mouth. Let it go back to where the ocean is big enough to take it all in and make it part of the world again."

Álvaro nodded and the two of them rested together, Álvaro's cheek on the old man's chest, his ear cocked to hear the prayers coming like easy breath from Walter's mouth, the weight of his head measuring the struggle as the old man's chest rose and fell. When Álvaro woke up, the chest was still and the prayers came in turn to Álvaro, his thumb making the cross on the old forehead.

It was only after everyone had been called and they'd come to get Álvaro that the others told him Walter wanted him to celebrate his funeral mass.

Part IV

22

SPRING CAME QUICKLY to the Bulkley Valley and the bulbs in Alejandro's garlic patch bloomed profusely. Isabel's mother's peony produced three luscious flowers for Lily Thomas's windowsill. Her dahlias made a surprise appearance in a new bed dug at Pioneer Haven. In Isabel's garden, Janna's tulips survived the winter to bloom in May. In ten days, many more flowers will be cut and driven up to the hall in Kispiox for Trevor and Soryada's wedding.

In the morning sunlight of this particular July day, Isabel stands on her small back deck. She wears cut-offs and a T-shirt and has cut her hair so short she just scrubs her hands through it to comb it. Her feet are bare. Lance and Dustin are upstairs. Janna is asleep in the living room. Álvaro is across town in, he says, the same bed where they made love. At least the springs feel that old, he says. The window she broke has been replaced and the priest is careful to lower the blinds whenever he changes. About time, she told him. Lily Thomas knew about them all along. And she saw a lot more shenanigans after theirs, she said to Janna before snapping her mouth shut.

Isabel watches Perro stalk the neighbour's cat. Rump in the air, tail wagging, he crouches down, growling at the clump of dahlias where she's hidden. They are all getting used to each other. Time together and time away. Janna has walked through the streets of Shaughnessy with Álvaro and swum in the pool at the provincial house where he now lives. The novice has gone back to school in Ottawa or they would be worried, but the rest of them are truly too old. They doze in the sun and wake up happy to the sound of her voice, wondering where they are. Álvaro has told her about how he became a priest and came to Canada. About meeting Isabel and even how they were found out. He has told her about his mother and Cesàr and the village he grew up in. He has told her about the planting and harvesting rituals, about his mother's prayers. He has told stories in loops and circumlocutions that they both recognize for the evasions they are, and for the moment, she is not pushing him. They both have a sense of time stretching out ahead.

Janna has moved into a basement suite near the university. She works long hours on her summer courses, one of which is Spanish. But she won't practise with Álvaro. Not yet, she says. When she was a child, Isabel told him, she refused to say a word until she was ready to speak full sentences. She has taken a week off to help prepare for Trevor and Soryada's wedding. Álvaro has agreed to perform the service. They are all getting used to each other.

Lance moves easily now and brings his coffee out onto the porch where Isabel stands, her feet cold on the damp wood. He stands beside her, close, but not touching. His hands, warmed by the coffee cup, the fingers curious and agile, are waiting for her to close the gap. She bends to the dog that has come to wriggle against him. She squats and leans, very lightly, against his thigh. Against the scar that curves up into his groin. He shifts his weight to return the pressure and Janna rattles the cords of the blinds pulled shut over the window just behind them. Isabel stands and steps away. He smiles at her. She's never known a man so unhurried. He sips his coffee. The neighbour opens his door to call for the cat.

"You're very patient," she says.

A lazy morning bee buzzes around his red hair and he stands still until it flies away. "When they were stitching up my leg, there was damage. They weren't sure if everything would still work. It took a while. My friend, the one in Terrace, she got impatient. And now, every time I look at you and feel that feeling, I'm a happy boy. I was a bit anxious about taking it to the next step."

Perro flops at her feet. She puts one foot on his warm fur, pokes her toes in under a floppy ear to scratch. "Not anymore."

"No," he says. "Not anymore. I'm not sure, now, what it is we're waiting for."

"In ten days this will all be done."

He raises his coffee cup. "Ten days," he says.

†

Janna is surprised how much she likes playing basketball with Dustin. He's a funny kid. Pudgy in the way twelve-year-olds often are, but a good hoop thrower. He doesn't mind sweating and Janna has to work to get the ball away from him. He still looks like a little boy but there's a squawk in his voice and a couple of hairs sprouting on his upper lip. He claps a surprisingly big hand on her shoulder when they're done and thanks her politely for the game. As they walk back from the basketball court, he tells her about his mom. She works for the railway. He tells her how he didn't really like to visit his dad when he lived in the bush.

"This is better," he says. "Isabel's nice. She's friendly, but leaves you alone. Mom says they're lovers, but I'm not sure." It's a question.

Janna doesn't think so. The men who came into the house back when she lived at home, the ones who opened cupboards looking for a bowl to dump the chips into, or sat on the back porch drinking a coffee, they were never her mother's boyfriends. Old friends from high school. Uncles. Cousins. It was a place they were comfortable. Lance is probably one of these. Besides, he seems too young. Dustin says he's forty.

"Should I find out?" she says.

He dribbles the ball down the ally. "What about your dad? How'd he feel about it?"

Janna tells him she doesn't think it's his business, really. But she doesn't know him very well, she says, and explains as best she can about Álvaro and Isabel, leaving out the priest part. "Holy," he says, drawing out the o and doesn't understand why Janna is laughing so hard.

"Are you coming to the wedding?" she asks.

He shrugs. "We're going out to Lance's tonight. He says there's going to be a lot of coming and going and we'll be in the way. And you should have your bedroom back, he says."

"Don't go because of me. We could work on my game."

He twirls the ball and tosses it above Perro's dancing. "It's out of my hands," he says and throws the ball at her, hard. She isn't ready for it. It hits her shoulder and bounces off into the brush. Perro follows it.

"What's that supposed to mean?" she yells as Dustin dives in behind the dog.

A flock of small birds flushed by the dog and the boy and the ball scatter around her as she turns into the back alley, rubbing her shoulder. She is lifting the latch on the back gate when Dustin catches up.

"Sorry," he says and she knows he is. He opens his mouth to explain, then closes it again. She waits. "It's complicated," he says.

"No kidding." She opens the gate and follows him and the dog into Isabel's garden.

Isabel is taking a photograph of Álvaro against the flowering linden tree, the mountain in the background. She calls Janna to stand beside him.

"I will submit to pictures, but only after I clean up."

Isabel puts down her camera. "Your hair needs cutting anyway," she tells Álvaro.

Janna groans.

"Yours could use a trim, too."

"She needs to do this," Janna tells Álvaro. "There's no point arguing. There might, however, be a point to prayer."

Álvaro sits on a chair in the centre of the garden and Perro pants at his feet. Isabel's fingers trace his scars, rubbing the lumps and knots until the jagged currents settle down and he relaxes. He closes his eyes. Then Isabel is showing Janna how to hold the scissors and she is there on the other side of him. And then Janna is in the chair and Isabel is showing Álvaro how to hold his daughter's hair in the comb and snip it so the cut ends blend in. Something is being exchanged. A shoulder leaning into a hip, a head pressed against a stomach. The small clumps of hair, receptacles for their DNA, fall to the ground where they mingle with the particles of dirt, of ash, and insect bodies. With flower seeds. As the boxcars crash together in great groans across the road, they relax into the gift of time and attention passing between them.

Dustin stands at the back door, watching. He looks pale and soft in the shadow. Janna calls him and he submits to the scissors. She brushes out the twigs caught in his hair and snips at the wispy curls around his ears. His hair has his father's red hidden in the brown and it is as fine as her own. Isabel sees the way he leans against her and relaxes under her hands and wishes that she had had more children, that Janna wasn't the youngest of all the cousins, that she had had, while still a child herself, the feel of a child's arms around her neck as she carried it, shivering, out of the lake or put it to bed. Álvaro feels the prickle of hair on the collar of his shirt and wishes that he could give the story a happy ending, that Clara could bring Lucía Madriela to have her hair cut in this garden.

When Trevor and Soryada arrive, Isabel takes dozens of pictures. Soryada is big now and her face is pale, a little puffy. They will take Álvaro to the priest's house in Fraser Lake and then set up their camper down at LeJac, in time for the Rose Prince Pilgrimage. They want to be there for the midnight vigil, to say prayers for Trevor's father.

"You take care of Soryada," Isabel tells the men as they drive off.

Lance is in the kitchen packing up food. Dustin is in the living room chatting online to some friends in Terrace. His father's place is off the grid, he tells Janna. No power, no phone, no Internet.

"Where exactly is it?" Isabel asks.

"You've never seen it?" Janna says.

Isabel shakes her head, suddenly shy.

"She sticks pretty close to town," Lance says and Janna wonders if that's a criticism. She wants to defend Isabel from something.

"There's nothing to stop you both from coming with us," he says.

"Don't fall for it, Janna," Dustin calls. "There's no TV. No phone."

"No telephones," Isabel says. "No calls from Trevor's sisters, no long talks about where to sit all the white folk coming from our side of the family." The phone rings as she speaks. "It sounds like paradise," she says, taking the call outside.

"There's mosquitoes," Dustin yells.

Janna laughs when she sees the frustration on Lance's face.

"I'm more of a city girl myself," she says, shrugging. "Thanks, but…"

"Just for the weekend," Isabel says, coming back inside. "Blessed peace."

"You go right ahead," Janna says, "but not this girl." And then she finds herself telling Isabel that she, Janna, will babysit Dustin for the weekend so that Isabel can see Lance's mysterious place in the bush.

"Take the bug dope," Dustin yells as the truck pulls away.

†

"A boat," Isabel says as Lance stops the truck beside a dock at the edge of the small lake at the end of a long track that wound in from Jasmine and Frank's farm through an aspen bush.

He turns to her, assessing the timbre of her surprise. "Yes," he says. "It was my father's gillnetter."

She stares at the wooden planks curving in the sun. Nasturtiums spill over from a pot on the deck and trail almost to the water shivering around the hull. Portable steps lead onboard through a little gap in the railing. She is surprised at the boat, surprised at the lake, surprised at Lance. She never expected this out of someone so practical. Someone who wasted not one movement. He is, she realizes, nervous. For a moment she wishes she were back in her house, alone. Everyone travelling in, but not yet docked.

She follows him on board. He unpacks and stows the food in the small cupboards in the cabin. Then he starts a tiny engine and takes them out to the middle of the lake where all they can see is the green of the trees, reeds, and shrubs lining the shore. He brings out washed vegetables, hooks up a propane tank, and puts water for the pasta on to boil. He asks her to make a salad and passes her a small board, a knife, and a wooden bowl. She tears the lettuce, chops the tomatoes, cucumber, and slivers the carrots. Behind her, he unfolds the bunk into a double bed, puts on sheets, a blanket, and folds it back into a bench. He hops out onto the deck and rigs up a small wind turbine, which is soon whizzing in the light breeze.

And suddenly she's shaking. She's on a date. She knew it before, but now her body knows it. She huddles on the bench, trying to stop shaking. To keep him from noticing her nerves. He offers her a glass of soda water but she shakes her head. Her hands are shaking. She doesn't know if she can swallow anything, but he makes some kind of joke and the feeling passes and they're eating at the tiny table tucked into one corner.

He tidies up the dishes and leads her out on deck.

"This is where the net used to be," he tells her, distracting her with stories of his time working summers with his dad off the north coast, until his dad took a buyout. She tells him about her dad, how close they were until her mother died and then he seemed to slide away. And so did she.

"Since his mom and I split, Dustin has been trying to take care of us. To keep something intact."

"He wants you back together?"

"He doesn't want strangers in his house."

Isabel thinks about the way Janna got into Lance's truck at the airport. His bush supplies in the back — a box of flares and safety equipment, rain gear and caulk boots, empty sample boxes. The mud dried on the door frame. Her slow walk through the backyard, keeping Perro at bay with her foot. Whose is he? she was asking with her toes. Assuming it was all Lance. Seeing Janna back sitting at the kitchen table made Isabel realize how the years she'd been away were gone. Irretrievable. And the time ahead was going to be different. Even more complicated. She is angry now, at herself. She keeps her nose clean for years and then within days of Janna's arrival she takes off with some guy.

"It might have been good luck," Lance says, "not having her dad around. All we ever did when we were together was fight about Dustin and it's all we've done since we've separated."

"Fight?" Isabel is withdrawing. She does not want anything taken for granted.

Lance scoops water out of the lake to water the nasturtiums. "Well, she'd fight. I just get quiet. It seems pointless when you know you can't win. When you don't even want to win. You just want to go your own way."

"I think I need to go back home."

His hands hover in the air, glistening. "She could have come. Dustin and I could sleep on the deck."

"You don't like her," she says.

He sits back on his heels, one hand brushing the hair away from his face. "I'd expect it for me, but it's hard to watch her judge you."

"Janna can judge me all she wants. It's her way of being with me. She's trying to improve me. I didn't raise her to be nice all the time. That's bullshit."

"Are we fighting?"

"I guess so. Yes, I guess we are. Maybe I should go."

"I've always liked being on my own," he says. "I thought maybe that had changed."

"It's not you I'm fighting with," Isabel says. "It's me. I have to get back."

He nods. "We'll go. But the water's warm," he tells her, untying the laces on his shoes. "I'd like to swim first. Ten minutes is all. Will you come?"

She shakes her head as he slips off his socks. He tucks them into his shoes and stands to unbutton his shirt. He looks across the small space between them to where she's leaning against the galley door. He pulls his shirt out of his pants and he is close enough that she can see the goosebumps rise as the cool air touches his bared arms. The sun, low over the aspens, glints on the copper hair. She feels trapped, a strong emotion almost like fear. He turns without a word, strips off his pants and shorts, and dives so quietly he disappears under the surface with scarcely a plop. She shivers in the doorway, holding on as the boat rocks from his departure. She is alone.

She is alone long enough to walk around the boat looking for him to surface. She is alone long enough to wonder about how to start the boat and get back to shore. She is alone long enough to be afraid and to not want to be alone anymore. When his head pops up and his hands reach for the boat, she is relieved. He uses his shirt for a towel and she watches him dry himself. First the face and then the shoulders. Down the arms. And then his chest, the hair springing up as it dries. One leg and another. The muscles in his thighs bunch as he lifts first one foot and then the other to the low railing. Neither of them speaks. The silence builds between them, becomes thick and tangible, strains against her resistance. The sun is setting behind him, and the air is full of cottonwood fluff and insects drifting in a halo around his head. She looks at him and her hands are the ones that finally move through the light and land upon his skin. His heat is already rising through the surface chill, and her hands move over his body to find the warmth. Only when she has made her reconnaissance does he move toward her.

†

"My mom tells me to get used to complications," Dustin says, sitting with Janna in the movie theatre. She has pulled a toque down low and slumped in the seat because she doesn't want anyone to recognize her. She dreads the wedding. There will be lots of jokes about Àlvaro and Isabel, lots of giggles and elbows in the ribs. Here there's no one over seventeen. She pulls off the hat. Dustin is talking about his mother's boyfriends and Lance's one girlfriend who dumped him last Christmas.

"It isn't easy," he says. "You keep talking if you can. It's way worse if you don't. I tried that for a while and you get a little crazy." He sounds like an old man, exhausted with life's endless twists and turns. "But you kind of get used to it."

He stuffs a handful of popcorn into his mouth. The trailers begin and Janna watches the light splash across his face. He's staring at the pictures without seeing them. His lips are moving and she bends to listen.

"I'm going to have to talk to Lance about it. I mean I can't tell my mom because she's really stuck on this guy. And he's nice enough. It's just his kids."

They are mean, he tells her. They're younger than he is and they seem nice, but they're mean. They tell their dad lies about him. They could pretty much wreck his life, he says.

Twenty minutes into the movie, Janna realizes it's a mistake. A group of kids alone in a big house are all turning into monsters except this one little nerd who's waiting to get axe-murdered. Dustin's eyes are closed.

"It's actually worse when you close your eyes," he says as if he's just conducted an interesting experiment.

She takes him out of the theatre and they sit against the warm cement wall of Janna's elementary school. A group of older boys are shooting hoops. He slurps the last of his drink through the ice at the bottom of the cup. The basketball ricochets off the wall and before it hits Janna she jumps up and catches it. The boys cluster at the edge of the court. One laughs and comes toward them. She bounces it a couple of times. Passes it to Dustin. He rises to his feet.

"You're as good as they are. Go play."

He looks at the boy holding out his hands for the ball. "Only if you do," he says and passes it back. She dribbles it toward the boy and passes it back to Dustin, now on the other side. They pass back and forth, approaching the hoop, and the boys don't clue in until they've scored and when the oldest boy checks her a little too hard she stops with the ball in her hands and says don't and he backs right off and then all they're doing is playing ball and Dustin isn't thinking about his mother's boyfriend's kids and she isn't thinking about her mother fucking yet another man.

She sends Dustin upstairs to wash. She wanders through the house, trying to find the old feelings. This was her home. The place she got maddest and the place she carries inside her, like her liver or her appendix. It has changed. The kitchen is tidier and there's different food on the shelves. Herbal teas. Jars of dried things — mushrooms? Tomatoes? Rice crackers and tahini. The dog's basket behind the door. A pair of men's sandals. A bird identification book full of paper scraps.

Upstairs, Dustin rummages behind the closed door of what used to be her room. She drifts up the stairs. In her mother's room, she sees no sign of shared accommodation. No condoms in the night table drawer. No stains on the sheets of the unmade bed, but a drawstring bag of worry dolls is tucked under the pillow. Janna squeezes Christmas girl in her pocket and laughs. You are part of one goofy family, she says. And you and me, we definitely fit right in around here. She pulls her out to show her the dozens of hangers stuffed into her mother's big closet: sweaters, blouses, dresses, skirts, scarves draped over a chair, and a pile of shoes on the floor. A chest of drawers pushed into the back corner.

Her grandmother's dresses, folded neatly with tissue and lavender sachets between the layers. Isabel used to bring them out at every birthday and she and Janna would try them on. She pulls out a white summer frock with a light floral print and a turquoise sash. The cotton is so threadbare, it's almost transparent. She strips off her T-shirt, tucks Christmas girl into her bra, and pulls the dress over her head. She stretches to do up the buttons in the back. She turns to look in the mirror on her mother's vanity, the glass warped with age. The girl who looks back at her is a stranger with a haircut she doesn't really like. The dress is loose and sags around her small breasts. The sash has a stain at one tip. On the vanity, squashed between a jar of face cream and a bowl of cotton balls, sits her old plush pig, more grey than pink. Its sideways smile infuriates her. She picks up the nail scissors open on the pile of magazines stacked on the floor beside the bed. The tiny blades snip and tear at the fur, revealing a layer of clear pink underneath the years of grime. She sticks the point of the scissors into the fabric and cuts until the stuffing comes out in matted clumps. The pig is in pieces when Dustin, watching from the doorway, asks if she would please give him the scissors.

Why am I so angry, Janna thinks, handing them over.

"It takes some getting used to," he tells her and asks if she'd like some nachos.

"Maybe they'll fatten me up enough to fill out this dress," she says as they stick the heaped plate into the microwave. "So I can wear it to the wedding."

"It looks very nice," he says. "I wouldn't change a thing."

"Will you be my date?"

"A pleasure," he says, bowing.

A few shreds of cheese glued to the plate are all that remain when Lance's truck pulls in. Janna is surprised to find herself pleased. Relieved. Happy, really, to see the look on Isabel's face when she notices the dress Janna is wearing.

†

Álvaro parks the priest's car between a big diesel pickup and an old brown station wagon. The vinyl upholstery's smell fills the air as the car's black metal gathers all the heat of the engine and the midday sun to pin him into place. A feathery dream catcher dangles from the rear-view mirror. A crucifix is glued to the dashboard.

The mown fields fall away in terraces to the lakeshore below where campers are parked, some pulled into the shade of the big cottonwoods that line the edge of the water, others arranged in circles on the rough grass. Small tents are scattered among them. A long stairway brings pilgrims up to the smoke rising from the cook shacks just below where he sits, the driver's window cracked open to let in air, flies, and the smell of fry bread. It is like the big powwows he went to when he lived in Winnipeg. The open sky and the rumbling of thunder. The line-up snaking into the dining tent, people hungry for lunch.

He sees the priest in the line-up and knows he should return the car keys. Instead, he locks the door and walks away from the food across to the booths set up beside the weed-strewn lot where the residential school used to be. A couple of power lines and thistles. A water tank. Scapulars and rosaries. Abortion is murder T-shirts. Small paintings of Christ. Two little girls dance around the long blue-jeaned legs of their mother — she is bent over the beads. Butterfly barrettes in their hair.

Inside a picket fence, the graveyard. Marguerite Jeanne Coudbert-Chabanet. Born March 13, 1866, in Augerolles France. Died Oct. 11, 1940, in Smithers. And all his Oblate brothers. RP Nicolaus Coccola. Corsica 1854. Smithers 1943. Rev. Jean Donze. Odil de Keyzer. At the far corner, women kneel beside the fence around the grave of Rose Prince, the Carrier Rose. She first came to the Indian Residential School at LeJac in 1922 as a student. She stayed there until her death in 1949 and was buried there. When the graves were moved to this spot, her casket broke open. Her body was intact, a smile still upon her face, a withered bouquet on her chest. The smell of flowers filled the air. What started as a small gathering has grown to attract hundreds of pilgrims. Rosaries and lockets are draped over the headstone. The women pray for miracles; some bend to scoop dirt from the grave into margarine tubs and plastic bags.

From a loudspeaker set up in a big marquee, flags fluttering from its peak, a woman speaks of the sacred symbol of the feather. Its central line bridges our humanness and our divineness, she says. It bridges our Christian faith as Catholics and our faith as Native people. Álvaro is drawn to her voice and her calm certainty. Outside the open back of the tent, people sprawl in beach chairs, bottles of water or cans of pop stuffed into the pockets in the arms. Wraparound sunglasses and braids. A shaved head and jean jacket with a wolf embroidered on the back. A man in his sixties tips his hat to Álvaro as if he recognizes him. He's slim through the hips, a Leatherman tidy at his belt of silver coins, cowboy boots, jeans, a shirt well cut for his broad chest, and a scapular dangling off the back of his collar. His brown face is weathered. Álvaro follows him to sit on one of the hard benches under the cover of the tent just as the speaker sits down.

In his black jeans and T-shirt, the sneakers that roll his feet outward, his Indian face, his scars, and the black toque so warm on his head and soothing the jangling nerves, Álvaro knows he looks like he belongs here. He can sit alone on a bench under the tent where a man now talks of losing his family to cocaine, about giving it all up to God, and the long way back, and feel part of the pain visible all around him. The people in wheelchairs, the people leaning on canes. The old woman shivering in the heat, bundled in her long purple woollen coat, her head covered with a flowered scarf, her eyes blurred behind thick glasses. The plump women and the skittering kids bringing up their bottles of water and oil for the priest to bless. The bags of holy dirt piled in front of the altar. We must give up shame, the man says. He is a big man, his beaded leather vest spread wide across his white shirt. He wears sunglasses and his thin grey hair is braided down his back. We must not bend under the responsibility for that which has been done to us, this is not our cross to bear. Those who have abused us, those who have stolen our land, those who have stolen our children. We must call for justice.

A little boy is brought in and laid down, curled up, on a blanket. Beside him, a girl sits, ripping open the Velcro on her pink running shoes, pressing the tabs together, ripping them apart again. Her face is bent to one side of her brown bony knees, her eyes intent.

But we are not victims, the speaker says. We must give up self-pity. We must accept responsibility for our own actions and atone for our own past. Resolve to not carry this pain forward into our children's lives, their children's lives. We must live inside our own lives and accept the help God will give us. To look around and see what we can do right now.

The man sits down and some prairie Indians sing, I saw the light, yes, I saw the light. No more darkness. No more night. Flatten the hills and Álvaro is in Manitoba. Angle them a little more steeply, add a few more straw hats and brighten up the women's clothing and he's at a re-dedication in the highlands of Guatemala. The rustling dryness of the corn, the small puff of dust where a foot hits the path. The same stocky Indian bodies, though the fat sits heavier on them here. The thin ones, gaunt.

He looks like he belongs because he does. His pain and sorrow is no more or less than anyone else's. He is made of more than his pain, but it will be with him as long as he's alive. Lucía Madriela, he says. Ana Elisabeth. Moises Osorio. Armand Guzman. Emilia Estuardo, Marta Barilla. Juan Tzul.

Trevor ushers Soryada to a bench on the far side of the tent and Álvaro feels a pang of fear for them. Fear and the old anger. That it will all begin again with the child in Soryada's belly, a child linked to him by the blood that Trevor and Janna share. The infinitesimal and infinite branching of capillaries that link the floating child to Clara and Vinicio, Vinicio as much a part of him as Janna is and it's almost more than he can bear, his tiny juncture in the great branching out and out into the world, the huge gnarled trunks of the cottonwoods, the tracery of their leaves overhead, the leaves turning in the breeze generated by the waters of the lake.

It was less than an hour ago that he'd felt some peace. He puts his elbows on his knees and drops his head between his hands and tries to recreate the binding together of his spirit.

He took Walter's ashes to the place where the lake becomes a river. He crouched there in the long shadows of the aspens. Here it is lake. Here it is river. A riffle of dark water marking the division.

He lit the braid of sweet grass the priest had given him and hung it from a willow branch bending over the outlet. Its smoke eddied in the currents above the water. He opened a small box and set the first spoonful of Walter's ashes right inside the line. It exploded in an arc on the surface, spiralling back into the lake before it was pulled into the river's turbulence, beginning its journey down the long fall to the ocean. It took him a long time, waiting for each spoonful to clear before adding another, sending his prayers into the ash, into the river. His shoes damp in the grass at the edge of the water, the heat of the day rising from the ground all around him. The insects drifting on the surface of the water, floating in the invisible currents of air just above the water, the sun behind him illuminating them in the long lines of early light. A little gust of wind blew ash into his face, into his hair, and into his mouth, his tongue curdling around its bitterness. He splashed water into his mouth, driving out the taste.

A memory came bubbling up, one so early he wasn't sure at first that it was his. He sat back on his heels, his mouth wet, the water drying on his face, trying to find the shape of what he was feeling. It was as if he'd dipped something out of the water, something that came from a time before memory, a time when he was simply in the world and never out of reach of his mother. He is making his way over uneven rocks and can feel the teetering difficulty of it in his small legs. He drops to his hands and knees to bridge the distance to the small dish the women dipped their clothes into before scrubbing them on the river stones, the insects floating like this, the sun slanting across his back. His mother's angry chatter explodes at the same moment the bitter taste of the ash explodes in his mouth, his tongue trying to push it out, his fingers clotted with it, smearing it across his face. Her worried scrubbing as she tries to get him clean, the women gathering around, talking to him, touching his face, saying his name over and over.

This was the moment she had talked about. The day the river first tried to snatch his spirit. The reason she was always looking into his eyes and saying his name. The ceremonies. The incense and the calling of his name. Come back, come back, she'd say when he was standing right there beside her.

Álvaro pulled off his hat and ducked his head into the water, the cold a shock of jangling nerves. He scrubbed himself clean of Walter's ashes, scrubbed his toque in the cold water, and dried his hands on the small napkin he'd brought with the kit the priest had lent him. He set out the implements of the mass. The small chalice, the box with the host, and the cloth spread on the grass. As he said the words he'd said thousands of times, he was a child again standing in the rocks at the water's edge, smoke rising from the incense and the candles, hearing his mother's voice call out his name. He was making room for that little boy inside of him, her son, making room, too, for the brother, the father and the priest, making a place where all of the currents that ran through him joined into one.

A hand on his shoulder brings him back. It is the priest in his robe and the tent is all but empty. Álvaro stands to return the car keys and follows him outside into the heat of the full afternoon sun. He is stopped short by what he sees. Big wooden Stations of the Cross curve around the edge of the top field.

Beneath each cross, a priest arrayed in all the splendour of his office sits on a lawn chair, the long white robes luminous against the green of the grass, the blue of the lake, and the bright sky. Some wear sun hats, some wear ball caps, some have bare heads, but all of the hair he sees is white.

What will become of us, he wonders, watching the men, each knee to knee in earnest conversation with a person come to make confession. A discreet distance away, penitents line up in the sun. Their patience is something beautiful.

Hunger stirs in his stomach and he turns back toward the cook shack. But the priest touches his arm and points toward one priest sitting bare-headed in the sun, his head sunk deep between his shoulders, a woman kneeling in front of him. He is the old man who'd asked Álvaro if he had a picture of Janna. The one, he remembers now, who offered to hear his confession.

"There are many more people here than we expected," the priest says. "Father John is exhausting himself. Perhaps if you offered to relieve him?"

Álvaro looks at the people waiting. Each person, each encounter, full of possibilities. Each moment as transient as his moment of being knit together down beside the river. When the woman gets up from her knees, is blessed, and leaves, Álvaro helps John out of his vestments, turning him into a small grey man in tan slacks, running shoes, and a green polo shirt. The skin on his hand as soft as a baby's. Álvaro's eyes fill with tears as he fastens the robe over his T-shirt and jeans and become a reflector of light in this bright place. Yes, he thinks. This is something I can do. Who he is — his pain, his mistakes, his faith — is immaterial. When he puts on the robes he becomes something that can be useful.

A tall woman waits for him. Two little girls skitter around her legs, giggling and shaking their long dark hair, the butterfly barrettes holding it out of their eyes. The woman's face has none of their joy; it is rigid with pain and worry, the hair reddened with dye or ill-health, the fierce resolve a strong light in her eyes. He looks at her and nods. She bends to the girls and they run toward a man standing alone, looking out over the lake. She comes toward him and he empties himself, prepares to receive this woman's story with his full attention. It doesn't matter where God is in all of this. This is, simply, something he can do.

Acknowledgements

Many generous people helped me over the years spent researching and writing *The Taste of Ashes*. Patient Oblate priests in northern BC, Vancouver, and Guatemala welcomed me into their communities to answer my many questions and my Catholic friends tried to enlighten me about some of the more esoteric aspects of the faith. I used, with permission, excerpts from the English translation of *The Liturgy of the Hours* © 1974, International Commission on English in the Liturgy Corporation. All rights reserved. Please note that none of the priests (or any other characters in the novel) are derived in any way from those I spoke to; they are entirely fictional. A special thanks to Vigil Overstall for taking me to the Rose Prince Pilgrimage near Fraser Lake. Thanks also to Ruth Murdoch who showed me some of the possibilities for art therapy. The painting described hanging at the foot of Álvaro's bed is *Little Girl with a Big Head* by Paula Scott.

Thanks to Grahame Russell of Rights Action both for the social justice work he does in Central America and for putting me in touch with Global Exchange Tours. Once I was in Guatemala, Marie Manrique showed me aspects of the country that many visitors never see; namely, the work done by the brave and dedicated Guatemalans who risk their lives every day in the struggle for social and economic justice. Thanks also to Merran Smith and Mike Simpson for telling me stories and sharing films about their work there. And of course, Amnesty International, whose efforts in Guatemala and around the world shine light into dark places.

Thanks to Bonnie Burnard who first encouraged me to turn Isabel's story into a novel and to the other mentors at the Banff Writing Studio; to David Bergen for his assistance at the Wired Writing Studio; to Luanne Armstrong who not only housed me in Vancouver, but gave valuable feedback on early versions of the manuscript; to John Harris and Vivien Lougheed for their encouragement and attentive readings; to Gillian Rodgerson for her insights and attentive eye; to Vici Johnstone of Caitlin for believing in this story; to Morty Mint for his enthusiasm and support; and, of course, to my friends and family who remind me, from time to time, to go outside and play.

Resources

The Art of Political Murder: Who Killed the Bishop? by Francisco Goldman. Grove Press, New York, 2007.

The Blindfold's Eye: My Journey from Torture to Truth by Sister Dianna Ortiz with Patricia Davis. Orbis Books, Maryknoll, NY, 2002.

The Body in Pain: The Making and Unmaking of the World by Elaine Scarry. Oxford University Press, 1987.

Guatemala: Eternal Spring, Eternal Tyranny by Jean-Marie Simon. WW Norton, 1987.

Guatemala: Never Again! Recovery of Historical Memory Project – The Official Report of the Human Rights Office, Archdiocese of Guatemala. Orbis Books, Maryknoll, NY. 1999.

Guatemalan Journey by Stephen Connely Benz. University of Texas Press, Austin, 1996.

Liturgy of the Hours. Catholic Book Publishing Co., NY, 1975.

The Long Night of White Chickens by Francisco Goldman. Atlantic Monthly Press, New York, 1992.

Maya Resurgence in Guatemala: Q'eqchi' Experiences by Richard Wilson. University of Oklahoma Press, 1995.

The Maya Textile Tradition by Margo Blum Schevill. Harry N. Abrams, 1997.

The Mirror of Lida Sal: Tales Based on Mayan Myths & Guatemalan Legends by Miguel Angel Asturias, Translated by Gilbert Alter-Gilbert. Latin American Literary Review Press Series: Discoveries, Pittsburgh, PA, 1997.

Popol Vuh: The Definitive Edition of the Mayan Book of the Dawn of Life and the Glories of Gods and Kings. Revised and Expanded Edition. Translated by Dennis Tedlock. Simon & Schuster, New York, 1996.

Silence on the Mountain: Stories of Terror, Betrayal, and Forgetting in Guatemala by Daniel Wilkinson. Houghton Mifflin, New York, 2002.

Textiles from Guatemala by Ann Hecht. University of Washington Press, Seattle, 2001.

Other books by Sheila Peters

Canyon Creek: A Script (1998) non-fiction

Tending the Remnant Damage (2001) fiction

the weather from the west (2007) poetry